A
Splendid
Country

A Splendid Country

T. Austin Cumings

Illustrations by Russell Autrey

EAKIN PRESS ꝟ Fort Worth, Texas
www.EakinPress.com

To
Samuel D. Logan—
journalist and gentleman.

The Cumings Family

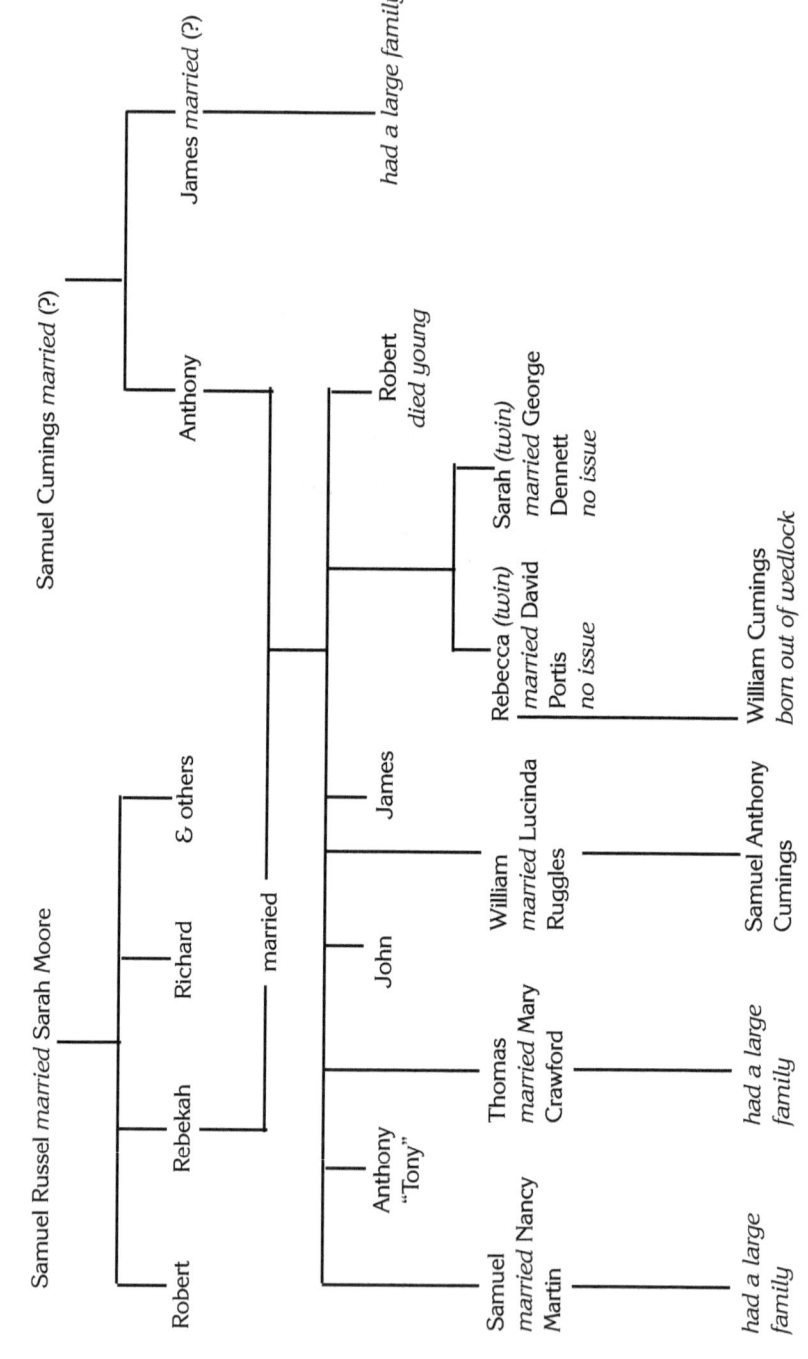

Contents

Part I   Before the Storm (1875)   1
Part II   The Journey (1776)   37
Part III   The Ohio Valley (1777–1821)   97
Part IV   Texas (1821–1874)   261
Part V   The Storm (1875)   449

*"They hesitate not to call it **a splendid country** . . ."*
— MARY AUSTIN HOLLEY,
writing of Texas in 1831

PART I

Before the Storm
(1875)

Chapter 1

Rebecca Portis was not feeling her normally robust self.

The doctor, unwilling to cite a diagnosis of advancing age, remained mysterious and simply prescribed a temporary change of climate. A cool sea breeze and inhalation of salt air should do wonders for her, he said. So, on a hot and humid Saturday in September 1875, she and a maidservant departed San Antonio by stagecoach for the Texas Gulf Coast port community of Indianola.

Reflecting on travel's varied discomforts, Rebecca found herself wondering whether the projected benefits of the seaside were going to be worth the ordeal of getting there. For her young companion, though, the outlook was much different. Kate Donahoo had scarcely traveled beyond the outskirts of San Antonio since her birth there two decades before. Now, several months into employment as the personal servant of the prominent Mrs. David Portis, she was beginning a journey to the coast.

Kate's excitement over the sojourn, and fascination with the unfamiliar terrain, eclipsed the rigors of the opening leg to Sutherland Springs. For her, the dust, ninety-five-degree heat, and endless rocking of the coach were overshadowed by the panorama of rippling, brush-covered hills, rock-lined creek bottoms, sturdy live oak and mesquite trees, and clumps of prickly pear cactus.

The clatter of hooves and metal-rimmed wheels against the uneven road of packed earth and scattered rock intruded on the quiet of the lonely wasteland. The noisy approach of the conveyance, punctuated by the crack of the driver's whip over the heads of his six-horse team, provoked scrambling retreats by jackrabbit and fox and roadrunner, and sudden bursts of aerial escape by bobwhite and white-winged dove. Deer and javelina suspended their hillside foraging among blackjack and huisache to eye the interlopers.

At mid-afternoon the stage pulled into Sutherland Springs, where its passengers were hailed by the portly driver of a waiting surrey. "You are here to visit the Señora Sutherland?" he inquired of the women, pressing a sweaty straw sombrero against his equally sweaty shirt.

Rebecca, invariably aloof and sometimes openly rude to Mexicans, stiffened and frowned. Kate waved in response to the inquiry and hastened to precede her mistress out of the coach. She helped Mrs. Portis to the surrey while the man struggled with the baggage.

Twenty minutes later, they were climbing a substantial hill, wheels rattling on a caliche driveway sandwiched between rows of cedar trees. Once clear of the cedars at the top of the slope, they abruptly passed through the open gateway of a rock fence and rolled across the spacious lawn of a large, two-story frame home.

Dr. John Sutherland's business successes had far exceeded the rewards of medical practice, as evidenced by the ample improvements to the expansive grounds surrounding his home and the richness of the furnishings within. His death in 1867 left Madge Sutherland, the doctor's third wife, heartbroken but financially secure.

Rebecca knew that a letter to Madge, sent well in advance of the departure for Indianola, would prompt a warm and firm invitation to stay over. Madge's late husband and David Portis had enjoyed social, political, and fraternal ties. Upon Sutherland's demise, Portis afforded Madge his considerable expertise as a lawyer while Rebecca spent several weeks at Sutherland Springs in selfless companionship with the dowager.

As Rebecca freshened up in Madge's rooms, Kate and a taciturn Polish housekeeper arranged the travelers' temporary quarters upstairs. By the time Kate had tended to the guest accommodations and then to herself, the older women were at leisure in the coolness of the east verandah. Rebecca invited her to join them and introduced her to the hostess as "really more of a companion than a servant."

Madge smiled while taking thorough visual stock. Youth was stamped all over Kate's round, pug-nosed face. Not beautiful by classical standards, she was nevertheless quite pretty when she smiled. Sandy locks accompanied a freckled complexion, from which gazed large, honest, blue eyes. There was enough shape to her five-foot, two-inch frame to elicit a veiled second glance from men.

In contrast, Rebecca (who admitted to sixty-two years of age and was in fact seventy-six) retained a vestige of truly arresting beauty. Neither skin nor hair betrayed her true age. A fashionable amount of gray was woven into auburn strands that flashed red in the sunlight. Wide-set, green eyes flanked an aristocratic nose. Her full lips were complemented by large dimples still distinguishable from the furrows of time. These features graced an oval face stamped with strength, yet totally feminine. Wrinkles encircled her eyes and tugged at her mouth, and loose flesh had gathered under her chin, but there was no doubt she had been one of Nature's finest works of art.

Until the last couple of years Rebecca had held her slim figure ramrod-straight. But, while advancing age was kind externally, it had wreaked havoc invisible to others. Those green eyes, damaged by internal bleeding, could no longer see well enough to aim a rifle, thread a needle, or read anything smaller than newspaper headlines. The handicap was alleviated only slightly by eyeglasses; hence an instinctive movement of the head to get closer to an object, and the resulting stoop.

Kate's prowess at reading had therefore been a major factor in the success of her job interview with David Portis. The illustrious attorney carefully described his wife's sight-related frustrations, allowing Kate from the first day of employment to anticipate Rebecca's visual needs.

When the widow Sutherland suggested that Kate accept a glass of fruit juices and rum, a favorite concoction of the late doctor, Rebecca cheerfully came to her servant's rescue. "Our little Baptist here doesn't take anything with spirits," Rebecca interjected with an affectionate smile. "Her leisure time, in fact, is spent with head bowed over her New Testament."

Kate did accept the substitute offer of a tall container of sweetened tea. While the old friends carried on what was essentially a two-cornered conversation, Kate sipped her drink and took in the shadow-sharpened features of the manicured grounds.

"There are ladies I would be worried about if they were traveling without a man, this day and age," Madge was commenting. "But I know you, my dear, and this young lady also seems very sensible. You said Mr. Portis will be joining you in Indianola?"

"Yes, he hopes to be there by Thursday, or Friday at the latest," Rebecca replied. "He is off speaking to the Democrats in Houston. There's talk once again about splitting Texas up into five states, and David thinks that is so foolish. He has a regular speech on the subject, you know. Kate and I will make out fine until he arrives."

"Yes, well, I was really thinking more about your trip tomorrow and Monday," Madge said. "You may not know that there has been new trouble in those parts with the State Police."

Rebecca chuckled to show a lack of concern. "That's all a case of men shooting other men," she observed. "I doubt they would bother an elderly lady and her servant girl. At any rate, I do have my pistol with me, and have not forgotten how to use it."

The conversation lapsed as Rebecca and Madge resumed their drinks. After a respectful moment, Kate took the opportunity to indulge her curiosity. Pointing to a far corner of the rock fence, some forty yards away, she commented, "That carving, or whatever it is down there, reminds me so of the Alamo. See it, just behind the tree stump?"

Rebecca sat up straight in her chair and, frowning, snapped her head in the general direction indicated. She, of course, could make out nothing at that distance.

"Yes, young lady," Madge responded. "That is indeed the Alamo. At least, it is Dr. John's Alamo. You may certainly go examine it, if you wish."

Thanking her, Kate alighted from the verandah. As she moved away, Madge said to Rebecca, "I suppose the big oak I lost to lightning last year always hid that fence corner from view. It's just something poor John felt compelled to do. Would you like to go and see, too?"

Rebecca, wearing a look of slight distress, declined.

Forty years had passed since the rebellion of colonial Texas against its parent country of Mexico. Armed conflict lasted only from October of 1835, with the opening skirmish near Gonzales, until the following spring, when on April 21 at San Jacinto the ragtag forces of Gen. Sam Houston surprised and routed those of Mexican dictator Antonio Lopez de Santa Anna in one of the world's least likely battlefield outcomes.

But no other heroes of the revolution equaled in stature that of the men martyred at the Alamo, a onetime Catholic mission at San Antonio de Bexar converted into a fortress. Almost every Texas town would later name streets in honor of William B. Travis, the young, fiery Alamo commander; Jim Bowie, who relinquished that command only after becoming incapacitated by illness; Davy Crockett, the elder statesman whose immortality had already been assured; and James Bonham, the brave and tireless horseback messenger who returned to die with Travis, his relative and boyhood friend.

For thirteen days beginning in late February 1836, Santa Anna with somewhat in excess of three thousand soldiers laid siege to the Alamo. The self-proclaimed "Napoleon of the West" finally ordered an attack before dawn on March 6, and every defender in the mission compound ultimately fell. The Mexicans' own losses in killed and wounded, though, approached four-to-one.

Kate reached her destination and found a recess carved into the fence corner at a forty-five-degree angle. Peering out was the familiar facade of the mission chapel, recognizable worldwide as the face of the Alamo.

Yet there were differences.

Kate knew every feature of the famed old structure in downtown San Antonio. The mission ruins had fallen on less-than-glorious times. Although the Alamo was the premier symbol of the revolution, and therefore nothing less than a shrine in the hearts and minds of most Texans, it currently served as a depot for U.S. Army quartermaster operations. The dilapidated condition was something of a scandal in the city.

The miniature chapel front facing Kate from the fence corner, rendered in adobe, reflected the serenity of a bygone era. Its lines were clean and unsullied by age or cannonade, yet contained much detail. The twin bas-relief columns to either side of the arched entrance bore hints of the intricate designs that adorned the originals. This Alamo even had little wooden doors.

Kate examined at length the handiwork of the late doctor, aware of something amiss but unable at first to identify it. Perhaps —yes, that must be it! Where the actual structure had upper-story windows to the far left and right, there was only blank adobe on Sutherland's model.

Then the main difference dawned on her.

The facade of the real building, restored a decade after the battle, featured a distinctive, rounded crest. Sutherland's replica was flat on top. A little cross of polished gold was inserted directly above the lone second-story window.

Kate did not recall any such cross in artists' depictions of the Alamo during its siege and fall. Yet crosses were certainly prominent on other Spanish missions in and around San Antonio. Judging from the attempts at accuracy exhibited in the pillars and doors, Sutherland would hardly have made such a mistake replicating the top of the chapel. Were these dramatically different details gleaned from firsthand knowledge—observations made prior to the revolution?

The cross, throwing back the rays of the late evening sun, took on a dull glow. The overall effect of Sutherland's creation was that of a sacred grotto. Despite the September heat, Kate clasped her arms and shivered. She was looking at a man's soul laid bare.

Confirmation came as soon as Kate regained the verandah.

"What you've just seen, my dear," Madge volunteered, "was one of Dr. Sutherland's ways of dealing with a very painful memory. You see, he was in the Alamo with the others, but unlike the others, he lived."

Prior to the siege, she explained, Sutherland had left the fortress with another rider, a man named Smith. They were under orders from Travis to determine the precise location of the approaching Mexican army. The advance guard of the enemy proved to be much closer to Bexar than had been thought. When the two scouts made this unpleasant discovery, they began a furious return ride.

"John's horse lost its footing and fell on his leg," Madge recounted. "It was a bad injury, but John remounted and made it back to the Alamo.

"Later, after the Mexicans had begun the siege, Colonel Travis ordered John and Mr. Smith to ride out in search of reinforcements. They avoided the Mexican pickets and rode hard to Gonzales. But there were no reinforcements to be found."

Sutherland, still in great pain, his leg stiff and swollen, felt unable to rejoin his encircled comrades. "Even if he had endured his injury and managed to make it through the enemy lines," Madge said, "he was afraid he would be more of a hindrance than a help to the others.

"No one had more personal courage than John Sutherland," she added, her voice suddenly husky. "But those who knew him back then have since told me that, when the Alamo fell, a part of him died with it."

"Only a part," murmured Rebecca. Her words drew a quick stare from Madge. Rebecca added, in a flat tone, "Parts of a lot of people died that day."

Blinking back tears, Madge reached over and squeezed her friend's hand. Following a strained silence, she cleared her throat and announced: "There is something else that John did . . . something that you both may be interested in. Perhaps after dinner we can share it."

Chapter 2

*M*adge Sutherland turned up the big reading lamp while Rebecca and Kate nestled into nearby chairs. This after-dinner assemblage in the drawing room held an air of expectancy, underscored by the sight of a large stack of papers on the table at Madge's elbow.

"I will not attempt to share all of this with you," their hostess said. "In fact, I will need help from you, Kate, in just reading those portions I believe to be of most interest to the present audience."

The papers, she explained, represented John Sutherland's recollections and research regarding the siege and fall of the Alamo. "This was written in 1860," she noted, "and may yet be made public. Fortunately, John's hand was still strong and steady at the time."

Madge adjusted her spectacles and commenced reading:

"'Though many years have elapsed since the Alamo fell, I have never, until recently, thought it necessary for me to publish anything in regard to it, supposing the facts would appear from some other source substantially correct. But, since several conflicting accounts have been published, some of which differ widely from my own knowledge of facts, I have deemed it my duty to history and to the children of the worthy patriots, to write out and publish my version of the last noble struggle of the gallant Travis and his noble band.'"

Madge, as she had promised, read only selected passages. Still, her throat grew dry and she yielded to Kate while several pages remained. After some initial difficulty, Kate found Sutherland's penmanship not too hard to decipher. Madge handed her the passage

10

regarding the evening of March 3, when the hopelessness of their situation was obvious to all of the Alamo's defenders.

Kate read aloud:

" 'What dark emotions they must have experienced in this extremity. All the sacred associations of the past crowded upon them, whilst the embittering prospect of the future silently admonished them that they would never witness that glorious dawn which should hail their country free and independent of despotic sway. But it was not theirs to falter. The rights of their countrymen were seized by the oppressive arm of a tyrant, and they were called upon to rescue them from his grasp . . .

" 'That pride of character, love of home and country, the true soldier's noblest attributes, enabled them to sustain with cheerfulness, if possible, their position, in this, their hour of extremity. It was thus, surrounded with the enemy, and awaiting the hour of attack, not knowing how soon it might arrive, that Travis addressed a letter to the Convention, and several others to private individuals . . .

" 'Those letters from Travis and quite a number of others from his comrades to their relatives were sent out on the night of the third of March by John W. Smith . . .' "

Kate paused, having noticed an unpleasant look on Rebecca's face. Both listeners, though, immediately urged her to continue.

Finally came the account of the Mexican attack, and Kate found herself rushing through the text in her excitement.

" 'The struggle did not last longer than half an hour, yet in that half hour more blood was drawn, perhaps, than ever issued before at the hands of the same numbers in the same length of time and under like circumstances.

" 'Travis and his boy [Joe, a slave] cut their way through the thickest of the ranks of the enemy and finally came near the northeast corner of the church, when Travis, seeing that the enemy were still rushing over the wall, mounted it, cheering his men to the conflict. After discharging his pistol he continued the slaughter with his sword, dealing blow after blow. As fast as they loosed their holds, they tumbled to the ground beneath him.

" 'But he was not long to occupy so conspicuous a place. Receiving a ball through the head, he fell on the inside. His boy, ever faithful, had continued near him, doing good service, but seeing the fate of his master and thinking that all was of necessity, lost, concealed himself in one of the small rooms of the barracks, where, after the action was over, he and another man were found by an officer.

" 'The former's life was spared because he was a Negro. The latter was promised protection if he would show the bodies of Travis and Bowie which he did, but Santa Anna soon rode within the walls and seeing him, asked, "What is that fellow doing here?" On being informed of the condition upon which he had been spared, he replied that they had "no use for any such men," and ordered him shot. A file of soldiers executed the order at once.

" 'So soon as the bodies of Travis and Bowie were shown by this man they were brutally mutilated by the sword and —' "

Madge stood up suddenly, placed her hand on Kate's shoulder, and said, "You need not indulge me further. I thank you for allowing me to share Dr. Sutherland's treatise." She took the sheet of paper from which Kate had been reading. "It is getting late, and I give you my apologies."

Madge's last words were lost on Kate, who, having glanced casually at her mistress, was struck with alarm. Rebecca was leaning forward in her chair, both hands squeezing a kerchief held against her face. Glistening rivulets trickled from between her fingers and down the backs of her quivering hands.

"Perhaps this was not, after all, the proper type of chamber reading for ladies—young or mature," Madge remarked. "I tend to forget just how detailed poor John did make his account."

She again placed her hand on Kate's shoulder, and, indicating Rebecca, said quietly, "She will be all right. It has been a long and tiring day for her—for both of you, I'm sure. Anna has already retired for the evening, so I will personally see you to your rooms."

When, following a short night, Sunday dawned at the Sutherland home, Kate became glumly aware that they weren't going to church services. Before the new week was spent, she would be desperately asking herself whether this transgression against the designated day of worship had caused God to turn His back.

Following a breakfast filled with light chatter, the time came for Kate and Anna to pack. In Kate's absence, she drew praise from Madge.

"If anything, dear Rebecca, she is probably more like a daughter to you than either a servant or a companion. Just imagine—a daughter already raised, whom you can enjoy without having suffered through the pains of her birth and adolescence." Then Madge, aware that the Portises had no children, silently cursed those unweighed words and changed the subject.

"Your trip today, you said, is going to take you to Helena and Yorktown, and on to Clinton." This drew a nod from Rebecca. "Then you need to know that Helena is Sodom and Gomorrah combined into one Hell on Earth. There are fights and murders and hangings every week, it seems."

"Sweet Madge! Always warning me about the world and its evils." Rebecca smiled. "I've seen much worse than what these times have to offer. But I appreciate your love and your concern, always. I promise you, we will take care."

Madge started to speak, hesitated, and then gathered her resolve. She took both of Rebecca's hands into her own and looked into those green eyes. "There is something else, dear, I want to say, and you are to take it as a friend should."

She felt the captive hands stiffen, but Rebecca said nothing. "You need to lay down the past. Enjoy the fullness of what you have now. Please, hear it from one who knows. Live for today, not for old dreams, while you have the choice."

The captive hands relaxed, then squeezed those holding them. "Madge," Rebecca said, her tone of voice sincere, "I know that your little reading last night had a purpose to it. I appreciate you, and I cherish your friendship."

Within the hour, formal good-byes had been said and the trip made into Sutherland Springs. The stagecoach was not long in arriving. Luggage loaded, they rumbled over the rock-ribbed crossing of Cibolo Creek and turned south toward Helena.

Madge had not greatly overstated the rawness of conditions in Helena, although the community no longer openly embraced the practice of its notorious Helena Duel. In this ferocious pastime, two combatants' left wrists were bound together while (usually stripped of clothing) they hacked away at each other with sharp but stubby knives. The short blades precluded the piercing of a vital organ, so that the excitement usually continued until one of the adversaries collapsed from loss of blood.

But even with public banishment of its namesake contest, Helena still offered peril to life and limb—especially when the Chihuahua Trail disgorged its cattle drives and ox-cart caravans, and the town's cantina and quartet of saloons became raucous and overflowing with rowdy drovers and teamsters.

Rebecca and Kate changed stage lines at Helena, necessitating a lengthy wait at the livery stable for the Clinton coach. Seated in the stuffy little office, they became aware as noon approached of an increase in traffic on the wooden sidewalk and in the dusty street. Men and women, some in formal church attire, passed by the open doorway on foot, on horseback, and in wagons and carriages—all headed in the same direction.

The office clerk, a thin, neatly dressed man in his early thirties, volunteered an answer to the unasked but obvious question. "Those folks are goin' to the hangin's," he explained. "There's three of 'em today. The men who'll do the swingin' robbed and killed an old couple here last month. The judge generally sets the hangin's for Sunday noon, after church, when more folks are in town."

Kate gasped in disbelief, but Rebecca turned to her and said dryly, "It's an acceptable form of entertainment, dear. They've had their precious Helena Duel taken away, so this offers perfectly legal amusement in its place."

The clerk issued an unsolicited rejoinder in a lowered, knowing tone. "Oh, the duels still go on, ma'am. They've just been moved outta town to a place on the San Antone River, and people don't talk about 'em in public anymore. Our sheriff don't like to hear it."

Kate looked quizzically at Rebecca at the mention of the Helena Duel. It was a surge of curiosity she soon regretted, for Rebecca gave her a detailed response.

What manner of devilish place is this? Kate wondered, clutching the small New Testament volume that lay in her lap.

Momentarily, the stagecoach arrived. The clerk carried their luggage out to the sidewalk and he and the driver began changing out horse teams. That done, the two men loaded the luggage while Kate helped Rebecca into the coach. The clerk, after a quick glance at his pocket watch, shut the office door and climbed up beside the driver.

The way out of Helena took them past the new, two-story Karnes County Courthouse. On the front lawn a noisy swarm of people stood, pressed in around two large live oak trees. Visible over the hats, bonnets, and scattered parasols of the spectators were the shoulders and bared heads of three men, mounted on horses. A rope stretched tautly between the noose snugged around each man's neck and a sturdy limb above.

The stagecoach driver reined in his team long enough for the clerk to alight. Kate initially stared without comprehension at the grim tableau. Finally recognizing it for what it was, she turned her head and shrank back in her seat.

Just seconds after the stagecoach resumed its journey, a great shout arose from the throats of Helena's citizenry in tribute to justice at high noon on the Sabbath.

That night was an uncomfortable one for both women, but especially so for Kate. They spent it in a frame hotel in Clinton, and the thin walls only slightly muted the frequent shouts, bursts of song, and occasional gunshots evidencing that the local cowboys were enjoying their evening in town. Kate watched, fascinated, as Rebecca inspected her revolver with squinting eyes to make sure it was loaded, then placed it under her pillow.

"Those are happy sounds out there, and I doubt they are shooting at one another," Rebecca ventured. "Just being little boys. But liquored-up, they're unpredictable, and we should be prepared."

Reflecting on the limited eyesight of her mistress, Kate made early use of the chamber pot and vowed not to get out of bed again before morning.

Even after the street celebrations died out, Kate's sleep was not sound. She was victimized by confused, disquieting dreams about the fall of the Alamo, public hangings, and riverbank knife fights between naked, bleeding men. Throughout, she was aware of a demonic symphony of groans and cheers from an unseen audience clamoring for more.

Chapter 3

$\mathcal{R}$ebecca found it difficult to crawl out of bed.

Two days of stagecoach riding had left her stiff and sore, and she did not sleep well in Clinton. It took a generous helping of determination, encouragement from Kate, and a pending train departure to force her into movement.

The travelers crossed the quiet, tree-shrouded Guadalupe River by ferry amid rising streamers of fog. Their hired buckboard was soon rattling into the new and thriving village of Cuero. They pulled up to the depot of the ambitiously named Gulf, Western Texas and Pacific Railroad.

The morning train to Indianola stood ready. The black locomotive, trailed by its tender, two freight cars and two passenger cars, already had a blazing firebox and was vomiting smoke from the dramatically flared stack. Red and antique gold trim adorned the huge drive wheels, cow-catcher, and headlamp. The initials of the railway company were emblazoned in those same colors across the tender.

This particular departure had drawn an abnormally large number of passengers. The final day of the San Antonians' journey coincided with the opening of a murder trial in Indianola which was of great interest to residents of the region, and many were choosing to cover the distance by rail. Even with her damaged eyes, Rebecca spotted the tell-tale bulges of weaponry under the coats of the men boarding the train. Most of them, in fact, appeared to be packing more than one pistol.

Reconstruction, that wretched Civil War aftermath which pro-

16

duced the lowest morale ever in Texas history, had not wiped out chivalry. Though both coaches were full when Rebecca and Kate stepped aboard, most of the male passengers rose immediately to offer seating.

Still, it was not a comfortable journey. The aisle was full of standing men who swayed with the irregularities of the rails. The women's high-necked, ankle-length apparel intensified the effects of heat, humidity, and closely packed bodies. There was also an abundance of cigar smoke, making the very act of breathing a conscious effort.

Things only worsened at Victoria, where far more people wanted on than off. Even though numerous men chose to make the balance of the trip on the boarding steps of each car, not everyone seeking a ride succeeded in getting one. Those who were packed inside tried to comfort themselves with the knowledge that the train would not stop again until it reached Indianola.

Kate, at Rebecca's urging, had taken a window seat. The rolling, chaparral-covered hills of the past two days were rapidly evolving into a flatter contour, with few trees of any real stature. South of Victoria the terrain became level and nearly treeless, and pockets of marsh began to appear. The lone redeeming feature, to Kate's way of thinking, was the sky. It was cloud-clear from horizon to zenith, and royal in hue.

Rebecca learned much from her audit of several ongoing conversations around them. The defendant in the murder trial at Indianola was named Bill Taylor. He and his brother, Jim, had killed former State Police officer Bill Sutton and another man at the city's wharves more than a year earlier. All four of the principals in this tragedy were from the vicinity of Clinton.

While no one ever produced a precise number, scores of men lost their lives in the events surrounding the bloodsoaked Sutton-Taylor Feud. Its antecedent, spawned immediately after the Civil War, was a recurring clash of wills between the occupying Federal troops and the free-spirited sons of Creed Taylor. This conflict spread like wildfire to other causes and other factions, including the Suttons, before finally burning itself out more than a decade later.

After Indian problems took Federal occupation forces elsewhere, hatred for unwanted authority was transferred to the State Police of Reconstruction Governor E. J. Davis. These officers, in dealing with the lawlessness of the coastal cattle country, used brutal enforcement methods such as intimidation, ambush, and the murder of captives.

Bill Sutton became the acknowledged leader of the State Police in the Clinton area. He purportedly took part in the slayings of the Kelly brothers, Taylor in-laws who at the time were unarmed prisoners, as well as the fatal ambush of old Pitkin Taylor. Pitkin's sons, Bill and Jim, swore at their father's funeral that Bill Sutton would pay with his own life.

In March 1874, Sutton, his pregnant wife, Laura, and a companion, Gabriel Slaughter, boarded a steamship at the Indianola docks. While standing with Laura on the lower deck of the departing steamer, Sutton and Slaughter were gunned down from the wharf by the Taylor brothers. Laura Sutton was not physically harmed, but the explosive horror of those few seconds remained with her for life.

Kate's initial sight of their final destination was less than inspiring. Against the horizon of the coastal prairie appeared a scattering of weather-scarred frame homes and outbuildings. But when the train began its slow, curving approach into town, whistle wailing, Kate realized Indianola was larger than it first appeared, and much busier.

As they entered the outskirts, the rail route was joined by that of a heavily traveled dirt thoroughfare. Plodding oxen, tended by whip-cracking teamsters on foot, drew wagons of varying sizes and lengths, most covered with hoop-supported canvas to protect their contents. Shouting men on horseback moved to and fro among the bellowing members of a Longhorn cattle herd, compressed by the railroad tracks on one side and a series of picket-fenced yards on the other. The movements of men and animals sent up a perpetual cloud of dust, which drifted slowly to the northwest on the currents of the prevailing breeze from the Gulf of Mexico.

These sights and sounds were hardly new to Kate, raised in the major center of commerce for South Texas. But Indianola did offer something that land-locked San Antonio could not. Before the train eased into the business district, Kate caught glimpses of sparkling Matagorda Bay and its nautical traffic.

Further slowing, and a final series of whistles, produced

heightened chatter and movement among the passengers. They began their quest for freedom and fresh air even before the train grated to a stop.

Swooping seagulls and thin, curling wisps of white clouds were all that occupied the brilliant blue sky over the bay.

Seated on the second-floor gallery of the Magnolia Hotel, Rebecca and Kate luxuriated in the fresh breeze playing across their faces. The late afternoon sun was behind them, as were the discomforts of their journey. A narrow strip of shell-strewn beach, all that the encroaching bay waters had left of Water Street, lay between them and the light surf.

Kate watched the activity on the bay, the opened New Testament lying all but forgotten in her lap.

Great wooden wharves reached out hundreds of feet into the dark waters. Lined up alongside them were sailing ships and steamships, moored after travels from as far away as New York. Beyond the T-heads of the wharves other vessels rode at anchor, low in the water under the weight of cargo. Most waited on an opportunity to dock, but the cargoes of a few were being lightered where they lay by crews manning single-masted scows.

The wharftops were acrawl with discharged or prospective passengers, horse- and mule-drawn carts and wagons, and swaggering sets of stevedores. A trainload of cattle was being backed onto an especially sturdy-looking wharf. The Longhorns were to be the cargo of the steamer *Stephen F. Austin,* whose crew was readying a gangplank rigged with a chute.

"Becky! Becky Cumin's!"

Both Rebecca and Kate turned their heads in reaction to the loud and unexpected salutation. Its source was a giant of a man who appeared to be in his early seventies, his ruddy, mustachioed face wrapped in a wide smile. One meaty hand gripped a walking cane; the other, when the two women met his gaze, lifted a wide-brimmed hat. Keen gray eyes spoke delight as the man took a couple of heavy steps forward in anticipation of a return greeting. Not immediately receiving it, he hesitated.

The cane was driven to the oaken floor of the verandah with a thump. "It's Seth!" he bellowed, impatiently knitting his brow.

Although her eyesight had let her down, Rebecca's memory

rescued both parties from further embarrassment. "Why, Seth Swearingen!" she responded with genuine enthusiasm. "Can it really be you? Oh, yes! How wonderful!"

Swearingen wrapped Rebecca's hand in his, leaned over and pecked her on the cheek, and lowered his great frame into an adjacent chair with an exhalation of pleasure. "It's shore great t' see ya, Becky," he rumbled. "Excuse me," he added abruptly. "I should be callin' you Miz Portis." This was said tenuously, more like a question than a statement.

Rebecca nodded, then introduced Kate as her traveling companion. "Mr. Swearingen's family and mine go back many years," she told Kate.

"That's right, Miss," Swearingen reinforced. "In fact, all the way back t' Kentucky. We was raised together on the Ohio River. Why, Becky and me—uh, Miz Portis and me—we seen the first steamboat ever t' run the Ohio."

Thus granted equality in the conversation, Kate asked how close to Cincinnati the site of their Kentucky upbringing might be. "I was born in Texas," she said, "but both my parents were from Cincinnati."

"Our home places," Swearingen reflected, "must of been about a hundred miles or so upriver. I been to Cincinnati a few times."

"Are you here for the Taylor murder trial?" Rebecca asked.

"Oh, no," came the reply, "though I would like to try and hear some of it if I kin squeeze into the courtroom. They was about t' finish jury selectin' today, I understand. No, I come here t' see if I kin find out who's been buyin' my cattle hides."

Encouraged by puzzled countenances, Swearingen continued. "I ain't the one been sellin' the hides. My cattle has been killed an' skinned, up north of Yorktown, and the Meskins doin' it have been bringin' the hides to Indianola to sell. Once I find who's doin' the buyin' . . . well, I reckon I kin discourage 'em from receivin' any more," he said, with a meaningful smirk.

"Are you sure it's Mexicans taking the hides?" Kate asked, a bit irritated at the rancher's manner.

"We caught one of 'em red-handed, Little Miss," Swearingen said, the unpleasant smirk broadening. "Him, now, we won't have no more trouble with. After we shot him, we cut open the belly of the cow he was skinnin' and tucked his head up inside. Then we pinned a sign to his chest, so as to let his *amigos* know they'll be next."

To what extent Kate failed to mask her revulsion, Swearingen took no notice. She glanced toward the bay, knuckles whitening as she gripped her New Testament.

The man returned Rebecca's gaze with a huge smile. "I can't believe it's been more'n thirty years!" he exclaimed. Leaning forward for emphasis, he added in a softer voice: "You're still the finest-lookin' lady I ever set eyes on."

His compliment went unchallenged. It did, though, prompt a change in subjects.

The ensuing chatter, rife with remembrance, revealed that Rebecca's family had forsaken the Ohio Valley to join the colony of Stephen F. Austin in Mexican Texas. The Swearingen clan soon followed, and the expatriated Kentuckians reunited at San Felipe de Austin on the Brazos River. Kate, a rapt listener, heard several references to family tragedies on the Texas frontier. She also learned that San Felipe ("San Phillip," Swearingen called it) was where Rebecca met and married David Portis. Shortly after that marriage, Swearingen moved away and developed his ranching operation in the brush country. He never married. It occurred to Kate that the big cattleman's first and possibly only love was now seated within three feet of him.

Abruptly, Rebecca turned to Kate and asked her to arrange with the hotel for a carriage ride.

"We'll go in the morning to Alligator Head," she said, an uncharacteristic sparkle in her eye. "It's the best place to see the ships come and go." She then surprised Kate by asking Swearingen if he cared to join them. He responded in the affirmative, although conditional upon the demands of his business in Indianola.

His interest in the Taylor murder trial, Kate reflected, was certainly short-lived.

Rebecca had returned to their rooms when Kate arrived to report on the success of her errand. The older woman asked if she knew who their driver would be.

The question both surprised and flustered Kate, and her face turned pink. Before she could stammer out an answer, Rebecca said mockingly, "Why, it's probably going to be that nice German boy who met us at the train. Yes, I believe I must be right. What's his name?"

"Mr. Schroeder," Kate said, embarrassed over being forced to admit that she knew.

Rebecca stopped the needling. "Don't be uncomfortable, dear." A knowing smile played over her lips. "Sometimes I see more with these old eyes than you might think. He is a rather nice-looking young man, at that."

Chapter 4

*F*or several thousand Germans who left their homeland in the 1840s for a new start in the fabled Republic of Texas, the point of entry into this land of promise was the remote, mosquito-ridden marshland on the west rim of Matagorda Bay.

These adventurers entrusted their futures to a colonizing venture funded and run by German noblemen. When the first cramped, sickly shiploads of prospective settlers landed, they found preparations woefully inadequate to ensure their survival. Shelter, food, medicine, and transportation were scarce, and many immigrants, already weakened from the grueling, pestilential voyage, died at the tiny company camp of Karlshafen.

Most of the surviving families ultimately reached the intended destination of New Braunfels, nearly 150 miles inland, or struck out on their own for more promising places. But a few entrepreneurs, knowing that more waves of fellow countrymen would be washing ashore, chose to stay in Karlshafen. The new town was several hundred souls strong when Texas joined the United States in 1846. Three years later, it changed its name to Indianola. Growth was rapid and the future apparently bright.

However, the community remained vulnerable to two ruthless adversaries: disease and tropical storms.

Yellow fever in epidemic form first gripped Indianola and other coastal Texas towns in 1853. Quarantines and quick burials were the only measures available to the panicked populace.

Seth Swearingen, by that time already ranching in the brush

country north of Clinton, had taken several slaves to Indianola and offered his help. He had not considered the mission suicidal; it was an accepted premise that those from outside the stricken areas were immune to the contagion.

Every member of his party lived to tell about what they saw and did. None, in fact, could forget.

"People died so fast that they couldn't dig graves for all of 'em," Swearingen recounted afterwards. "Finally, we just dug a long trench in the beach north of town and buried 'em in it."

An eruption of black vomit, he recalled, "meant a yellow fever victim was done for. In some cases, even before they had done twitchin' they was put into boxes. And I mean boxes, not real coffins—just that and nothin' more. I had to help take two little girls from their beds and put 'em into boxes before they was completely gone."

Among the casualties of the epidemic were the parents of Konrad Schroeder, who was then three years old. Konrad and a younger sister were raised by relatives who worked at the Magnolia Hotel. By the time he reached manhood, Konrad himself had become a valued member of the hotel staff, with permanent quarters in the stable.

Sharing those premises was Enrique Guzman, who from his last name had acquired the sobriquet of "Goose." Guzman's privileges of residency came in exchange for upkeep of carriages, harness, and horseflesh owned by the hotel and its guests. His spending money came from employment on the waterfront, hard work which had built strength and endurance into a deceptively slight body.

Close in age, Konrad and Goose were frequently companions by choice in their spare time. The people of Indianola grew accustomed to seeing the big, blond German and the dark, mustachioed Mexican together on the street. This pairing might have triggered some disapproval in caste-conscious Victoria, Guzman's hometown, but almost everyone in youthful, plebeian Indianola was on equal social terms.

The morning after the Portis party arrived at the Magnolia, Konrad and Goose took an early stroll downtown to learn the status of the Bill Taylor murder trial. Konrad kept close track of the time; he intended to be punctual in driving Miss Donahoo and her mistress to Alligator Head.

Taylor was facing trial for gunning down Gabe Slaughter, the young man who had so unwisely joined Bill and Laura Sutton at Indianola. Since Jim Taylor remained at large, eighteen months after the twin slayings, Bill Taylor's day in court was uppermost in the minds of all parties to the Sutton-Taylor Feud.

After more than a year in jail at Galveston, placed there by law officers who feared he might be either rescued or lynched if kept in Indianola, Taylor was back in the Calhoun County calaboose, a block from the courthouse. This morning, he was due in court to hear the state's formal charge against him.

The azure skies of the past few days were gone. Dark clouds ruled, and a damp, unpleasant wind out of the east blew across the bay.

The route Konrad and Goose were taking to the courthouse led past the jail. As they approached the lockup, a quartet of armed men stepped briskly from the front door. Steely eyes shaded by wide-brimmed hats swept the street, and quickly settled on the big German and his companion. Hands tightened on four rifles, bringing Konrad and Goose to an abrupt halt. Neither of the companions was carrying a gun, and the surprise and alarm stamped on their youthful faces seemed to reassure the armed men. The four sheriff's deputies turned their attention to three other figures emerging from the jail.

Konrad knew two of those three: District Attorney Bill Cain and Sheriff Fred Busch. He figured that the man in between, each wrist handcuffed to the inner wrist of his escorts, had to be Bill Taylor.

The accused did not present an especially evil or intimidating image. Not much older than Konrad, he was short, already balding, and decidedly plump—the last attribute probably due to a year of confinement and square meals. He seemed unconcerned about what awaited him. As the entourage started up the street toward the courthouse, two deputies in front and two at the rear, Taylor was the only one in the procession wearing neither a hat nor an officially grim visage.

Maintaining a prudent and respectful distance, Goose and Konrad followed.

Gathered on opposite sides of the front steps to the courthouse were some of Bill Taylor's best friends and worst enemies:

the Taylor faction to the left and the Sutton crowd to the right, equally well armed. Unnaturally silent, they all watched his heavily guarded approach.

"Keep moving, men," Busch quietly told his deputies. "We ain't stopping for nobody." Raising his voice, he addressed those waiting at the steps: "Stay out of our way, boys! Calhoun County is gonna see to it that Mr. Taylor has his trial before a judge an' jury. No trouble, now!"

Wide-eyed, Konrad and Goose came to a stop once more. Each faction before the courthouse boasted more than a dozen members, and every one of them was intently eyeing the sheriff's little band. Busch's warning created such a hush that the crunching of boots against the seashell-surfaced street seemed magnified as the lawmen maintained their course.

When they reached the bottom step and began their ascent, Taylor exchanged eye contact and a couple of phantom nods with certain of the Taylor group. From his right came grumblings and muttered curses. Every onlooker stood with arms loose and extended, ready for someone else's sudden move.

It did not come.

Once the prisoner was safely inside, two deputies took a spot at the top of the steps and faced those below. They announced that no firearms would be allowed in the courthouse.

Most of the men appeared willing to yield their weapons for a view of the proceedings. The process, though, was going to take time, and Konrad did not intend to be late for his appointment with the ladies from San Antonio. Goose, for his part, was less concerned about the time than he was over the prospect of a personal frisking. He carried a knife concealed on the inside of his left boot.

They were on the verge of shrugging off their disappointment and returning to the hotel when Konrad recalled having seen an emergency ladder at the rear of the courthouse. The pair rounded the building and to their delight found that the ladder was unattended. It led straight to one window of the courtroom on the second floor.

They decided to take turns peering in. Goose went first, scurrying quietly up the rungs until his head was level with the coveted view. The first thing he saw was the judge's raised bench, occupied by a black-robed, gray-bearded gent who calmly cradled a carbine in his left arm. On the near side of the bench stood Sheriff Busch, hands cupping the oversized buckle on a two-holster gunbelt weighted by identical Colts. On the far side of the judge was the jury box—empty for the moment.

Facing the bench from separate tables were prosecutor Crain and accused murderer Taylor, the latter seated next to a well-dressed man who was doubtless the attorney for the defense. A wooden rail separated them from the spectators. Armed officers shared the front row of seats with a young woman whose hat, veil, and dress were black.

Goose inhaled sharply. The veil could not mask the hatred blazing from the eyes of the widow Sutton as she glared at the back of Taylor's head.

Without warning, the window sash was jerked open and a rifle barrel thrust out. Goose instinctively threw up both hands, lost his balance, and fell off the ladder with a loud cry. He landed on Konrad, who had tried to catch him, and they went to the ground in a heap.

Shaken but not hurt, they sat up slowly and faced each other. Alarm gave way first to relief, then to laughter. But sobriety swiftly returned. Following a rush of footsteps, two more rifles were stuck in their faces.

"Who the devil are you? What were you doing up there?" an angry deputy sheriff shouted at them. "Keep your hands up!" he snapped as they rose painfully to their feet.

A second officer searched them. "They ain't got no guns," he reported.

"W-we just wanted to get a little look-see at the trial," Konrad stammered after he and Goose identified themselves.

"You sure picked a hell of a way to do it," came the disgusted response. "That was a fool stunt. We'll likely see enough trouble around here without any bone-headed moves like that. Go on, now. Get outta here."

Sheepishly, and a little stiffly, the companions picked up their hats and obeyed. By the time they were a half-block away, though, the laughter returned full-blown.

"I s'pose we're lucky we didn't break our necks," Konrad said, wiping tears from his eyes.

"*Sí*, and also not in jail," Goose responded. "Anyway, they no find *mi amigo*," he added, reaching down and patting the inside of his boot.

"What did you get to see?" Konrad asked.

Goose, growing serious, expounded on the firepower visible in the courtroom. "The Taylor gang," he said, "they mos' be gonna try to save Bill Taylor, *sí*?"

"And the Sutton gang may have come here to kill him," Konrad rejoined. "I guess that's why the law is actin' so spooked. Maybe you and me are lucky we didn't catch a bullet just now."

Rebecca did not feel at her best, and the weather was far from pleasant. But an early-morning note from Swearingen saying he would join the outing bolstered her resolve to go. Kate, meanwhile, was preoccupied with new and confusing thoughts and sensations.

How, Kate wondered, could Rebecca sense her attraction to Konrad Schroeder? He had simply met them at the train depot, driven them to the hotel, and brought up their bags. Yet, Kate reflected, *Mrs. Portis knew, better than I myself did, that I seem to have an interest. Well, we'll see how things go today.*

At first, they went well.

Promptly at ten, Konrad pulled up in front of the hotel atop a handsome, mahogany-trimmed brougham drawn by a matched pair of chestnut geldings. If his choice of vehicles appeared ostentatious for a casual country outing, Konrad stood ready to justify it with a reminder that Mrs. Portis was an established and esteemed patron of the Magnolia.

Swearingen assisted Rebecca into the carriage, then turned to help Kate. Impulsively, Konrad asked Kate if she might wish to ride up front and help with the reins. She hesitated, then picked up the nod from her mistress and acquiesced. As Konrad accepted her little gloved hand, the sensation was everything that either of them had anticipated.

During the hour-long drive Konrad gave Kate a synopsis of his early-morning adventure, followed by a general dissertation on the Sutton-Taylor Feud. Their conversation then moved into a cautious exchange of personal information.

Inside the carriage, the old friends worked diligently at fanning Swearingen's flame even though both knew the effort was pointless.

There's no fool like an old fool, Swearingen was telling himself even while turning up the charm a notch.

Alligator Head, the point of mainland nearest Pass Cavallo, offered a panoramic view of the marine traffic moving to and from the Gulf of Mexico. Kate was awestruck by the criss-crossing parades of stately schooners and smoking steamships, behemoths of grace and power trailed by intersecting wakes. She was unmindful of the choppiness of the bay water, made turbulent by the damp gusts of wind from the gulf, and did not recognize the signatures of storm damage written on the rigging of several incoming vessels.

After watching for a few minutes from the carriage, Kate accepted Konrad's offer to get an even closer view by walking to the riprap-reinforced shoreline. Their elderly associates, conversationally embroiled in events long past, declined to join them.

"I do miss the ol' Ohio River," Swearingen was saying. "Texas is bigger and better in a lots of ways, but it ain't got a river like the Ohio. Why, the Brazos is hardly any wider than Brush Crick was."

Rebecca nodded. "I recollect that when we came to Texas," she said, "my brothers had to build and run a sawmill and grist mill in exchange for their big, five-league grant. The creek that ran through the grant, you'll recall, was hardly more than a trickle, between the rains. But they made do."

"Did you ever go back to Kentucky?" Swearingen asked.

"No," Rebecca replied firmly. "I've never gone back to any place. Not to Kentucky. Not even to San Felipe." There was, though, a strain of wistfulness in her voice.

Swearingen studied her face, then said, "I been back to both places. Neither one has ever growed. When we left Kentucky for Texas in '29, they was layin' out a town on the Ohio that they called Concord. It was down below your family's place, across Sycamore Crick. The next Cincinnati, they called it.

"I went back there in 1860, right before the war. I recollect the time as bein' late September. Concord was still alive, but just barely."

He gestured at the scarred, brass-tipped walking cane leaning against his carriage seat. "Picked that up on the same trip. It's hickory."

Rebecca kept her eyes on the bay. The real images before her, though, were sharply focused memories of Indian summer in the Ohio Valley. "Was the goldenrod out?" she asked dreamily.

"Yeah," the big rancher responded. His intended amplification was interrupted by the return of the hired help.

While helping Kate back onto the driver's bench, Konrad told Swearingen of the storm-damaged ships. "They took a beatin' somewhere out in the gulf," he said. "It's beginnin' to get nasty here, too." Peering in at Rebecca, he added, "If it's all right with you, Mrs. Portis, maybe we had best be headin' back."

Chapter 5

A soft rain began as the little party re-entered Indianola. Konrad reluctantly reined in the geldings so he could help Kate find shelter inside the carriage and fetch a poncho for himself.

Taking a seat next to Rebecca, Kate saw immediately that her mistress was gray of face and in discomfort. "I'm glad you're here, Little Miss," Swearingen said in a worried rumble. "Becky seems t' have faded a mite."

Once at the hotel, Rebecca needed help to leave the brougham, and it took both Kate and Konrad to get her upstairs to her rooms. Kate had never seen her mistress stricken in this fashion. But she repeatedly waved off offers to summon a doctor, insisting that such spells had come and gone before and she would be fine.

This lame climax to the once-promising sojourn left Swearingen standing alone in the hotel lobby, scowling and thumping his cane against the floor in agitation. "Can I help you, sir?" the desk clerk asked.

Interrupted from morose thoughts, Swearingen glared at the clerk and then nodded. "Yeah," he growled. "Send a bottle of your best whiskey up to my room. Water, too." He stomped off toward the staircase.

At the stable, Konrad had to rub down the horses and clean the harness and brougham himself. Goose, doubtless pulling a shift at the docks, was not on hand. "Not having much fun, either, I'll bet," Konrad mused aloud, glancing out through the parted wooden doors at the falling drizzle.

The damp, clean scent of the rain crept into the stable, blending with the aromas of horses, leather, saddle soap, and hay. As he worked, Konrad kept a smiling image of Kate in his mind's eye. He considered various intrigues that would bring them in contact. Idly, he also wondered whether Mrs. Portis had recovered from her spell.

Around midafternoon, a soaked and exhausted Goose trudged in. "Plenty work for everybody," he announced to Konrad in a hoarse voice, pulling off his sodden shirt. "Big storm coming in, maybe here. They want to unload everything in the harbor. I just come to get my poncho and a dry shirt and rest a little while. Good money to go back."

As if to underscore his news, a gust of wind shook and swung the stable doors. The erstwhile drizzle was growing steadily into a downpour.

"Well, Goose," Konrad responded, "if we have something blowing in from the gulf, there is work to be done around the Magnolia, too. Guess I better get moving." He donned his poncho and hat and strode decisively out of the stable, attracted to the hotel by more than a mere sense of duty.

Rebecca, running a fever, slept most of the afternoon under the unwavering vigil of Kate. The rise in humidity and an intermittent rush of rain against the roof and bayside windows put Kate herself into a drowsy state. Stubbornly, she resisted the urge to sleep and delved into her beloved New Testament. Every few moments, she reassured herself that her mistress was still sleeping peacefully.

The only time Kate left the room was to order their supper. When it was brought up, she felt a pang of disappointment that the delivery was not made by Konrad.

Konrad had intended to put in an appearance at the Portis quarters after latching up and tying down everything on the premises that might be vulnerable to a gale. Those rounds made, he came inside, dried off as thoroughly as possible, and climbed the stairs, his heart picking up tempo.

Swearingen's room was just off the landing. Aware that the old cattleman had ordered two bottles of whiskey since their morning ride, Konrad decided to look in on him.

He had to knock twice before getting a responsive bellow. He opened the door and glanced in. Swearingen, still wearing coat and boots, was piled up on the bed, whiskey glass in hand. The hickory cane was hooked over the brass bed frame behind his pillows. An empty bottle lay on its side near the lavatory cabinet, apparently at journey's end after a roll across the floor. A second bottle, still two-thirds full, rested next to an empty water pitcher on the bedside table.

"Come in, boy," Swearingen said, a note of affection in his thickened speech. An inviting but erratic wave of his free hand toward the bottle on the table just missed knocking it over. "Hab a drink, and I'll tell yuh aw about women. Damn 'em!"

In light of the rancher's advanced intoxication, Konrad made a quick decision. If he closed the storm shutters over Swearingen's windows, it would mean having to light a lamp—always a major hazard where a drunk was involved. Since the windows were on the town side, facing away from the expected blow, Konrad decided to leave the shutters alone.

What he did not leave alone was the whiskey.

When Kate answered his knock, Konrad snatched off his hat with an exaggerated motion, smiled broadly, and asked a bit too loudly how Mrs. Portis was doing. Kate's welcoming smile froze as she looked intently into those large, blue eyes so like her own. They were reddened. And from the caller came an unmistakable whiff of the detested odor of whiskey.

The joy left Kate's face. "Mr. Schroeder," she asked with a decided lack of warmth, "have you been drinking?"

Konrad's unwary smile threatened to split his face. His dulled senses had not yet sounded an alarm.

"I looked in on Mr. Swearingen," he confided, "to make sure everything was in order in his room. I was a li'l worried 'bout him. We had a coupla drinks."

Inwardly, Kate was crushed. Outwardly, manifesting her Baptist upbringing, she radiated mounting disapproval. Konrad stepped back, belatedly intimidated.

"Mrs. Portis is resting comfortably, thank you," Kate managed to say in a cool tone. "If there is nothing else, Mr. Schroeder, then good night." The door was abruptly shut.

His surprise and hurt turning to frustration and anger, Konrad slapped his hat on and stomped away. Totally forgotten was his official mission of securing the storm shutters in the Portis rooms.

Leaning against the door, Kate lowered her head and bit her lip until it was bruised. More painful, though, was the stab of disappointment in her heart.

"Kate," Rebecca called out in a tremulous voice. She had raised her head off the pillows and was looking blankly around the shadowy bed chamber.

"I'm here, Mrs. Portis," Kate said, casting her own distress aside. The elderly woman said nothing else for a moment, though she reached out a hand for assistance. She slowly sat up on the side of the bed. Kate helped slide Rebecca's bare feet into a pair of slippers and draped a shawl over the hunched shoulders.

When Rebecca next spoke, her voice was stronger. "Please, dear," she said. "In my blue bag, inside a leather wrapper, is a book. Would you get it for me?"

Kate went to the bag indicated and fished out a thin rectangle of leather secured by a frayed red ribbon. She carefully removed the ribbon and unfolded the brittle wrapping. The book cover, consisting of cloth stretched over board panels, was so faded as to be neutral in color.

She cautiously opened the aged volume, anticipating a request to read from it. The badly foxed title page proclaimed the contents to be the four Gospels of the New Testament, printed at Oxford, England. The frontispiece crudely but effectively depicted a haloed Jesus delivering the Sermon on the Mount to an awestruck assemblage.

The rain rattled heavily on the windows for several seconds, then subsided to a soft staccato. The daylight had grown so wan that the room was virtually in twilight. Kate positioned the book to get as much light as she could on its yellowed pages.

"Read the inscription, please, in the front of the book," Rebecca requested.

Kate parted the front cover and the flyleaf and found, in boldly penned strokes that had withstood the years:

> To our beloved Rebekah, on the blessed occasion of her marriage to Mr. Anthony Cumings. 14 September, 1775. May ye always abide within His light.

Kate's eyes widened. "A hundred years ago today!" she exclaimed.

"Yes, dear, one hundred years ago," Rebecca echoed. "My grandparents gave this book to my mother on her wedding day. She would have been very close to your age then. No, that's not right. She had just turned eighteen. Imagine! Two years younger, even, than you."

"So you were named for your mother," Kate said.

"Yes, though as you see, her name was spelled differently. She always told me that her name was spelled the Old Testament way, and mine was the New Testament spelling."

Rebecca closed her eyes.

"My mother never loved any man but my father. She met him young and married young, and within the year went out into the Kentucky wilderness with him. My mother had been raised enjoying the comforts of that time, but she agreed to live far from home where hardly any of those comforts existed. She did it because she was committed to my father.

"She spent her last twenty-five years without him, but she never loved anyone else."

Rebecca opened her eyes, and those damaged orbs tried to search out Kate's gaze through the gathering gloom. "That is the way to fall in love, Kate. When you're young, and only once."

A lump formed in Kate's throat and something very much like a sob forced its way through her lips. She could not speak.

The rain grew loud again. Its flowing patterns on the windows were reflected in the vanity mirror, and then thrown against the rapt face of the young listener. The shadows intensified.

"I am sure you wondered, though you would never have asked," Rebecca resumed, "why I chose to include Mr. Swearingen on the ride today. You may mark it down to vanity. Poor Seth always tried to be there, at my doorstep—that is, up until I married David. I realize that I probably did him no favors this morning by taking him with us."

She sighed. "I used to believe I would someday have the man of my desires, but something kept getting in the way—always something. And the one time when I thought what I had waited and prayed for was finally going to work out . . . ." Her voice trailed off. Even in the darkness, her eyes twinkled with tears.

Kate, still holding the book, remained silent and motionless while the other woman regained her voice.

In the back of the book, Rebecca explained, was a cloth pouch. "Please be very careful, my dear," she cautioned, as Kate turned the book over. "You will find a letter in the pouch. Unfold it—be careful—and read it out loud. Any parts you may not be able to make out, I can give you from memory."

PART II

The Journey
(1776)

Chapter 6

South of Harpers Ferry, that durable little community sandwiched by the spectacular confluence of the Potomac and Shenandoah rivers, the tree-shrouded Loudoun Heights rise to greet travelers entering the Virginia county of the same name.

Beyond the initial rocky ascent, the land opens into flowing hills so reminiscent of Scotland that the comparison has been made repeatedly for three centuries. To the east lies the meandering Potomac; to the west, a thin strip of the Blue Ridge Mountains flanking the Shenandoah Valley.

In February 1755, when the area was still part of Fairfax County, Welsh immigrant Samuel Russel secured acreage along the Northwest Fork of Goose Creek. Two years later, the same year Loudoun County was formed, Russel and his Irish wife, the former Sarah Moore, celebrated the birth of their third child—a daughter they christened Rebekah.

Two decades following, early in the momentous year of 1776, the newly married Rebekah and her family were poised on the brink of tumultuous change.

One wintry January evening, Samuel Russel stood backed up to a robust fire in the study of his hillcrest manor house. The only other person in the room was a much younger man who stood with hands on hips, his full attention directed toward Russel. He gave the appearance of expecting to disagree with what Russel was about to say.

Outside, the somber, fading sky had begun to emit snow. Red oak, hickory, maple, and walnut trees huddled in dark clumps, their barren branches spread like a skeletal canopy against the drifting flakes. The surrounding hills, criss-crossed with stone fences and hedgerows of cherry and locust, would soon turn from patchwork brown to uniform white. Far below the manor house, ice had formed thickly against the banks of Goose Creek and threatened to creep out and merge at midstream.

"Anthony," the older man said, anxious to present his thoughts before being interrupted for dinner, "I want you to consider a proposal. As you are now my son-in-law, I view Rebekah's happiness and your own as inseparable."

Anthony Cumings had a general idea of what was coming, and he intended to express his own desires before the matter could be considered settled. However, he owed his father-in-law and host the initial courtesy of attentive silence.

There was also, on Anthony's part, some deference in regard to age and financial status. The contrast in the clothing worn by the conversationalists was as obvious as the difference in their ages.

Russel, although not sporting a wig on this occasion, was substantially clad in silk breeches and hose. His waistcoat of royal blue was finely trimmed with gold embroidery; the buttons, and the buckles on his elegant shoes, were of silver. His white linen shirt sported ruffles at the neck and cuffs.

The shirt Cumings wore (his best) was similar to Russel's. But the breeches and unadorned waistcoat were of wool, their buttons and buckles made from bone. His yarn stockings were stuffed into leather shoes charitably described as acceptable.

Cumings had youth and other personal assets on his side of the ledger. His was a rugged build, earned through the back-breaking rigors of farming, and he owned a clean-shaven, friendly, moderately handsome face topped by thick brown hair. Marginally under six feet in height, he still measured several inches taller than the round, gray-headed, balding gentleman by the fireplace. Cumings's naturally fair complexion ran to ruddiness and freckles, in contrast to the dark skin of Russel.

Weighing on the minds of both men were the disintegrated relations between Britain and its American colonies. All else having failed, full-scale war was in the offing. Though the Declaration of Independence would not be issued for another half-year, the Continental Congress in July 1775 had taken two rather obvious measures: appointing George Washington commander of the Continental Army, and three days afterward declaring that the colonies were taking up arms against their heavy-handed parent nation. While the official stance of the congressional delegates in 1775 invited the possibility of reconciliation "when hostility shall cease on the part of our aggressors," the ultimate desire of most of those unhappy with Britain's yoke was nothing less than independence.

The declaration of war gave new importance to the colonists' earlier encounters with British troops at Lexington, Concord, and Breed's Hill in the vicinity of Boston. They were embraced as moral victories, if not tactical ones, stirring hopes the entire length of the Atlantic seaboard from Maine to Georgia.

Virginia had witnessed rebel heroics of its own in 1775, in the seaport towns of Hampton and Norfolk.

Lord Dunmore, who proved to be Virginia's last governor of royal appointment, had displayed little diplomatic genius even while his subjects' demonstrations of ill-will toward King George III were limited to the published word. When the unified resolve of the Continental Congress was made clear, Dunmore first fortified, then fled, his official nest in Williamsburg. He took refuge aboard a warship harbored at nearby Norfolk and soon decided he could hold that community against the colonials with a force made up of Tories, "freed" slaves, and a sprinkling of seasoned British soldiers and seamen.

The siege of Norfolk came to an earlier-than-anticipated end in December, when Dunmore inexplicably ordered his small, motley force to attack the Americans' position outside the city. The Battle of Great Bridge produced no long casualty lists, but its outcome in favor of the Continentals did serve to remove Dunmore as a further obstacle. He took his wife and winsome daughters and fled Virginia by ship.

Meanwhile, American forces undertaking to run the British out of Canada had captured Montreal and at year's end were preparing for an onslaught of Quebec.

American leadership believed, and advertised the belief, that France for certain, and probably Spain, would become active allies in the near future. In all, the spirits of those colonists who yearned to break the hated British rule were high indeed.

The reflections of Russel and Cumings on these events were as different as day and night.

Anthony Cumings burned with patriotic fervor. He fully expected to take part in the pending conflict. As far as he was concerned, his wedding to Rebekah last summer had only temporarily delayed enlistment in the Continental Army. Even now, he was building up a resolve to announce to his bride and their families his intent to join Washington in the spring.

On the other hand, Russel, who as a young man had witnessed the might and ruthlessness of the British military machine, foresaw nothing but bloody, bitter defeat and long-term consequences awaiting his adopted country. Painfully aware of his son-in-law's passion, he had for weeks quietly schemed to devise a sure-fire plan of deterrence. Finally convinced that he had created one, the wily Welshman was choosing this pre-dinner fireside chat for the opportunity to spring it.

Russel pointed to a large tapestry hanging between the east windows of the study.

"There, my boy, is one of the few sons of Kymru—excuse me, Wales—who the English are pleased to honor as a fellow Briton. And that is because he gives the British a claim to America that is ages older than the claim Columbus made for Spain."

Cumings had frequently admired the images on the heavy rectangle of cloth, crafted by none other than Russel. Dominating the work were the head and shoulders of a young man whose flowing red hair and full beard encircled a mystical, serene countenance. Tranquil blue eyes met the gaze of all observers. Across his temples ran a woven headband of various bright colors. His purple tunic bore gold trim vaguely nautical in design. From the chain around his neck hung a large gold disk bearing the likeness of a winged serpent or dragon with undulating body and coiled tail.

Behind him, under a sky of white, puffy clouds, rolled the sea. Over his right shoulder billowed a square-rigged sail, propelling a small ship. A white Maltese cross occupied the otherwise scarlet field of the sail. A red-haired figure clad in purple (obviously the same man in the head-and-shoulders portrait) stood in the bow, gazing forward while crew members tended the ship.

"Prince Madoc," Russel identified the subject of his intricate work. "Half Welsh, half Irish—like your own little wife, my boy."

Madoc, he continued, was one of numerous sons born to a feudal warlord whose death produced bloody competition for his throne. Madoc spurned the strife and chose the sea, and became a mighty mariner whose praises would be sung by Welsh bards.

"He discovered a new land, far to the west, sometime around 1170 A.D.," Russel said. "He supposedly made three voyages there, the last from which neither he nor any of his sailors returned. After the success of Columbus three centuries later, the storytellers decided Madoc had reached America first.

"What you see here was copied by memory from a painting I studied many times when I was but a lad. It quite impressed me, as may be evident.

"Prince Madoc was generally credited with being a Christian and therefore probably martyred for the cause by the savages in America. If the serpentine figure on the gold disk mystifies you, understand that we Kymry must always celebrate our ancient national symbol, the dragon."

Cumings was indeed mystified, but not by the dragon. This discourse was not at all what he had expected.

"You may or may not know," Russel said after a moment's pause, his heavy black eyebrows knitted, "that as a young buck in Wales I held a petty magistrate's position. Suffice it to say that I later made some unfortunate alliances, necessitating my departure. Like Prince Madoc, I took to the sea to avoid trouble, and came to the land that I somewhat wistfully choose to believe contains his bones.

"I became an indentured servant to a man named Hardin, who very kindly rewarded my labor and diligence of five years by giving me clothing and a gun. He also allowed me to earn a small corner of this present estate. And like Prince Madoc, who secretly lies in state in some valley or atop some mountain, my bones will be buried in America."

The rotund Welshman studied the blazing fireplace for a while, as his guest maintained a puzzled silence. Then he turned to face his son-in-law, and resumed.

"This relative wealth and comfort now enjoyed by my family became mine even though Virginia was a colony of England." He held up a hand, open palm forward, to still the agitation those words stirred in the listener.

"At present," Russel continued, "there are those of us who

believe the Englishman's yoke is too tight, that the colonies are being treated in an arrogant, unfair fashion. I have no quarrel with those conclusions; the English throne has never been celebrated for its charity or tenderness.

"But as I grow older, and continue to think on these things, it occurs to me that the best course of action for Americans is not bloodshed. How can we accomplish anything, in the name of God, by using methods which He does not condone?"

Cumings's discomfiture increased. While Russel was not a Quaker, he had in recent years become close friends with his Quaker neighbors, many of them also of Welsh descent. Russel was allowed (as were other non-Quakers) to attend the monthly meetings of the Religious Society of Friends. In truth, Cumings respected the pious speech and reverent attitude displayed by most members of the sect; they stood for righteousness in a society where many professed Christians and their clergy tended to make a mockery of religion. In fact, some Friends had risen to leadership status in Loudoun County.

Now, though, the Quakers' steadfast belief in the immorality of war placed their integrity at loggerheads with popular sentiment. This pacifist stance was fast eroding their influence and good name. A confrontation was brewing over the Friends' refusal to give tithes beyond the regular tax levy for support of the Continental Army.

Cumings chose to break his silence. "I can understand," he began, with what he intended as great tact, "that one born in Great Britain would feel a strong loyalty to his king and country. Most of us born in America, though, do not necessarily share that bond."

Russel's round features clouded with impatience. The black brows contracted. "Young man," he responded, "I am a Welshman. The King of England rules my homeland, but he does not care for it. The English view the people of Wales—and of Scotland, too, for that matter—as wild, uncouth, uncivilized dreamers who represent something of a wart on the posterior of the British Empire.

"No, Anthony, I am not full of blind allegiance to the King of England. I am, though, quite mindful of the teachings of a far greater King who has seen us all through trying times. In brief, I have prospered in this young country under His hand, regardless of taxes and of who sits upon any earthly throne. It would be ungrateful—nay, sinful—to go counter to His instruction by raising the sword against those in authority."

Russel was finally showing his hand. Cumings had wondered to what lengths his father-in-law would go in attempting to dissuade family members from taking up arms against the British. What lengths, indeed!

Russel gave the glowing logs a vigorous once-over with the wrought-iron poker, prompting an eruption of sparks and flame. The reborn fire sent increased warmth and light billowing over the study. The Welshman turned and faced Cumings.

"I have reached some personal decisions," he said, "as regards my life on this earth as well as my eternal soul. If you would be kind enough to listen a bit longer to an old man, I shall attempt to sum up my thoughts."

Anthony Cumings locked his hands behind his back, smiled, and nodded. His affection for the other man was genuine. Russel had been a family friend for many years prior to the recently consummated courtship; whatever was on his mind, Cumings believed his heart held nought but kindness and good intentions.

"In order to better please my heavenly Lord, and have peace within myself," Russel said, "I am going to surrender certain of my properties, as well as the practice I have employed in accumulating them. I am speaking of my slaves, and the institution of slavery."

The Quaker influence again, Cumings told himself. Russel could never attain full acceptance from the Religious Society of Friends as long as he owned slaves. But Russel, almost as if he had read the other's thoughts, added, "I am doing this not to please any other man, but because I believe it is right."

This voluntary loss of manpower, Russel continued, would mean reducing the activities of his farm. Specifically, he cited the raising of tobacco. He had, he said, planted his final crop.

"It may be that some of the Negroes will stay on," he conjectured, "but that remains to be seen. In any event, this decision puts me in a position to dispose of other things I will no longer need. For instance, I will not be taking tobacco to market. Therefore, one or more of our fine Pennsylvania wagons will be available for other use. But I get a little ahead of myself.

"You have expressed a perfectly natural desire to join other young Americans in going to war. However, I am opposed to the initiating of violence and bloodshed. Please understand—I will not, unequivocally, oppose you in that endeavor. But I am prepared to offer you an alternative to consider and pray over."

Smiling, he rolled his eyes upward and spread wide his arms. "Imagine," he said, "a wilderness garden where every man, woman, and child can enjoy all of life's necessities in abundance. A heaven on earth where worship of our Lord comes first and continues un-interrupted, unsullied by the avaricious natural lusts of mankind."

At a recent meeting of the Friends, Russel said, he learned of such an Eden, newly created on the far side of the Allegheny Mountains, in the lush, fertile Ohio River Valley. "Its inhabitants live peacefully as neighbors to the red savages, whom they are winning over as worshipers of Christ," Russel related. "How I would love to see it myself . . . to take part! But it cannot be! I have determined that I must remain where I am and see the storm of war through. I cannot desert my friends in what is going to be their greatest time of need.

"My older sons will follow my wishes so far as the war is con-cerned. But they are, neither of them, interested in giving up the furthering of their farms for such an adventure. My two youngest children are still part of this household.

"That leaves you and Rebekah."

In his eagerness, Russel placed his hands on Anthony's shoul-ders, his beaming face turned up to that of his son-in-law. "By the providence of God," he said, "I have found out that this Paradise is wanting an upstanding Christian man who can assemble and oper-ate a mill to grind meal and flour. Not many Christians are mill-wrights or millers, and vice versa. What an opportunity for you, who are versed in both mills and the Scriptures! The materials and much of the labor for erecting the mill will be provided, needing only the millwright's direction."

Thus exhausting his prepared text, Russel stepped back and lapsed into the expectant silence of one ready to field questions and parry arguments.

Cumings shook his head as though to clear his mind. It was all too quick, too fantastic. He had heard nothing over which to raise an objection or stake a debate, but neither was he instantly sold on the plan so boldly laid before him.

He and his younger brother James were doing little more than scratching out an existence on the adjoining tracts they had inherit-ed after their father's death. James, still single, shared the family home with their mother. Anthony and Rebekah lived in Russel's first house and the birthplace of the Russel children, a comfortable stone cottage nestled into the foot of the hill alongside Goose Creek.

Anthony frequently spent his daily horseback rides to and from the brothers' farm deliberating on his prospects. Frankly, he had found them wanting. In fact, one lure of military duty lay in the absolute separation it offered from the ceaseless, frequently unresolvable problems of the farm.

From a day-to-day work standpoint, Anthony preferred the outdoor regimen of farming to most of what milling entailed. However, he had helped his uncle Benjamin construct or rework several grist mills, learning a great deal about their operation in the process. The challenge of directing such an endeavor appealed to him.

His contemplations were interrupted by the appearance of Rebekah at the doorway. "If my two gentlemen are ready," she announced cheerfully, "dinner awaits you."

Anthony glanced at his father-in-law, who responded to her summons with a smiling nod over clasped hands. Both men basked in Rebekah's presence. Like Prince Madoc, as Russel had pointed out, she was a favorable blend of Welsh father and Irish mother. She had her father's dark complexion to go with her mother's emerald eyes and finely wrought features. The radiant, dimpled smile of this brown-haired country lass charmed men and women alike. These days, she smiled almost constantly.

As Anthony took Rebekah's arm, Russel caught his eye with a quick touch of an index finger to the lips.

The Welshman trailed the young couple, his unwatched countenance growing solemn. The thought of Rebekah moving far away, into primitive, perhaps perilous environs, was a painful one. Russel knew that the western waters glistened red with the blood of pioneers who dared to invade the domain of the Indians. But he had determined to his own satisfaction what was best for everyone involved, and Samuel Russel's mind was seldom changed.

Chapter 7

*F*aced with such a favorable prospect, it was only a matter of time before Anthony acquiesced. True, he was giving up his dreams of battlefield glory; but they paled in comparison to the opportunities offered by Russel and this modern Eden—and the comfort of having Rebekah by his side throughout the adventure.

In their next conversation, held once again under the tranquil gaze of Prince Madoc, the sagacious Welshman removed Anthony's last major apprehension by promising to bring the Cumings brothers' little farm into his own operation. "I pledge to you also that I will personally look after James and the widow Cumings," Russel declared.

They shook hands on it. The next step was to inform their unsuspecting relatives. Anthony, near to bursting with youthful excitement, could hardly wait to share the news with Rebekah. To the master weaver fell the much less savory task of telling Rebekah's mother.

Russel discreetly chose the sanctity of their bedchamber, but the deed still sorely sapped his courage. Sarah Russel did not take well to her husband's news, nor to the fumbling manner, with eyes averted, in which it was delivered. His revelation struck her with the force of a sudden death in the family.

"But why?" she wailed, her eyes flashing with tears as well as anger. "Why a place so far removed from us? Why have you done this, Samuel?"

He knew it would be worse than useless (for the moment, at

least) to offer a comforting embrace. Instead, he turned from her agonized, accusing glare and intently studied the floor.

"We cannot be so selfish as to keep those children here, with all the present uncertainties," he said, "when such a good life awaits them elsewhere."

"Good life!" Sarah's voice choked with reproach. "They will be hundreds of miles from all that's civilized. They will have no slave or servant labor, instead depending solely upon the strength of their backs, with all manner of dangers around them. If the war does indeed reach Loudoun County, and you be forced to take up arms, at least our adversaries shall be the British, not the murdering Indians. Rather to fall into the hands of civilized men than to be tortured by soulless savages!"

"Civilized?" he echoed loudly, going on the offensive with gusto. "You call the British civilized? These wonderfully civilized men are the brutes who perpetrated the public hanging, the drawing and quartering of David Morgan and other noble, God-fearing Welshmen, right before their families! The King himself had Morgan's burnt heart served up on a platter! I find no positive distinction in favor of the British!"

Sarah offered no rejoinder. Though both of them knew Russel's diatribe was a diversion from the real bone of contention, he continued: "For their crime, which was the support of Bonnie Prince Charles to regain the throne of England for the Stuarts, these men were hanged until just short of death. Then they were cut down from the gibbet, their bowels cleavered out and burned before their faces. Finally, they were beheaded and their bodies quartered."

Russel at last looked his wife in the eye. "That is how King George II made an example of those he believed to be involved in treason against the Crown. What do you think his beloved grandson will do to punish colonial rabble for equally treasonous, seditious actions? Would you like to see—or for our daughter to see—Anthony subjected to such atrocities?"

Sarah answered in a low but firm tone, baring to judgment the heart of a mother: "Since we are talking of unhappy choices, I should prefer that to having both of them lose their lives and scalps to the savages."

His attempt at rationale thus checkmated, Russel ruefully fell silent. Then he smiled tenderly and moved close to his wife. Frowning, she nevertheless allowed him to wrap her in his arms. "We simply have to trust in God's mercy, do we not?" he asked softly. Knowing he was resolute in his decision, Sarah began weeping. But she did not pull away.

Benjamin Cumings didn't know quite what to make of his nephew's news, but he readily agreed to hold school on building and operating mills.

The old widower lived with three sons in rooms adjoining his grist mill on Red Fox Run at one end of Cobbler's Gap, a short day's ride south of Goose Creek. Anthony, too, had lived there for parts of the past several autumns while helping his uncle and cousins construct and rework mills. Now he was back, in order to confirm what he already knew and to glean additional knowledge before departing for the Ohio Valley.

A soot-encrusted stove in the middle room of Ben's ill-kept habitat cradled a crackling fire to warm the chilled traveler. Anthony backed up to it and gulped down a fiery shot of his relatives' corn whiskey while explaining the sudden need for information. Ben, too, was huddled near the stove, a dirty blanket around his shoulders. He had a nasty cough, but it didn't deter him from enjoying his perpetually lighted pipe.

"Sounds like a rare prospect, indeed," Ben said between puffs. "But what confounds me, lad, is that ye won't be gettin' a thing in return fer your work. Now, what kind of miller would agree to that? After all, we are well known fer havin' a good head for business." A wink and a sly grin accompanied this observation, reminding Anthony of Samuel Russel's comment regarding millers and Christians.

"According to Mr. Russel," Anthony countered, "I will receive the payment I think fit for work done for those outside the settlement. In addition, I'll get a portion of the meal from those within the settlement—enough for my own household."

Ben erupted in a spasm of coughing. Upon recovering, he asked, "Who will own the mill, lad?"

"No one," came the response, prompting the old man's eyebrows to lift. "That is," Anthony amended hastily, "it will belong to everyone. Mr. Russel thinks I will be allowed to have quarters at the mill, just like yours."

"Quite an honor, that," the miller muttered dryly.

Despite the old man's ill-concealed cynicism over the idea of a community-owned venture, he was willing to impart knowledge. Anthony spent the next few days making drawings of the mill apparatus and jotting down notes from the wheezing words of wisdom proffered by his tutor.

Because Anthony could not know what to expect in the way of stream conditions, Ben explained the four basic water wheel designs—overshot, undershot, breastshot, and pitchback—and amplified the benefits and drawbacks of each. He also drilled his nephew on the various types and patterns of millstones, expressing a strong preference for the French burrstone.

It was the second afternoon of Anthony's stay at Red Fox Run when Ben's daughter Ellen showed up with lively little twin girls in tow.

Anthony had never thought his loud, lanky, awkward cousin was particularly winsome. Five years of marriage and four of motherhood had not improved her appearance or disposition. He was, though, touched by the care she gave her father, and her concern over his continuous cough.

"You must give up that filthy pipe," she remonstrated with the miller. "It is going to be the death of you."

Ben tightened his jaw on the offending instrument and defiantly exhaled a large, noisome cloud. "Yes, I'm scarce expectin' to make another ten or fifteen years," he retorted. "The truth is, this here pipe is me last real pleasure in life. 'Twere the dust from the Indian corn, all these years of grindin' it, that give me the cough."

"Corn whiskey, more apt," she shot back.

"And how is the health of Squire Leachman?" her father asked with substantial sarcasm, eager to change the subject. "Did he not wish to visit Red Fox Run? Ye give the appearance of a widow—drivin' your own team, bringin' the children with ye."

Ellen refused to be baited. "He is still down in the back, and allowed as how he could use a time of quiet," she said matter-of-factly. "Besides, you taught me how to handle a team as well as any man. And the girls do love to see their Pa-Pa."

At the close of what proved to be a brief visit, Ellen kissed her father on the cheek and forbade him to see her off. "Stay inside," she admonished. "Anthony will walk us to the buggy. I'm going to bribe him to hide that horrible whiskey from you," she added darkly.

The late-afternoon sun threw the deep, chilly shadow of the mill over the front yard, where Ellen had tethered her two-horse team. Both cousins shivered from the cold as they walked to the buggy. The twins had already climbed aboard and were snuggled under a heaping pile of furs, clamoring to be off.

"They are pretty little ladies," Anthony noted honestly. Struggling to make conversation, he added carelessly: "Would you not like to be mother of more?"

Ellen looked directly at her questioner, as was her way. "I had so much trouble with the girls," she replied, "that the midwives have warned me not to bear any more children. But William does want a son, so we will see."

She cocked her head, and narrowed her eyes ever so slightly. "Where in the Ohio Valley does this Eden of yours lie?" she asked. Anthony sensed real interest behind the question.

"All I know," he said frankly, "is that it is a fortnight's journey on the river below Fort Pitt."

Excitement crept into Ellen's face, coloring her thin cheeks. She gripped his arm.

"Promise me," she said in an impassioned tone, "that, should you meet up with a certain man there, you will tell him that it is all right for him to come home."

"What man is this?" Anthony asked, surprised by his cousin's sudden intensity and the change in her demeanor. For the first time in his experience, Ellen seemed feminine.

"A giant of a man, I suspect," she responded, her voice uncharacteristically soft, "though he was scarcely more than a boy when I saw him last. His name is Kenton. Simon Kenton."

Chapter 8

*Y*oung Rebekah Cumings did not expect her new life on the wilderness trail to be a continuous serving of peach cobbler. Nevertheless, steeped in self-centered romantic bliss, Anthony's bride was scarcely prepared for the battering her pampered ego was about to undergo.

She had reacted to Anthony's announcement of their impending adventure with naive excitement. Finally, she would see for herself what lay beyond the beautiful, mysterious Blue Ridge Mountains! Even though Anthony did make an obligatory reference to hardships and perils, Rebekah shrugged off those words. She declined to believe that the two men who most loved her would subject her to very much in the way of unpleasantness.

The day of departure—a clear but blustery April Fool's Day—was, predictably, far less painful for those leaving than for those left. Even so, Rebekah suffered a tightness in her throat when she hugged and kissed each parent for the final time. Anthony refused to dwell on the prospect that he might never again behold his mother's fragile, beloved features; she had made it easy for him, staying put in her little cabin following their good-byes the evening before.

The party of four—Anthony and Rebekah were joined by her younger brother Richard and Ben's oldest son Malachi—set out from Goose Creek in Russel's Conestoga wagon, drawn by a team of four frisky horses and trailed by a reluctant milk cow on a tether.

Plans called for Richard and Malachi to accompany the travelers as far as Redstone on the Monongahela River. They would return home with the horses while Anthony and Rebekah continued the journey by boat.

Richard, about to turn eighteen, was a late replacement for Anthony's brother James. Harsh words had broken out over James's unattractive lot of tilling the soil and looking after their mother while Anthony started a new life in the West. Actually, the spark that led to a pushing, rolling, grunting tussle was struck over another topic. Speaking more out of frustration than from deep thought, James indicted Anthony's manhood for abandoning his pledge to take up arms in the colonists' cause.

They parted under a truce, Anthony promising to send for James and their mother to join him in the Ohio Valley when the time was right. However, feelings still ruffled, the siblings mutually abandoned the prospect of James making the initial trip.

Late on the first day of travel, the adventurers ascended the eastern slope of the Blue Ridge Mountains to Williams Gap. Here the mountain chain was very low and narrow; the afterglow of sunset still filtered through the trees when they reached the summit and located the crude log home of the oldest Russel son, Robert. The cabin was situated so as to offer a nice overlook of the Shenandoah River Valley, though in the twilight it was smothered under a hazy blue shadow.

Robert's hospitality was limited only by the furnishings of his rough abode; Rebekah received the host's own bed, while he and the remainder of the party wrapped themselves in quilts and pelts to spend the night on the dirt floor before the fireplace.

After Rebekah was presumed to be asleep—her first night spent apart from Anthony since their marriage—Robert informed his audience in low, authoritative tones that travel conditions would become more primitive from this point westward. But, he added, the real dangers of the journey were not those offered by Nature or even by Indians.

Bands of renegade blacks occasionally surprised and robbed unwary travelers, Robert revealed. "They will help themselves to everything, most especially the horses," he said. "In truth, though, they are less likely to take your lives than are the white cutthroats who also haunt the roads.

"Learn, as I've learned," Robert continued, "to keep your rifles within reach at all times. You should, of a certainty, post a guard

over every camp. Each morning when you wake up, slip your powder horn and hunting pouch over your shoulder."

Just after sunrise, the little party left Williams Gap and wound
its way down into the wide river valley. Soon they were carefully
fording the shallow Shenandoah.

Signs of civilization became less frequent, but the road was
straight and well-traveled. At the close of the following day they
reached Winchester, the point of departure into frontier Virginia.
Primarily for Rebekah's sake, Anthony decided to take a room at an
inn. He reasoned that he might not be able to offer her such a nice-
ty again for some time. Malachi and Richard, after enjoying their
turns in a tubful of scalding water, stepped out for the night to
guard the wagon and give privacy to the exercise of matrimonial
privilege.

As he and Rebekah bathed and prepared to share an honest-to-
goodness bed, Anthony sensed from his wife's unusual quietness
that she was waiting for the right moment to spring some petition.
In some ways she reminded him of her father.

Scrubbed clean, dried off, and clad in his knee-length night-
shirt, Anthony licked his thumb and forefinger and pinched the
flame off the wick of the bedside candle. This left the ruddy, dancing spits of light in the fireplace to illumine their room. He crawled
into the rickety four-poster and gently pulled Rebekah close.

"Dear," she began, as they snuggled under the covers, "do we
really have to continue this trip into the wilderness? Couldn't we
just go back home? It's exciting and all of that, but I can't keep
myself groomed for you the way I wish, and I get so tired of jiggling
about in that old wagon."

Though it should not have, this bold request caught Anthony
by surprise. He seldom denied her anything, but to him the idea of
turning around was unthinkable. It threatened his pride, his very
self-respect. How could he go back and face everyone, dissuaded
from the great adventure by the whimsy of his wife?

An awkward silence fell between them, and froze the expectant
smile on Rebekah's face.

"No," Anthony said at last, sitting up and placing his elbows
on his knees. His voice was firm, almost defiant. "We can't disappoint your father—nor, for that matter, the people we are going to

join. Word has been sent ahead that we're coming, and I am expected to build them a mill. We are not quitting. You must put this out of your mind."

Rebekah was shocked by the flat refusal, the cutting off of any discussion. She had spent half a day summoning the courage to ask, and dreading the possibility of hearing the answer just given. To her the denial meant countless hours, days, weeks consigned to misery: exposure to the unfriendly elements day and night, virtually no privacy, and, worst of all, the endless bouncing of the wagon.

She flung herself away from Anthony, hugging her side of the bed, angry tears stinging her eyes. Anthony placed his hand on her bare shoulder, but she shook it off. He sighed deeply, and dropped back into the bed.

It was at this unhappy juncture that they fell prey to the bedbugs.

The terrain became rougher as the party encountered a succession of steep hills and deep hollows. Rebekah's unhappiness with the shortcomings of extended travel degenerated from an initially cheery facade to open pouting, and finally to sulking martyrdom. For the first time in her life, she was unable to do what she wanted with face, hair, and dress. As a result, she felt neither pretty nor clean. Even though her companions cajoled her and catered to her, she found little gaiety in arising each morning to monotonous breakfasts of milk and biscuit, the breaking of camp, and resumption of the torturous trip. The charming smile that had so brightened life at Goose Creek had turned upside down.

Conestoga wagons, built for hauling freight and farm goods for short distances, had a high, flat panel in place of a driver's bench. Teamsters rode their team's wheel horse (the horse just in front of the left wheel) or walked alongside that animal within quick reach of the brake. Anthony spent each day in the latter fashion, handling the sturdy single rein, or "jerk line," connected to the bit of the left lead animal. Rebekah sometimes walked with him or rode the wheel horse, but more often spent her time perched behind the front panel, moodily entertaining dark thoughts under her bonnet.

Despite the strain on his connubial life, Anthony remained enthralled with the expedition. As they trudged along, every hill, every turn in the road, held for him the cloaked promise of something new. Even overcast skies and frequent, chilly rain, which perpetuated the muddy condition of the road, failed to dampen his spirits.

Malachi and Richard plunged daily into the surrounding forests in search of game, augmenting the supply of pickled pork and beef with the fresh flesh of hare and partridge. Malachi, the only accomplished hunter among them, decided Anthony needed tutoring in that regard and convinced him on occasion to turn the jerk line over to Richard.

While the world's armies still used muskets, which were powerful and deadly at close range, the rifle was the American pioneer's choice as a hunting tool. Its grooved barrel, in contrast to the smooth bore of the musket, discharged a spiraling ball with greater accuracy at greater distances. A rifleman had to determine the optimum powder charge and diameter of bullet for his particular weapon; that done, he wielded the deadliest hunting piece yet devised by mankind.

Because firearms were essential to everyday life, Anthony had not thought it out of character when the peace-loving Samuel Russel presented him with a fine flintlock rifle before they parted. "I know you are taking the musket your father used against the French," Russel said, "but this is, quite frankly, a superior weapon. Please take it as well. The Lord saw fit that David have a sling and five smooth stones. I risk no disapproval with this gift."

The forty-two-inch iron barrel of the rifle was set into a slender forepiece of black walnut. Three brass rings joined the barrel and forepiece and also held the ramrod. The stock, twenty-five inches of matching walnut, finely carved, featured a curved brass butt plate. On the right side of the stock was a patch box; on the other, a cheek plate. Both were fashioned of brass, as was the ornate trigger guard.

Under Malachi's tutelage, Anthony settled on a size of ball and charge of powder he deemed appropriate for the rifle. In a short time, he became a dependable marksman. He looked forward to those hours in the woods, so that Richard wound up handling the team with increasing frequency. This voluntary absence from the company of his wife only deepened her gloominess, but Anthony had reached the point of avoiding that which he could not change.

Three days after leaving Winchester, they took a ferry across the Potomac River into Maryland. The ferryman said they would reach Fort Cumberland by following the river upstream past Cresap's stockade. He also said there might well be "a coupla things t' watch fer" in the neighborhood of the stockade.

"First," he said, after a long draw on his corncob pipe, "there'll more'n likely be Injuns camped 'round the stockade. You needn't worry—they'll be harmless enough. Old Colonel Cresap feeds 'em right good, so's to keep 'em friendly to us Americans an' not the Redcoats.

"Also, you need t' know that Colonel Cresap is a right strong believer in the war fer independence. Since you're a'goin' west, and not joinin' in the fight, you mought want t' avoid any meetin' with the colonel. He kin be right insultin' about them he considers Tories, or worse."

Anthony flushed at the phrase "or worse," which could only mean something like "coward." These things considered, he agreed that Cresap's stockade was best avoided.

But they couldn't totally avoid the little fortress, having to pass between it and the river a couple of afternoons later. Sure enough, the occasion provided the travelers with their first glimpse of Indians en masse. A large contingent of them was camped on the hillside below the stockade. Rebekah grew alarmed at the fierce, gloomy faces, and was repulsed by the dark objects hanging from their belts after Malachi identified them as scalps.

Finally, the river bluffs opened into a broad valley. Fort Cumberland came into view, rising over the far bank. Once within the fort's satellite village of Washington Town, the travelers managed to acquire a fat, rested milk cow in exchange for their own travel-worn bovine and a cash incentive. Although public lodging here was nothing special, they again luxuriated in hot baths at the local inn.

Heeding unsolicited advice about safety in numbers, Anthony forged an informal alliance with another westward-bound family before leaving Fort Cumberland. This clan—Nathan Cash, his wife Dot, and four children—hailed from Richmond, and they too were bound for the Ohio Valley. Cash, though, planned to cross the Monongahela River at Redstone and continue overland to Fort Fincastle on the Ohio River, where two brothers awaited him.

Separating Fort Cumberland and Redstone were the formidable Allegheny Mountains. A quarter-century before, a daring party of scouts for the Ohio Company, led by the Indian guide Nemacolin, had blazed a route over and around the rugged mountain ridges. They were followed four years later by the ill-fated British military expedition of Gen. Edward Braddock, whose incredible feat of moving an army across such adverse terrain was wasted in a blood-bathed ambush by French and Indian forces near Braddock's intended target of Fort Duquesne.

From the time of Braddock's defeat until the Treaty of Paris in 1763 brought an official cessation of hostilities between the British and French, French-inspired Indian attacks stymied the advance of settlers into western Pennsylvania, Maryland, and Virginia. Once the menace of the red man appeared to be removed from those regions, Nemacolin's Path swelled with adventurers. Indian resentment and resistance continued to reach flash points, but the white man soon gained an insurmountable advantage in numbers.

In the Battle of Point Pleasant in 1774, fought at the confluence of the Ohio and Great Kanawha rivers, colonial troops clashed with a force consisting of Shawnee, Mingo, and Delaware. Although the Indians suffered only half the number of casualties they inflicted before retreating, their leader, Cornstalk, saw the futility of continued warfare against superior odds and initiated a treaty.

This accord would by no means, however, signal the end of bloodshed in the Ohio Valley between the mortal enemies.

One morning after departing Fort Cumberland, the tandem of wagons, with Cash in the lead of Cumings, completed a brutal, seemingly endless mountain ascension. After resting their teams, the travelers set off again with a sense of relief across a wooded, rather level crest. Soon, though, a new form of misery manifested itself.

They entered a region made preternaturally dark and gloomy by tall, close-standing white pines. The sky was totally closed off by the treetops. Recurrent rains had turned the trail, already low and rutted, into a virtual bog. This stretch, Anthony thought, was undoubtedly the storied "Shades of Death," dreaded domain of merciless highwaymen talked of in Washington Town.

Faced with the possibility of an unfriendly encounter, or of a wagon bogging down, no one ventured off to hunt. This precaution proved wise when both right wheels of the Cash wagon became mired up to the axles.

The grunts and exclamations of the men as they worked to free the wagon stirred mocking echoes from the forest. Dot Cash and her children stood under a large pine, watching the progress and offering words of encouragement. Rebekah, loathing the prospect of becoming dirty so early in the day, sat viewing the tableau from inside her wagon. Abruptly, she became aware of eldritch noises from afar that prompted the hair to rise on the back of her neck.

After a few seconds of listening with pounding heart, she identified the sounds as the sobbing and wailing of little children in horrid disharmony. Rebecca shook off her fear and became consumed with pity and wonder. She held her breath and tried to determine where the heart-wrenching sounds were coming from. She climbed out of her perch and softly stepped around to the rear of the wagon.

Sloshing along the shadowy road with slow, agonized, barefoot steps came a girl of six or seven years. Her long woolen gown was torn and muddy. Tears had cut grotesque streaks through the grime on her face, which was also criss-crossed with scratches. She hugged a squalling, muslin-wrapped infant to her heaving chest.

"Mrs. Cash!" Rebekah called out, alerting the lone mother in the group. She walked gingerly down the rutted road toward the girl, her concern for the small pair mitigated by a desire to keep her own clothes clean. The latter preoccupation was all for naught; the distraught child embraced Rebekah, smearing her with mud, the wailing infant muffled in between them.

Milk met the immediate need of the baby, but the girl was not to be comforted. She only continued to cry when asked her name and the whereabouts of her family. Having freed the Cash wagon from its boggy moorings, the men began backtracking the girl's footprints in hopes of solving the mystery.

Two hundred yards away, they found traces of horses' hooves and wagon wheels leaving the roadway. These led through the thick pines to a Conestoga wagon standing in a small clearing. Leather harness lay nearby, all in a heap, but the team was missing. The campfire had burned itself out, rather than its ashes being scattered. Shouted halloos from Anthony and Nathan Cash failed to bring any response, other than echoes and the cautious emergence of a cur dog from the brush.

Unspoken foreboding swept over the members of the search

party as they approached the wagon. One side of the canvas cover was split and agape, exposing two wooden hoops.

Malachi went to the front of the wagon, stepped up on the doubletree, and peered over the front panel. His head jerked forward, then recoiled. He glanced down at the other men, revulsion written on his face.

"They're dead," he finally managed to say. "Their throats are cut."

Chapter 9

Malachi's grisly discovery un-
leashed feelings of sorrow
and rage on the one hand, and
a chilling sense of mortality on the other. Robert Russel's warning
about banditry and death on the road had not been a hollow one.

Amid the thick shadows of the forest, within a few yards of
where they had been found, the bodies of a man and woman in their
early twenties were buried side by side in a common grave. It
dawned on Anthony, about to speak words over the dead for the
first time in his life, that he could only presume they were Christians—presume, as well, that they were married. Nothing in the
wagon helped determine their identities. Six-year-old Mathilda
knew them only as "Mama" and "Daddy," and between sobs she
called out for them again and again.

Meanwhile, her eight-month-old sister, Elizabeth, slept peacefully in the lanky, experienced arms of Dot Cash, who had produced a leather nursing apparatus and administered a long-overdue
feeding of milk.

"Heavenly Father," Anthony prayed, after everyone gathered
around the fresh mound of earth, "we ask Thee to extend Thy mercy
and grace to the souls of this man and this woman, to accept them
into Thy kingdom." Mathilda screamed and tore away from Rebekah's encircling arms. She ran toward the silent wagon, even though
it no longer held any comfort for her. Rebekah made a move to follow, but Dot Cash stopped her with a frown and a shake of the head.

Anthony's voice grew hoarse as he continued: "We pray for
Thy vengeance to be wrought upon those who committed this

deed, and we ask Thee to send Thy comfort to these young children." He opened a little book containing the Gospels, a wedding present from his in-laws, and read aloud the Lord's Prayer from Matthew:

" 'After this manner therefore pray ye . . .' "

Mathilda sat down on the wagon tongue, her face in her hands, her body heaving with sobs. The cur dog came up behind her, and shoved his muzzle into her back. She sat bolt upright and turned around.

"Tory!" she cried, a faint note of joy in her trembling voice. She attempted to put her brier-scratched arms around the dog's neck, but the animal ducked her embrace and backed away with a whine. A great, bloody knot on the side of his head had closed one eye, and the canine was avoiding any contact with it.

The brief rites completed, Richard walked over to the wagon. "You need to be gentle with your dog," he told Mathilda softly. "That's a pretty bad place on his head." He slowly stretched a hand toward Tory, who growled at first, then permitted a light, scratching caress under the chin.

The killer or killers had taken the victims' horses and weaponry, and some of the food. After hashing over the realities of the situation, Anthony and Nathan Cash appropriated and divided the remaining property they deemed useful. They left the nearly empty wagon where it stood. Within the hour, the pioneers had resumed the trek toward Redstone. Tory tagged along in the roadside mud.

Dot Cash let it be known from the outset that she regarded her own four offspring enough of a burden. With a flourish, she had handed over the baby and the nursing gourd to Rebekah. Clearly, both Mathilda and Elizabeth were henceforth the concern of the Cumingses.

Mathilda, disconsolate, ate little and cried much in the ensuing days. Nighttime became unpleasant for everyone. The girl tended to wake up suddenly, screaming or sobbing, and in so doing would rouse the baby. Those unidentifiable nocturnal sounds from invisible sources beyond the glow of the campfire embodied more sinister possibilities now than they had before. Tory, tied up at night to the Cumings wagon, frequently burst into short salvos of barking at presences he alone sensed.

The travelers had reached the toughest terrain on their route.

Once through the "Shades of Death," they encountered no more level ground. Instead, slowed to a crawl, they struggled from ridge to ridge across the frowning Alleghenies. Even at this snail's pace, the rocky roadway sent endless jolts and tremors through the wagons. To compound the problem of navigating the tortuous descents and ensuing climbs, the gray skies frequently discharged rain.

Twice, faced with long declinations made treacherous by the drizzle, the men locked the rear wheels and laboriously skidded their conveyances to the foot of the slope. The horse teams were handled with great care, as the uncertain footing increased the chances of a broken leg. For the same reason, the clumsy milk cows were led by hand.

Rebekah, placed by fate at a sort of crossroads, finally laid down her self-pity.

Already enduring the journey under protest, she could have entertained further gloominess at being burdened with the two orphaned children. Instead, her heart went out to them; she committed herself in an earnest effort to be, as much as possible, the mother they had lost. In the process, her self-encouraged misery began to fade.

By degrees, Rebekah gained Mathilda's confidence. Soon they were talking freely about Elizabeth and Tory, and of others in the present party of travelers. The one remaining wall was the topic of Mathilda's parents, and what had happened to them. At last, even this barrier tumbled, and the youngster poured out her heart about the murders of her father and mother. Even told in her limited vocabulary, the account was hair-raising; many years afterward, she could still recount with great vividness the details of that terrible event.

On the night they died, Mathilda's parents were in their customary sleeping place at the front of the wagon, little Elizabeth tucked in between them. Mathilda lay slightly more than an arm's reach away in a nest of pelts and blankets. She awoke to the sounds of men's voices, their rasping whispers filtering through the canvas cover of the wagon. From underneath the wagon came a low growl, unmistakably Tory. He barked once, twice, a few feet away—then came the thud of a heavy blow.

A frightening series of sensations followed one another in the darkness: a creaking and rocking of the wagon, her father's sleep-thickened voice raised in alarm, frantic struggling, a muffled scream from her mother. Then, after a momentary lull, the resumption of the strange voices, no longer whispering.

Terrified, Mathilda had yanked a blanket over her head. Her heart pounding wildly, she tried to keep perfectly still.

Elizabeth started to cry.

"A baby!" a man's voice expressed astonishment. "Damn me, if there ain't a baby in between 'em!"

"It won't bite," a second voice jeered. "Just make sure we get everything out o' there we kin use."

Flickering light penetrated the single thickness of Mathilda's refuge. In mortal fear of discovery, she held her breath. From very close by came the sound of canvas being cut and ripped apart. Abruptly, her bursting lungs had their way and she gasped loudly for air.

"Well, now, what's this?" a gruff voice asked. The next instant, her blanket was snatched away.

A bearded man in a fur cap and deerskin shirt glared at her, his scowling face less than two feet from her own. He was leaning through a great hole in the canvas, his left hand holding aloft a flaming pine torch. His right hand flung down the blanket and seized the petrified Mathilda by one arm. He dragged her out of the wagon and swung her roughly to the ground.

Mathilda sat up, clutching her arm and moaning in pain. She glimpsed, nearby, the dim, outstretched form of Tory.

With his free hand, the man reached for a blood-stained knife projecting hilt-first from the sideboard of the wagon. As he yanked it free, Mathilda's terror was channeled into flight.

She jumped to her feet and ran away, screaming. A second man suddenly appeared before her, a menacing shadow in the flickering light. The girl evaded his lunging reach and raced past the dying campfire and into the forest. The explosion of screams, curses, and sudden movements spooked the wagon team, tethered by a common line to one of the pines. The horses reared up, snapping the line, and all four bolted in different directions.

Running barefooted through the inky darkness, the terrified youngster was impervious to the lashing and tugging of brambles. But she finally tripped and fell face-first to the ground.

Straining for breath, Mathilda realized no one was chasing her. In fact, she could hear the two cutthroats shouting at each other and cursing as they attempted to round up the scattered team. She curled up, aching inside and out, the night stirrings around her generating new fears. Whimpering, she pulled her gown tightly around her in response to the chill. She closed her eyes, hoping with the unreasoning, desperate hope of a child that the nightmare would soon end and everything would be all right.

At last, when the sky began to lighten, the only sound that Mathilda heard was the ragged crying of Elizabeth.

Nemacolin's Path brought the wearied wayfarers out of the mountains at Chestnut Ridge, then paralleled twisting Redstone Creek to where the tributary plunged into the Monongahela. They made their way south along the wooded bank, and shortly reached Redstone.

The village was scattered across a sloping embankment that rose sharply several hundred feet to a knob, where squatted a military stockade. Under the vigilant eye of the fort, this shapeless infant town was struggling to grow. Though ugly and primitive, it did offer a sprinkling of humanity and a double dose of boat-building—to all appearances the leading industry.

Having spotted a waiting ferry, the Cash clan called out their good-byes and hustled away to make the next crossing of the river. Nathan Cash was eager to join his brothers at Fort Fincastle on the Ohio. Anthony and his entourage established a camp near the stockade. He and Malachi then set out to find either a completed boat or a boat-builder.

A quick tour of the riverfront revealed that Redstone's true leading industry was sin, in the forms of gambling, corn whiskey, and frowsy women. However, the cousins also located saw-pits and scaffolding crowded around a natural little harbor, and several watercraft were under construction there. Anthony approached the nearest man who had his hands on his hips, the universal pose of one in charge.

This fellow, Miles by name, affirmed that he had the perfect boat under way and available soon. The prior prospective owner had run afoul of a cottonmouth, and his discouraged survivors were making their mournful way back home. Miles, his beard badly smeared with tobacco juice, waved one sleeveless arm toward a large, rectangular frame resting on skids that ran to the water's edge.

This structure, shortly to be the bottom of a boat, measured sixteen feet in width and forty feet in length. Made of solid wood beams a foot and a half thick, it was squared off at both ends. Planks had been fitted into the mortised beams and secured with wooden pins. Workmen were placing upright timbers at certain points on the frame, to which oak siding would be fastened. Once the sides were in place, and the fitted wood caulked throughout, the craft would be placed in the water and completed there.

"It'll be up t'you," Miles said, "to tell us where you'd be wantin' your cabin, and how big. Then we kin cut the oarlocks and nail down the mast and caps'n. You kin be ship-shape and on your way in under a week, no more."

They struck a deal, although the boatwright appeared reluctant to accept the coin of the realm until Anthony offered nearly twice what he thought the boat was worth. Shrugging, the young Virginian reflected that his own need for currency of the conventional kind would be next to nothing in the wilds of the Ohio Valley.

Each product of the builder's art was distinctly different. No two finished flatboats looked the same, except for the common characteristics of great size and ugliness. Yet thousands of them successfully floated the western waters and ended their nautical lives in dismemberment, only to reappear in the form of houses.

Anthony was elated with his luck in securing a craft more than half completed, meaning a delay of a few days instead of the anticipated fortnight. But his spirits cooled when he began to consider how large and awkward the flatboat was, and how clumsy and dangerous its maneuvering might prove to be. The Monongahela had already discharged most of its spring crest, and the water level was dropping daily. There were rocky shorelines, shoals, islands, snags, and eddies to duel. Rebekah, who he had naively supposed would be available to assist, was now burdened with Mathilda and Elizabeth. Malachi and Richard had work agendas awaiting them in Loudoun County, and intended to stay in Redstone only long enough to help load the boat before beginning their return. Anthony realized he would be faced with handling the craft by himself. It was an impossible situation. And, to make matters worse, he had not seen a single soul in Redstone with whom he would consider sharing a boat.

Anthony voiced his newfound anxiety to Malachi as they walked back toward the camp. His cousin, apparently preoccupied with other thoughts, had no answer. When they reached the wagon, Malachi told Anthony he had "somethin' to do" and parted without another word.

It was well after nightfall before he returned. The remainder of the little party was gathered around the campfire when Tory began to bark and growl. Anthony came to his feet and moved quickly in the direction of his rifle. Malachi and a taller companion lurched out of the darkness and into view. The second man gave a friendly wave and hailed the campers. "I believe I have a kinsman of yours here," he called out.

Rather than subsiding, Tory's growls grew into snarls and he jumped about ferociously at the end of his rope. Neither man paid the dog any attention as they approached the campfire.

Malachi's appearance spoke eloquently of a recent bout of fisticuffs and a current state of intoxication. His gait was wobbly. He smelled strongly of spirits. His shirt was torn and bloody, his nose—the apparent source of the blood—was bruised and swollen. Helping him keep his feet was a tall man clad in deerskin breeches, a wool shirt, and a cocked hat.

The stranger also radiated an aura of whiskey, but his dark, clean-shaven face bore no marks of fighting and he obviously held his liquor better. He helped Malachi to a sitting position before the fire.

Richard was the picture of amazement, eyes and mouth agog. Mathilda, frightened by the stranger and by the dog's behavior, hid behind Rebekah's skirt. At a word from her husband, Rebekah took Mathilda into the wagon. Anthony ordered Richard to remove Tory to the far side of the wagon. Then he gave full attention to the newly arrived twosome.

"He's all right," the stranger said of Malachi, with a smile that flashed white teeth. "He'll be fine. He was holdin' up well agin' two others, on the river bank. They took off when I come along."

Anthony peered closely at Malachi. Dull, bloodshot eyes peered back. They shifted to the tall man, and a puffy smile appeared. "My frien' is here," Malachi said needlessly, through purple lips. "He kin go witcha on th' boat," he told Anthony.

"I hear you're goin' down the Ohio," the tall man said to Anthony. Then, aware he had not introduced himself, he doffed his hat. Unruly black hair dropped to his shoulders. "My name is Abbott," he said.

"Pleased to make your acquaintance, Mr. Abbott," Anthony replied, methodically looking over this new friend of Malachi. He liked what he saw.

The gent standing before him was a woodsman, probably in his early thirties, lean but broad-shouldered, exuding an air of confidence not born of whiskey. Despite having absorbed a few shots of that liquid, he stood lightly on moccasined feet.

Anthony made an effort to control the sudden eagerness within him. "Yes, we are going down the Ohio, after we stop at Pittsburgh for further instructions. The Lord has given us a great opportunity."

"Well, Mr. Cumin's, your kinsman here said you was the only man in your party," Abbott noted. "He was a mite troubled about you handlin' th' boat all by yourself. I'm a trapper. I know the Ohio River, an' I'm eager to get back thar. I'm also a purty fair shot, and you never know when them savages is goin' to make trouble on the river."

It all sounds too good to be true, Anthony thought. *Just when circumstances begin to create doubts, along comes a full-sized man experienced in dealing with the perils of the river. As Samuel Russel would have said, how just like God it is to anticipate every unforeseen need!*

"If you are looking for a place on our boat, Mr. Abbott," Anthony said, "I believe we might be able to accommodate you."

On the other side of the wagon, Tory leaned stiff-legged against his hempen restraint and continued to growl.

Chapter 10

The adventurers could make out the massive earthen parapets of Fort Pitt, looming impressively on the right-hand side of the river, long before they reached "The Point"—that spearhead of land between the merging Monongahela and Allegheny rivers where the proud Ohio begins.

Built by the British following the French and Indian Wars to command the headwaters of the Ohio, the fort was a sprawling concoction of dirt, stone, and brick straddling The Point. Scattered about it were the squat frame dwellings and business houses of rapidly growing Pittsburgh. Beyond this encroachment of civilization crouched rugged hills; across the Monongahela, to the southwest, rose a high, steep, wooded incline.

"Just t'other side of the fort is the Allegheny," Abbott told Anthony as they methodically worked the big sweeps to keep the flatboat aligned with the current. "Straight ahead of us is whar it meets the Monongaheely an' becomes the Ohio."

Pittsburgh marked the end of their first leg of river travel. The trip from Redstone convinced Anthony that he and Rebekah—even were she not attending to the orphan girls—could not have directed the clumsy, ponderous ark through the myriad dangers within the deceptively serene waters. He was equally sure that God had sent Abbott to provide the expertise and confidence needed to navigate the swiftly flowing stream. The trapper maintained a steady hand and easy manner in dealing with the river hazards and in directing Anthony's assistance. While Rebekah had to lend a hand in steering to and from shore, the men managed the rest of the navigation.

The vessel presented an awkward sight, though hardly an unusual one for the time and place. Open decks fore and aft flanked the cabin, the flat roof of which served as an upper deck where the three long sweeps were manned. The single mast was mounted in the bottom of the boat and projected through the cabin roof. Three-foot-high gunwales ran the full perimeter of the craft. The squared lines of the bow and stern were so nearly identical that only the location of the stern sweep indicated which was which.

In one corner of the foredeck was a sandbox used for cooking; broken limbs and quartered wood were stacked loosely beside it. In the other corner stood the rope-swathed capstan. Close by lay Abbott's overturned birch-bark canoe, under which the frontiersman took his sleep. Most of the foredeck, though, was occupied by the Conestoga wagon, which still contained many of the Cumingses' possessions. Its wheels were removed and the canvas cover stripped off the supporting hoops, to allow an unobstructed view forward from the upper deck. A section of the canvas had gone to furnish the seldom-used sail.

Anthony had kept one of Samuel Russel's horses for a mount. This animal, along with Abbott's horse and the milk cow, shared a common bed of hay and leaves that took up virtually the entire afterdeck. The trio of beasts accepted their tethered status and appeared to be at ease in the new environment.

Once the ark was launched, the remnants of Rebekah's ill humor had all but vanished. After all, the event marked an end to weeks of shaking and bouncing over rough terrain. There was a tranquility to be enjoyed from the gliding movement of the boat, and in watching the lazy passage of scenery. Gone, too, were the intolerably close sleeping quarters of the wagon. The suspension of a large, heavy quilt to partition the cabin gave the young couple a sense of privacy despite having the children asleep only a few feet away.

Mathilda, just tall enough to see over the gunwales, was captivated by the river travel. She loved to play in the bow, and needed frequent reminders from Rebekah to don her bonnet for protection against the warm May sun. Her nightmares came less and less frequently, illustrating the amazing, God-given resilience of the young.

Her little world, in fact, seemed to have nearly righted itself until an incident occurred with Abbott.

The woodsman had made overtures of friendship even before they departed Redstone, and was close to conquering Mathilda's fear of him. At the shank of their first day on the river, having moored the ark to a big locust tree, Anthony and Rebekah went about preparing a partridge for supper while Abbott sat cleaning his traps. Mathilda, whose duty of watching Elizabeth abated when the infant slipped into slumber, drifted back and forth between the two scenes of adult activity.

She sat down cross-legged on the deck near Abbott, who was running a rasp over the iron teeth of a great, hinged trap. He glanced up and smiled, then spoke as he resumed his cleaning: "Do you know what I got here?"

Mathilda shyly shook her head.

"This is to ketch big varmints with."

"So we can have them to eat?" she inquired.

Abbott's teeth flashed in a quick grin. "Yep, that too," he acknowledged. "But the main thing is their pelt. You know, like the skins you wrap up in to sleep."

As he spoke, the trapper put down the rasp and unsheathed a large knife, intending to use it on the tighter clefts between the jig-saw teeth. Mathilda gasped and jumped to her feet. As she stared at the knife, eyes and mouth wide open, Abbott playfully pointed it at her.

"Aw, c'mon," he said carelessly. "It won't bite."

The little girl screamed, terror contorting her face. She ran pell-mell over to Rebekah and ducked behind her, grabbing two small fistfuls of skirt. Abbott stood up, the knife in one hand, the other hand outstretched palm-up in a gesture of helplessness. "I don't know what it was, made her act so," he said lamely, wearing a perplexed expression. Anthony and Rebekah looked first at Abbott, then at each other, and finally down at the cowering form of the girl.

Mathilda resisted every attempt to pry an explanation out of her, but was clearly terrified of Abbott. She stayed as far away from him as she could, and her playfulness returned only after he left the boat to set out traps. The next day, she kept to the cabin to avoid the woodsman.

Tory evinced a continuing dislike of Abbott as well. The cur spent his time at one end of a rope tied to a peg just inside the doorway of the cabin. He appeared always to be watching the trapper as the latter moved about the craft, uttering a throaty growl whenever the man ventured close. Since Abbott made no attempt—nor had any reason—to enter the cabin, the tension between man, child, and beast assumed the form of a standoff.

Once ashore at Pittsburgh, Anthony made his way to the fort to ask the whereabouts of an aged recluse known simply as Micah. This ancient worthy, Samuel Russel had told him, lived in the woods somewhere around Pittsburgh and was in possession of the directions to the New World Eden.

Unfortunately, that was the extent of Russel's information. Anthony felt a bit foolish. He hardly knew enough about the old solitary to even frame an intelligent inquiry. Nevertheless, he located what appeared to be the main gate of Fort Pitt and approached a bored-looking sentry. Surprisingly, the soldier wore the garb and accoutrements of a Virginia militiaman; Anthony had expected to find Pennsylvanians in possession of the fort.

Though directed at uninterested ears, Anthony's question of the sentry was overheard by a thin, sharp-featured man carrying a large bag of flour over his shoulder.

"Pardon me, sir," the gent with the flour bag said to Anthony. "I don't mean to be attendin' to your affairs—the good Lord forbid. But I'll confess to a chance bit of eavesdroppin' just now."

He eased the bag of flour to the ground. Keen gray eyes made a sweeping appraisal of Anthony, who returned the attention in wonderment. Apparently satisfied with the result of his scrutiny, the stranger continued: "Are you wantin' to find a certain place down the Ohio River"—he lowered his voice slightly—"that is a sanctuary for Christian worship?"

The look on Anthony's face was answer enough, though he added an affirmative nod.

"Then, sir," his questioner said with an engaging smile, "allow me to suggest that we go and find Master Micah together. I'm after those same directions, and have found out where the keeper of them lives."

The gray eyes twinkling, he touched the brim of his cocked hat and stuck out a large, bony hand. "My name is Nimrod Ellison," he said. "I come from Philadelphia in search of a better life for me and mine."

"Anthony Cumings." The name and handshake were given together. "From Virginia. Are there many of us, then, headed for this promised land in the west?"

"I presume so," Ellison replied. "The hermit who bears the prophet's name can surely tell us."

He returned the sack of flour to his shoulder in one easy motion. "My flatboat is at the river bank," he said. "Allow me to deliver this load, and we'll take my canoe to the other side."

Anthony squinted into the afternoon sun, studying the steep slope across the Monongahela. Ellison followed his gaze, and chuckled. "Yes, my newfound friend," he said. "Our Micah lives somewhere up yonder."

Breathing heavily from the long, steep climb, Anthony sat and looked in appreciation at the panorama below.

Blanketed in shadow, even Fort Pitt was less impressive from this lofty perspective. Passing either side of the fort, the sparkling waters of the twin tributaries merged at The Point, sacrificing their identities to become the Ohio. That majestic, alluring stream flowed away into tree-shrouded mystery among the hills, flinging a challenge to the adventurous wayfarers of young America. The grandeur of the encircling terrain dwarfed the fortifications and village clinging to the spit of soil where the rivers met.

Anthony could just make out the details of his flatboat, nestled among the half-dozen similar craft lining the far shore of the Monongahela. There was sunbonneted Rebekah, working over the sandbox to cook supper. Abbott, returned from peddling pelts, squatted Indian-style near his canoe with head bowed. He was doubtless cleaning or mending traps.

Nimrod Ellison, puffing less heavily than his companion despite several years' seniority, put a friendly hand on Anthony's shoulder. "Quite a view!" he commented.

Anthony nodded, conserving his wind.

At that moment, there sounded behind them a shuffling, uneven tread. They turned, then removed their hats in deference to the advanced age of the little man who approached.

A single loose garment of linsey-woolsey hung from thin, bent shoulders down to the ankles of his moccasin-shod feet. His head was covered with an unruly mass of long, white hair, strands of which drifted across his wrinkled brow in the soft evening breeze. "May I be of service?" he asked, his ivory beard bobbing with every syllable.

Ellison smiled, then jauntily stepped over to the ashes of the hermit's fire. He took up a piece of limb and dragged one end through the blackened debris, producing a crude ellipse with crossing tails. All three men knew the image was intended as that of a fish.

The beard lifted into a smile. "God bless you both," said Micah, "and welcome."

"We could see that you were in prayer, so we waited," Ellison said as they filed into the crude assembly of timber, canvas, and skins that made up Micah's abode. He and Anthony introduced themselves.

"So you are among the chosen," Micah murmured. "They come from every colony, though most especially Pennsylvania. All bring a special calling to the flock. What might yours be?"

"I am a miller and a millwright," offered Anthony.

Ellison beamed at him. "Even so!" the Philadelphian exclaimed. "I'm a carpenter and cooper—as well as the best man with a rifle to ever come out of Bucks County." He immediately blushed at his own braggadocio.

Taking note of the fading light, Anthony asked if there were a map to study and help them find their destination. Micah slowly shook his head. "But the directions are simple," he said. "Listen closely."

From Pittsburgh, the hermit said, there would be nine days of river travel before they need concern themselves about landmarks. By the tenth day, they should be watching closely for a certain island, lying opposite the mouth of an intersecting stream on their right. "You may well see the same combination of landmarks on two or three occasions earlier in your journey," Micah cautioned, "but the island I speak of, you will not reach for at least eight or nine days.

"At the foot of the island," he continued, "you will see a wooden cross. Look well, for it is all but hidden among the willows. Less than two miles downstream, a bluff will appear on your left. It conceals a small creek. That creek runs to the Ohio from the place you seek."

Micah gently drilled his pupils on the directions. When he was satisfied they had them down, his face grew solemn.

"There are dangers between here and there," he admitted. "What you should beware most are the Indians. They are full of deviltry and deceit, and know not the meaning of mercy. Remember, the left-hand or southern shore is much safer for you than the other. The red man rules the north side of the river but is less sure of himself on the other side.

"Whatever their tricks, their attempts at deception, do not be lured into landing on the north side."

He paused, his words casting a pall over the listeners. Then Ellison asked, "When we reach—well, whatever it's called—who is it that we should seek out?"

Micah smiled. "The trappers and other outsiders know the place you are going as the Three Islands area. In truth, it has no name, but we refer to it as New Ephrata.

"God's chosen leader for us is David Singletary," he said, a quivering reverence in his voice. "His is indeed the heart of David, beating in the breast of Goliath. But," he added, his eyes resting on Ellison, "you will not have need to seek him out. He will find you."

Chapter 11

A thick mist stirred sluggishly across the bosom of the Ohio, reducing the timber on the near shore to a blurry gray shadow and completely hiding the far shoreline. It intercepted and diffused the struggling rays of the early morning sun, creating a dazzling white veil.

Abbott had long since returned with his traps and the night's disappointing catch of two rabbits. Now he stood firmly gripping the bankside sweep of the ark, shaggy black head cocked in anticipation.

Squinting into the fog beyond the stern, Anthony hallooed at the formless image he knew to be Nimrod Ellison's flatboat. The voice of Ellison floated back, surprisingly loud, in affirmation that the Pennsylvanian was ready to follow.

"Very well, Mr. Abbott," Anthony called out. "Let's shove off!"

The backwoodsman gave one hearty push on the sweep, then lifted the big paddle, dark and dripping, swung it forward, dropped it, and pushed once more against the yellow water. The ark rocked and moved away from the bank. Anthony went to work at the opposite sweep, while Rebekah held the stern sweep clear. Anthony soon came to relieve her and dropped the stern sweep for use as a rudder. Abbott, meanwhile, clambered down into the bow past the ever-vigilant Tory and began straining his eyes in search of hazards.

They encountered none. Within an hour, the mist had dissipated to the point where the river could be scanned for many yards ahead. Abbott returned to the upper deck and took over the stern sweep.

"I'm reckonin' we'll reach Yeller Crick afore dark," the trapper said. "We have one more night we kin rest easy, then after that, we'll be needin' to post a guard. If we had a full moon, which we don't, we'd be safer to just keep on driftin' with the current all night long."

Remembering the words of Micah, Anthony suggested that the left-hand bank of the river would be the prudent place to put in for the night. Abbott shook his head in disagreement.

"It's true the Injuns don't live on that side o' the river," he said, "but they hunt there. No, the best place for us to tie up at is an island. That way, they can't get to us 'less they come by canoe. And it's quicker to get this here flatboat loose from an island than from the shore."

The last point made especially good sense to Anthony. The shallows near the riverbanks were packed with the debris of past freshets, souvenirs of broken and fallen timber swept up by cresting waters in the spring and autumn. The accumulation of half-submerged tree trunks, limbs, and branches extended dozens of feet into the stream. A hasty nocturnal departure through a network of such snarls and snags would not be easy.

Ellison's flatboat, floating some thirty yards behind, was now clearly visible. Traveling with the cooper were his wife, Hannah; their sons, Elijah and Jacob, ages fourteen and nine; and Hannah's father, a dour old individual named John Evans.

It was Evans who, in campfire conversation the evening previous, had waited for Abbott to go trapping before voicing an opinion that the backwoodsman behaved more like an Indian than a white man. "I've been around them that lived in the woods," he said, "and them that lived with the savages. I think this one has lived with the savages."

The observation had rankled Anthony. "Mr. Evans," he had rejoined, "I truly don't know that much about Mr. Abbott. He appears, though, to detest the redskin as much as anyone. He's very alert to the dangers facing us."

Evans had grunted sarcastically. "Mr. Cumin's, just remember that the Injun has not only the whites fer his enemies, but other tribes of Injuns as well. They've been hackin' up one another fer years before our people come along an' attracted their heathen hatred. If'n they ever settle out their own differences and get after us in a body, we'll be in a heap o' trouble."

The old man's remarks had chilled Rebekah and rendered all the more ominous the inky darkness hovering about the little radius of campfire glow. *How far we are from everyone else but the savages,* she thought. *How helpless we are, really, except for the hand of God.*

The Ohio, nearly a quarter of a mile wide, wound its way through a stunning mix of verdure. Beyond the piles of ruined timber at water's edge, solemn willows drooped their yellowish-green foliage from heights of up to twenty feet. Above them rose stately maple and ash, mantled in darker greens. Towering over the rest, like tremendous sylvan palisades, were sycamores, beeches, and poplars, whose mighty limbs shaded the peripheries of the river corridor.

Great, forest-clad hills met the sky in every direction. Snuggled around their rugged feet were semicircles of bottom land whose wooded terraces sloped gently down to the river.

The valley throbbed with animal life, although most of it remained unseen. Small, chirruping birds gathered in the shadowy boughs. An occasional eagle or hawk soared high overhead. Insects skipped across the surface of the stream, risking a lightning-quick demise as the target of a striking fish.

During the afternoon, Elijah and Jacob Ellison took advantage of the finny aggressors and caught several fine catfish. This string of successes became the main course of the evening meal, prepared over a fire on a sandy spit at the mouth of Yellow Creek.

After supper, Rebekah took Mathilda and little Elizabeth to the ark and put them to bed. She had just returned to the campfire when Abbott renewed his advice regarding future camps. "Yeller Crick is safe enough for us," he said. "But I'd suggest us a'stickin' to the islands startin' tomorrer night."

Old Evans, keenly studying the woodsman, asked him about their present surroundings. "I have somethin' in my head, Mr. Abbott, about Yelluh Crick and red devils," he said. "Wasn't there a fight here between Injuns and whites sometime back?"

At the question, Abbott's congeniality vanished. He flung down his piece of catfish and sprang up, glaring at Evans. His jaw muscles rolled. In a tone made husky by emotion, he replied: "What you speak of wasn't no fight, sir. It was murder—nothin' less than murder."

Evans smiled thinly, though his face had lost some of its color. He remained seated. "Tell me, sir. Might it be a matter of who is doin' the killin'—whites or redskins—to call it murder?" he queried casually.

All eyes in the camp were on Abbott. Struggling for self-control, he clenched his fists but kept them by his side. Anger smoldered in his eyes.

"D'ya know what happened at Yeller Crick, Mr. Evans?" he asked at last.

The older man shrugged. "I'm not clear on it a-tall," he said evasively. "Seems to me it had t' do with a bunch of drunk savages and some of our folks. I think we got the best of 'em."

The woodsman had regained his composure, but continued to return the sarcastic gaze of Evans. He also remained standing.

"What it involved, sir," he replied quietly but ominously, "was the ambush of unsuspectin' Injun braves and a squaw who was near to havin' her baby."

Rebekah gasped and moved closer to Anthony, who put his arm around her. The two Ellison boys grew big-eyed. Their mother instructed them sternly to go and get ready for sleep.

"The Injuns was Mingoes," Abbott continued, "from the village of Chief Logan, a few miles up Yeller Crick. In spite o' warnin's from other tribes, Logan and his people was friendly to the whites. A party o' white hunters was camped here one evenin' and invited some o' the Mingoes over to enjoy a sportin' round o' marksmanship—and lotsa firewater. When the Injuns got good and drunk, the whites shot 'em down like dogs, fer no reason.

"Other Mingoes heard the shootin' and come to see what'd happened. They was ambushed, too. Two of 'em was Chief Logan's father and brother."

Among the listeners, only Evans failed to evince shock at Abbott's account. "A sad story, Mr. Abbott, to be sure," he responded. "But I kin tell you of many deeds done by the red savages, sadder'n this—much, much sadder. By the way, you spoke of a squaw with child. Did they kill her, too?"

The trapper's eyes blazed anew. "Sir, could be you already know the answer to that," he shot back. "But maybe no one else here does."

Abbott stared at the pale, upturned faces around the fire. "The squaw," he told them, teeth gritted, "was with the Mingoes first invited to the whites' camp. She tried to run away when the shootin' started. She was shot through the throat, but not killed—not then.

She didn't die until them whites had strung her up by the heels and opened up her belly with a tomahawk."

Rebekah hid her face against Anthony's shoulder. Hannah Ellison gasped and squeezed her husband's hand.

"That squaw," Abbott continued, "was Logan's sister. This all happened 'bout two years ago. Chief Logan moved his village from Yeller Crick to a place further down th' Ohio. Since that time, he's been busy killin' every white he kin get his hands on to pay for the blood o' his family."

"There's plenty o' white men, Mr. Abbott," Evans retorted, "who're on the same mission against the red devils, for the same reasons." Scowling, he leaned forward and added, "By God, sir, you seem awfully sympathetic with them savages!"

Nimrod Ellison could contain himself no longer. "That's enough!" he said sharply to his father-in-law.

Without another word, Abbott wheeled about and stalked out of camp. Stunned into silence, the others heard him board Anthony's flatboat to pick up his traps. Tory barked once and followed up with a long, subsiding growl. A moment later, the woodsman passed noiselessly into the forest.

His silent, sullen departure ended the evening's social time on an ominous note.

Once they were in the confines of the ark's cabin, Rebekah asked Anthony, "Do you think Mr. Abbott will come back? He really does frighten me, at times." Without waiting for an answer, she added, "I'm going to find out, once and for all, what it is about him that puts Mathilda into such a state."

Anthony took her gently by the shoulders. "He'll be back, no doubt," he answered. "But I certainly don't think you have anything to worry about. If I did, Mr. Abbott would not be traveling with us."

Unconvinced, Rebekah pulled away and began to undress. "Maybe it's Tory you should be asking about Mr. Abbott," Anthony quipped.

After they lay down, Rebekah whispered into her husband's ear: "In the morning, I am going to find the pistol Richard left with us. I want you to show me how to load and shoot it."

Anthony, both amused and irritated, tried to dissuade her. "I can tell you," he replied, "that we have this precious pistol only because Richard could never hit the same target twice. It's totally useless as anything other than a toy."

"All the same, I would like for you to make it ready to shoot, please," Rebekah insisted, no touch of levity in her voice.

Anthony argued that she would be more likely to hurt herself with the pistol than anyone else. But eventually her persistence won out. "Okay, my love. I'll do as you say," he pledged, hoping she would forget about it overnight.

Abbott was indeed back by morning, though he had nothing to show for his nocturnal trapping efforts. While he seemed genial enough, Anthony sensed a new distancing between the woodsman and the remainder of the party. Reflecting on the confrontation with Evans, he ruefully admitted it could hardly be otherwise.

That night, and for several to come, the flatboat tandem was moored at islands in the middle of the river. Anthony, Nimrod Ellison, and old Evans split the nocturnal watch duties, for Abbott invariably took his canoe and spent the night trapping. Despite the frequently voiced suspicions of Evans as to the woodsman's true activities, the canoe returned most mornings with a cargo of game.

Abbott seemed to thrive on remarkably little sleep. Once the boats were launched and appeared to be following the current, he would take a quick nap underneath his overturned canoe. A similar ritual occurred in the early afternoon.

On the third day following the departure from Yellow Creek, the trapper was preparing to indulge in his morning slumber. Anthony, manning the stern sweep, watched him kneel in order to crawl under the canoe. Suddenly, he regained his feet and looked intently over the bow. Then, after waving at Anthony to attract his attention, Abbott pointed downstream.

Several hundred yards distant, a great cloud of dust was rising above the trees along the southern shore. Anthony heard a deep, growling rumble, like the roll of summer thunder, but the sky was blue.

Ignoring the hostile reaction of Tory, leashed near the cabin door, the trapper sprang up the ladder to the top deck. "We'd best pull to the north bank and sit still for a spell," he said rapidly, all the while signaling to the Ellison ark to do the same. "See that dust? It's buffalo, and I reckon they've been spooked by Injuns. It'd be a good idee for us to lay low and hope the huntin' party don't see us."

Chapter 12

*T*wo sharp, distinctive sounds cut through the vibrating rumble of many pounding, heavy-laden hooves: the snapping of wood and the whooping cries of Indians.

The flatboats were swung quickly toward the opposite shore and eased into its bristling mantle of floodswept timber. From this vantage point upstream, the voyagers soon witnessed the vanguard of the buffalo herd bursting through the trees and plunging blindly into the river. There the mighty beasts compounded the confusion, snorting and bawling and thrashing around in the muddied shallows. Those behind veered as they came upon the leaders, turning parallel to the bank and trampling the willow trees in their path.

Emerging from the dust came a handful of riders, bronzed, black-haired men who straddled their horses without benefit of saddles. These hunters, naked except for buckskin breeches and headbands, bent their bows and sent arrow after arrow into the shaggy brutes floundering in the water. It took several shafts to dispatch an animal, and the shower of the deadly missiles seemed endless.

"Like fish in a barrel, eh?" Anthony said to Abbott. Even as he spoke, though, a pair of bison suddenly regained firm footing on the bank and charged their tormentors. One hunter was thrown by his panic-stricken mount right into their path, and his death-shriek reverberated up and down the river.

Two braves alighted and went to where he lay. They knelt briefly by the broken body, then stood while the remaining hunters gathered. The dead man's horse was captured and the owner draped across it. With this sad burden in tow, the quintet of red men rode slowly into the woods from whence they had appeared, leaving nine buffalo carcasses in the water and on the bank.

"Are they Mingoes?" Anthony asked.

"No," the trapper responded. "I've not seen those Injuns afore, though from their looks I reckon they might be Cherokees. If so, they're a long ways from home." He looked Anthony in the eye. "You've a choice to make, Mr. Cumin's," he said. "I'm believin' them's only a part of the huntin' party. In any event, they'll be back pretty quick t' skin off the hides and take the meat.

"We kin stick it out right here the rest o' the day, hidin' from 'em, or push off and hope to get past them dead buffalo afore the Injuns show back up."

"If they see us," Anthony asked, "how likely are they to attack?"

Abbott shrugged. "Bein' as I don't think they're from these parts, we are prob'ly safe. But anyhow, for my part, I'd sooner take my chances on the river than sittin' next to the shore."

That was enough to sway Anthony. He motioned to the Ellisons to push off, and he and Abbott did likewise.

Keeping as quiet as possible, with only the stern sweeps breaking the water, they floated out into the stream and drifted toward the spot where nine hunted and one hunter had died. The children were agog at the prospect of seeing the horned, hulking beasts up close; every adult scanned the deserted, hoof-shredded bank with anxious eyes.

Ellison's milk cow broke the silence with a mellow cry. Seconds later, his horse snorted. The unwelcome sounds nettled the edgy pioneers, and Evans soundly cursed both creatures under his breath.

Just five minutes more and they would be past the carcasses, and could apply the side sweeps for added momentum.

The woodsman cocked his head, then turned to Anthony. "Too late!" he muttered. "I hear horses." In a louder voice he called to Nimrod Ellison and his father-in-law, each of whom gripped a rifle: "You'd do best to lay them guns down at your feet, out of sight behind th' gunnels, an' grab a sweep. The Injuns is about to spot us, but I don't think they'll attack. If I'm wrong, you kin grab 'em up quick enough."

Ellison promptly laid his rifle down, but Evans, a sneer on his face, shook his head. Angered, Ellison reached over and seized his father-in-law's weapon as if to wrest it away. The old man's face turned pale with rage, but he, too, lowered his rifle to the deck.

No fewer than a dozen Indians rode out of the forest, and the drifting flatboats attracted their full attention.

Abbott shouted something at the savages, held up both hands with the palms out, and looked around at the other men. Anthony, Ellison and Evans followed suit. Hannah Ellison grabbed her mesmerized sons and yanked them down behind the gunwale. Rebekah regained her wits and swept Mathilda off to the cabin, where Elizabeth lay sleeping.

The Indians aligned their mounts at water's edge and studied the flatboats and pale-face crews in silence. They made no move for their bows, which they wore diagonally around the torso. Each man, Anthony noticed, had a quiver stocked with arrows and also carried a knife and tomahawk.

With deliberate slowness, Abbott lowered his arms and took the handle of the sweep nearest him. He waved once to the savages, then told Anthony to go to the other sweep and begin rowing. Ellison and Evans did the same, and soon they had left the hunting party behind.

Abbott calmly returned to his canoe and napped until well past noon. When the frontiersman awoke, he dipped out some of Rebekah's root tea from the pot suspended over the sandbox fire. He then passed by the bristling Tory and ascended the crude ladder to the upper deck. There he took the rudder from Anthony, who was full of curiosity regarding the Indian hunting party.

"First Injuns you ever saw, eh?" Abbott's tanned face briefly flashed white teeth, the first smile he had displayed since the Yellow Creek episode.

"The second," Anthony replied, and told him of the encampment at Cresap's stockade near Cumberland.

Abbott grunted. "Big Spoon," he said. "That's what the Injuns call Cresap. He feeds 'em, hopin' they won't go over to th' British side."

He reiterated his belief that the hunters were Cherokees, whose homeland lay to the southeast as far away as Georgia and the Carolinas. The advance of the white man, he said, had driven the incumbent tribe of the upper Ohio Valley—the Shawnee—further west.

"Lord Dunmore's War took place in these parts nearly two years ago," he said. "When they smoked th' calumet, an' signed the treaty, it was like openin' up the gates. In come the whites. Away go the Injuns."

Just the day before, Abbott cited as an example, the travelers had passed the bustling village of Zane's Station, nestled around the wooden stockade known for the moment as Fort Fincastle but soon to be patriotically renamed Fort Henry. "That was just a lonesome li'l outpost afore last year," Abbott said.

Fort Fincastle . . . The name reminded Anthony of the Cash family, whom they last saw crossing the Monongahela. Nathan Cash had intended to join his brothers at that fort and continue his westward journey in their company. Wistfully, Anthony wondered if he might see Cash again.

Abbott, waxing unusually loquacious, continued on the subject of Indians and their domain. "To th' north of th' river," he said, "we'll pass Mingo territory first, then the land of the Shawnee."

"Whose land is it to the south?" asked Anthony, recalling that their destination lay on that side of the Ohio.

The trapper smiled again. "That's Kain-tuck land," he said, seeming to savor the name. "All Injuns hunt there, but none of 'em live there."

His eyes sparkled. "You've never seen such huntin'—never! Lotsa game. Deer. Bear. Buffalo. Grass as high as your head. Lotsa clear cricks an' lakes. And it'll stay thataway, on account o' it's guarded. Least-ways, the Injuns think so."

"Guarded?"

"Yep. By the Azgens." Abruptly, Abbott's face clouded and he fell silent. So quick was the change in him, almost as though he had caught himself saying too much, that Anthony didn't even ask the obvious question: Who were the Azgens?

At dusk, closing out the eighth day of their journey, the voyagers came upon a large island. They directed the arks around the right side and discovered a willow-fringed inlet, an inviting place to tie up for the night.

Anthony, a long stick in one hand to chase off snakes, went south of the inlet foraging for firewood. As he searched and collected, there came to his nostrils an odor as of something long deceased and decaying. He grunted in disgust, but an abundance of fallen limbs led him toward the stench rather than away from it.

As the odor thickened, it aroused Anthony's curiosity. The island was not a likely home for any large animals. Fighting off nausea, he parted the high, reedy grass and shuffled forward through the willows and locust trees. The noise from a swarm of buzzing insects helped guide him. His nose burned, and tears blurred his vision.

But tears were not enough to blot out the horror of what he finally found.

The bodies, sprawled face-up, were those of two men and three young boys. All were white. All had been scalped.

Despite the swollen and blackened features, Anthony recognized Nathan Cash and two of his sons. The other man, of similar build and complexion, might have been a brother to Cash, the third boy possibly a nephew. Mutilations were disclosed through the gaping, bloodied holes in their clothing.

A thorough search of the island by Anthony, Abbott, Ellison, and Evans turned up no sign of the other family members—the third boy, his sister, or their mother, Dot Cash. It was impossible, too, to tell whether the murders had taken place on the island or whether the bodies had simply been dumped there.

The burials were completed by torchlight. Abbott did his share of that task, until the frequent glares from Evans became too much for him to tolerate. As the spadework was winding down, off he went in the canoe.

The others wordlessly collected around the graves. To Anthony's relief, Ellison took it on himself to pray over the dead. The Pennsylvanian, who at dawn each day opened his Bible in meditation, stood with the leather-bound book in his hands near the flickering torch. Anthony drew solace from Nimrod Ellison's unassuming, yet truly reverent petition to the Lord God of Hosts on behalf of those who had met with this sudden and violent end.

But the cooper's words held no relief for Rebekah. She somehow managed to feed Mathilda and Elizabeth, and induce them into an early sleep. Then she broke down.

Her sobs drove Anthony nearly frantic. She would not lift her head from their makeshift bed, nor stop crying, no matter what he said or tried to do. Her present distress was much different, he realized, from the pouting anger of before. This outpouring, like Mathilda's on the day she joined them, embodied despair and hopelessness.

Anguished, Anthony stepped out onto the deck. Tory, curled up just outside the threshold, gave one sleepy growl, determined who had disturbed him, and resumed his slumber.

The night wind stirred the willows around the inlet and at least momentarily dispersed the ever-present mosquito cloud. A crescent moon struck rippling highlights across the mighty Ohio. The trees along the riverbank stood in black silhouette against a glowing multitude of stars. Insects and frogs raised their familiar choruses.

Anthony inhaled the fresh air in gulps, trying to drive from his nostrils the lingering stench of death.

What was going to happen next in this godforsaken place? How, he wondered, could the Creator of Heaven and Earth allow the beings made in His own divine image to practice such cruelties on one another?

Two more days, he told himself. Two more days, and they should be entering the gates of New Ephrata, where the Lord was truly king and white men lived peacefully in the wilderness among their red brothers. At this moment, the persuasive promises of Samuel Russel seemed so remote and foolish. Had it not been for the reinforcement by the hermit Micah of what lay ahead, the expedition would seem to be the most insane folly.

Should he have heeded the pleadings of his wife, back in Winchester, and returned home? If so, what would have happened to Mathilda and her baby sister? For that matter, what was going to happen to all of them now? It was impossible not to reflect on the gruesome fate of the Cash clan.

Anthony knew he must shake his doubts, and that he could not do so alone.

"Holy Father," he mumbled, "send us Thy Comforter. Give us safety and rest in the shadow of Thy wings . . ." He tried to concentrate solely on the things of God.

Chapter 13

*A*lthough the tenth morning on the Ohio dawned clear, marred only by a light fog, it didn't stay that way long. Soon there were gray clouds collecting, and a gusting northeasterly wind began to buffet the sterns of the flatboats.

This should be the day, Anthony declared to Abbott, that they would at last come upon what Micah had described: a large creek opposite a single island, intersecting the river from their right. "At the foot of this island, so that we'll know it from any other," Anthony repeated the hermit's directions, "will be standing a wooden cross. Only a mile or so further, on the left, there will be a bluff and the mouth of a little creek. That's where we find New Ephrata."

The trapper offered only a superficial response, appearing to be caught up in an excitement of his own. His eyes glittered, and his actions seemed quick and nervous. He had not returned from his nocturnal trapping foray until after sunrise, with no game to show for the extended time.

Eager to reach journey's end, Anthony for only the second time on the voyage hoisted the sail. Ellison, his craft similarly equipped, did the same. Despite their boxlike contours, the arks cast foamy wakes once driven by the wind.

Anthony, manning the stern sweep, observed that Abbott was foregoing his customary morning nap. The woodsman sat in the bow, hatless, his black locks blown by the breeze. As he studied the river, he primed his flintlock. Abbott had said nothing of his own intended destination, but Anthony surmised it was the "Kain-tuck land" of unsurpassed hunting.

Evidently, New Ephrata sat right in the thick of Kain-tuck. Anthony wondered again about the shadowy Azgens, cited by Abbott as the guardians of this unclaimed territory. If they were Indians, as he surmised, the New Ephrata colonists must be on friendly terms with them.

The river shifted its direction decidedly to the north of west, and the northeasterly gusts became a crosswind. The boats lost some of their momentum. Anthony, not enough of a sailor to manipulate the simple, square-rigged sail to his advantage, was debating whether to lower it when he thought he heard a voice calling from somewhere ahead.

Sure enough! Just a few hundred feet downstream, against the north bank, a solitary figure was perched on a willowy sandbar, alternately waving arms wildly and shouting through cupped hands: "Help me! Please, please help me! In the name of God!"

Abbott jerked his head around. "That's a woman thar!" he exclaimed. "A white woman! Swing over!"

A vague discomfort stirred in Anthony's gut. He remembered Micah's warning about the north shore and Indian treachery. Hand on the sweep, he hesitated. Abbott gestured excitedly, almost fiercely, at the pleading figure. "Swing over!" he repeated impatiently. "We have t' help her! Quick, man!"

Still standing where they had first seen her, the woman continued her cries for help. She was bareheaded; her long blond hair blew in tangles about her face, and her dress was ripped apart at the bosom.

As she lowered her hands from her mouth, Anthony recognized the gaunt figure.

Dot Cash!

He pushed hard on the stern sweep. The flatboat veered toward the sandbar.

Several things then happened in very quick succession. First came the hoarse shout of Evans, from the trailing ark. "No, Mr. Cumin's, don't stop!" Anthony glanced back. The old man was bouncing frantically around Ellison's foredeck. "Don't stop!" he pleaded. "Keep to the channel! It's a trap!"

When Anthony again looked shoreward, Dot Cash was running awkwardly toward the water. Her right ankle dragged a rope. Recognition and horror were written on her face in terrible twin strokes. Thin arms flailing the air, she screamed, "Go 'way! Don't come no closer! Go 'way!"

But the most astonishing sight was that of Abbott, standing in the bow, raising his long rifle toward Anthony. The eye drawing the bead was cold and merciless.

Instinctively, Anthony dropped to the deck just as Abbott discharged his weapon. The Virginian would ever afterward credit God with sending him that life-saving reaction.

Abbott threw the rifle aside and charged the ladder for the upper deck, tugging at his hunting knife as he went. Tory, at rope's end, exploded in a furious salvo of growls and snarls.

Anthony scrambled to his feet and looked about hastily for his own rifle, which was propped against the starboard gunwale. As he lunged for it, he heard a savage chorus of Indian cries. Several braves burst out of the willow grove and sprinted after Dot Cash. She had run the limit of the rope and was sprawled face down in the sand.

Just as Abbott reached the base of the ladder, Tory made a heroic lunge and the slip knot in his leash jerked loose. The sudden release cost the cur his balance, but he bowled into Abbott's legs and knocked the trapper down. Simultaneously, man and beast sprang to their feet. Tory gathered himself to fly again at Abbott even as the trapper readied his knife.

Then came the explosion of a gunshot. Abbott gasped, dropped the knife, and grabbed his stomach with both hands. The leaping dog struck him high in the chest, knocking him against the gunwale. Abbott managed to turn and hurl himself over the side.

Rebekah stood in the doorway of the cabin with a smoking pistol clenched in her hands, green eyes wide in disbelief. Abruptly, little Mathilda pushed past her and trotted over to where Abbott's knife lay. She snatched the weapon off the deck and fiercely hugged it to her breast, screaming tearfully, "Daddy's knife! Daddy's knife!"

Anthony seized the stern sweep in both hands, and with all of his strength swung the flatboat back toward the channel. A shot rang out from Ellison's flatboat, sparking louder howls from the Indians. Anthony did not see who fired the shot, nor at what target it was delivered. "Come and help!" he shouted at Rebekah, who numbly dropped the pistol and with a sob forced herself up the ladder.

While she handled the stern sweep, trying to wipe away her

tears, Anthony utilized the sail as best he could. Ellison's ark was close behind, its canvas billowing. The screaming of the Indians grew fainter, and there was no immediate sign of pursuit.

Within minutes, the dark shape of an island ahead loomed dimly against the sullen hills and lowering sky. As they neared its head, Anthony instructed Rebekah to steer to the right side. Shortly, the mouth of a stream opened up on their right.

"This fits Micah's account!" Anthony declared. "It has to be the island he spoke of!" Soon they were clearing the foot of the isle. The black clouds had opened to dump their burden, and the sheet of rain further hindered visibility.

But there it was: a cross, made modestly of unhewn timber, standing maybe four feet high among locust saplings.

"Just another mile or more!" Anthony shouted back at Ellison. "We're nearly there!" He then took his weeping wife in his arms.

"Oh, Anthony!" she sobbed. "It's all so awful, so hard to believe . . . Dot Cash, at the mercy of those savages . . . and Abbott! He tried to kill you! He was in with the Indians after all! Mr. Evans was right about him, the entire time! And I—I had to shoot him! Do you believe he's dead?"

He gently shook his head, placed his cheek against her forehead. "I don't know. Everything happened so fast. I didn't see anything of him after he jumped overboard."

Rebekah recounted Mathilda's retrieval of the knife. "Poor little thing! No wonder she feared Abbott so! She must have known or felt, all along, that he was one of the men who murdered her parents. How horrible!"

Anthony nodded. "She and Tory," he said hoarsely.

They were interrupted by the excited voice of Evans. "The Injuns!" he yelled. "I kin see 'em a'comin' after us!"

They descried, far upriver, several dark objects—almost surely canoes—slicing through the choppy water. Neither wind nor rain had dissuaded the red men from their ill intent. Now the fickle wind was blowing north to south, and the sails that had so providentially spirited the flatboats away from danger were once again flopping about uselessly.

The travelers could only take up the side sweeps and row hard, and hope to somehow outlast the determined savages.

Over the next few minutes it became obvious that the skilled pursuers were diminishing their distance. Wicked gusts of wind and driven whitecaps pummeled the ungainly flatboats, hindering their progress, while the four canoes full of savages seemed to glide through the foamy turbulence.

How cruel, it occurred to Anthony, to be so close to the end of their journey and perhaps not make it! He could hear Rebekah gasping for breath as she doggedly plunged her sweep into the water again and again. The storm clouds had intensified, the rain beat down, and now flashes of lightning gave vivid detail to the fast-gaining canoes and their whooping, war-painted crews.

Of a sudden, a new surge of hope animated Anthony. To their left rose a sheer limestone bluff about twenty feet high—perchance the very one described by Micah. Somewhere around its base should be the mouth of the little creek serving New Ephrata. Even now, Anthony realized, they might be within earshot of succor.

He scrambled over the wet deck to the rear sweep and pulled it hard, turning the flatboat toward the bluff. The trailing Ellison ark did the same. Through the rain and gloom, Anthony frantically scanned the base of the formation, not initially spotting an opening. Oh, yes! There it was, almost hidden by the willows.

The chopping waves drove the arks shoreward, and here the voyagers' lack of skill betrayed them. Anthony misjudged the approach, and before he could prevent it his flatboat swooped screechingly into a clutching network of half-submerged timber. A violent collision followed as Ellison's craft blundered into Anthony's, driving both into a snarl of wood from which there could be no escape.

The tomahawk-waving Indians yelled in exultation, and flash after flash of lightning highlighted their confident movements to reach the stranded flatboats. The white men turned to their rifles out of instinct and desperation, though grimly aware that the rain had certainly fouled them. The women, seeking at least temporary safety, joined their children within the cabins. There, in virtual darkness, Rebekah, hugging Mathilda and sleepy Elizabeth, fought back panic and sank to her knees in forlorn but passionate prayer: "Please, merciful God! Please, Lord Jesus! Don't let it end this way!"

Anthony, his rain-streaked face pale with emotion, appeared momentarily at the cabin doorway. "If Mathilda still has that knife," he ordered, his voice cracking, "do not hesitate to use it—in whatever way you must!" He ducked inside and pressed his lips to Rebekah's, then pulled away from her embrace to contest the impending assault.

The Indians brought the canoes in close and prepared to board, weapons in hand, their leering faces made doubly grotesque by the rain-smeared war paint. They sent triumphant war whoops echoing off the water and the limestone bluff.

All at once, the screams died in their throats, and the victorious smirks turned to open-mouthed alarm.

A booming, sonorous voice, calling out in a tongue Anthony did not know, brought the Indians' frenzy to a shocked halt. Anthony followed the stares of the awestruck, upturned faces to the top of the bluff.

There stood a manlike figure of immense proportions, its full-length, hooded garment billowing in the storm. The next flash of lightning disclosed a pointed beard and aquiline nose protruding from the dripping cowl.

The figure extended a long arm, the folds of the sleeve rippling in the gusting wind, and pointed to the flatboats. The deep, hollow voice directed a question in English: "Where do you travel?"

Anthony, heart pounding, cleared his throat and responded: "To New Ephrata!"

The voice returned to the language first spoken, addressing the petrified Indian audience. The powerful tones rose in intensity, and one did not have to understand the words to know that an answer had been demanded. An older warrior of some evident authority stood up gingerly in his rocking canoe and offered a stammering reply.

There came another question in English: "The Shawnee say they pursue you because you fired upon them. Is this true?"

Nimrod Ellison snatched off his soaked three-cornered hat and raised his voice in reply: "The Injuns had a white woman tied up on the sand, to bait us into a trap. She bravely warned us away. Then these mighty warriors—" His voice broke, but he held up a hand to indicate he had more to say. Hoarsely, he continued, "What I aim my rifle at, I do not miss. Ask the brave Shawnee if I did not kill the woman with a single shot, even as they were close around her, trying to cut out her tongue!" He covered his face with trembling hands.

The cloaked figure's voice resumed the Shawnee tongue in ringing tones, doubtless administering a verbal lashing. With reluctance, the Indian spokesman bowed stiffly, dropped his head on his chest, and sat down.

With an imperious wave, the mysterious figure hurled a command at the Indians. In hasty compliance, they turned their canoes and began the difficult task of paddling upstream through the storm.

The great voice once again spoke in English. "Come ashore in your canoes. You can safely leave your boats where they rest. You will have help on the morrow to retrieve your beasts and belongings.

"Meanwhile, I, David Singletary, welcome you to New Ephrata in the name of the Lord Jesus Christ."

Part III

The Ohio Valley
(1777 - 1821)

Chapter 14

*T*he wearied miller watched the stream of yellow powder slow to a trickle as it tumbled down the mealspout and dropped into the trough. Satisfied that the final load of Indian corn had been exhausted, he pushed down on a lever to separate the upper, spinning burrstone from the lower, stationary one. Then he threw a second lever, disengaging the millstone spindle. Gears squeaking and popping, the wooden apparatus shuddered to a stop. In the sudden stillness there drifted up from the wheel pit the soft splashing of water and a rhythmic groan as the water wheel continued to turn the main shaft.

Anthony used his left shirtsleeve—marginally the drier one— to mop the gooey mixture of sweat and cornmeal dust from mouth, cheeks, and neck. He ran an index finger under his cotton kerchief headdress, across his eyebrows, and through the contours of each ear, dislodging further damp accumulations.

A breeze entered the north window and stirred the particle-filled air. It danced lightly over the back of Anthony's sodden shirt, and beckoned him to the aperture with its whisper of impending change.

This year, late September in the Ohio Valley found the temperatures and humidity unseasonably high. Indeed, Anthony could not remember the last time a breath of fresh air had filtered into the gristmill. Probably not since sometime in May, he reflected. He grasped the window frame on either side, buckled his elbows, and greedily thrust out his head for more clean air.

Two stories below bubbled the tail water, rushing from the

gloom of the wheel pit into the waning sunshine. It played along a narrow stone race and joyfully reentered Sycamore Creek, from whence it had been diverted upstream at the millpond and channeled under the mill.

The creek continued north on a slightly bowed course of several hundred yards to a limestone bluff, or natural wall, under which it disappeared. But Anthony well knew that it emerged on the other side of the bluff and emptied there into the Ohio River. This point of confluence, screened by willows and river debris, was where his and Ellison's flatboats had been hung up and overtaken by Shawnees sixteen months before.

Sixteen months? More like sixteen years! Anthony thought. *Sixteen exciting, wonderful years.* For everyone in the two flatboats— even, wonder of wonders, the irascible John Evans—it had been a time of spiritual rebirth.

It had also been a time for physical birth, as tiny Samuel joined the Cumings household on a frozen February evening.

True to the practice of community in New Ephrata, a bevy of midwives helped usher in Samuel. His and his mother's wants were fully addressed by a tireless procession of volunteer domestics.

Dedicated both spiritually and physically to the glory of God, the residents of the community functioned as a corporate body. Within six weeks of their arrival, Anthony and Rebekah were comfortably lodged in a snug cabin raised by the menfolk. The Ellisons were treated in the same fashion. Since then, Anthony had taken part in nearly a dozen house raisings for other newcomers.

Though the dwellings became home to the families for which they were built, legal ownership was not conveyed. Having asked who owned the property on which his house sat, Anthony was told simply, "The Lord," and was gently discouraged from giving it any more thought.

Hunting and the agricultural fields were tended to by the men, and (except for the slaughter of livestock) the women handled food storage and meal preparations. A single large kitchen produced the entirety of each day's three communal meals, which were first placed before the men and then served to the children, the women helping themselves last.

The dining hall occupied the bottom of a two-story structure. On the second floor, children pursued lessons in reading, writing, and arithmetic, along with heavy doses of the Holy Scriptures. Their instruction came in the daytime; at night, adults who had not mastered those skills took a turn.

No one in the colony or its environs—including twoscore families of Shawnee converts to Christianity, who lived across the river—wanted for food, clothing, shelter, safety, society, spiritual edification, or educational opportunity.

There was, though, a great price affixed to life in New Ephrata, one which its residents paid gladly for the most part. This was the surrender of individual possessions and fleshly comforts, the abandonment of personal ambition, the quelling of lust for temporal things. That which had been important (but not of God) in the outside world was forsaken—even its memory.

Clothing and home furnishings were almost painfully austere, underscoring the theological point that man was put on Earth to further the glory of God, not his own vanity. The colonists replaced the secular thoughts and values they had brought to New Ephrata with the worship of God the Father, God the Son, and God the Holy Spirit. Ceaseless worship. Each waking hour marked with prayer and praise. Every activity dedicated to the greater glory of the Godhead.

Dying to self as the Bible instructed was the single most important lesson. To this end, all adult newcomers were required to spend a fortnight in solitary prayer and meditation before rejoining their family circle. For Anthony, this was a powerful experience; for Rebekah, it was nothing short of supernatural.

The gristmill was up and running within a year.

Anthony, after prayerful consultation with a body of men designated by David Singletary as the elders of the community, chose the site on Sycamore Creek. While the millpond and millrace were being excavated by others, Anthony and Nimrod Ellison designed and assembled the wooden milling apparatus. Next, they crafted the big undershot wheel.

All hands labored to dig the wheel pit and reinforce its walls with stone. A three-story frame building followed, and the young millwright then turned his attention to the great French burrstones Singletary had brought into the wilderness. Lovingly, Anthony spent days dressing them, cutting spiral grooves that would shear and grind the corn particles while pushing them from the center to the perimeter of the stones.

Among those who showed an unflagging interest in the building and operation of the mill was Luke Higgins. This oldster, despite an ill-concealed appetite for corn whiskey, enjoyed a deferential treatment within the colony due to David Singletary's special love for him. Once the milling process started, Higgins asserted himself as Anthony's right-hand man. At the miller's beck and call, he opened and closed the watergates at the dam and on the millrace and performed sundry other duties.

He also turned out to be a thorough source of information on Singletary and the colony's history. This was due in some measure to the old bachelor's affection for Anthony—and for John Barleycorn.

Other than Communion wine, no strong drink was tolerated within the colony. Yet, on any given afternoon, Anthony's milling companion might magically produce a jug of whiskey. Tongue loosened, old Luke allowed soliloquies to flow freely. One such afternoon, the topics he chose were himself and Singletary.

By his own account, Higgins had spent virtually all of his adult life among the Indians. As a fur trader wandering the forested land beyond the vanguard of American settlement, he forged close bonds with the various tribes, some of whom were enemies of the others. A preference for the wilderness decided the course of Higgins's life. Retaining no fond memories of the crowded, comfort-softened East, he opened a trading post across the Ohio River from what was to become New Ephrata. For a season, he was the only resident white man.

Then, unexpectedly, comradeship arrived in the person of a dynamic young preacher of the Gospel of Jesus Christ.

Higgins, wise to the ways of the frontier, never initiated conversations about a man's past. As a result, despite nearly thirty years of close friendship with David Singletary, the trader had learned little of David's family or upbringing. Some things, though, became obvioius early on: Singletary had a keen mind sharpened by a fine education, as well as a passion for the Gospel and a compulsion to spread it among the red men.

While a very young man, David once related, he had spent some years with a monastic camp in the Pennsylvania backwoods.

At this commune, Singletary pursued pottery-firing, glass-blowing, and the shadowy study of alchemy, all of which he would later find useful in the Ohio Valley.

But it was as a missionary of the Word that he plunged into the trackless western forests to preach salvation to the Indians. He ultimately stumbled upon Higgins's trading post, and an unlikely bond of friendship formed.

The kindnesses of Higgins had attracted numerous red-skinned satellites. The way Singletary saw it, their souls were ripe for holy harvest.

"I've no doubts the Lord knew what a team in harness we'd make," old Luke said softly to Anthony, eyes moist. "I always thought o' myself as a godly man, but it just weren't in me to win over the savages to Christ. So the Lord, He equipped Davy and sent him here t' do it."

In stark physical contrast to those he sought to convert, Singletary was almost seven feet tall, with arresting blue eyes, shaggy brown hair, melodious bass voice, "and a wondrous great strength," Higgins said. Potential converts, in awe of such a commanding presence, generally were spellbound by his simple but powerful presentation of the Gospel.

For a time, the happiest in Higgins's life, the two white men joined forces to do God's work among the red heathens. But an ever-increasing number of light-skinned heathens began to worm their way into this fruit-laden paradise. Neither Higgins nor Singletary was able to deal effectively with these coarse, brutal, and often greedy representatives of their own race. Inexorably, the bloodshed began between red men and white.

To further complicate matters, the celibate fell in love.

"She was a real winsome little red lass," old Luke recalled fondly. "Poor Davy! Ye could see it blowin' across him like a great north wind. And she, too—she loved him mightily." The girl was a Mingo, Luke said. She was sister to Chief Logan, who after marrying into the Shawnee nation had become greatly esteemed among them.

The prospect of raising a family in the midst of a mounting frontier war between his wife's people and his own deeply troubled Singletary. He turned to his first source for direction. Having sent his pregnant wife to live with her family for a while, Singletary found a hideaway in the forest where he could fast and pray. There in undisturbed solitude, among massive trees so tightly clustered that their intertwined foliage blotted out the noonday sun, the missionary sought the will of God.

At last a plan was revealed. Singletary should establish a community of white Christian families, assembling various skills and abilities to teach their red brothers. The only chance for peace on the frontier, he understood God to declare, lay in the assimilation of the Indian culture within that of the whites.

"So," old Luke resumed after a whiskey-punctuated respite, "we moved t' this side of the river and began t' spread the news of New Ephrata and who an' what we wanted. God is seein' to it that men like you are drawn here, each an' every fortnight."

"But why did you move across the river?" Anthony asked. "Weren't you already established on the other side?"

"We was only two white men with a tradin' post and an encampment of pacified Shawnees," the old man replied. "As you know, the north side is th' Injun side. With trouble heatin' up between Injuns and whites, a settlement of whites over there would never of made it."

"Why are things different on this side?" It was a question Anthony remembered having asked before. Higgins gave the answer that had been given before, only in greater detail.

"The Injuns believe the south side of the river is bad medicine," Higgins said, a smile flitting over his lips. "All the tribes hunt game here, but none dare t' live here. They're a-feared of the Azgens."

Anthony started at the term. It was like hearing the voice of Abbott once again . . . Abbott, the traitor, doubtless long since found floating face-down in some snag-infested shallows.

"The Injuns say that, hundreds o' years ago, there was a tribe of whites that lived south o' the river," the aged narrator expounded. "These whites had sailed across the big water. They weren't full of war; in fact, they tried t' keep to themselves. But the Injuns still feared and hated 'em, and the red tribes joined forces to free up this huntin' ground from the whites.

"They finally killed ever' last member of the white tribe—men, women, and the youngsters. The last of 'em were driven west to an island in the Ohio an' massacreed. But this bloody deed caused the restless spirits o' the murdered whites t' be loosed in the dark forests below th' river, and for many generations, now, no Injuns have dared t' set the poles of their wigwams on this side.

"The Injuns call these ghosts the Azgens. And them red men that aren't Christians are most 'specially scared of Davy 'cause of his awesome size and his ways."

Higgins shrugged. "I s'pose that's one way the Lord chose to protect New Ephrata," he said. "We've yet t' have a single soul here killed or captured by Injuns of any tribe. Yet, the bloodshed goes on all 'round us. You've seen the signs of it, floatin' down the river."

Anthony's party of adventurers could personally attest to the miracle of New Ephrata. Flatboats snared in a tangle of deadwood, rifles rainsoaked and useless, two dozen grinning Indians circling their canoes . . . But certain death or worse, Anthony mused, had been averted by the sudden, providential appearance of Singletary— evidence of a sovereign God.

The old man's story had proven quite revealing. For one thing, Anthony did not know about Singletary's wife and child—had never seen or heard of them. He said as much to Higgins.

A look of pain captured the old man's countenance. He rocked his body back and forth, hugging the near-empty clay jug to his chest. After licking his lips, he took a gulp of whiskey.

"Don't ya know what happened to Chief Logan's fam'ly?" Luke asked, watery, blinking eyes nervously meeting Anthony's. "They was done in by a band of murderin' whites on Yellow Crick. Davy's wife, big with his child, was among 'em."

Chapter 15

For the remainder of their years together, Anthony never quite understood what Rebekah experienced during her time of solitary prayer. Nor could she adequately explain. It was simply, in that most mysterious of terms, a miracle.

Within a month of arriving in New Ephrata, in accordance with Singletary's practice, the adults from the Cumings and Ellison families were separated and placed in individual "prayer closets." There, with only water and meager portions of bread for sustenance, they spent a fortnight in what was intended to be purifying prayer and meditation. Each came away moved by the experience, but none so profoundly as Rebekah. When she rejoined her husband, Rebekah's self-centered vanity had given way to an attitude of selflessness—coupled with a burning love for the Lord Jesus Christ.

She was still vivacious, still subject to interwoven spells of the serious and the lighthearted. And still, on occasion, maddeningly independent. But her bouts of pouting and primping were gone, replaced by a serene composure and simple neatness of toilet. And the doubts and fears that so haunted her on their westward journey also vanished.

As far as Rebekah was concerned, God had personally touched her. Many times over, she offered thanks. So, too, did Anthony, whose incomplete understanding did not hinder his gratitude.

There was no way to know on which of the fourteen days of seclusion Rebekah received the supernatural visitation. Daylight and dark were not distinguishable in her windowless room, lighted solely by a supply of candles and furnished only with a pallet, a small table, and a Bible.

From the beginning, Rebekah struggled against the gentle instructions to concentrate on prayer while reading and considering the word of God. A thousand thoughts distracted her. She longed for Loudoun County and her family; wished she had never agreed to this flight of madness. Worst of all, she seemed to be constantly recalling the sight of Abbott at the instant she shot him. Abbott, clutching his punctured stomach with both hands as the mongrel Tory flew at him . . . unbelieving eyes, wide with pain, meeting hers. His desperate lunge overboard, and the tell-tale bloody palm prints left on the gunwale.

In wrestling with such reflections, Rebekah knew that she was not alone. Somewhere close by, locked away in his own Spartan surroundings, Nimrod Ellison must be suffering the tortures of the damned over his mercy-driven snap decision to kill Dot Cash.

Rebekah determined she must read aloud from the scriptures in order to drive other thoughts from her mind. The practice soon became a habit. She at first sought out the four gospels, so familiar from the book given her as a wedding present. As time passed, she ventured into something different: a strange and wonderful narrative concerning the Apostles.

" 'And when the day of Pentecost was fully come, they were all with one accord in one place.

" 'And suddenly there came a sound from heaven as of a rushing mighty wind, and it filled all the house where they were sitting.

" 'And there appeared unto them cloven tongues like as of fire, and it sat upon each of them.

" 'And they were all filled with the Holy Ghost, and began to speak with other tongues, as the Spirit gave them utterance.' "

When Rebekah began to read the next verse, a singular thing happened. The words she saw—solid, stilted, King James English— were not the words she spoke. In fact, the sounds issuing from her own mouth were not words Rebekah knew.

She gasped. "Oh, my God!" was her thought, but she voiced something utterly different, followed by a moan.

Fear suddenly beset her. Just as suddenly, it departed.

More accurately, the perception Rebekah had was of Fear— personified as a hideous little imp from Hell—being seized by the scruff of its repulsive neck and hurled away. Her next sensation was of something warm and wonderfully reassuring draped over her shoulders and radiating throughout her being. A magnificent, infinitely loving presence filled the room. She fell upon her face—not in fear, but in reverential gratitude and worship—and allowed the sobs and tears to have their way.

Old Luke Higgins, standing at the upper gate to the millrace, luxuriated in the first cool breezes of this unusually hot and humid September. The incessant gurgling of the diverted creek water as it chased itself down the long, rocky channel kept Higgins from hearing the rattle of the millworks or sensing their cessation. Surely, he thought, glancing repeatedly at the second-floor window of the mill, the final load of Indian corn had by this time run its course.

Luke was finally rewarded by the sight of Anthony leaning out of the window and waving to him. He loosed the rope from around the capstan (a relic off the Cumings flatboat) and lowered the gate into the neck of the millrace. The weighted sluice slid easily to the bottom of its frame, squeezing the stream of water to a trickle. Over the next few minutes, as Higgins watched idly, Sycamore Creek recovered its normal flow.

Without warning, Luke felt himself seized around the ribcage by a mighty pair of arms and lifted into the air. He was lowered and released almost before he could react, and a booming laugh smote his ears. He staggered about to face a buckskin-wrapped barrel chest, whose owner gazed down at him with twinkling brown eyes.

"Why, Simon Butler, you whippersnapper!" Higgins gasped angrily, though relieved at the identity of his playful assailant. He half-heartedly punched the young Hercules in the stomach. "Lucky for you," he growled, anger now feigned. "I mighta done ya in before I learned who ya was!"

The big man stooped and picked up his long rifle, which he had laid down in order to grab his prey. "I'm worried about you, Mr. Higgins," he rumbled. "Where's your rifle? Where's the sentries? Don't you know it's dangerous times in Kaintuck?"

"We don't need t' fear the Injuns here, Simon," rejoined the older man, rearranging his twisted tunic. "You for one surely know that, even if no one else believes it."

The young man's face grew serious. "Things may be different now," Simon contended. "The Shawnees has been raidin' our side o' the river since early last winter. It all started over that rotten cur,

Chief Pluggy. He only got what he deserved, but it stirred up Chief Black Fish mighty bad. We've been under attack ever since, different times at Harrodsburg and Boonesboro and McClelland's Station. We've lost some good men—women, too."

Higgins was aware of the bloody clashes of the past eight months, provoked by the death of the vicious subchief whose Indian name the Kentuckians had derisively shortened to Pluggy. Black Fish, having previously felt bound by the three-year-old peace treaty between Chief Cornstalk and Lord Dunmore, used Pluggy's demise as an excuse to cross the river and give the settlers a lesson in fear. After all, Black Fish argued, Dunmore's subjects had turned on him and their own king across the great water. What good was Cornstalk's treaty now?

"We've had no trouble here," Higgins reiterated. "For that matter, I've lived in this same spot for a full score o' years and never drew bead on another man, red or white. There's been some thought given lately t' buildin' a blockhouse, but Davy says it would show a lack o' trust in th' Lord."

"And lack of trust in the Injuns, as well," the young giant noted with a touch of sarcasm. "I kin tell you I've spent time inside the blockhouses west an' south o' here, and they're all that kep' my scalp from decoratin' a Shawnee belt."

As they talked, the pair watched Anthony emerge from the mill and step to the bank of Sycamore Creek. There he washed from the waist up, ruefully slipped back into his damp, soiled shirt, and sauntered over to meet the visitor.

"Praise the Lord!" He gave the salutation common to New Ephrata and extended his hand. "I'm Anthony Cumings, Mr. Higgins's milling apprentice," he added jocularly.

This lighthearted dig brought a smile from old Luke but did not produce the same result in the stranger. Anthony found himself the subject of a quick, hard stare before the big man struggled to assert his manners. "I'm Simon Butler," he finally said, perfunctorily wrapping a big paw around Anthony's hand.

"Simon here has known these woods since he was a boy," Higgins said. "He's the finest scout in the Ohio Valley, an' no one's better at bringin' back meat in the dead o' winter."

Butler seemed embarrassed by the praise. "Where do you come from, Mr. Cumin's?" he asked abruptly, as if to change the subject. But the question came across too bluntly.

"Northern Virginia," Anthony answered, piqued at the frontiersman's attitude. "Loudoun County, on Goose Creek. And you, Mr. Butler? Where are you from?"

Butler clearly did not relish answering. "Winchester," he said at last, in a tone which cast doubt on the veracity of the reply. He glanced at Higgins. "Guess I better get back to th' woods, where I belong," he said stiffly, shouldering his rifle.

Anthony abruptly felt ashamed. Butler, despite his great size and self-confidence, was clearly younger than Anthony—in fact, could not be much more than twenty years of age. Whatever the lessons offered by forest life, social graces were unlikely to be in the forefront.

"Mr. Butler," Anthony said hastily, "I'd be remiss by not sharing the bounty of our Lord with you. Please be good enough to wait here." He turned and strode down to the mill, and, stooping, disappeared through the doorway. In a moment, he emerged with a filled sack and offered it to the hunter. "Corn meal, Mr. Butler. The cakes go well with game of any kind."

Gratitude shone from the scout's whiskered but youthful face, more for the chance to redeem a potential friendship than for the gift itself. "Thank you kindly, Mr. Cumin's," Butler said with a broad smile. "I'm powerful fond of johnny-cake an' milk. Thanks again." This time the handshake was warm and vigorous.

Higgins smiled approvingly. After Butler departed, rifle in one hand and meal sack slung across the opposite shoulder, the oldster waxed apologetic. "Beats me, what got into his manners," he said. "Sure did act odd towards you, for a fact. But Simon is a fine lad. He's also a good one to have around in a scrape, and I'm afraid our people—outside of New Ephrata, that is—are goin' to need all the ones like him they kin scare up.

"I can't help but believe that young Butler has somethin' in his past he's run away from. But then, how many of 'em around the Ohio bottoms hasn't? Well, we'd best be gettin' on. We don't want to miss the readin' of the word over the evenin' meal."

As Anthony and Higgins headed in the direction of the dining hall, they spotted the towering, cloaked figure of David Singletary brooding atop the limestone bluff overlooking the river. Anthony speculated as to what had attracted Singletary to that post. Might he be watching for the arrival of new colonists? Or was he worriedly contemplating the heightened hostility and brazenness of Chief Black Fish?

No, certainly not the latter; to know David Singletary was to recognize that his thoughts and decisions reflected full and abiding faith in God. And through him, God had promised safety for New Ephrata.

Then again, Anthony asked himself, just who had the people of New Ephrata, the followers of David Singletary, put their own faith in: God or man?

Chapter 16

*I*n terms of armed conflict, 1778 was among the quietest periods of the Revolutionary War. Only one major encounter took place between the American and British armies, this during an unsuccessful summer offensive directed by Washington at Monmouth, New Jersey.

More important were two actions taken that year by King Louis XVI of France—the recognition of the United States as an independent nation and the forging of a military alliance with the Americans. The alliance gave a badly-needed morale boost to the Continental Army, which had incurred terrible hardships in a winter-long encampment at Valley Forge.

On the frontier, the continuation of the British-inspired Indian depredations finally prompted Virginia to move—however feebly—in defense of its far-flung Kentucky settlements. Lt. Col. George Rogers Clark, who knew how to fight the Indians on their own terms, took an expedition westward.

Residents of New Ephrata remained blissfully unaware of the war's progress, no matter the proximity of the events. As though God Himself had ordained it, they led an undisturbed, prosaic, worshipful existence even while surrounded by bloody conflict—dwelling peacefully in the eye of the storm.

They did, however, learn to their dismay that, in an episode only indirectly related to the war, the Shawnees had taken captive the young hero Simon Butler.

Butler and two other men had trailed a contingent of horse-stealing Indians across the Ohio and recovered some of the horses. A bit slow in heading for home, Butler and Alexander Montgomery were surprised by pursuing Shawnees and Montgomery was killed and scalped. The third member of their party escaped to tell the sorry tale. Butler, known and feared by the red men as a great adversary, would be considered a prize prisoner and no doubt had already suffered slow death by torture.

Anthony Cumings and Luke Higgins were lamenting the loss of Butler one evening at the close of their day's work. Anthony, kneeling on the bank of Sycamore Creek, was wriggling out of his shirt to wash up when he heard Higgins greet someone. Hastily, he slipped back into the grimy garment and glanced around.

The caller was a deerskin-clad squaw, plain of face and grim of expression, who told Higgins in her own tongue that she had come for corn meal. The old man turned to Anthony and translated the request.

"She's a Miami," Luke added, "an' a slave of our so-called Christian Shawnee bunch across th' river. If Davy ever learned of it, he'd have her set free. But sometimes I know better'n Davy. She'd only be worse off. Her own people won't take back one who's been disgraced like she has."

Anthony went into the mill for the requested food. Returning with a bulging sack, he heard Higgins lecturing the squaw in rough tones, and saw him reach out and grab something dangling from a string around her neck. A knife flashed in the woman's hand and she promptly severed the leather thong. The squaw's dark eyes glittered with anger, and she was not fully mollified even when Anthony presented the meal. With a curt nod and grunt of thanks, she stalked off, back bent under the weight of the bag.

Higgins wordlessly extended his hand, palm up, displaying a flat piece of wood which had been pierced to accommodate the thong. It was scraped and rubbed smooth on one side.

Painted on the polished face, in fine, black lines, was the likeness of a dragon or serpent with batlike wings. The long, undulating body tapered to a coiled tail; the head essentially consisted of gaping jaws and a single, baleful eye. It was a wholly evil creation, Anthony thought as he studied the work.

The image was tantalizingly familiar. He had seen it, or something very like it, many times before. But where?

"This is one o' the gods the Miami worship," Higgins said, disgustedly. "It's a holdover from the past, but now we've only the one true God in New Ephrata. I told the squaw she couldn't wear it no more an' that she'd best not make another."

"If she made this, she's quite an artist," Anthony said in frank admiration. "Just look at the details! The jointed wings, the hint of scales on the body . . . that glaring eye! Impressive . . . almost as if it were inspired."

"It's inspired, all right," the old man retorted. "The devil's own inspiration! And speakin' of eyes, did you see hers? If looks could kill, I'd be with my Maker right now! She loosed that knife so fast, I thought I might be a goner."

"Madoc!" Anthony blurted out, excitedly. "Prince Madoc! That's it!"

Higgins gave him a puzzled look.

"I knew I had seen something like this before," explained Anthony. "Rebekah's father, Mr. Russel, has a tapestry in his house, portraying a Welsh hero of olden times called Prince Madoc. My father-in-law always said he believed that Madoc and his crew sailed to America back in the twelfth century, long before Columbus did.

"Mr. Russel weaved this portrait from a childhood memory of a painting in Wales. In it, Prince Madoc wears a gold medallion on a chain. There's a flying dragon on that medallion, with the body curling just like this one does!"

Skepticism and alarm chased one another across Higgins's lined, anxious face. "Say, now," he queried, eyes narrowing, "you don't mean t' tell me . . .?" He paused midway through the question, as though interrupted by a more pressing thought. "Kin we go back inside, Anthony? Let's talk this over."

Translated, the suggestion meant having a swallow or two of whiskey. Anthony sighed, but followed the old trapper into the mill.

After temporarily satisfying his thirst, Higgins sat the jug in his lap. "Now, me lad," he said, a quaver in his voice, "kin you tell me what this sailor prince looked like?"

"Yes, I remember. He had red hair, a headful of it, and a beard. His eyes were blue, not so very different from the water his ship sailed on. There was, as I said, the medallion hanging against his chest."

Higgins held up a trembling hand to interrupt. "His shirt, or whatever he wore . . . the color wasn't purple, was it?"

Anthony nodded. A flood of astonishment swept over him.

"You've seen something of the same man, Mr. Higgins!" he said, passionately. "What did you see? Where did you see it?"

"All in good time, lad," came the subdued, thoughtful reply. The old man wiped gnarled fingers across his mouth and peered at Anthony. "So these Welshmen, these sailors, they came to America. Whatever happened to 'em? Did they get back home?"

Anthony's brow furrowed. "I think the way the story went, they made three voyages to America. They never returned from the last one. Rebekah's father said he believes Prince Madoc is buried somewhere . . ." His throat turned dry. "Somewhere out here in the western lands." Stunned, Anthony sat down opposite Higgins, staring hard at him. Finally, he heard the answer he was by now anticipating. But there was more.

"What you just described," Higgins admitted, "fits right smart with some paintin's in a cave acrost the Ohio. This same cave also holds the bones of a man that many o' the Indians believed to be the chief of the Azgens."

Anthony let out a long, slow puff of air. It was as close to a whistle as he could muster.

Could the Azgens—the legendary white "Indians"—be the crew of Madoc's last voyage? Or, perhaps more likely, their children and grandchildren? Had they brought women with them? Anthony wished now he had paid greater attention to the whimsical ramblings of Samuel Russel, especially on this subject.

One more detail, though, he did recall. "Mr. Russel believed that Prince Madoc was of the Christian faith," Anthony pointed out. "The tapestry showed a great cross on the sail of his ship. The dragon on the medallion was just a popular symbol of Wales. I'm sure the prince would've taught Christianity, not the fable of dragons. Why would the Miami take the dragon for a god?"

Higgins smiled darkly, the effects of the whiskey beginning to show. "We don't always get t' control what happens after we've gone. In fact, it's seldom that we kin."

The jug was subjected to one last, greedy pull, then Higgins tenderly and regretfully returned the vessel to its hiding place. He shot a look at Anthony. "I know, I kin tell: you want real bad t' see that cave, don'cha?

"Well, after th' first good snowfall chases the Shawnees to their wigwams, you shall. And there's somethin' else you'll be gettin' to see as well."

The first "good" snowfall found Anthony's thoughts far from any pilgrimage to the final resting place of Prince Madoc. Its mid-November arrival coincided with that of little Anthony, the second Cumings child.

This latest addition to the household helped finalize a long-pending decision to place Mathilda and Elizabeth with the neighbors, a warm, loving couple named Bowen. The Bowens' only child had fallen overboard and drowned in the Ohio River on the way to New Ephrata, and they accepted with eagerness the challenge of taking the girls.

Early in December, Anthony and old Luke Higgins decided they had fulfilled—in fact, exceeded—their responsibilities for seeing to corn meal reserves and mill maintenance. The marauding Shawnees, whose villages lay several days' marches to the north, were presumably home for the balance of the winter. Although the temperature remained below freezing for the third consecutive day, the wind was negligible. It seemed to be an opportune time for the promised expedition.

Nimrod Ellison accompanied them, giving the party a crack rifleman. They intended to hunt game on the return trip.

Securing jerky from the Christian Shawnees, the warmly clad adventurers set out northward on horseback. "We'll meet Brush Crick 'bout noon," said Higgins, referring to the stream which emptied into the Ohio opposite the island with the cross.

They traveled through dense clusters of great, denuded hardwoods. Occasional snow-flecked cedars and spruces provided green relief to an otherwise white landscape. The sky, though still the color of lead, no longer surrendered snow. That which had already fallen crunched lightly underneath the horses' hooves. Ellison silently pointed out traces of animal activity on the cottony blanket; conversation was low and infrequent, out of deference to the remote prospect of an Indian hunting party in the vicinity.

Near the hour predicted by Higgins, they reached ice-encrusted Brush Creek. Old Luke then directed them upstream along the meanders of the creek. Shortly, the party came to where a smaller stream entered the creek from the far shore. Without hesitation, the old trapper dismounted and cautiously led his horse and fellow travelers over the frozen surface.

The course of the smaller creek took them into low, rippling hills crested with cedars. Finally, Higgins stopped before a high limestone cliff which was fronted by twin spruces.

"Make ready the bull's-eye," he told the others. Then he lay on his stomach between the trunks of the trees and crawled out of sight beneath their branches.

Dropping to one knee, Anthony pushed away the snow. On the exposed stony surface he placed the bull's-eye lantern. This device consisted of a boxlike iron frame containing two fixed ovals of convex glass with a tallow candle mounted in between.

Anthony produced a strip of cloth and twisted it tightly. Rifle in hand, Ellison knelt beside him. The hunter prepared the flash pan and Anthony dropped one end of the twisted cloth onto it. Ellison twice ignited powder before the cloth caught; Anthony hastily touched the tiny fire to the candle.

"What's takin' you lads so long?" the voice of Higgins boomed out from behind the spruces, unnaturally loud and echoing.

"It's lit, Mr. Higgins," Anthony replied. He flattened himself as Luke had done, and scooted a short distance underneath the tree limbs. Ellison carefully handed him the lantern.

Soon the three men were standing in a cave, illuminated only by the magnified candle flame. The atmosphere was humid, close, and stale. Their lantern picked up faint reflections, whether from moisture or rock particles Anthony could not be sure.

Higgins made out the long outline of Ellison's rifle in its owner's hand. "You kin leave that gun here, Mr. Ellison," he said. "I don't know as you'll need it, and anyway I'd kindly hate to have it go off inside this cave."

Ellison hesitated, then respectfully demurred. "Unless you can promise me we're not goin' to meet any bears or catamounts," he rejoined, "I'd as soon keep it with me." Higgins shrugged, the simple movement mimicked monstrously by his shadow high on the wall, and they proceeded with caution over the uneven floor.

They hadn't gone far when Anthony, straining his eyes in the dim light, saw something ahead. For a moment, he thought Ellison's precaution in bringing the rifle was well-founded. "Bones!" he said in a hoarse whisper. "Maybe this is some animal's lair, after all."

Higgins hoisted the lantern head-high to better see what lay in their path. The light revealed a human skeleton in a sprawled position on the cave floor. The rib cage was collapsed, almost as though crushed by a giant's foot. A disembodied skull, sans jawbone, sat upright a foot or so away from the other bones. It glared sightlessly at the intruders.

"This lad has been lyin' here for years—prob'ly centuries," the old trader said. He lowered the lantern for a closer inspection. "You'll take note, Mr. Ellison, how dry these bones are. An' you'll see they've not been gnawed."

Resting on the rocky surface underneath the flattened ribs was a hammered stone spearhead. "I s'pect that spear was put through our friend, here," Higgins mused, "though it's anyone's guess as to why."

Higgins stepped around the human rubble. "What we came t' see is this way," he said. Lantern suspended knee-high, he eased into a damp, narrow passageway.

The rocky corridor lasted only a few dozen steps. They entered a second cavern whose shapeless gloom overwhelmed the feeble illumination from the bull's-eye.

Higgins moved to his left, stopped for a moment, then gave a grunt of satisfaction and lifted the lantern.

"Here, Mr. Cumin's. Is this your Prince Madoc?" he asked rhetorically, confident of the answer.

Anthony gasped. There could be no doubt.

The surreal, gaudily painted visage looking at them from the limestone wall was twice as large as life. A twisted band of gold crossed the temples and pressed against full, flowing locks of red hair. Beneath the pale brow, large blue eyes gazed dreamily from half-closed lids. The mouth, encircled by a flaming mustache and beard, wore a subtle, tight-lipped smile.

A loose-fitting tunic of lavender (perhaps the nearest thing to a royal purple at the artist's disposal) fell from broad shoulders. Against the man's breast, supported by a chain necklace, dangled a large disk of gold. Writhing across its surface was the familiar winged serpent.

As Higgins moved deliberately along the wall, the passing rays of the upheld lantern revealed other murals. His companions caught dark, momentary glimpses of tableaux recounting a relentless, mortal conflict between red men and white. "I'm afraid we have t' move along," Luke said. "We haven't enough candle here t' dawdle."

He did, though, pause a bit longer in front of the last two paintings.

Madoc reappeared in the first of these depictions, identifiable by his lavender clothing and gold jewelry. His hair, though, was entirely white, and the once-handsome features were furrowed with age and, in all likelihood, with grief as well. He was kneeling, eyes closed, withered hands clasped and lifted heavenward. Behind him crouched two scowling Indians, spears poised to enter their victim's back.

The final scene was as terrible as it was spectacular. The white "Indians" were huddled together on a river island, surrounded by red attackers pouring out of their canoes. All too vividly, Anthony could recall a similar predicament. The last remaining whites—men, women, and children—were being slaughtered among piles of their dead.

Ellison groaned and shook his head.

"We've one last thing t' see in here!" Higgins rasped. They crossed the cave to the opposite wall and stopped before a sort of natural stone bench about two feet off the floor.

Here was another skeleton, this one lying face-up—had there been a face. A twisted band of darkened gold encircled the skull. Within the crumpled ribs rested a round object which, upon closer scrutiny, appeared to be the gold medallion depicted in the murals.

Anthony reached in gingerly, his gloved hand brushing against the paper-thin bones of the Welsh seafarer. He picked up the disk and attempted to rub and brush away from its face the grime of centuries.

There was the serpent! The curled tail, the jointed wings, the forbidding eye, the parted jaws. All three men took turns examining this ancient icon of Welsh nationalism. Decisively, Higgins returned it to the rightful owner.

"No one's stolen from th' Azgen king all these years," he said. "We'll leave to him what's his."

As they moved away, Anthony took a last look at the skeleton, which was scarcely five feet in length. *How diminutive a frame for such a celebrated explorer,* he thought. Gleaned from Samuel Russel's tapestry, his perspective had been of a physical giant akin in stature to the Vikings.

Chapter 17

When the riders returned to Brush Creek, Higgins had yet another surprise in store. Instead of turning south toward home, he renewed his upstream push. Anthony and Ellison exchanged glances, but were not loathe to pursue additional adventure.

The gray cloud cover finally broke. Late afternoon sunshine struck dazzling highlights off the snow and threw a network of tree shadows over the terrain. The creek described a long, lazy semicircle, with an open field of low land inside the crescent and a high ridge to the outside. "We're goin' t' climb up there," Luke said, pointing to the crest of the ridge.

Ellison ventured a word of caution. "We've found no sign of Injuns, to be sure," he said. "But wouldn't we be easily seen, runnin' about on that ridge?" The formation at its highest point appeared to rise better than a hundred feet above the frozen creek bed and was visible for miles in at least two directions.

Higgins smiled. "I hear your concern," he replied. "But in this instance, we'll be ever' bit as safe as if we was back acrost the Ohio." Without further explanation, he climbed off his horse and was soon scaling the near end of the ridge with an energy and nimbleness belying his years.

Once again, Anthony determined that he was no climber. When at last they reached the top, the youngest man among them was the most winded. The cold air cut painfully into his throat and chest. The view, though, was worth the exertion.

The ridge projected off a plateau, initially declining as it narrowed to front the bend of the creek. The last few hundred feet, however, rose to a bluff overlooking a panorama of bottom lands to the west and north. Between the plateau and the ridge ran a deep ravine, fanning out where it reached the creek far below the bluff.

A scattering of leafless trees occupied the snow-covered crest. Deep evening shadows hugged the ground, outlining massive bulges that struck Anthony as rather peculiar. The old trapper rubbed his mittens together in exultation. "Just as I hoped!" he exclaimed. "The snow makes things easier t' see." He stomped over to a mound about three feet high and began kicking away the powder.

As Anthony and Ellison watched in bafflement, the efforts of Higgins uncovered a bizarre sight. "Behold," the old man cried, belching puffs of frosty air from his exertion, "the tail of th' serpent!"

They distinguished a humpbacked spiral of snow-draped earth, growing continuously in size from the central point of origin. It described three smooth coils and then headed north down the crest. Finally realizing what old Luke had brought them to see, Anthony followed with an amazed eye the contours of the huge, undulating body as it ran the length of the ridge. Even the sprinkling of trees could not hide it.

"You could be here most times of th' year," Higgins said, "an' not be able to see it as well. The snow sure helps."

The three men followed the writhing effigy, which swelled up to five feet high and twenty feet across before beginning to taper. Approaching the bluff, they came to a crude but unmistakable attempt to outline the beast's head and distended jaws. From tail to snout, the serpent was well over a thousand feet long.

Separate from the jaws, but partly within them, an earthen lip formed an oval. The enclosed area reached almost to the terminus of the ridge. In all, the effigy represented a remarkable accomplishment by a primitive people.

Twilight had arrived, softening the glare of the snow. The adventurers took in the panorama before them: smooth fields rising to rolling hills, the latter outlined in pink and orange by the dying rays of the sun. Brush Creek meandered off to the northwest, where a pair of sparkling tributaries joined it.

"Well, Mr. Cumin's, is this not the dragon of th' gold disk we saw today?" Higgins's voice fairly dripped with triumph. "And th' very same ungodly image the squaw painted?"

"Yes, certainly it is . . ." Anthony began, but added: "And yet, not quite. The gold disk and the squaw's sketch both showed a winged dragon. This one hasn't any wings."

Ellison spoke up. "You'd hardly be able to lay out such a spread o' wings on this ridge. It's not near wide enough."

Higgins wagged his head. "That's not why there's no wings, Mr. Ellison. The Miami tell that the 'old ones' who did this, many lifetimes ago, had a purpose in makin' the likeness of th' serpent wingless. They sought t' lure the real snake-spirit into this rock-and-clay likeness, where it would be trapped without havin' its wings to escape."

Ellison snorted in derision. "Snake-spirit! So, did the 'old ones' succeed with their clever trap? Is the snake-spirit captive here now, beneath our feet?"

His contempt nettled Higgins. The reply came quietly, but with an edge. "Yes, Mr. Ellison. The Miami say the 'old ones' lured the serpent by offerin' up some o' their own people —" he pointed to the oval enclosure—"in there."

"Offering up!" Anthony exclaimed. "Do you mean they made blood sacrifices, like in the Old Testament?"

"Yes, lad, I'm afraid so—except'n they wasn't bullocks and lambs." The old trapper ran his tongue over dry lips.

The chill of the winter twilight seemed to sink more deeply into their bones.

"Anyway," Higgins said to Anthony, "you've seen, now, all that I've seen. You've an idea 'bout what happened to the people we've always called the Azgens. It appears the Azgens an' your Welsh sailors might've been the same lads. The Azgen king an' Prince Madoc . . ." he shrugged.

Looking at Ellison, Higgins continued. "Now maybe you kin figger out why it didn't worry me none to risk bein' seen up here. No Injun from any tribe would risk his red soul to come after us. Though I don't intend for us t' do it, we could've burned a fire up here tonight an' have it seen for miles without a worry—about the Injuns."

They opted instead for a small blaze in the ravine behind the ridge, making camp in a small, rocky hollow sheltered by a stand of cedars. The fire was for warmth only; the trio satisfied their hunger with some of the Christian Shawnees' jerky.

Although Higgins reiterated his belief that they were safe from Indian attack as long as they remained in the neighborhood of the serpent effigy, he nevertheless insisted that a watch be rotated among them. "Th' dragon on that hill is an idol," he said, his voice quavering. "Practicin' idolatry is sinnin' against God, and begets evil. Lots o' evil has been done on that hill. We need t' guard ourselves tonight."

Ellison stared hard at the old trapper. Then he commented, "You're right, Mr. Higgins, when you say that man sins against God by makin' idols of other things—includin' himself. But the evil we truly need to guard against is in our deceitful hearts, not in some ancient pit of idolatry."

Surprisingly, Higgins had no reply except for a tired smile. He wiped his lips with the back of his hand, and Anthony knew he badly wanted a pull on that jug back at the mill.

They settled themselves into the hollow, nestling under a pile of fur pelts. The campfire would be kept burning all night while they took turns at the prescribed watches. The flickering light penetrated only a few yards into the gloom of the ravine. Far above was a slice of night sky, clear but moonless, a starry wedge caught between the black, hulking masses of the ridge and the plateau.

Seething with all that it had absorbed, Anthony's mind kept returning to a single, tragic thought. Madoc was, by Samuel Russel's account, a zealot who would have tried to win the people of his adopted land to Christ. Instead, he had left only his dried bones and a terrible legacy of pagan sacrifice, spawned unintentionally by a patriotic emblem.

Why did Higgins insist on the round of watches? Was there some dark, nameless residue still astir from the hideous worship of the "old ones"? The Indians (according to Luke) must certainly think so. Yet the old trapper was known to ridicule the Christian Shawnees over their own lingering superstitions.

It seemed to Anthony that he couldn't have slept for long before Ellison woke him with a shake on the shoulder. Resolute to do his part, he accepted the ice-cold rifle. He got up, worked on the fire, and sat down under a wrap of furs, enjoying the rekindled warmth. Gazing into the ruddy flames, Anthony realized abruptly that this night was the first he would not be spending with Rebekah in more than two years. They hadn't slept apart since undergoing the fortnight of solitary meditation and prayer mandated for new arrivals at New Ephrata.

His thoughts turned to his sons, Samuel and Anthony. The latter, only a few weeks old, already presented an identity problem to his namesake. They would have to call the new arrival by some other name . . . Tony, perhaps . . .

He drifted into slumber.

Just a few feet away, Ellison screamed. The ear-splitting cry was high-pitched like that of a terrified woman.

Anthony tried to leap up, but his cold, cramped legs did not respond. The rifle fell from his numbed grasp. Dulled by the uninvited sleep, he could only turn his head.

Ellison was lying on his stomach, his arms and legs thrashing frantically, sending the snow flying in every direction. He did not scream again, but instead was whimpering like a child.

In a few seconds, Higgins had straddled the hunter and began shaking him stoutly by the shoulders, meanwhile bellowing "Jesus!" repeatedly into Ellison's ear. The whimpering slowly died, the thrashing ceased, and old Luke cautiously climbed off the stricken man.

Ellison rolled over and sat up. Tears streaked his cheeks, and his teeth were chattering—not as much from the cold, Anthony discerned, as from abject fear.

"You all right, laddie?" Higgins inquired, his voice incredibly tender. Ellison nodded, but stared at the ground and continued to shudder. He then closed his eyes and placed clasped hands in his lap. His lips moved in silent prayer.

Higgins and Anthony helped Ellison into the little hollow and squeezed in on either side of him to offer reassurance and share bodily heat under the covers. Gradually, his shaking subsided. Not another word was spoken. They all faced the fire and awaited the dawn without resumption of sleep.

Days later, at a time he felt was opportune, Anthony asked Ellison what manner of nightmare he had dreamed the night they spent below the dragon on the hill.

His eyes telling more than any tongue could describe, Ellison managed only one word: "Evil."

Chapter 18

With great peace of heart and mind, even as their colony grew in numbers and in spiritual strength, the people of New Ephrata awaited the fulfillment of Holy Scripture predictions.

David Singletary had determined early that this sylvan sanctuary would be well-grounded in the tenets of the Bible and built on the ashes of things temporal. In the final accounting, he proclaimed repeatedly, there would be celestial reward for sacrifice and faithfulness.

At the worship services held in the great meeting house, Singletary raged to and fro across a high platform and reminded his enthralled listeners about the glory that would accompany the materialization of the New Jerusalem.

"And John wrote of the holy city coming out of heaven, prepared by God like unto a bride for her bridegroom," he would thunder. "When that matchless moment has come, God will dwell with us and gather us to Him, and we will be His people. He will wipe the very tears from our eyes, and there will be no more death or pain, for those things shall pass away!

"And He who sits on the Great White Throne, the Alpha and the Omega, will declare that those who overcome shall inherit all things and be sons of God! But the unbelieving and the abominable, the sorcerer and the murderer, the idolater and the liar, will find their part in the lake of fire and brimstone!"

Clenched fists raised high, the mighty figure of Singletary seemed almost to physically touch Heaven. The orator's piercing blue eyes would sweep the mesmerized assembly at his feet. The occasional smile illuminating his handsome but normally solemn features might have been characterized by detractors (had there been any) as sly, even vaguely mocking. But the people of New Ephrata held nothing in their hearts except love and gratitude for this demigod and his untiring leadership.

True enough, some of the menfolk felt a passing uneasiness at the way their wives and daughters appeared to respond so strongly to the presence of Singletary. These feelings, though, were immediately rejected amidst pangs of guilt and self-reproach. What carnal, unworthy thoughts! So the men of New Ephrata, Anthony among them, silently rebuked themselves and forced the foulness from their minds.

Still, Anthony felt a sense of relief when he heard that Singletary intended to take another bride—this one a Cherokee. Thereafter, the aura of tragedy surrounding Singletary began to fade. Rebekah voiced her joy at the news. It struck Anthony's spirit, though, that she also seemed a bit chagrined. Had he expressed this notion to other men instead of suppressing it, he might have uncovered kindred thoughts.

There was a practical side to David Singletary's vision for New Ephrata.

Having cleared the land for tilling, grazing of stock, and home sites, the colonists planted more than just staple crops. Under Singletary's direction, they made preparations for fruit orchards, vineyards, and white mulberry trees, the latter imported as a first step toward the development of a silkworm industry.

Across the river, Singletary oversaw the building of stone-lined kilns. The Shawnee converts were taught how to make and properly fire clay bricks, pottery on a potter's wheel, and a rude form of glass. Later, at the same site, a shaft was sunk for the purpose of operating an iron furnace.

While any mention of the war was discouraged, Singletary inwardly chafed at the seemingly endless state of conflict between British and Americans, red men and white. He considered New Ephrata neither American nor British; the longer his little colony could remain essentially insulated from the outside world, the better. Yet, there was one facet of Singletary's plans that could not be implemented until hostilities ceased: establishment of trade with distant New Orleans.

So long as the war raged, and the British stoked the fire of Indian hatred for Americans and furnished the savages with weapons, navigation of the Ohio and Mississippi would have to wait. Even the inhabitants of New Ephrata could not expect protection to extend beyond their own boundaries.

Late in the summer of 1779, the white settlers along the Ohio Valley received wondrous news: Simon Butler was alive and well and back in Kentucky, having survived a year of captivity among the Indians and British.

His treatment by the red men had been, as feared, unspeakably inhuman. Eight times he was forced to run the gauntlet, a life-or-death trial wherein the naked, unarmed runner was forced to dash between long, parallel lines of weapon-wielding Indians. Three times he had been tied to the stake, prepared to suffer death by burning.

By the hand of Providence, Butler survived these ordeals and was finally turned over to the British military authorities in Detroit. With the help of others, he made his escape and returned to Kentucky, a young man who had aged many years within the span of only one.

Butler's Herculean body bore terrible marks from his mistreatment, the most severe of which was an indentation of the skull. Cracked by a tomahawk blow, the bone had knit.

The ordeal left emotional scars, too. What the Indians had been unable to damage, though, was his courage. After a time of rest, Butler returned to the border warfare against the savages.

Anthony and old Luke Higgins were as joyous as anyone over the tidings of the frontiersman's return. Anthony had long since forgotten the rude, puzzling behavior of Butler on the occasion of their first meeting.

He was reminded of it the following year, by none other than Butler.

Late spring of 1780 witnessed an unprecedented flood of pioneers loosed on the Ohio. No amount of bloodletting by the lurking, merciless Indians (and it was considerable) daunted the foolhardy whites in their scramble for new land. In part or in whole, family after family fell victim, easy marks for an ambush as they careened helplessly downstream on the spring crests. Standing on the limestone bluff overlooking the river at New Ephrata, an observer might at any hour spot, bobbing ominously in the current, prosaic household or personal items from some ill-fated flatboat.

On the first of June, Anthony had just completed the arduous job of sharpening the great millstones. The underside of the top, or "runner," stone and the upper side of the stationary, or "bed," stone were grooved in patterns to grind meal and push it to the outside, from where it fell into the bin. Prior to the first corn harvest, the miller's rites of spring included the backbreaking use of hammer and chisel to redefine the patterns.

Because of Anthony's loathing for the task known as "dressing the stones," it was the last preparation he made for the milling year. This done, he and Higgins were carefully lowering the stones into place when the bellow of a man's voice reached them from the lower floor of the mill.

"Mr. Higgins! Mr. Cumin's! I need to talk with you!"

Heavy footsteps hurried up the wooden steps. The shaggy head of Butler burst into view, full beard parted in a large smile.

He was forced to wait until the bed stone was adjudged level, whereupon Anthony released the grip of the iron tongs. The miller and Higgins then turned their attention to Simon Butler, whose face was shining with boyish joy.

"Could I speak with th' two of you?" he demanded, unable to suppress his excitement.

Both men nodded, wearing puzzled smiles.

Butler's demeanor sobered a bit. "I need t' ask your forgiveness—both of you," he said, "but more 'specially of Mr. Cumin's."

Anthony shook his head, but Butler held up a giant hand. "Yes, sir, I do," he insisted. "I've been a-livin' a lie. My name's Simon, but not Simon Butler. It's really Simon Kenton."

He chuckled at the blank looks. "That's what I shoulda figgered. But I thought I'd killed a man back home in Virginia, an' that everyone would be lookin' for me to take me back an' be hanged. So I've been a-hidin' out here like a lot of others, lyin' about who I was—but, as it turns out, for no reason.

"The other day, my brother John arrived here," the scout continued. "I knew him on sight, but he didn't know me. I wasn't even sure I could trust my own brother. Well, it did come up in th' conversation that the fella I thought I had killed was still alive. In fact, everyone back home thought it was him who'd murdered me, though they couldn't prove anything since they didn't find my body. John was powerful surprised when I finally told him who I was.

"Me an' this other fella were fightin' over a girl. To be truthful, he had just married her. He was older'n me and had already whupped me pretty good once. But I had growed some since, and was itchin' t' get even."

After a fairly even start to the fight, Kenton said, he managed to get the upper hand "an' I beat him up pretty bad after that. I thought I had killed him. I got scared and ran away. I've been Simon Butler ever since."

Kenton looked Anthony in the eye. "The man I thought I'd murdered was William Leachman. The girl he'd won from me was Ellen Cumin's. Know 'em?"

Anthony was thunderstruck. "Yes, of course I do! Ellen is my cousin, the daughter of my uncle Benjamin at Cobbler's Gap. She's married to Leachman."

The pieces started to fall into place. Anthony recalled Ellen visiting one wintry day when he was staying at Benjamin's, learning how to build a mill. Aware that Anthony was heading for the Ohio Valley, she had asked a favor of him. Her words came floating across the gulf of nearly five years' time: *"Promise me that, should you meet up with a certain man there, you will tell him that it is all right for him to come home . . . A giant of a man, I suspect, though he was scarcely more than a boy when I saw him last. . . ."*

Almost certainly, Anthony thought, she had identified the man as Simon Kenton.

"So you kin see, Mr. Cumin's," Kenton continued, "why I behaved a little queer when you told me your name and whar you were from. I thought you might be kin to Ellen, and maybe even knew my name in connection with Leachman's death. I thought him dead, for sure.

"I'm askin' your forgiveness—and yours as well, Mr. Higgins —for lyin' to you and actin' rude."

Both men shook Kenton's hand warmly. "I think," Anthony said, "Ellen must've known you weren't dead. She described you to me, though not as her husband's adversary, and sent a message that you could safely return home. She believed you to be somewhere in the Ohio Valley."

Kenton's face fell. "I've got one other piece o' news for you, Mr. Cumin's," he said, somberly. "My brother told me Ellen died last year havin' a baby boy. She'd been warned 'bout havin' any more children. At least the boy lived."

So, Anthony thought, with a sudden sense of loss, *Leachman finally has a son to go along with his daughters . . . acquired at great cost.*

Chapter 19

*A*lmost six years from the day Lord Dunmore fled Norfolk, abandoning his royally appointed governorship of colonial Virginia, another prominent British aristocrat suffered like humiliation on the same Atlantic coastland just a few miles away.

In early autumn of 1781, about 8,000 redcoats under the command of Maj. Gen. Charles Cornwallis found themselves surrounded at Yorktown. Continental and French forces of about twice their strength had them hemmed in by land, and a fleet of French warships had chased off British support from the sea. After initial fighting and a subsequent siege lasting three weeks, Cornwallis saw the hopelessness of it all and had a subordinate surrender his forces to General Washington's subordinate. Though a final, formal treaty with Great Britain was two years away, little Yorktown had witnessed the last major encounter of the Revolutionary War.

The Treaty of Paris, signed in September 1783, recognized the erstwhile colonies and a huge portion of western lands as the domain of the United States of America. Westernmost Virginia, known as the District of Kentucky, by this time boasted several bona fide little cities sprinkled about its interior. Residents of those cities were already talking about separate statehood.

But signatures affixed to paper promises in Paris meant nothing to the first natives of America. This was hardly surprising, since no Indian interests were addressed in the agreement. For better than a decade following ratification of the treaty, the Shawnees and others continued their border warfare with the whites in the Ohio Valley.

Throughout this period, the people of New Ephrata kept their eyes on the things of God. While they were free to correspond with family back east, discussion of the news found in letters from the outside was discouraged. When Kentucky gained statehood in 1792, the event touched off celebrations in Louisville, Frankfort, Lexington, and Danville; in New Ephrata, statehood might as well have been granted to the moon for all it mattered.

Or, at least, so its blissful residents believed.

Anthony suffered two personal losses in 1784: his mother and Luke Higgins.

Higgins's death, of course, saddened all of the colonists and David Singletary in particular. Singletary had shared a bond of love with the trapper for more than thirty years, and for a season the old look of mourning returned to blight his countenance. Anthony took on one of the Ellison boys (now grown men) as an apprentice to replace Higgins. The young man's work was adequate, but Anthony sorely missed the camaraderie of the old trapper.

The bad news from Loudoun County was presented cautiously in a letter penned by Samuel Russel, who wrote that Mrs. Cumings had "passed Peacefully & without undue Suffering." Russel added that Anthony's brother James had taken a wife and was raising a growing family. James continued to till the brothers' farmland with the ongoing assistance of Russel, who faithfully paid the land taxes each year in the brothers' names.

In the fall of 1793, nine years after their mother's death, James left Virginia and joined his brother in New Ephrata.

He arrived without prior announcement, surprising Anthony at the mill on a gray October afternoon. James had brought with him his wife, Mary, and nine children. He was also in possession of cash from the sale of the farm, and had an official-looking sheepskin document signed by Virginia Governor Beverley Randolph.

"Mr. Russel's son Robert has purchased our farm, including the home place," James reported during the brothers' initial visit. "He paid me—us—in British silver. You'll be wanting your portion now, of course."

To his brother's surprise, Anthony declined the offer. "Keep it, if you wish," he said. "There's simply no need for money in New Ephrata."

Recovering nicely, James agreed to hold the money, but added, "I still consider half of it to be yours. And anyway, we also have something of considerably greater value to discuss."

The sheepskin document was a military land warrant, issued in 1792 to the widow and children of Samuel Cumings from a grateful Commonwealth. Anthony was nonplussed. Their father had served in the French and Indian Wars in 1756 and 1757. The award of the land grant, an event their mother fruitlessly awaited for the remainder of her life, had taken thirty-five years to process.

"I think," Anthony said finally, "the set-aside land is considerably downstream from here."

But James, more informed, shook his head and replied, "The land you refer to has long been exhausted by claims. The reserve we will have to examine is to the north, across the river."

Indian territory! Anthony didn't know whether to laugh or console his brother. It was true that Nathaniel Massie, a bold and energetic entrepreneur, had established a heavily fortified station on the north side of the Ohio at the Three Islands. It was also true that numerous claims there had already been surveyed. However, the Shawnee, Wyandot, and Miami had little sense of humor about their territory being summarily seized and divided among the presumptuous palefaces. The land above the Ohio would change hands only at the cost of shed blood.

"Why don't we put aside this prospect of the land grant, for the present," urged Anthony, "and settle you down here? It's a blessed life, without want and without strife, dedicated to the Lord and to His return. The men will build you a house, and the women will feed you and your family. All that's asked in return is for you and Mary to willingly labor for the common good and to the glory of God. There's a fine homesite near our own home."

James looked skeptical, as well as a little uncomfortable. "That may be a possibility," he said politely. "What price are you asking?"

"You don't understand, James," Anthony replied. "The land is not mine—nor anyone's—to sell." He smiled at the look on the other's face. "Actually," he continued, "it's the Lord's. He owns the cattle on a thousand hills. But our leader and brother in Christ, David Singletary, acquired ownership as a gift from the Cherokee nation after he married into their tribe. The whole of New Ephrata, and much more, was included in that gift. It is up to us to be good stewards and make wise use of it."

Clearly, James was wavering. Finally, he voiced what was of most concern to him. "This is a religious place—nothing wrong with that, of course. But tell me, Anthony. Do they have church often? Must everyone go each and every time?"

The older brother's smile broadened. "We have church in the field by day, and before the hearth by night. I have church daily, in the mill. We carry church with us in our bosom. James, I ask you only to give it a try. You'll never have cause to regret it."

And stay James did. Sometimes, though, Anthony doubted that the prescribed fortnight of solitary meditation and prayer had fully purged the world from his brother's heart and replaced the love of temporal things with a love of Jesus. For one thing, James did not discard the land warrant.

Several years earlier, Singletary had established a governing structure for New Ephrata that included multiple offices for elders. Seated as an elder, Anthony was given charge of several hundred acres of riverside grazing and farm land in addition to his duties at the mill. James joined the men under Anthony's direction in the raising of livestock and crops.

Everything their work produced was for the use of the entire colony. James adapted well to the system, except to wonder aloud how they would get by when the colony and its communal ways ceased to exist. Fresh from the outside world, he knew of the incredible migration already on the way to Kentucky and points beyond. To him, New Ephrata was a mere moment in time that would soon pass.

Unperturbed, Anthony stated his belief that Jesus would return before New Ephrata became overrun by outsiders. James's rejoinder was that, should Jesus tarry and the colony disintegrate, the brothers still had the land warrant and both shares of proceeds from the sale of their farm—a reaffirmation to Anthony that his younger brother retained a bit too much worldliness.

Anthony's share of the British silver coin did come in handy, much sooner even than James expected.

Widespread ice and snow ushered in 1794. The cold grew so relentless and intense that the Christian Shawnees crossed the frozen river to huddle before roaring fires in the superior structures of their white brethren. Except for instances of necessity, travel had come to a halt.

It was surprising, then, when the tranquility of the Cumings house was disturbed one January morning by a hasty knocking at the door. Young Samuel, soon to turn seventeen, slid back the bolt while his four younger brothers—Tony, Thomas, John, and toddling William—suspended their various enterprises to see who was outside and wanted in.

"Wait, Samuel," called their mother. "Ask who it is, first," Rebekah ordered as she put down her sewing. Anthony was at the mill, replacing worn gears, and even in New Ephrata families whose men were away had become cautious about opening their doors to unexpected callers. There were more and more strangers on the road these days.

"Who is it?" Samuel bellowed, and placed an ear to the door.

"This is Reverend Craig, of Minerva," came the muffled reply. "I have business with Mr. and Mrs. Cumings."

The Reverend Lewis Craig had led a traveling flock of Baptist pioneers into the region the summer previous, establishing a church in a little community downstream from New Ephrata near Limestone. A native of Virginia, Craig in 1781 felt himself called to Kentucky, where, as he said, "the harvest truly was plenteous and the laborers few." Over the next decade, his gypsy congregation migrated step by step from Cumberland Gap to the Ohio Valley, leaving in its wake a growing crop of converts.

Rebekah had never heard of Reverend Craig. But his office impressed her, and she did not suspect trickery. Nevertheless, as she opened the door, Samuel sought out his grandfather's old musket.

Doffing his snow-sprinkled fur cap, Craig stepped inside. Twinkling gray eyes surveyed the house and its inhabitants, and quickly settled upon Samuel and the youth's proximity to the musket. "You'll have no need o' that, laddie," the visitor said cheerfully. He did not, however, move far from the threshold.

"My husband is away, though he will very soon be back," Rebekah said frankly, studying the caller. A man of medium size and middle age, Craig presented a pleasant appearance overall. The most remarkable feature was a strawberry mark on his face, running from one ear to the corner of his mouth and lifting the lips into a perpetual half-smile.

An ordained preacher for a quarter of a century, Craig was not so perfected by his profession that he failed to admire the woman before him. Assuming that all five boys in the house were hers, the visitor judged her to be well past thirty-five, an age considered old for pioneer women. Yet Rebekah stood erect, shoulders back, green eyes bright, rich brown hair untouched by gray, and dark skin still young. Only her hands revealed the years of labor. Many women in the civilized east would have given much to share her enduring beauty.

"Madam," Craig said, recovering himself, "I bear what you and your husband might well believe to be bad tidings. But years from now, you will thank me."

Rebekah's only response was to fold her arms. Craig cleared his throat and continued. "I realize that the people in New Ephrata have lived a life apart from the world. In many ways, I admire them. Ye must know, though, that this is no longer an unclaimed wilderness. Kentucky has been a state of its own, severed from Virginia, for more than a year. Where we are standing is now within Mason County. In fact, I have been commissioned as a stonemason to construct the courthouse at the county seat of Washington."

The minister dropped his eyes, examining the fur cap he held in one hand. Then he looked again at Rebekah. "Recently, while in Frankfort, I purchased from the state a large section of land along the river. At that time, I had no knowledge of whether anyone might already be on it—illegally, of course.

"As it turns out, much of what is known as New Ephrata occupies the property I have bought. There can be no mistake." Craig's voice grew very gentle. "This homesite, that of Mr. James Cumings, and the surrounding acreage all belong to me."

Rebekah placed both hands against her stomach, which suddenly felt as though it had been kicked. Craig saw a hurt look clouding the green eyes.

He abruptly donned his cap. "I pray we can reach a solution suitable to all," he said, forcing a smile. "I do not anticipate tossing anyone out in this weather. Even now, my horse may be almost too stiff with the cold to move. However, I am going to the mill to discuss this with Mr. Cumings."

After hearing him out, Anthony was incredulous.

"This land was given to David Singletary by the Cherokee Indians," he told Craig.

"I have already visited with Mr. Singletary on this matter,"

Craig said dryly. "The Cherokees failed to register their ownership of this land with the governments of either Virginia or Kentucky. Likewise, David Singletary has filed no notice of ownership with any state or county authority. On the other hand, I suppose, neither has he been pressed for taxes."

The minister's voice grew courteous, even solicitous. "Mr. Singletary understands the situation perfectly," he said. "I am of the mind he will make things right. I felt it was my duty, however, to see that everyone involved knows what is expected."

"And that is . . .?" Anthony asked.

"That I be fairly compensated for my land."

Ready to depart, Craig offered his hand in a gesture of peace. Anthony ignored it, and instead requested the price of the land under and adjoining his and James's houses.

Pursing his lips, Craig asked how many acres Anthony wanted.

"One hundred," the miller replied.

Without hesitation, Craig named his price: "Fifty pounds sterling, which I assure you is very fair. I will," he added, "give you a year—perhaps somewhat longer—to pay it out. When that is done, you shall receive a deed."

This time, Anthony took Craig's hand. "We will meet your terms. You have my pledge on it," he said, trusting that James had not disposed of the proceeds from the Loudoun County sale.

The minister appeared greatly relieved. He would not be haunted by the memory of those clouded green eyes after all.

Chapter 20

*I*t is doubtful that Lewis Craig ever intended to become an agent for change in New Ephrata. On the other hand, it is equally doubtful that he ever harbored any regrets.

A product of the great wave of evangelical preaching in 1760s Virginia, Craig achieved notoriety in his home state even before becoming an ordained minister. Arrested and placed on trial for "holding unlawful conventicles and preaching the gospel contrary to law," he challenged the jurors over a bowl of grog in the local tavern.

"Gentlemen," he is reported to have said, "I thank you for your attention to me. When I was about this courtyard in all kinds of vanity, folly, and vice, you took no notice of me; but when I have forsaken all the vices and am warning men to forsake and repent of their sins, you bring me to a bar as transgressor. How is this?"

Tradition has it that one juror, celebrated for his hell-raising, was so convicted by the confrontational Craig that he spontaneously renounced his profligate lifestyle and accepted Christ as Lord and Savior.

Thirty years, hundreds of sermons, and thousands of miles later, the tireless evangelist remained bold enough to beard the lion in his own den. So it was that, prior to visiting with Rebekah and Anthony about his land, Craig had called on David Singletary.

They sat facing each other on wooden stools in Singletary's Spartan front room, the patriarch of New Ephrata and the interloper bearing bad tidings. The former, despite almost seventy years of age, held his immense torso ramrod-straight. A lesser man on Craig's errand would have been badly intimidated.

The atmosphere within the room seemed almost as frigid as the elements outside.

"Mr. Singletary," the visitor opened, "I'll get straight to the point. I have recently acquired land along the river, reaching quite some distance from either bank of Sycamore Creek. This acreage is occupied by a number of houses and farms, including your home. I cannot find in the land records a single claim of ownership from anyone on the property. Is there any legal right of possession here?"

The great blue eyes returned Craig's gaze unblinkingly. "The earth is the Lord's, and the fulness thereof," Singletary rumbled. "Men may claim this or that piece of land for their own. When they and their progeny have returned to dust, the Lord's land will endure, as it always has."

The minister kept silent.

"Brief generations ago," Singletary continued, "the Cherokee nation claimed this entire territory—the heartlands of Kentucky and Tennessee. When I took one of their princesses as my wife, they gifted me with a section of that land, including that which lies under our feet. But no, sir, there is nothing of paper record, nothing in writing, filed with any governmental authority, red or white."

The blue eyes momentarily closed. "It has been my prayer that the Lord would return before the question of land ownership became the divisive issue it always is. The Lord has seen fit to tarry, so here we are." The eyes snapped open and fixed on the visitor. "Have you a proposal to make?"

Craig cleared his throat. "I am humbly aware," he said, "that you and these others, residents of what is rather whimsically christened New Ephrata, have been here for many years. You have, it is said, led lives of peace and solitude, dedicated to the glory of our Lord Jesus Christ. I do not want to interrupt your lives, should it be possible to avoid doing so."

He leaned forward, looking up at the impassive face of his host. "I am prepared to sell the land to you at what I believe is a very reasonable price. Further, I can give you some time to perform the payments. The price is a half-pound per acre, in sterling. I believe a year is really sufficient time, but that can be extended if we both believe it necessary—and the Lord tarries."

Eyes narrowing, Singletary drummed giant fingers against his knees. "How much land do you reckon that you own within New Ephrata?" he asked.

"I should say close to two thousand acres," Craig replied blandly.

Singletary was silent for several heartbeats. Then he exhaled slowly. "Reverend Craig," he said at last, "the people of New Ephrata eschewed all personal property, all accumulation and gain, to dedicate themselves and their labors to the Lord's work. They knew that the pursuit of Mammon would hinder their service to God. Man cannot serve two masters, Reverend."

The implication stung like a slap across the face. Coolly, the minister sidestepped the challenge. "We do seem to have a dilemma on our hands. Well, sir, you know the price and terms," Craig said, rising to his feet. "You seem to be in charge of these people. I leave it to you to forge a resolution. By the by, sir, do you hold a position or title? I was referred to you as the man to seek out in New Ephrata. Are you the mayor?"

The blue eyes radiated frank dislike. "The sheep know the voice of their shepherd," came the reply.

"Ah, then! You're a pastor. So you certainly do have a responsibility here. Tell me, Parson Singletary: in all these years of isolation, what has been the fruit of your labors? How many souls have you saved?"

Singletary lifted himself off the stool, dramatically unfolding to his full height. He waved one immense hand at the front door. "You have delivered your message, sir. I bid you good day and Godspeed back to where you are from."

Surprisingly, New Ephrata met Craig's challenge. The cost, though, was much greater than a thousand pounds.

Whereas the colonists had long lived apart from the world, buffered by the wilderness and its fearsome occupants, they at last awoke to find the world arrived at their doorstep. They had to acquire the land they lived on and farmed, and pay taxes; they had to make public their family affairs, through probate court and marriage licenses. The men would now be expected to serve in the militia and on the county road crews.

No one was inclined to comply fully with these onerous new laws, and in fact few did. With Singletary showing the way, New Ephrata transformed itself from an open, communal society to a secret one. The public records of Mason County did not reflect the clandestine agreements made and carried out among the faithful to continue the old ways whenever possible. Many of life's watershed events went unreported. From this point on, there were two separate and sometimes conflicting sets of records for Singletary's followers—the official one on file in the courthouse at Washington, and the more extensive and accurate one maintained and kept privately in the homes of New Ephrata.

One unwelcome change faced by all inhabitants of the region was the irreversible decline in the population of game. More people meant more mouths to feed, and their increased presence drove the wildlife farther away. Nimrod Ellison and his band of hunters also complained about how the advent of other settlements created a new hazard for foragers. "We have now, in these woods," Ellison reported dryly, "many more rifles and far fewer marksmen."

In the earliest days, buffalo meat was a staple. Many times had Ellison followed the great beasts' sunken trail to the salt licks and waited out the arrival of the herd. The secret to success lay in picking out and dropping the leader; after that, it became a matter of shooting as many of the milling, befuddled brutes as was deemed sufficient.

The bison had long since vanished from the Ohio Valley. Now, as the nineteenth century neared, residents found they must either devote more hours to the hunt or settle for less bounty.

Money, though, remained the hardest commodity to come by. And New Ephrata, having been forced into relations with the outer world, was not exempt from this problem. Singletary's thoughts returned to the river, and to the prospect of trade with New Orleans. His community could offer not only staples like corn, tobacco, and pickled meat, but more exotic exports such as silk, iron, pottery, bricks, and glass.

Like an answer to prayer, events soon favored the notion.

First, the victory of Gen. "Mad" Anthony Wayne and his troops over a confederacy of Indian tribes on the Maumee River smashed the red men's defiance and led to the Treaty of Greenville in 1795. This opened up safe passage for boat traffic on the Ohio. Later that same year, the United States and Spain entered into a pact known as the Treaty of San Lorenzo. Among other things, it freed the lower Mississippi River from adverse Spanish control and gave Americans the right to utilize the port city of New Orleans to reach the markets of the world.

Of the community's younger generation (especially the boys), few were immune to the lure of the river. The Ohio flowed from the world many of their parents had left, and where grandparents whom they had never known still lived. The majestic stream drifted tantalizingly past New Ephrata and continued west, carrying on its broad bosom flatboat flotillas of families bound for a rendezvous with an unknown fate.

Despite each day's regimen of school and chores, it was common to see upwards of a dozen youngsters sprawled on the crest of the limestone bluff under which Sycamore Creek merged with the river. Their eager eyes searched the Ohio's clay-yellowed waters for the smallest floating object, and each sighting touched off excited and fantastic speculation as to said object's identity and origin. The actual appearance of flatboats would bring the audience to its collective bare feet, accompanied by a chorus of shouts and waving of arms at the passersby. The envious landlubbers usually remained standing and staring until the arks had drifted out of sight.

Young Samuel Cumings participated in the river-watching with as much enthusiasm as anyone. But his fascination went beyond what bobbled on the surface; it extended to the most minute characteristics of current, depth, wildlife, and hazard. He loved to walk the bank, with or without companionship, tirelessly cataloguing the details. Despite a sternly enforced ban against swimming in the river, twice tragically underscored by the loss of young lives, Samuel occasionally took clandestine plunges into the shallows to explore the murky waters.

Though none of their parents ever knew it, Samuel and two other game youths once used a big log to take them to Brush Creek Island and back. This intrepid trio, on a humid June afternoon, shrugged off the fear of marauding Indians and, under Samuel's expert direction, picked a spot slightly upstream of the island from which to launch their makeshift conveyance.

Clinging to the log and kicking their feet, they challenged the sluggish summer flow of the river successfully enough to reach the island before being swept past it. The young explorers stalked about in exaggerated crouches among the willows and locust saplings, more acutely concerned about being spotted by sharp-eyed New Ephrata adults than by scalp-seeking savages. The islet had little to offer visitors besides sand, pools of stagnant and foul-smelling water, mosquitoes, gnats, frogs, and several brown snakes. The serpents, any of which could possibly have been the dreaded, deadly water moccasin, were respectfully left to their own devices.

It was in his nineteenth summer when Samuel, at that time a tender of vegetable gardens under the good-natured tutelage of his uncle James, received the first opportunity to utilize his river lore.

News of the treaties of Greenville and San Lorenzo had reached Singletary, who understood their import and wasted little time in taking action. He commissioned Anthony Cumings and Nimrod Ellison as boat builders.

Both men eagerly accepted their assignments. Cumings would construct and operate a sawmill. Ellison, by trade a cooper, would direct and oversee the building of the New Ephrata mercantile fleet.

The contemplated site for the mill and boat yard was on Sycamore Creek, between the gristmill and the limestone bluff overlooking the Ohio. Anthony, though, developed second thoughts. "It will be hard to get your finished boats over or around the bluff to the river," he commented to Ellison. Also, he added, the debris from the sawmill, expected to be substantial, would sooner or later clog the creek's subterranean path to the river.

Anthony shared his thoughts in prayerful counsel with Singletary, but the latter showed little concern over either perceived problem. "The Lord's arm is not short," he said mysteriously. Then he retreated to his house, where he remained sequestered for the remainder of that day and all of the next.

Late into the night following, long after bedtime, the inhabitants of New Ephrata were shocked out of their sleep by a series of prodigious blasts and violent quakes, as if the world's largest munitions depot were being exploded. While terrified children howled, crazed dogs barked, and panicked men yanked on their breeches and scrambled for their rifles, a deep-throated rumble came from the general direction of Sycamore Creek at the river. Showers of rocks, large and small, descended with rattles and thumps upon shingled roofs.

Armed men emerged from their homes to find the night air thick with dust that stung the eyes and nose. Within five minutes, much of the male populace was thronging excitedly along the creek below the mill. The rumbling had ceased. Their flickering torches revealed little except for the dust, though it seemed to be thinning.

Singletary appeared among them, his cowl pushed back to reveal disheveled gray hair, his face and beard smeared with dirt. But he wore a smile, the blue eyes flashing.

"There is no cause for alarm, brothers!" he announced loudly. "On the morrow, you will see that the limestone bluff which stood between us and the vision of trade with the outside world is no more. We spoke to the mountain, and it moved." The smile broadened and grew a bit cynical. "We can now offer the Reverend Lewis Craig all the stone he needs for building the new courthouse."

Reaching far into his past, refreshing the lore of alchemy gleaned as a young man at the monks' camp in Pennsylvania, Singletary had indeed caused the movement of a mountain—or, at least, a bluff twenty feet high. After a week of industrious rubble removal, the confluence of Sycamore Creek and the Ohio was restored for all to see.

It was then that young Samuel's river lore and the future economy of New Ephrata became intertwined. Anthony turned to his oldest son and said, "Samuel, I'll need your help to build the sawmill. After that, you must begin preparing charts on the course and the hazards of the river. There may no longer be any threat from the Indians, but our boats could still fall prey to the river itself."

Samuel's thoughts raced ahead of his father's. Eyes glowing, he replied, "Yes, sir! That means charting both the Ohio and the Mississippi down to New Orleans, does it not?"

Chapter 21

*L*ike a man possessed, David Singletary drove his charges hard at their various tasks—harvesting crops, smelting iron, weaving silk yarn, firing pottery and bricks, and blowing and pressing glass. He was determined to develop a wide array of fine products to offer to the world's marketplaces.

At the start, Nimrod Ellison and his carpentry force were busy assembling boxes, crates, and barrels of different shapes and capacities from a stockpile of wood scraps. It wasn't long, though, before the cooper had to set aside his tools and send his apprentices to do other jobs while awaiting lumber from the slow-producing Cumings sawmill. He had not even begun his most important assignment, the production of keelboats to carry New Ephrata products to New Orleans. The scaffold wherein the boats were to be built stood stark and empty, its skeletal hulk looming as a constant reminder of delay.

Twenty years before, when the gristmill was erected, the prospect of its great wheel also powering a sawmill had not been considered. In hindsight it was an astounding error, though back then the community was building only log structures and had an abundance of flatboat planking for doors and shutters. Now, a freestanding sawmill was the only option, and Anthony selected what he considered the best site. The millrace was deepened and reinforced just above where it rejoined Sycamore Creek, and the sawmill soon straddled it.

From the outset, this enterprise was unsatisfactory. The operators found the languid movement of the sash saw maddeningly slow, and chafed at the great amount of wood wasted in the process. Even more discouraging was the miserable performance of the logging crew. Novices all, the loggers learned the hard way that felling a tree and getting it to the mill took much more planning and exertion than first thought. The best stands of favored species—red and white oak, walnut, ash, maple, and buckeye—were not found in the vicinity of Sycamore Creek, meaning the suitable forest giants generally had to be dragged over a series of steep ridges.

It was a two-pronged problem: the limited capacity of the mill, and an inadequate supply of harvested timber. Finally, there came a solution from an unexpected source.

Jonathan Ruggles had joined the community as a lad of ten. Escaping the violent fate met by the remainder of his family at the hands of cutthroats, he was picked up along Braddock's Road by travelers bound for New Ephrata. A decade later, he married another orphan of the same trail—Elizabeth, who as an infant in the arms of older sister Mathilda had aided their rescue from the "Shades of Death" with her crying.

Apprenticed to the colony's aging cobbler, Mr. Carr, Jonathan secured a temporary release from that obligation to try his hand at logging. As no one in the logging party was experienced at moving felled trees any distance, the assertive young man soon assumed the leadership role. After a cruel, wrenching fortnight of pitting teams of men and horses against thick forests and steep terrain, Jonathan conceived a better plan and took it to David Singletary.

Much of the desirable timber, he pointed out, stood on or reasonably close to the river and upstream of Brush Creek Island. "How 'bout," Jonathan suggested, "floatin' a sawmill on canoes 'twixt the island and riverbank, and lettin' the river current bring the trees to the mill and drive the saw, all at onc't? We kin get timber to th' Ohio a lot faster than haulin' overland."

The plan, declared Singletary, smiling for the first time in days, was nothing short of divine inspiration. The present mill should be kept in operation, he decided, to receive timber harvested downstream. Anthony Cumings would see to the construction and placement of the floating mill.

Anthony did so, although he wished Samuel were back from his expedition to chart the Ohio and Mississippi. No one was more familiar with the vagaries of the river currents than Samuel, hence no one else could as precisely choose the optimal spot for the mill. However, his absence could not be helped. Singletary would brook no delays. The next-oldest Cumings boys, Tony and Thomas, were left in charge of the Sycamore Creek mill while their father assembled the floating mill at Brush Creek Island.

For the next forty years, Samuel Cumings would spend most of his waking hours in traveling what were then called "the western waters." As deckhand, pilot, and captain of many river vessels (and tireless, perpetual chronicler of the streams he rode), he enjoyed a career filled with adventure. Yet, to his dying day, the memories of that first river journey in 1796 remained fresh and unclouded.

The trip was not particularly dangerous, nor even full of hardships. What set it apart from subsequent outings was that it gave Samuel his first encounter with the world outside New Ephrata. Upon returning, he remarked to his father that God had succeeded remarkably well in fashioning the wonders and beauty of the earth, but appeared to have blundered badly with the being created in His own image.

Samuel's lone companion in the charting endeavor was Noble Grimes, not actually a member of the Singletary community. Grimes, along with his mother and two brothers, had settled two years before on the Ohio side of the river near the mouth of Brush Creek. They lawfully acquired the property where the Christian Shawnees lived, and put them off the land. They did this, however, with such fairness and kindness that even Singletary was favorably impressed. Before the turn of the century, Singletary would buy "back" from the Grimes family the lion's share of this same property.

Noble Grimes was in his early thirties, large of build and formidable of countenance, though easy in disposition. He was educated, capable, and ambitious, and had visions of empire. He exhibited a strong interest in the prospect of downriver trade, and made a suitable senior partner for the little expedition.

Grimes and Samuel followed the waterways to New Orleans on a keelboat, the younger man doggedly taking notes and drawing charts several times daily despite an aversion to the crew. Raised in an environment of piety and love, mutual respect, personal cleanliness, modesty, and presentable social graces, he found the boatmen to be everything he was not. With the strength and endurance of brutes, they were crude, loud, boastful, profane, quarrelsome, viciously combative, incessant drinkers of everything alcoholic, and frequently filthy in appearance and smell. In the sweltering heat, few of them wore anything other than a ragged pair of pants held in place by a rope, and perhaps some manner of hat or cap.

They stood aside for nothing and no one. Even their token deference to the passengers was crudely feigned, although the intimidating appearance of Grimes tempered their tongues.

"I had no idea," Samuel confided to Grimes early in their trip, "that men could be so completely evil. Surely every man among our crew is rushing headlong to damnation."

A smile flickered across the older man's face. "They're no saints, to be sure," he said, exhibiting a touch of his late father's Irish brogue. "But there are worse rogues loose. I don't ken whether these lads would cut one's throat while he slept, just to get a coin off his body. I feel they'd at least offer one a sportin' chance."

The trip had begun in August, when the Ohio was at low ebb and its sluggish current often insufficient to propel the keelboat. So the barefoot boatmen walked from stem to stern along runners flanking the cabin, pushing long poles into the muck of the river bed. Naked torsos glistening with sweat, they moved rhythmically to the sound of their own obscene songs and chants.

The drop in the river level meant increased danger from hazards lurking just below the surface. Sunken timber bumped and scraped against the keel and the ribs of the hold, and on occasion unseen sandbars jarred the craft to a halt. Whenever a bar was struck, the boatmen's chants dissolved into loud and lusty cursing.

Despite their repulsiveness, Samuel ultimately found himself admiring the strength and toughness of the crew members. Even while pungently voicing complaints, they toiled almost continuously through the steamy hell of each day. They slept on the open deck without bedding or shelter. Their food consisted of what they caught on fishing lines and singed lightly over an evening fire, and their nonalcoholic drink was the turbid water of the river.

The keelboat made cargo deliveries and pickups at the infant cities of Cincinnati and Louisville, the first centers of commerce Samuel had ever seen.

He was especially enchanted by Cincinnati, located on the

outer bank of a sweeping bend in the Ohio. Its brand-new wharves and business houses occupied the immediate shore. Above them, nestled on graceful hillside terraces, rows of frame residences peeped out at the great river.

Louisville, unhealthily huddled on a marshy plain, was far less attractive. Its fascination lay chiefly in its proximity to the wild, intimidating Falls of the Ohio. Viewing this remarkable river feature for the first time, Samuel had no way of knowing he and the falls would later wage an important battle over the issue of supremacy.

Chapter 22

*I*t was inevitable that Spanish Louisiana should become part of the United States. The amazing thing was that, when it did occur, there was no bloodshed. Many Americans would have preferred a more sanguinary method of annexation.

A vast area west of the Mississippi, plus the "Isle of Orleans" on the river's east bank near the Gulf of Mexico, belonged to France until the Treaty of Paris in 1763 closed out the French and Indian Wars. Under terms of the treaty, Spain ceded Florida to Britain and received Louisiana from the vanquished French for use as a buffer in protecting Mexico. However, the dons did not long enjoy Louisiana in peace. While the sprinkling of French inhabitants up and down the Mississippi rather easily transferred their loyalty from one European monarchy to another, Spain's colonial officials saw early on that the westward flow from the Yankee colonies would pose a problem. By the close of the American Revolution, the tide of Anglo settlers rolling toward the Mississippi represented a full-blown threat to New Spain's northeastern hinterlands.

With no burgeoning pioneer stock of its own to colonize the western Mississippi Valley, Spain was dependent on a far-flung and woefully inadequate military presence there to check the inevitable incursions. All interested parties had to be aware that in the upcoming contest over Louisiana, whenever it happened and whatever shape it took, numbers and conditions would greatly favor the Americans.

Finally, at the close of the century, Spain chose an option it viewed as the lesser of two evils: ceding Louisiana back to the French. France by this time was a far cry from the ill-equipped nation which had lost its New World holdings nearly forty years before. Under Napoleon, the French would certainly brook no nonsense from Anglo interlopers. Above all else, the Spanish asked of France that Louisiana not be relinquished to any other sovereignty. This Napoleon pledged, in writing.

In late 1803, the emperor broke his word. To add insult to injury, the recipient of all Louisiana—for a paltry $15 million purchase price—was the United States.

William Charles Cole Claiborne, a hardened twenty-eight years old when he took the governorship of the Orleans Territory of the United States, was no one's fool. On the other hand, the Virginian had no natural sympathy for the people over whom he was suddenly handed great power.

The territory's inhabitants included the Creoles, a genteel group which by definition consisted of white New World natives whose ancestors were French or Spanish (and among whom much intermarrying had taken place). They enjoyed the privileges of money, education, and social rank, and by default had frequently filled offices within the Spanish colonial hierarchy. Catholics all, they were rightfully apprehensive over this radical shift in rule to a fiercely Protestant, essentially Anglo-Saxon republic.

Claiborne had to deal with the Spanish bureaucrats still technically in place during the long, drawn-out transition period. Furious at Napoleon, who further compounded his sins against them by failing to define the boundaries of the purchase, the Spaniards feared how the United States might act to settle those boundaries. For instance, Jefferson's government was already intimating that at least part of Texas—if not all—had been included in the transaction, a contention the dons hotly denied. Diplomatic discussions on this topic were not starting out favorably for Spain.

Whatever the dimensions of the Louisiana Purchase would finally be, federal leadership deemed it wise to split the known area into two functional segments. Claiborne's domain stretched from the gulf north to the Thirty-third Parallel, which was the south boundary of the Territory of Louisiana under Gen. James Wilkinson's administration in St. Louis.

Trouble was, no one had yet defined the western boundary.

Most of the population of the Orleans Territory was in New Orleans proper, a mature but as-yet unincorporated city of about ten thousand. Its residents in late 1803 were treated to a bizarre sequence of flag exchanges at the Place d'Armes, the Crescent City's central square. The Spanish flag was lowered in favor of the French Tricolor at one ceremony, followed three weeks later by the formal removal of the French flag and raising of the Stars and Stripes. The real transition of ownership and citizenship, though, could not be handled quite so neatly.

To his fellow citizens he was James Wilkinson, supreme commander of the army and currently governor of the Territory of Louisiana. To the Spanish government, he was Agent Number Thirteen, who over the long course of this secret relationship received something like $40,000 for services promised and services claimed.

To Aaron Burr, former vice president of the United States, he was a confidante and a fellow conspirator. To Jane Wilkinson Long, later immortalized as the Mother of Texas, he was the always supportive, immensely affectionate "Uncle Jamie."

Clearly, Wilkinson was ambitious. He also had a boundless appetite for what to him represented the good things in life. A dedicated family man, he wanted only the best for close kin, too. As a consequence, he learned early that no ordinary income could ever keep the Wilkinsons up in the lavish manner he desired. To him, having the means to live grandly was always more important than how it was gained—or at what sacrifice.

Typically, his first tour of military duty on behalf of his country was marked by extreme highs and lows. Early in the Revolutionary War, the field exploits of this young Marylander sent him on a rapid rise through the ranks of the Continental Army. By age twenty, he had bypassed older, more veteran rivals to attain the office of brigadier general. Then, within weeks, he allowed himself to be caught up in internal army politics, including an attempt to supplant Washington as commander-in-chief with a subordinate. This foolish episode, fueled in large part by Wilkinson's appetite for drunken carousing, led to his sudden resignation from the army.

Within two years, he bounced back to attain a less hectic and apparently more profitable position with the Continental Army, that of clothier-general. But here, too, despite hard work and some display of good management, he was forced to resign in the face of questions about irregularities in his accounts.

Wilkinson in 1784 moved to Kentucky as the representative of a leading Philadelphia mercantile firm, and there he enjoyed popularity for a time in Frankfort as a rising political figure. He was among the most vocal and least patient of advocates for Kentucky statehood. However, his extravagant lifestyle contributed to a breach with his bosses, and by 1787 he had run up quite a list of creditors. That summer, driven by the genius of desperation, James Wilkinson traveled downriver to New Orleans and audaciously engineered the bargain of his life.

Spanish authorities there, always paranoid concerning the giant young nation upriver, apparently believed Wilkinson when he told them he was a man of growing political influence throughout the western United States. They may even have believed him when he said he had grown unsympathetic with the government of his own nation, as it was controlled by Eastern power brokers who cared not a flip for the problems of the western citizenry.

His audience listened intently as Wilkinson said he could discreetly use his considerable influence in the interests of Spain, and—even more importantly—would be in a position to learn and pass along valuable information.

What he wanted in return was a stipend of $2,000 a year and an exclusive right to use the Mississippi as a route to market. The deal was struck, and Wilkinson took an oath of allegiance to Spain along with a designation as Number Thirteen.

He returned to Kentucky in an expansive mood, and for awhile seemed to have the means to support his appetite for the good life. By the time the Treaty of San Lorenzo was signed in 1795, ending his exclusive access to the Mississippi, Wilkinson had long since reentered American military service and was moving up rapidly through the ranks. If the Spaniards harbored early regrets about investing in Wilkinson, their misgivings must have dissolved entirely when, at the close of 1796, he succeeded "Mad" Anthony Wayne as commander of the United States Army.

Wilkinson's pliant ethics and position of great power eventually brought him into the confidence of the man sometimes described as America's first real politician . . . Aaron Burr.

Though Alexander Hamilton was the one mortally wounded in his duel with Burr, the fatal bullet just as effectively snuffed out the public life of the man who fired it.

Hamilton—the tireless adversary who had helped engineer Burr's political setbacks, including the whisker-close loss of the presidency—was at last dispatched. Ironically, his death left Colonel Burr as Colonel Burr's chief nemesis.

Further tragedy would stalk the suave, elegant New Yorker in years to come. In the spring of 1805, however, only the passing of his wife a decade before could match the crushing blow Burr received following the presidential campaign of 1800.

Thomas Jefferson was the presidential candidate and Burr the vice-presidential nominee of the Republicans. Together they convincingly unseated incumbent John Adams, whose Federalists were in disarray from warring among themselves. Interestingly, though, every electoral vote cast for Jefferson was matched with one for Burr, without distinction as to which office—president or vice president. While Jefferson clearly was the intended choice for president, Burr was equally eligible to hold the top post—and came within a single electoral vote of ascending.

Burr would not withdraw his name from consideration, and accordingly the messy deadlock was dropped into the corporate lap of the House of Representatives. The Federalists had taken a whipping, but their significant numbers in the lower chamber gave Burr hope for a coalition of the defeated party and his Republican backers.

Many Federalist congressmen preferred Burr to Jefferson, but Hamilton preferred anyone to Burr. Desperate, he threw his political weight behind Jefferson. After an embarrassingly long delay, the House began voting on the matter. Burr could never capture that extra vote, and Jefferson emerged as the winner on the thirty-sixth ballot. Burr, of course, became vice president.

When Burr ran for governor of New York in the spring of 1804, the Hamilton-led Federalists defeated him. The frustrated Burr, still occupying the office of vice president, challenged his archenemy to a duel. They met July 11 on a New Jersey hill alongside the Hudson River. Although by all eyewitness accounts the duel was fought fairly, Hamilton's friends immediately raised the cry of "Murder!"

As is not uncommon, revenge came at a high cost. Three decades of service to country, including Revolutionary War heroics (hence "Colonel Burr") and a glorious tenure as a U.S. senator from New York, suddenly went up in smoke. Burr completed his term of vice president in impeccable style, but he knew his political career in New York and Washington was over.

So it came to pass that the little colonel looked westward, to rekindle the dreams of empire he shared with James Wilkinson.

Spring, in glorious mantle of flowers and verdure, was sweeping northward into the upper Ohio Valley. Cottonwood, buckeye, and maple had already donned the livery of summer. Nature's matchless floral sprays carpeted the lush river bottoms. The whistle of the cardinal, the cry of the mockingbird, and the like calls of dozens of feathered kinsmen echoed through the dense woodlands.

A few miles below Marietta, the Ohio River turned abruptly to the west. A precipitous high hill, shrouded in trees, bounded the south shore. The late-afternoon sun transformed the rippled face of the great river into sparkling gold. Just ahead of Aaron Burr's gliding flatboat, the liquid gold parted to embrace the shadowy green bulk of a large island.

"Steer to the right, helmsman," commanded Burr, his dark eyes searching the island's shoreline for the first sign of a landing. Soon they saw it—an inlet resembling a small bayou, fringed with graceful sycamores just beginning to leaf. At a word from Burr the three-man crew swung the boat toward the opening, gave a couple of hearty braking tugs on the side sweeps, then suspended them in air as the craft drifted into the cluster of sycamores. The helmsman leaned gently on the stern sweep, maneuvering the boat toward the lone pier.

Burr's traveling companion, fellow New Yorker Gabriel Shaw, stood on deck with the colonel. "I say!" he exclaimed, and pointed excitedly to a white edifice gleaming through the trees. "I say! What a sight out here, in this howling wilderness! In the middle of a river!"

The two friends braced themselves—needlessly, as the flatboat slid smoothly alongside the little wharf with nary a bump. A crew member hopped out, rope in hand, and deftly captured a post. Only when the rope pulled taut did the boat scrape the wharf, and the other crewmen cushioned even that contact by placing their feet against the posts.

"Very fine work, gentlemen," Burr murmured, the ghost of a smile lighting his aristocratic features as he touched his hat in a mock salute. He followed the enthralled Shaw onto the wharf and up a graveled walk.

The travelers ascended the slope and came to a double gate of iron, hung from an immense pair of white stone pilasters. Through its ornate, opened wings they followed a hedge-lined route between an open meadow to their left and a beautiful, sprawling shrubbery on the immediate right. Sunlight struggled through the deepening shadows of the trees to reach the shrubbery, the fading rays highlighting a delightful collection of blooming plants. Next on the path was a garden, brilliant with color from a wild array of fruits, vegetables, and flowers. Smaller gravel paths meandered through the garden's scenic, scented interior and wound around pieces of pallid statuary.

"What pleasure grounds!" the flabbergasted Shaw muttered. "This horticultural paradise must represent a happy marriage of marvelous natural fertility and masterful gardening. I've scarcely seen the equal anywhere in the civilized world."

The curving walkway terminated at the pillared entrance to an imposing residence. This mansion, first observed from the boat, had been the initial titillater of Shaw's curiosity.

The main section of the house stood a full two stories, its elegant poplar exterior painted a gleaming white. Rows of windows, their green shutters pinned open, offered an inviting appearance. A pair of brick chimneys poked through the shingles of the hump-backed roof. From either end of the house swung graceful, curving porticoes leading to single-story enclosures—the kitchen at one end and a library at the other, the visitors would later learn.

The colonel lifted the brass door knocker and struck three solid blows. One of the double doors opened and an inquisitive black face popped out. "You may tell Mr. Harman Blennerhassett, if he is home," Burr impressively instructed, "that Colonel Burr and Mr. Shaw of New York are calling."

The man-servant blinked twice at the unfamiliar faces. Recovering smoothly, he smiled and swung wide the door. "Yes, suhs," he said with practiced gusto. "Come in! Come in!"

His backward step allowed Burr and Shaw to cross the threshold. Burr retrieved a letter from within his mantle and handed it to the servant. "For your master," he instructed.

The callers had a moment to admire the elegant entrance hall. The shining oak floor was partially clad in a long green-and-gold rug that extended to the base of a wide, graceful staircase. Midway between the front doors and the stairs of polished wood hung a ponderous chandelier, its lighted tapers provoking prismatic sparkles within the cut-glass pendants.

Burr and Shaw were shown into a handsomely appointed parlor. "Ah'll delivuh dis lettuh to de Mastuh," the servant declared, and the parlor door was pulled shut.

While the New Yorkers made themselves comfortable, the full-toned scrapings of a violin bow became audible from elsewhere in the mansion. The mournful melody was, the listeners thought, capably rendered. Abruptly, the music stopped. Footsteps echoed on the stairs and shortly the parlor door was flung open.

Burr stepped forward to exchange greetings with the master of the island. Shaw would later recall with amusement the visual disparity offered by the principals in this encounter.

The colonel was quite small, yet well-proportioned, and erect —almost regal—in bearing. Despite a rather weak chin, the aristocratic countenance was darkly handsome. His large brown eyes, appearing to be as black as the heavy eyebrows that shadowed them, glittered with intelligence. Nothing about him betrayed the rigors of the day's travel; he appeared to have just dressed in front of a mirror. Aaron Burr maintained command of himself, and frequently of those around him as well.

Harman Blennerhassett stood slightly more than six feet tall, awkward of frame and movement. He had a long, thin face, an equally long and prominent nose, and unruly brown hair plastered across his bulbous forehead. Extreme nearsightedness had produced a permanent squint and added to his clumsiness. Although born into lofty family circumstances, and therefore drilled in all of the graces reflecting his station in life, Blennerhassett sometimes appeared unsure, almost inept in certain social situations.

Burr's letter of introduction had just such an effect. The master of the island was literally gasping for breath, like a fish out of water. "What—what a tremendous thing!" he finally stammered, clumsily shaking the hands of his visitors. "Vice President Burr! And . . . friend! Sirs, you bring this household great honor!"

He is an Irishman despite the unlikely surname, Shaw thought. *His speech is polished, but surely smacks of Eire.*

The colonel offered their host a small, heavily wrapped package. "Here, sir, are your microscope slide-glasses from Philadelphia, which I agreed to deliver on behalf of the younger Dr. Wallace, of Marietta, in exchange for the kind epistle of introduction just given you."

Gushing with gratitude, Blennerhassett fumbled nervously with the package and almost dropped it. To the immense relief of Shaw (Burr seemed not to notice the near-disaster), he placed it on an end table.

"You are, of course, staying through dinner," Blennerhassett boomed, his nervousness giving way to more relaxed cordiality. "Excuse me while I inform Mrs. Blennerhassett."

Chapter 23

Like General Wilkinson, Aaron Burr never seemed to have quite enough money to meet his needs. Unlike Wilkinson, whose sole spark of fidelity was invested in home and hearth, the widower Burr never seemed to have quite enough female admiration to gratify his ego. The colonel's character was a mixture of great strengths and equally grand foibles, and his fondness for women was the despair of his friends. When Burr's eyes first met those of Margaret Blennerhassett, he immediately warmed to the challenge.

The lady of the island was certainly not what either Burr or Shaw had expected. Not yet thirty—younger than her husband by fifteen years—she was the epitome of feminine charm. There were, to be sure, certain physical characteristics oddly similar to those of her husband: above-average height for her sex, a long, pointed chin, ears protruding a bit too much, and rather large hands. Still, the lustrous blue eyes, finely formed nose, dimpling smile, long brown tresses, and witty, vivacious manner confounded the predispositions of the visitors. She was her husband's equal or superior in every way.

Following a sumptuous dinner, the two Blennerhassett boys were dismissed and the four adults retired upstairs to a spacious, richly outfitted drawing room. Shaw's participation in the evening's conversation was light, but his attention remained keen. It didn't take him long to realize that Burr was in possession of greater prior knowledge about this island and its owners than he had chosen to share with his traveling companion.

Responding to polite, apparently careless questioning by Burr, Blennerhassett divulged that he had spent in the neighborhood of $70,000 on the purchase of the property and erection of the ten-room mansion, and on continuing improvements to both. The attentive Shaw soon understood that what he and Burr had seen of this isolated estate at sunset was just a fraction of the whole. Substantial farmland was under tillage, and there was extensive improved pasturage for horses, cattle, sheep, and goats. Pigs had been introduced in a wooded section of the island. All of these agricultural endeavors were being looked after by a battery of slaves.

When Mrs. Blennerhassett spoke about the island, she lauded not only the splendid improvements but the natural beauty of the environs as well. Her poet's soul revealed itself in describing the mist-softened, dew-sprinkled early mornings; the refreshing play of afternoon breezes across lush pasture grasses and through ancient groves of oak and poplar; the pink-and-gold sunsets mirrored on the wide bosom of the river.

"You speak as though you are very much in love with this island, and justifiably so," offered Shaw in one of his rare comments. "But, as you are people of breeding and culture, do you not miss equivalent companionship?" Burr's head nodded slowly, as if he approved of the question.

Harman Blennerhassett answered. "There is a degree of loneliness here," he acknowledged. "However, a few miles upstream live the people of Marietta, whom you met just today. That village was established by some of the veterans of our late revolution, New Englanders who are reasonably well educated and refined in their own right. I have some business association with a local firm there. This home has an extensive library, and also a laboratory for scientific experimentation to occupy me. In all, I dare say we are content—at least, for the present."

Margaret Blennerhassett emphatically changed the subject. Flashing her dimpled smile, she asked, "And as for you, Colonel Burr, with your glorious term as vice president now run—what lies ahead for you when you have completed this adventuresome western journey and return to New York?"

Her femininity allowed her to get away with firing such a broadside at Burr, who returned the smile.

"This western journey, as you style it, is not solely for pleasure," he responded. "The people on this side of the Alleghenies are not enamored of their central government. I travel with an ear open to their thoughts and complaints. There is also the matter of Spain, with whom we may yet be embroiled in some difference over territorial boundaries, or the ill treatment of Spain's subjects in Mexico. I listen and observe, and I contemplate the critical issues facing the country."

Having completely circumvented her question, he smiled again. "I do indeed have affairs to be settled in New York," he added, "but my return there may be for only a brief time. I believe great opportunity lies in the West . . . for men of vision and courage." He glanced at the master of the island. "Don't you agree, Mr. Blennerhassett?"

The Irishman squinted back at Burr and nodded.

As a closure to the evening, the host acquiesced to his wife's repeated pleas to play the violin. Genuinely ill at ease, Blennerhassett nevertheless performed almost without flaw. Shaw thought it strange to see those clumsy hands move so artfully, tenderly producing such beautiful music. The final melody was a melancholy one, played with considerable passion.

After Blennerhassett had put down the instrument, and blushingly endured everyone's compliments, Burr said suavely: "I believe I recognize the last piece. It's magnificent! Isn't it of Irish origin?"

Blennerhassett confirmed the accuracy of Burr's memory. "It's an old air from the north of Ireland—Londonderry, as I recollect," he said musingly.

Under the wavering light of burning pine knots, the visitors made their way down to the boat. The Blennerhassetts accompanied them almost the full distance, even while offering a night's rest within the mansion. Burr declined, noting that "there is no companionship in sleeping."

No sooner were they left alone than Shaw began bombarding Burr with questions. "You were holding out on me, Colonel," he said good-naturedly. "I believe you know quite a bit about these people and their dream island. I heard Mr. Blennerhassett's statement about 'our revolution,' but I'll wager he's no American—nor she. He sounds Irish to me, and she sounds English."

"He became a naturalized citizen five years ago," Burr said blandly, and laughed at Shaw's mock indignation. "I did pick up a few tid-bits today in Marietta," he confessed. "Blennerhassett is an Irish nobleman, who unexpectedly inherited the family estate when both older brothers passed away prematurely. For some unexplained reason, he sold the entirety of the holdings and came with his lovely young wife to America. And not just to America, but as far from civilization as he could safely locate and still procure many of the fine things to which they are accustomed. The locals gossip about some dark secret in Blennerhassett's past, which they avow he is running from.

"He is educated in law but does not practice. He is a poor businessman and makes little from his enterprise in Marietta. As one of the rustics there had it, he has every kind of sense except common sense. I fear much of the family fortune has been foolishly sunk into the sand of this miserable island."

Shaw did not like Burr's final comment, nor his tone of voice. He heard in it contempt for Blennerhassett, coupled with an interest in Blennerhassett's finances. And Shaw also suspected the colonel of entertaining an unspoken but definite interest in Blennerhassett's wife.

Rebekah Cumings always referred to her first twenty-five years in Kentucky as the best years of her life. After that, things began unraveling.

In 1802, sickly little Robert was born after great difficulty, and the midwives of New Ephrata solemnly warned Rebekah against having more children. That meant, of course, the end of certain conjugal privileges until she was well past the age of fertility.

So Robert's arrival closed out the crop of young Cumingses at nine. The first six were boys: Samuel, young Anthony or "Tony," Thomas, John, William, and James. Then in the spring of 1799, Nature doubly surprised Anthony and Rebekah with twin girls. They were named Rebecca and Sarah, the latter in honor of Rebekah's mother. As for the former, the spelling was stipulated by Rebekah, who explained that her children were born "into full provision of the New Covenant and should not bear Old Testament names." Samuel and Sarah, she pointed out, had special dispensations as they were named for their grandparents.

Even as Robert was making his painful entry into the world, work had begun on the third generation of the family in Kentucky.

Samuel in early 1802 had married Nancy Martin, and Thomas soon thereafter wed Mary Crawford.

Despite his marriage, it could be argued with some force that Samuel Cumings's first love remained the river. He was gone from home for months at a time, leading the Singletary exporting flotillas to New Orleans. The return route meant traversing the Natchez Trace, an overland journey far more fraught with peril from pestilence, snakes, unfriendly savages, and ruthless highwaymen than was the descent on the waterways. From fledgling Nashville, northern terminus of the treacherous Trace, the New Ephrata contingent continued on foot or horseback to Lexington and the Ohio Valley.

Noble Grimes, with whom Samuel had taken his first river odyssey, remained interested in the younger man and his mapping and charting efforts. Grimes was of the belief that these aids to navigation should be published for profit, and once suggested that he and Samuel acquire a printing press. Then he came up with a better idea.

"I've made the acquaintance of a man of considerable means," he confided in Samuel. "Like myself, he's an Irishman. He owns an island up near Marietta, and has built there a great manse and has cultivated beautiful grounds.

"He's let me know that he could use a good return on his money just now, and he's investin' in my town at the mouth of Brush Creek. What occurs to me, lad, is for me to write the man and tell him of your fine work on chartin' the rivers. He'll immediately see the value it holds for boatmen. Might be he'll entertain a publishin' scheme himself."

As good as his word, Grimes wrote the letter. But the weeks passed into months and no response came. Samuel suspected that the apparent failure of the town at Brush Creek was probably uppermost in the minds of Grimes and his investor. On occasion he contemplated publishing the material himself, but this urge never progressed beyond daydreaming.

Then, in the summer of 1805, Grimes suddenly died. Samuel's mourning was cut short, though, by the calamity which befell his own father.

While operating the Brush Creek Island sawmill, Anthony Cumings fell into the river. His head became pinned in between two immense logs and was squeezed so tightly that he lost consciousness. Thomas and John rescued him, but he lay bedridden for months from headaches and fever. He never fully recovered, physically or mentally.

The following spring, word came that Samuel Russel had died. As Rebekah was still taking daily care of Anthony and also keeping a worried eye on frail little Robert, she realized she could not make the journey to her family home in Virginia. Son Samuel was away on a trip to New Orleans, and Tony, as the oldest son still at home, functioned as the head of the household during his father's illness. Rebekah decided that her representative to Loudoun County would be the ever-adventurous Thomas, who went gladly and took with him teenaged William.

The emotional load became almost unbearable. Rebekah had missed bidding a final farewell to her father, and would not be able to personally share in her mother's grief. Anthony lay feverish and incapacitated while Robert coughed and whined. Samuel, Thomas, and William were all making long, dangerous trips.

"Pray, Tony," she hoarsely told her second-oldest, despair tugging at her throat. "You're the head of the family now."

Chapter 24

Wile it didn't say everything
Samuel Cumings wanted to
read, the unexpected letter
from Harman Blennerhassett easily held his interest.

Weeks after being penned, it was delivered to Samuel by a
brother of Noble Grimes. Blennerhassett, obviously unaware of
Grimes's death, had written him and enclosed the separate epistle to
Samuel. The letter expressed an interest in reviewing and acquiring
the "navigational information spoken of so highly by your champion, Mr. Grimes," and requested a personal delivery of the charts and
notes to Blennerhassett at his island home "as soon as is practica-
ble."

The letter continued:

> This material may well be of some value to an important expedi-
> tion now being organized by myself and Colonel Aaron Burr, late
> Vice President of the United States. In fact, should your arrival
> here coincide with the next visit from the Colonel, he is desirous
> of making your acquaintance with the prospect of engaging you
> in the preparation of additional navigational aids. Please acknowl-
> edge receipt of this letter immediately and respond favorably to
> my request, if you are prepared to do so.

Blennerhassett mentioned nothing about publishing the material, nor did he venture a purchase price. However, Samuel told himself that a man of such wealth and connections would certainly
make a positive response worthwhile.

As though they were truly afterthoughts, a couple of post-
scripts appeared under Blennerhassett's signature:

P.S.—Should you know of any young men in your neighborhood, hardy of physique and venturesome in spirit, who would like to participate in the upcoming enterprise, they should without delay present themselves to Colonel Burr or myself at Blennerhassett's Island. Upon enlisting for six months, each will receive twelve dollars per month, clothes, and provisions, with a possible bonus of 150 acres of bountiful Southwest land. They are asked to provide their own weapons.

P.P.S.—The expedition is also in need of boats of a particular manufacture, and I recall Mr. Grimes speaking of a boat-yard in your vicinity. These boats are to be built much on the order of a large skiff, light of weight, with a shallow draught, pointed at either end, and otherwise capable of being moved upstream as well as down. They must be of such size as to accommodate up to thirty men, and supplies in like proportion. Should the local yard-master have an interest in constructing up to a dozen such craft, the plans are available from Colonel Barker, on the Muskingum above Marietta.

Samuel saw in Blennerhassett's addenda the potential for his brothers Thomas and John to earn money and perhaps acquire property as members of the expedition, and also for an infusion of capital into Nimrod Ellison's boatyard operation. Although New Ephrata retained the communal aspects of many of its activities, including kitchen, school, and agrarian pursuits, residents there had need of cash like everyone else. Samuel had been apprised of Blennerhassett's riches, and he assumed a former vice president of the United States must likewise be wealthy. It did not occur to him to question the solvency of the "enterprise."

Still, Samuel wanted someone to confide in, from whom he might solicit guidance. Due to the death of Noble Grimes, and the sometimes befuddled mental state of his father, Samuel turned to his mother. She, however, told him he should ask the counsel of the Reverend Lewis Craig.

"None of us within New Ephrata knows what is going on in the outside world," she pointed out. "Reverend Craig is well read and keeps himself informed. He probably knows all about this unexplained expedition, and all about the gentlemen as well. It seems to me there are answers you should get before involving yourself, let alone others."

Mother and son knew that a visit to Craig could throw the

Cumings household into disfavor with the community patriarch. There continued to be bad blood between David Singletary and the minister, exacerbated by Craig's public denunciation of Singletary as a heretic and blasphemer. This outburst came after Craig heard a New Ephrata resident assert that, at the time of the Second Coming, Singletary would appear at the right hand of Christ. Outraged, Craig confronted the patriarch with the statement and demanded to know its origin. He received no answer other than contemptuous silence.

Despite this unfortunate circumstance, Samuel followed his mother's advice. He found Craig at home, sharpening his stone mason's tools between glances at an open Bible on his workbench. Despite his industriousness, the minister was in a receptive mood.

After reading Blennerhassett's letter, Craig handed it back to Samuel.

"There's a bit of a scandal brewing, and our recent vice president appears to be at the center of it," he began. "It's hard to say what is fact and what is purely conjecture on the part of the newspapers. If we choose to take the scribes seriously, then Aaron Burr and his friends are indeed plotting any number of dark and seditious actions."

Samuel's eyes widened. Craig smiled, animating the cherry-red mark on his face.

"No one really knows the truth, young man, except Mr. Burr himself," Craig continued. "But wild stories are being told. The most fantastic of them, perhaps, goes like this:

"Mr. Burr and some highly placed acquaintances intend to divide the nation, causing the western states and territories to pull away from the federal government in Washington and form one of their own. I find this unlikely, because Mr. Jefferson is a very popular president in the West, and the pressures of a few years ago, when the lower Mississippi was in Spain's hands and closed to American trade, went away after the purchase of Louisiana. Surely, men in the positions occupied by the supposed conspirators realize these things better than I.

"Still, that rumor persists and is given credence by many. And there are other rumors. One has it that Mr. Burr is waiting for our country to go to war with Spain. I fear such a war is possible, because the United States wants to take Florida from the Spanish, and because there is disagreement and tension now between us and Spain over the western boundary of Louisiana. Too, there simply exists a mutual, long-standing distrust and dislike.

"Should war occur, and the Americans prevail, Mr. Burr (so our rumor goes) is somehow going to project himself in the thick of things and become emperor of Mexico. Or, perhaps, he will promote the joining of the conquered Spanish lands with the breakaway western states and forge an empire of his own. Many who claim to know him say that Aaron Burr is easily capable of such self-aggrandizement."

Craig carefully polished his glasses with a shirt sleeve, then resumed.

"Politics, is an ugly thing, all about power. Mr. Burr is an ambitious but frustrated man, denied by either fate or divine intervention from holding the office of president. He has powerful friends and even more powerful enemies.

"Amazingly, all of these real or imagined machinations I speak of appear almost every week in our Kentucky and Ohio newspapers and are talked of in the streets. If indeed Mr. Burr and others are designing such conspiracies, they are doing a dismal job of keeping them secret. The former vice president and his schemings are, at present, the leading topics of discussion in this country."

Samuel looked stricken. The minister smiled again, and playfully poked the young man's shoulder with a gnarled fist.

"Having said all that," he added, in a kindly tone of voice, "I fail to see any reason why you should not respond to this Marietta gentleman's inquiry. It's true that we don't know what the expedition is about, but all he and Mr. Burr want from you is help in getting down the river. What can be the harm in turning a simple business deal?"

Historians would later be undecided as to whether General Wilkinson was initially a follower of Burr or vice versa. Just how seriously they considered attempting the division of the young Union would be equally debatable. But most certainly, the intriguers at one point were in collusion to take personal advantage of a war with Spain. Wilkinson had apparently cooled on this prospect when, in September of 1806, the chance to spark just such a conflict was dropped into his lap.

The elements necessary to place Burr and Wilkinson in a position to succeed in their wild scheme never came together. Most critical of those elements was the financial and military support of Great Britain, solicited on the premise that the United States would indeed be split asunder into two greatly weakened halves. By the summer, it was made clear to the plotters that the British were unwilling to invest money or ships in the enterprise. Correspondingly, the general's eagerness to proceed with the project began to sag.

Spain had stubbornly laid claim to land east of the Sabine River, asserting that the border of the Louisiana Purchase was the Arroyo Hondo. Governor Claiborne's action in 1805 to expedite the American takeover of the fort at Natchitoches, not far from the disputed ground, embarrassed and angered the Spaniards. During the ensuing winter, they doggedly increased their military presence at the west bank of the Sabine, until in the spring of 1806 they had amassed about a thousand troops.

Alarmed authorities in Washington dispatched a flurry of directives to Wilkinson in St. Louis, urging him to increase the American military presence in Natchitoches and prepare for repelling an invasion. The general ignored the urgent tone of these missives, tarrying in St. Louis. Having failed to secure British aid, Burr was far behind schedule with his efforts to gather, prepare, and equip a strike force on Blennerhassett's Island, and at best would not be ready before winter. Whether Wilkinson was buying time for Burr, or whether he was simply unsure of which star to follow, could be answered only through conjecture. Nevertheless, he resisted until August the mounting pressure from Washington to take action.

Early in that month, about a third of the Spanish forces crossed the Sabine and established a camp near the Arroyo Hondo. This was Spain's land, the commander said, and they would not budge from it. Wilkinson in leisurely fashion moved down the Mississippi to Natchez, then further downstream to the confluence with the Red River. The journey up the Red to Natchitoches, site of newly built Fort Claiborne, was hard and slow.

Once there, Wilkinson at first appeared indecisive. Then, on October 8, a young man named Samuel Swartwout arrived at the fort under the guise of wanting to join the expected fight with the Spanish. His real mission was to deliver a coded letter supposedly written by Burr. The general spent most of that night deciphering the letter, which proved to contain a highly favorable and equally fictitious account of the state of affairs concerning the plot.

If the intent of the epistle was to draw Wilkinson into a firm commitment to the plot, it had the opposite effect. The general knew at least some of the statements were lies. However, the letter itself was a smoking indictment of its alleged author as a conspirator and traitor. Reportedly in imminent danger of being removed as supreme commander of the army by President Jefferson, Wilkinson saw a way to regain the chief executive's favor through a sacrificial offering of Jefferson's archenemy and former vice president.

Then, of course, the general would covertly notify the Spanish government of his role in scotching the widely advertised invasion of New Spain by the removal of its chief instigator, Aaron Burr. Surely that welcome information would extract a handsome reward from his secret employers.

Chapter 25

While General Wilkinson was taking his time journeying by water from St. Louis to Natchitoches, the crossing of the Sabine by Spanish troops had others responding quickly.

Claiborne in New Orleans and acting Mississippi territorial governor Cowles Mead in Natchez called for volunteers to join their militias. Westerners spoiling for a fight with Spain turned out in even greater numbers than requested. Learning of the militia buildups, and of Wilkinson's belated arrival in Natchitoches, the Spanish contingent near Arroyo Hondo prudently broke camp and recrossed the Sabine.

If Wilkinson had nursed any lingering thoughts of sharing Burr's pipe dreams, the ludicrous claims in the cipher letter whisked them away. First of all, western sentiment for a split of the Union no longer existed. Second, without aid from England, the conspirators were insufficiently financed to assemble a private force capable of seizing New Spain. Of all Burr's plots, the only one with a chance of success depended on the colonel attracting a large enough force of volunteers, such as Claiborne and Meade had just raised, for the "liberation" of Mexico.

For that to happen, the patriotic fervor and blood lust of Americans needed to be whetted by an incident—or outright war—with Spain. Ironically, Wilkinson now owned the opportunity and means to create that incident but had decided emphatically not to do so. Instead, he was going to please his president as well as his employers in Madrid by foiling Burr's last desperate try for glory.

To snuff out the prospect of another Spanish thrust across the Sabine, Wilkinson engineered the recognition of a neutral ground westward from Natchitoches to New Spain's Nacogdoches, a distance in excess of a hundred miles with the Sabine roughly at the center. This arrangement stayed in force until the United States and Spain settled their differences over the boundary of the Louisiana Purchase, which would not occur until 1821. On November 6, 1806, the general and Lt. Col. Simon de Herrera signed an agreement formalizing the proposal.

Previously, Wilkinson had sent a sensationally worded dispatch to Jefferson, claiming to have just learned of a treasonable endeavor supported by "a great number of individuals possessing wealth, popularity, and talents . . ." It was the intent of this powerful coalition, the general wrote, to "rendezvous eight or ten thousand men in New Orleans," revolutionize the territorial government, and seize the banks, as a prelude to unlawfully invading Mexico. While in this initial communication he pretended not to know names, Wilkinson had no doubt Jefferson would quickly conclude who was at the head of the conspiracy.

In a later missive, Wilkinson did name Burr as the moving force, adding indignantly that the former vice president had even tried to lure him into the plot in order to leverage support from the army. A modified version of the decoded letter was included with this dispatch as evidence of the allegations.

By the meanderings of the Ohio River, Blennerhassett's Island lay two hundred miles upstream from New Ephrata—a long, hard trip to make against the current. So in October 1806, Samuel, Thomas, and John Cumings, accompanied by another young adventurer named Tully Fenwick, chose to travel by horseback across southeastern Ohio to Marietta. Samuel had with him the river maps and charts as requested; the other three wanted to investigate the prospects offered by the mysterious Burr-Blennerhassett expedition.

"After all," Thomas reasoned, "this outfit is going down the Ohio. So if it winds up that we don't like the way things are, we can just hop off at New Ephrata."

From Marietta they rode downriver to Belpre, where the course of the river turned sharply from south to west. Below Belpre they happened upon a panoramic overlook of their destination—and, surprisingly, a waiting ferry.

The operator looked them over keenly as he took them out to the island. "Shore lotsa you boys a-collectin' here," he ventured. "Lately, it's payin' me mought near as good t' take folks back 'n' forth t' this island as it does to cross th' entire river from Belpre t' Virginny. What's a-goin' on here, anyhow?"

Samuel answered truthfully that they were not sure. "But former Vice President Burr and Mr. Blennerhassett are in charge of whatever it is," he added proudly, "so it's bound to be important."

The ferryman narrowed his eyes and spat into the river. "I reckon Mr. Burr's all right," he opined, "but that other fella is a sight. I think he's teched in th' noggin."

The grand appearance of the Blennerhassett mansion and its lavish grounds enveloped the young men with awe. None had ever viewed such a residence. Thomas, John, and Tully were led to recently erected barracks in a wooded area beyond the house. A servant invited Samuel inside the mansion and escorted him into the very parlor that had greeted Burr and his companion Shaw eighteen months previous.

There was not a chair in the room that Samuel dared sit in. They were all far too elegant. He felt uncomfortable, out of place with his backwoods apparel and upbringing, and wondered what kind of impression he was going to make on his host.

Immersed in admiration of the luxurious furnishings, Samuel did not notice the parlor door open. Suddenly, he became aware that someone was in the doorway, even as a musical female voice welcomed him to "our island home."

Margaret Blennerhassett stood before him, blue-eyed, dimpled, willowy, and wholly charming, dark hair coiled daintily around her head. Her silk dress and flashing jewelry lifted her into a realm of surreal loveliness unmatched in his tender experiences. His young wife, Nancy, was certainly pretty in her own plump, homespun way, and he had always frankly thought that no woman could ever be as beautiful as his mother. Now, for the first time, he was not so sure.

For her part, the mistress of the island found the young riverman's appearance to her liking. His serious, fine-featured face bore the ruddiness that comes from sunrays bouncing off water. The sincere hazel eyes peering from beneath a queued mop of black, curly hair bespoke a naive honesty. Nearly six feet tall, he was slender in build except for a powerful set of shoulders. Margaret surmised that he was within a year or two of her own age.

"I-I'm Samuel Cumings," he said at last. "I've come to see Vice President Burr and Mr. Blennerhassett."

"I am Mrs. Blennerhassett," she responded, her dimples deepening. "At the moment, neither gentleman is here. Colonel Burr has been in Kentucky, though he is due back very soon. My husband is out in the neighborhood, attending to the many details regarding our upcoming . . . trip. Please have a seat, Mr. Cumings, and make yourself at home. Will you have tea?"

He nodded, cautiously testing a chair, as she rang a small silver bell.

Emboldened, Samuel yielded to his curiosity. "You mentioned a trip, Mrs. Blennerhassett," he said. "I suppose it is the same journey for which my navigational materials are being considered. Could you tell me a little about it?"

"Why certainly, Mr. Cumings," she said graciously, taking a nearby chair. He had never heard so charming a voice.

"My husband and Colonel Burr are engaged in developing frontier land in Louisiana for settlement by those who can afford it. The property, originally purchased from a French nobleman, lies on the Ouachita River. The colonel says that the country there is even more beautiful than the Ohio Valley, and the climate far less prone to disagreeable winters."

A colonizing venture! Samuel felt a great sense of relief. None of the wild stories about invading Mexico or dividing the nation, then, held any relevance to the present project. Yet he had seen something earlier in the afternoon which still disturbed him, and he decided to address it.

"Two of my brothers and a friend came with me," he said, after gingerly sipping the hot tea. "They are interested in the advantages of joining the expedition as was outlined in Mr. Blennerhassett's letter to me. When we arrived, they were taken around behind this house, to where some men were marching."

Samuel placed the little cup in its saucer and looked intently at his hostess. "If this is not a military expedition," he asked, "why, then, are those men being trained as soldiers?"

Margaret found herself enjoying this conversation, and it had nothing to do with the topic.

"Why, Mr. Cumings," she responded, blue eyes wide, "there are red savages in Louisiana. Our party must be prepared for all eventualities. However, Colonel Burr assures us we will not be in any lasting danger."

Samuel blinked. "Then you yourself intend to take part in this expedition? You are going along?"

"Of course, Mr. Cumings," she replied, elevating her pointed little chin. "I go wherever my husband goes. And our two sons go wherever we go. It will be a grand adventure."

Glancing through the parlor window, Margaret rose abruptly. "You are about to meet my husband, sir. He is coming now." The faintest shadow of disappointment flitted across her face.

Cordialities exchanged, Harman Blennerhassett and Samuel at once began an examination of the maps and charts. Once they lay unrolled and unfolded, however, the Irishman seemed hardly able to keep his attention focused on them. Samuel seldom finished answering one question before Blennerhassett was hurriedly raising another. The master of the island was clearly distracted over something other than navigating the rivers.

This rather unsatisfactory interview concluded with Blennerhassett saying he wanted Burr to review the materials. "The colonel is due in tonight," the Irishman noted. He then suggested that Samuel join his brothers overnight in the barracks.

Darkness had fallen by the time the expedition's recruits finished their supper. Samuel, seated at the campfire with Thomas, John, and Tully, spoke freely about his interview with Harman Blennerhassett. But he avoided any mention of the earlier visit with the more charming member of the island family.

In truth, he was unable to sort out his feelings about Margaret Blennerhassett. There arose in his bosom a cloud of exhilaration whenever he relived any part of their encounter. Yet, along with this sense of delight came also one of caution and—yes, no doubt about it—just the slightest twinge of guilt. Thus absorbed, he lay awake after the others, exhausted from their drilling, had begun emitting the various noises of slumber. Finally, he decided he was so far removed from sleep that he may as well stroll around a bit.

A half-moon nearing its zenith glided free of the grasping clouds and cast just enough radiance for Samuel to make his way. His ambling walk led through the shadowy grounds of the mansion to the south portico, close to the kitchen, dark now but aromatic from years of consumed firewood and animal fat. To his left, the rear of the main structure loomed massive and spectrally white.

Faint but unmistakable, there came on the night air the musical voice of the lady of the house. Instinctively, Samuel paused in his walk to listen. A sense of shame warmed his straining ears when he realized that Margaret Blennerhassett was leading her sons in bedtime prayers. Chastened by conscience, he quietly crossed through the portico—and stopped again.

Before him, the variable grays of the front lawn dropped gracefully to the sparkling inlet. There a large flatboat, illuminated by a quartet of torches at its corners, lay moored to the wharf. The unsteady light of the pine knots silhouetted a pair of men walking toward the house, one excessively tall and lean and the other short but well proportioned. Samuel knew the taller man to be Blennerhassett, and easily guessed the other's identity. They were in animated discussion. To avoid a possibly unwelcome encounter, he stepped back into the shadow of the portico as they approached.

"I tell you, Colonel," the voice of Blennerhassett became intelligible, "it is a trifle uncomfortable in the neighborhood. The Hendersons, for example, remain unfavorably disposed toward our enterprise. They have created considerable ill-will directed at you and myself among their neighbors on the Virginia shore. I am even led to understand that the militiamen of Wood County are considering an inspection of the island."

When the shorter man spoke, his suave voice bore a trace of irritation. "It may be," he said, "that the articles in the local newspapers are partly to blame. They smack too strongly of a separatist viewpoint regarding the future course of the western states. Frankly, my dear Harman, those writings were ill-advised. It would not take much of an imagination to link the mysterious 'Querist' to yourself as the author."

Apparently wanting to conclude their conversation outside the house, the pair paused on the first step of the pillared entrance. Blennerhassett stood silent, head on chest and shoulders slumped in apparent dejection. The little man changed his tone of voice. It became upbeat, encouraging.

"But worry not, my friend. We shall soon have our boats and supplies, and this rude band of ragamuffins will yet make a disciplined, capable force to be reckoned with. Then it's down the river we go, for fortune and glory! Let the Spanish dons beware! Nothing is going to stop us, you and me, from recouping our fortunes many times over!"

Something heavy introduced itself to Samuel's stomach. He had just overheard proof of the tales only half-believed by the Reverend Craig.

Blennerhassett spoke timidly. "Then your trip was a success?" he asked. "You have raised additional capital?"

"I have received pledges of cash and supplies, to be secured along the way," Burr replied. "More boats will be available at Louisville, and again when we reach the mouth of the Cumberland. I have also heard from our New York agent, and many men, fully equipped, will depart soon from Pittsburgh and join us here."

The master of the island seemed reassured. Continuing in that same timid voice, he said, half-questioningly, "And . . . should General Wilkinson not be able to provoke an incident, and there be no war with Spain . . . we will simply proceed up the Ouachita on the colonizing project."

Burr chuckled. "Yes, yes, of course," he reassured the Irishman. It was apparent that Blennerhassett, the romantic dreamer, had no heart for riches won by bloodshed. "However, my dear sir," the colonel continued, "never underestimate General Wilkinson. He is a man of unlimited capabilities."

Chapter 26

Wilkinson's capacity to serve his own ends while sacrificing Burr seemed limitless.

Having nullified any further threat of Spanish confrontation on the Sabine through the "neutral ground" pact, the general turned undivided attention to maximizing his opportunities at Burr's expense. He hustled to New Orleans, where he ordered the city's antiquated defenses shored up to meet an expected invasion by a force of thousands. He repeatedly harangued the dubious Claiborne and other, more easily duped officials in New Orleans with tales of secret agents and intrigues within the city to aid the alleged invasion. Finally, Wilkinson got what he wanted: New Orleans was placed under martial law. Before year's end, the city was in turmoil over nothing more than the convenient figments of the general's sanguinary imagination.

Meanwhile, ignorant of Wilkinson's treachery, Burr blithely went about building up his expedition's forces and supplies. Then came word from Frankfort that the federal district attorney of Kentucky had ordered Burr's arrest on a charge of "high misdemeanor," related to a purported plan to invade Mexico. Intending to nullify the political strategy behind the action, Burr appeared voluntarily to answer the accusation. Even before the charge to the grand jury could be completed, however, the district attorney's case collapsed due to his inability to locate a supposed key witness.

The determined prosecutor was not finished. Within three weeks, Burr was back in a Frankfort courtroom facing essentially the same charge. This time the case did go to the grand jury, which in its deliberations found no cause to try Burr. It was a clear legal victory for the former vice president, but the adverse newspaper publicity nevertheless sent shockwaves through the fragile financial foundations of Burr's enterprise. Many high-profile backers now had second thoughts, and were abruptly less than eager to declare themselves friends of Aaron Burr and supporters of his latest scheme.

On the heels of Burr's no-bill, the nation also began to receive word of a riveting proclamation from President Jefferson. In it, without naming names, Jefferson called for a halt to the assembling of any military force to be used "against the dominions of Spain." Labeling such efforts "criminal," Jefferson commanded "all officers, civil and military," as well as "good and faithful citizens" to work vigilantly for the "discovery, apprehending and bringing to justice of all such offenders."

One of the fiercest winters in the country's short history was about to grip its inhabitants, and none would feel more left out in the cold of 1806–07 than the little colonel.

Snow was falling on Blennerhassett's Island.

Inside the barracks, scores of men grumbled over the weather as they stepped up preparations for embarking on the expedition. Harman Blennerhassett, even more nervous and less inspiring than usual, had made a general announcement in the morning that they would depart "any day now, sooner than expected" for Louisiana. All must be in readiness, he stressed, in anticipation of that as-yet undetermined hour.

The Irishman wanted to wait out the completion of additional boats at a yard on the Muskingum River. But two factors were pressing him to depart sooner—the worsening weather, and deteriorating relations with the neighbors on both sides of the river. Already, family pressures had forced a number of defections by men recruited from the immediate vicinity. Blennerhassett had never enjoyed much credibility in the upper Ohio Valley; now the reputation of Aaron Burr was rapidly sinking into disrepute as well. Dark suspicions dogged the activities on the island, widely viewed by the locals as part of a plot against the government. How long would it be, the Irishman wondered fearfully, before the crude elements of the Wood County militia worked themselves into a frenzy and forcibly descended upon the island?

For weeks, Blennerhassett had labored to contain his doubts and to maintain a positive demeanor before his family. But this day, after urging the diminishing corps of recruits to readiness, he clumsily confessed his fears to the lady of the island. Then he departed for the Muskingum, on one last, forlorn chance that the extra boats were finally ready.

Samuel was spending the morning in the Blennerhassetts' parlor, once more examining his notes on the stretch of river between the island and New Ephrata. This duty had been imposed by Blennerhassett, who told him tersely and without explanation that the flotilla might have to travel nocturnally the first few days.

The riverman had been in high spirits for weeks. His joy dated from the moment Burr personally honored him with the offer of piloting the expedition on its descent of the Ohio and Mississippi. This aggrandizement, so much more than Samuel could have expected, eclipsed his concerns about the real mission of the enterprise. He had sent home a glowing letter, telling Nancy of his upcoming role in Burr's colonizing venture. In the same missive, he reassured his parents that he, Thomas, and John were all doing well.

Having finished the ordered review of the river, Samuel collected the notes and placed them in a leather pouch. He then picked up a long brass cylinder propped against the table and unscrewed the cap. Carefully, he extracted a roll of papers, untied the red ribbon which bound them, and spread them out on the tabletop. They were maps created by Colonel Burr.

The top map depicted the entire course of the Ohio, and that of the lower Mississippi to the Gulf of Mexico. It also showed a large tract of land in Louisiana abutting the Ouachita River, with the inscription "Bastrop Grant" written beneath. According to the map, the flotilla must descend the Mississippi nearly to Baton Rouge, then enter the mouth of the Red River and ascend portions of it, the Black River, and finally the Ouachita to reach the grant. It was certainly a tortuous route, and Samuel once again contemplated the alternative prospect of a westward portage from Natchez.

He peered intently at the map, absorbed in thought. The snow beat noiselessly against the window panes. Then there came, he thought, the sound of someone crying. Puzzled and curious, he stepped to the window and looked out. A fur-wrapped figure sat on one of the wrought-iron benches which flanked the front porch, hooded head cradled in small, gloved hands, the snow accumulating unchecked on hunched, shaking shoulders.

It had to be Margaret Blennerhassett.

Samuel briefly considered honoring her right to privacy. But that was subordinated by a desire to rescue her from the cold, and to comfort her if at all possible. Decisively, he tapped sharply on the glass until she straightened and glanced around, one glove wiping her cheeks. He gestured for her to come inside.

A moment later the lady of the island was in his arms, face red and tear-stained, her slender body racked with sobs. Then, regaining his senses, Samuel led her to a chair and shut the study door. He knelt at her feet.

"What is it? What's wrong?" he asked, his voice shaking. He could not imagine what calamity had thrown the polished Margaret Blennerhassett into such emotional disarray. "Why were you sitting out in the snow?"

The sobs subsided. Margaret produced a handkerchief and wiped her eyes and nose. "I didn't want the children—nay, anyone —to see me," she said in a quavering voice. "We're ruined! We're totally ruined! Our sin has come home to us!"

Samuel was speechless.

"It's my fault," she continued, between sniffs. "I'm the one who thought we needed to do something new and exciting. Poor Harman! Truthfully, he wants nothing more than to somehow right his finances and stay where we are. Oh, he was excited, at first, about joining our fortunes with those of Colonel Burr. Well, we didn't know it would mean putting everything up!"

Another chorus of sobs escaped.

"You mean all that you own here has been mortgaged for the venture?" Samuel asked, aghast.

Margaret nodded tearfully. "All that we brought from Ireland, we put into this place. All of this place, we have now pledged to help finance Colonel Burr's enterprise. And it was my insisting that pushed Harman into doing it. And I love this place so, and now it's gone . . ."

Searching for any scrap of reassurance, Samuel countered, "But you will recoup your fortune in Louisiana, by developing the Bastrop grant as a colony for the wealthy. I was just looking at it, right over here on the table." He pointed to the maps, pinned flat by paperweights.

Margaret stood, shakily, and stepped to the table. She looked at the top map for a few seconds, then removed the paper weights on one side so that it rolled up, exposing the next map. "These other maps are what you need to be studying, Mr. Cumings," she said. "For these maps are the maps to Colonel Burr's heart."

Samuel had in fact examined the other two maps. One was of the northern provinces of New Spain, and the other was of the eastern seacoast of Mexico. "If Colonel Burr gets his way," Margaret continued, "we will never reach the Bastrop lands. We will be part of an invading force of Mexico! My poor husband, who cannot see across the room—who abhors bloodshed—is not the kind of man to participate in something like that. And yet, thanks to me, he has sunk our entire fortune in it!" She stared dolefully and then repeated, "Our sin has come home to us!" Covering her face with the handkerchief, she began to cry again.

Without thinking, Samuel blurted out: "What sin? In heaven's name, what are you talking about?"

Margaret lowered the handkerchief and studied him with red-rimmed eyes. She heaved a great sigh.

"Harman Blennerhassett, my beloved husband for nearly ten years—the sweetest, kindest man I know, the father of my two wonderful children—is also my mother's brother. He and I are uncle and niece.

"He fell in love with me from our first encounter as adults, when he came to escort me home from school in England. We were married before we even saw my parents. I was very young, and yet, within me, I knew it was not quite right. But dear Harman, who never saw any wrong in it, took the full blame as he was considerably older. In spite of that, my father disinherited me.

"We sold the Blennerhassett property and came to the United States. I feared that the social circles of even this remote little country would somehow learn our secret. So we continued west, as far west as was safe, and discovered the island. And we have been wonderfully happy here for years. It is truly a paradise, and I had reconciled myself to—" Here she stopped abruptly, then continued.

"Well, along came Colonel Burr, with what seemed like an answer to our financial problems and—and to my own little conceits. And now we have mortgaged our holdings, we are reviled and persecuted by our neighbors, and we must travel thousands of miles through the wilderness, prey to the ravages of winter, wild beasts and Indians! All because of our sin!"

Suddenly, the study door flew open. Through it, as Samuel sprang awkwardly to his feet, burst Harman Blennerhassett. The younger man's face turned crimson. Even eyesight as weak as Blennerhassett's should have revealed enough to provoke him to wrath. But he was full of his own news.

"Margaret, dear!" he exclaimed in a tone of great agitation. "The Ohio authorities have seized our boats on the Muskingum! The president has apparently issued some statement to the effect that our expedition is a threat to the nation and must be stopped! I also understand that the militia is organizing to take over the island. We must leave tonight!"

Chapter 27

*E*arly December of 1806 found Gen. James Wilkinson in frenzied control of New Orleans: intimidating civilian authorities, spreading rumors, erecting fortifications, commandeering private property, jailing accused conspirators without magisterial authority. All the while, the general pleaded and bellowed for reinforcements to help resist the thousands of armed fanatics who he insisted were swarming down the Mississippi in the company of Aaron Burr.

Just after midnight on December 11, Burr's actual forces numbered fewer than a hundred men, huddled in four boats clandestinely launched from Blennerhassett's Island into the icy waters of the Ohio. Meanwhile, their spiritual leader was hundreds of miles away, traveling to Tennessee to call on Andrew Jackson for further financial assistance.

The boats were lashed together in twos, one pair trailing the other by a few lengths. In the lead tandem, Samuel Cumings occupied one bow while a sharp-eyed Burr lieutenant named Comfort Tyler rode opposite him in the other.

The decision to flee under cover of night was not birthed by idle fears. Shortly before dusk, word reached the island that warrants were out for the arrests of Blennerhassett and Tyler, and that the Wood County militia planned a dawn raid.

A bone-chilling drizzle had replaced the snowfall of the day before. It further curtailed visibility, already poor on this overcast night, making even more difficult the challenge facing the flotilla and its pilot. The crews could not risk using any light, as sentinels from the militia of two states were doubtless posted atop the river bluffs. The oars were stacked to avoid noise; only the silent current propelled the boats. Samuel and Tyler strained their eyes and ears to detect any hazards that lay ahead. In addition, Samuel used a long sweep, suspended from the bow by a loop in the painter, to probe the water.

It was impossible for upwards of one hundred men to remain totally quiet while gliding over the amplifying surface of the river. Still, outside of occasional coughs and shuffling of numbed feet, they did remarkably well. Samuel soon grew irritated with the continued sniffling on the part of Blennerhassett, who sat close behind him. There arose in the breast of the river pilot a feeling of contempt only lightly laced with pity. The Irishman was probably bemoaning his newly acquired fugitive status, and belatedly second-guessing his decision to ransom the family assets and bankroll this bizarre venture into the unknown.

In fact, shortly before they launched, Blennerhassett appeared to have lost his wits.

Despite his urging, Margaret steadfastly refused to accompany him and expose their young sons to the elements and other perils of an open boat. Finally, to the embarrassment of those around him, the lord of the island broke into tears. At this juncture, Samuel boldly volunteered his brother John to look after Blennerhassett's family until a more suitable craft became available. "Take them to Belpre tonight," Samuel quietly instructed John. "There they have friends who will put them up. They shouldn't be on the island when the militia drops in."

So Harman Blennerhassett, born into a noble family of ample means and raised as a gentleman, found himself in the unseemly position of a patrician thrown in among plebeians. He sat shivering in the rainy darkness, a marked enemy of the republic, drifting away from his family and his mortgaged paradise.

Samuel's major navigational hurdle, simple enough by day but complicated by the murky darkness and the need for stealth, consisted of safely passing a small island several miles below Blennerhassett's. He recalled the advice in his notes: "Channel about the middle of the river between the head of the island and the shore to the right side; when half way down run close in to the shore to avoid a little bar at the foot of the island, and when opposite the point bear out to the middle of the river to avoid sawyers."

The feat was accomplished by prearranged signals. When at last Samuel and Tyler spotted the dark mass of the island, Tyler imitated the cry of an owl. Oars were eased into the water and both pairs of boats swung toward the right-hand shore. Once they drew even with the foot of the island, the same signal was used, and the boats were directed back toward the middle of the river. Everyone held his breath in dread of crashing into the sawyers—fallen trees with one end mired in the riverbed, their twisted members posing a ripping, gouging menace to boat hulls. The flotilla, however, incurred only a couple of harmless scrapes.

The fugitives rode the current until daybreak. Then, seeing no evidence of pursuit along the bluffs or on the river behind them, they separated the boats, broke out the paddles and, in single file, resumed the journey.

By afternoon of the third day, Samuel began to recognize friendly surroundings. Soon he spotted the familiar outline of Brush Creek Island looming downstream. As they passed by the island there was no sign of the floating mill; it had been disassembled for the winter. In a few minutes, the boats were crunching through the light ice formed around Singletary's Landing. Samuel, Thomas, and Tully Fenwick were back, however briefly, in New Ephrata.

Nimrod Ellison had long since become wrinkled and silver-haired. But as he approached the landing, Samuel thought the long-time family friend looked especially old and worn.

Flashing Ellison a wave and a smile, Samuel asked, "Ready to sell us some boats? We expect more men to join us downriver."

No smile came from the cooper, whose normally clear gray eyes seemed dull. "Howdy, Samuel," he said quietly. "I see Thomas over there. Where's John?" Even as he spoke, he beckoned to Thomas to join them.

An icy tingle not born of the weather ran down Samuel's spine. "John's coming in a day or so," he responded. "What's wrong, Mr. Ellison?"

Thomas sauntered up, some flippant word of salutation dying unspoken as he sensed an air of somberness.

"Boys," Ellison said, looking at one and then the other, "I'm afraid your pa's gone to be with the Lord. Passed away in his sleep. We buried him just yesterday, not havin' any idea how close you was to bein' back here." Tears welled up in his eyes, and he briefly hugged the younger men to him. Samuel choked back a sob, while Thomas turned red-faced and bit his lip, staring at the ground.

"Another thing, Thomas," Ellison continued in a kindly tone. "Your Mary's havin' a bit of a problem with her child-bearin'. You might want t' go see her before you see your ma."

Thomas stumbled off over the snow, hastily wiping his cheeks.

"How is Ma doing?" Samuel asked in a husky voice.

"You know, Sammy, we've seen some wondrous things since we been here in New Ephrata," Ellison responded softly. "But I've not seen the likes of your ma. She's cried some, sure, but she has mostly sung hymns and has been a comfort and blessin' to those around her. Nancy and your little boy were over at your ma's house a short time ago. They might still be there."

After an explanatory word to Blennerhassett, Samuel carefully ascended the icy river bank and began what seemed to be a very long trek to his parents' log home. Sympathetically, he thought of Tony. Times came when it was not at all glorious to be the first-born. And, at the other extreme, six-year-old Robert would have only limited memories of his father. The twin girls, Rebecca and Sarah, were just a year older than Robert. William and James, one just emerged from his teen years and the other still in them, might be hit hardest of all.

Samuel reached the front steps, wiped his eyes, heaved a mighty sigh, and knocked.

Rebekah Cumings opened the door, tentatively at first, then swung it wide after recognizing her caller. There was a long embrace, and tears shed, but the sobs were stifled. Short-legged Robert and the twin girls, both almost a head taller than he, swarmed around Samuel and demanded that he pick each of them up "to get some lovin'." While thus occupied, Samuel briefly told his mother about the trip from Blennerhassett's Island, and assured her that John was fine.

"Where are Tony and William and James?" he asked.

"James has gone to the stockpile for firewood," she answered. "Tony and William are hunting. So, as you can see, my young men are taking good care of me." She took his hand and clasped it between her own work-worn hands.

"Your father," she began, her voice trembling, "was very proud of you. He thought this expedition must be an important event, what with the men who are involved in it. In fact," she added, with a ghost of a smile, "he was a little put out with Reverend Craig for inferring that Colonel Burr might be anything less than a patriot."

Rebekah squeezed her son's hand tightly. "What I'm getting to, Samuel," she said, her voice now strong and warm, "is that I want you to complete your work with this expedition. It is what your father would have wanted. Thomas, of course, needs to stay here with Mary because of her difficulties, but his part in the expedition isn't as important. Your brothers are taking good care of me, and we will also look after Nancy and little Will for you. I don't even know whether you have considered not completing the trip, but please finish it . . . for yourself and your father.

"Now, go to your family, and be with them for whatever length of time you have here."

"It's just overnight, Ma. But I'll be back."

There was one last hug, a final tear or two, and Samuel found himself trudging toward his own home in the gathering dusk. He did not see the giant, habit-clad figure standing under the branches of a nearby cedar. After Samuel was out of sight, David Singletary, still erect and powerful at eighty-plus years of age, stepped away from the tree and knocked at Rebekah's door.

When it opened, Singletary pushed back his cowl. Pale blue eyes stared straight into the face of the surprised Rebekah as he announced in a rumbling voice, "I am sent to comfort the widows and orphans. May I come in?"

Singletary placed one large foot onto the threshold, but Rebekah did not step back. Nor did she release her hold on the door. Green eyes narrowed, she coolly returned his bold gaze.

"There are no orphans here, Father David," she said, using the community's stock salutation of Singletary with a touch of insolence. "And One greater than any of us has already sent me His holy comforter. Who has sent you? Mrs. Singletary?"

It was Singletary who stepped back, making an effort to control his surge of anger at this rebuke. "I only thought . . ." he began.

"I believe that I understand your thoughts," Rebekah interrupted, "and I further believe that you should leave my doorstep and turn your thoughts toward home."

Without waiting for a reply, she closed the door and shot the bolt. Singletary slammed fist into open palm, and bellowed, "I will not be mocked!" He yanked his cowl over his head and stalked off.

A few dozen yards away, he encountered James, manfully pulling a sled laden with firewood. Singletary ignored the youth's breathless greeting and stiffly marched past him.

It was five days before Christmas, but Aaron Burr was not in a festive mood. He sat with Andrew Jackson at a small table in a Nashville hotel room, listening to the general and scarcely believing his ears.

"It's finished, Colonel," Jackson was saying. "The Mexican thing is up in smoke! Tarnation, man, there's probably a dozen warrants out for your arrest! The president's seen to that. I never suspected just how scared of you he must be.

"You can take the two boats I've already built, but that's all I'm contributin' to this. My advice to you is to either scrap the whole project or head for the Ouachita River and develop your Bastrop holdings. I'm afraid, though, you'll be hauled in by some eager somebody before you even get to Natchez."

Chapter 28

*A*t long last, the leader of the expedition was about to meet up with his forces, on a little island where the Cumberland River emptied into the Ohio. The rendezvous was due at a time when the prospects for success were not encouraging.

The sky continued to be full of winter storms. When it wasn't snowing or sleeting, a chilly drizzle usually set in. Ice had formed on the river's backwaters and in some of the shallows, and there was ample evidence that the weather would only worsen.

Despite Samuel's efforts to explain the process involved in navigating the Falls of the Ohio—in actuality only a sloping series of fierce rapids—one of the boats had somehow entered the wrong chute, floundered, and was beaten apart against the rocks. Miraculously, everyone aboard was plucked alive from the icy water, but the boat and its provisions were lost. So, while two new boats had been added at New Ephrata, one at Cincinnati, and two more at Louisville, only eight boats made it to the mouth of the Cumberland.

The number of adventurers had likewise fluctuated. Men joined the expedition at Maysville, Cincinnati, and Louisville, but the unrelenting winter storms and the growing notoriety of the enterprise caused defections along the way. Fewer than ninety hardy souls were now on hand awaiting Burr's appearance.

After two days on the island, Harman Blennerhassett became alarmed over the failure of his family to appear. In particular, he feared for their safety in descending the falls. Samuel reasoned with him that John would not have settled for anything less than a ship-shape craft for Mrs. Blennerhassett and the boys, and that navigating the falls was an accomplished art among rivermen. He omitted the fact that John was not a riverman.

Finally arriving at the island three days before the new year, Burr first conferred privately with Comfort Tyler and then called a get-acquainted session. He made the rounds of the recruits, individually shaking hands and asking names.

Samuel suspected that, before the briefing from Tyler, the colonel had known nothing of the events and rumors which prompted the hasty departure from Blennerhassett's Island. Burr's composure, when only minutes later he addressed the assemblage on those topics and others, was remarkable. Once again, he proved himself master of the situation.

"I personally apologize," he said, in a strong, reassuring way, "for the actions of my political enemies in creating the confusion and concerns which led to your early start on this expedition. There are, unfortunately, certain men who have willingly circulated rumors and untruths in order to damage me.

"Among these despicable rumors is one to the effect that Mr. Blennerhassett and I conspired to cause a separation of the western states from the balance of the country. There is not now, nor has there ever been, any seed of truth to that allegation. In fact, I have just come from a conference with General Jackson, before whom I solemnly pledged anew my oath of allegiance to our country. In return, the general sent with me the two fine boats you see here now."

Burr resumed walking among the men, looking each one in the eye as he passed. "You have also heard about the prospect of our participating in a liberation of the downtrodden citizens of Mexico, should there prove to be ample provocation to intercede. At present, I am inclined to believe we are unlikely to see that eventuality any time soon."

He knew only too well the validity of that last statement. On his way down the Cumberland from Nashville, the colonel, to his consternation, had learned about the establishment of the neutral ground between the Sabine and the Arroyo Hondo. While it illustrated General Wilkinson's fine diplomatic skills, the episode also clearly indicated that Wilkinson was suddenly unwilling to create an incident with Spain.

News of the general's frenetic activities in New Orleans had not yet reached the Ohio Valley.

"The purpose remaining before us," Burr continued, "is the colonization of the Bastrop lands in Louisiana.

"The Baron de Bastrop—who despite his title is not French, but rather is a Dutchman—some years ago received from the Spanish government in Louisiana a grant of more than a million American acres on the Ouachita River. His bargain was to settle five hundred families there, and to receive an exclusive right to flour milling for that locale.

"There was disagreement and squabbling among the Spanish authorities as to the wisdom of this pact, thus preventing the baron from completing his prescribed performance. Then came the purchase of Louisiana by our nation, and Bastrop's scheme fell into complete disarray. Through a series of transactions, I have acquired ownership to about a third of the original grant, and it is this land that I propose to colonize."

Burr then painted an inspired oral picture of the advantages of the Ouachita River bottom lands. He reminded his men of the 150 acres each would receive upon doing his part to render the land habitable. This exhortation completed, he offered a parting wave and retired with Tyler and Blennerhassett onto his keelboat.

The performance by Burr (for so it was) had the desired effect, lifting the spirits of the venture's participants. For Samuel, though, there was stinging disappointment at the colonel's glib denial of his efforts to split the nation. Etched in detail in Samuel's memory was the nocturnal conversation he had overheard on Blennerhassett's Island.

New Year's Eve found the expedition entering the Mississippi River, and bows soon pointed south toward New Orleans. According to Burr's map, they must descend the Father of Waters to the Red River, near Baton Rouge, then ascend that tributary to the Black River and, finally, the Ouachita. Samuel asked Burr about the prospects of a portage from the Mississippi to the Black, eliminating nearly a week of travel. The colonel responded that the boats were too large and too heavily weighted with provisions to make a portage.

The flotilla crossed the imaginary line between Tennessee and the Mississippi Territory. Several days later, Burr, joined by Tyler and a couple of his other confidants, utilized a swift bateau to precede the main body of boats down the river. After hours of searching the eastern shore of the Mississippi, they located the mouth of the Bayou Pierre.

Their ultimate objective was to find the rambling, comfortable house of Judge Peter Bruin, a member of the territorial tribunal and a longtime ally of Burr. Soon after entering the bayou, the bateau was fighting through shards of ice to reach the judge's pier.

The former vice president would shortly have ample cause to remember this day above many others.

In addition to hot buttered rum and warm bread, Judge Bruin offered his visitors a copy of the Natchez newspaper. From it, the incredulous Burr gleaned that General Wilkinson had shared the decoded contents of the Burr cipher letter with President Jefferson, and that the president had shared it with Congress as well as the nation's reading public. In fact, passages of the damning document were reprinted in the newspaper columns.

Then the stricken colonel was told by Bruin about Wilkinson's military takeover of New Orleans and of his histrionic assurances that Burr and an army of thousands would soon attack the Crescent City.

The worst blow, delivered in as cushioned a manner as the old magistrate could manage, was verification that the acting governor of the Mississippi Territory, responding to orders from Washington, had issued a proclamation ordering the arrests of the "Burr conspirators."

"On what possible charge?" Burr inquired weakly of his host.

"As I understand it," Bruin responded, "for 'designs unfriendly to the peace and welfare of the Territories of Mississippi and Orleans.' But I am afraid, my dear friend, that the implication is treason."

A moment of flabbergasted silence overtook his listeners. Then Burr, ever able to bounce back from adversity, managed to find grim humor in the situation. Wilkinson, the consummate Judas, had weighed his alternatives and had chosen to freshen the fading favor of Jefferson by betraying Burr. And to silence forever the sacrificial lamb, the general had somehow engineered a charge which carried with it a trip to the gallows.

When, on the following day, the flotilla reached the mouth of Bayou Pierre, there awaited the travelers an order from Burr to encamp at the first favorable site on the Louisiana side of the river. The message did not include any explanation, nor did it divulge when Burr might rejoin the expedition.

Blennerhassett, temporarily distracted from worrying about his family, seized upon the truth. "We must be wanted men in the Mississippi Territory," he lamented.

They found a patch of relatively high and dry Louisiana ground a mile or so below Bayou Pierre, studded with grotesque cypress trees clad in Spanish moss.

At temperatures well below freezing, sleet mingled with ice fell continuously in the river bottom for two days and nights. The resulting glaze encased every limb of every tree in the great forests crowding the Mississippi. The long strips of moss congealed into titanic batches of icicles reaching to the earth. Under this crushing weight the forest giants dropped limbs, or were split down the trunk, and did so with such frequency and number that the sounds of grinding and snapping wood were almost constant. The river itself grew heavier and heavier with ice. In all, the scene was more reminiscent of Siberia than of the sunny South.

Burr did not appear, personally or vicariously, during this time. But there was great relief in the meantime for Samuel and Blennerhassett, due to the tardy arrival of refugees from the mortgaged island. They included Margaret Blennerhassett and her sons, who after nearly a month in the tireless care of John Cumings were safely delivered to the head of their uprooted household.

Samuel embraced John and led him over to one of several roaring fires the expeditionists kept kindled around the clock. He filled his younger brother in on the events of the journey between Blennerhassett's Island and New Ephrata. Then Samuel hesitated and began fumbling with his words.

"If you're tryin' to figure out how to tell me about Pa," John said quickly, "it's okay. I already know. We stopped there for provisions. It was pretty hard t' take. But I knew I had to stay with the Blennerhassetts. I wasn't too sure about the other men in our boat . . . trustin' them, I mean. Besides, you and he"—John indicated Harman Blennerhassett, who was still hugging his sons—"were dependin' on me to get them here. I thought sometimes we'd never catch up with you."

Samuel nodded. "We were concerned about you, too. I wondered whether you might have had trouble at the falls."

John shook his head. "Naw. Luckily, some o' the men knew how to get through them. It was a little scary, because big chunks of ice were bouncin' around as we came down the chute.

"No, the delay was all in gettin' away from the island. Samuel, the Blennerhassetts' house and grounds are ruined. The militia from Virginia is a herd of soulless pigs. There's no other description for 'em that will do. I feel badly for Mrs. Blennerhassett.

"By the way," he added, lowering his voice, "she certainly thinks highly of you." He smiled at the sudden redness in his brother's face.

"What do you mean about the house?" Samuel asked brusquely.

John's smile faded. "You'll remember," he said, "tellin' me t' take the family to Belpre. We did just that, and went on to Marietta the next mornin' to see about locatin' a suitable boat. We saw the confiscated boats Mr. Blennerhassett had ordered built. But there was nothin' to be had for our use.

"Finally, Mrs. Blennerhassett insisted on goin' back to the island, so we did. The militia was there, and they promptly put us under arrest. They had almost destroyed the place. Someone had found the wine cellar, and I never before saw such a bunch of belligerent drunkards. The commandin' officer was absent; once your escape was discovered, he took some of his veterans and rode down the Virginia side of the river as far as Point Pleasant. I guess they never saw you.

"Meanwhile, the drunken louts he left behind were breakin' the furniture, puttin' their bayonets into the walls, and eatin' and sleepin' where they pleased. They turned out the livestock, and the grounds were soon a trampled mess.

"I had to tolerate bein' arrested, o' course. At least, until one of the men began payin' too much attention to Mrs. B. I'm afraid I have t' confess, Samuel," John confided, his smile returning, "that as soon as th' opportunity presented itself, I put that gentleman into a deep sleep. Mrs. B. hid me out in the attic when his comrades came lookin' for me.

"Thankfully, they were distracted by the arrival of several more boats, includin' the one we later left in. These boats were manned by some of Comfort Tyler's recruits from New York, who o' course were immediately placed under arrest. For three days I hid out while the militia held a mock trial for the New Yorkers and did lots of other drunken, insane things. Finally, the commandin' officer returned, and I must say he was furious at what he found. He personally apologized to Mrs. B., for whatever good that did.

"I came out o' hidin' and we were free to leave. Only six of the New Yorkers were willin' to try and catch up with the expedition. We all boarded one boat under the command of a Mr. Butter, and here we are."

Samuel picked up the thread of his own narrative, and concluded by recalling a remark of Blennerhassett's. "He apparently believes," Samuel said of the Irishman, "that Colonel Burr had us camp on this side of the river because we are all wanted by the authorities in the Mississippi Territory."

"But what for?" John asked, and Samuel had no answer.

That evening, Comfort Tyler arrived in camp after a hazardous crossing of the frigid river. He had only one order, and it was carried out immediately. Half of the muskets brought by the expedition were gathered up and placed in a single boat. The craft was taken to the middle of the river, where a hole was punched in its bottom. With a sense of foreboding, Samuel and John witnessed this act, which evidenced admission of some vaguely defined guilt.

Chapter 29

Dearest Nancy—

First of all, I am writing to let you know that I am safe &
sound. However, our expedition has met with an untimely end,
we having gotten no farther than a few miles above Natchez on
the Mississippi R. where we are now encamped. If there be good
news from this turn of events, it is that I shall prob'ly be returning to New Ephrata by the Summer.

Col. Burr's enemies have proven to be powerful. When we
reached this Vicinity about the middle of January, the Col. learned
he was being arrested for treason against the Nation. He parleyed
with the Mississippi Territory Officials over the terms of his surrender and the arrests of all other members of the expedition.
Doubtless, he believed no jury would indict him, due to the
absence of any evidence, and that we could then freely resume our
journey to the Bastrop Lands.

Altho he was right about the jury, the Col. failed to reckon
with the power of President Jefferson, who is determined to see
him to the gibbet. The Territorial prosecutor and the jurors
assembled to hear the case against Col. Burr found no evidence to
merit a trial, but the judge denied him release from his bond anyway. It is also believed that the hand of Gen. Wilkinson, who (it
is said) has good reason to silence the Col., can be seen in the
unfair action of the judge.

Last night, Col. Burr presented himself at our camp, very
briefly, to assure us that we will come to no harm. "I am the man
whom Jefferson and Wilkinson are after," he said. He advised us
that we may be compelled to give statements, and asked us only
to tell the truth. In truth, we know little to tell. He wished us
well, and said that all who desire to go on to the Bastrop Lands

will have his assistance in laying claim to their promised share of the property.

Men are strange, fickle creatures. In the Col.'s absence, he was roundly cursed by many of the expedition, and there were others who deserted. Yet, last night, after he had done speaking, we all stood as one and gave him a rousing ovation. Tears were in the eyes of some as he departed. Tho he did not say so, I am sure the Col. is fleeing the country, most likely to Florida to ask sanctuary from those against whom he really did plot—the Spanish.

The weather is still very bad, but the snow has turned to rain. Once we are done with the Authorities, and the mud has had a chance to dry, John & Tully Fenwick & I intend to start up the Trace for home. Please pass this news on to Mother & Tully's folks. I love you and miss you & Little Will.

Samuel.

Even before the letter left Samuel's possession, it became outdated in one respect. The same evening that he finished, folded, and sealed the epistle with wax, John came and urged him to consider a new adventure.

"Tully and I are goin' to stake our claims on the Bastrop Lands," his younger brother said excitedly. "We want you t' come along and make yours, too. All together, we'd have 450 acres and a decent start. We've already packed us some provisions, and Mr. Blennerhassett is allowin' us t' take one of the bateaus. We plan on leavin' right away—tonight—before we're further detained by th' authorities."

Samuel immediately found issue with the proposal. "You may have a hard go in establishing a legal claim to the property," he warned. "It is my suspicion that making future contact with Colonel Burr will be difficult for a long time to come."

John chuckled. "You're probably right, brother," he acknowledged. "That very thought led me t' secure a letter from Mr. Blennerhassett. It says that he an' the colonel were equal partners in the colonizin' scheme, and that he owns half o' the Bastrop Lands. It further assigns Tully, me, an' you full ownership of 150 acres each. Come on, brother! We need a good pilot for our bateau!"

Anger welled up inside Samuel, but he did not argue further. Surely, Blennerhassett recognized the worthlessness of such an unsubstantiated claim. His letter was hardly worth the time he'd taken to compose it. Then again, the man's common sense always seemed open to question. "I hereby give you my 150 acres," Samuel finally said. "As for me, I intend to start for home as soon as the Trace dries out."

John was subdued for a moment, disappointed that his older brother was passing up this fresh adventure. Finally, he said matter-of-factly, "In that case, I'd like for you t' put into writin' that you're givin' us your share." Samuel stared at him, then grinned and reached for his makeshift pen and ink. Their father had remarked more than once that John showed some of the shrewdness of Uncle James when it came to business dealings.

After Samuel had scribbled a short missive to satisfy John, the latter accepted it with a word of thanks. Then, the boyish smile reclaiming his face, John said in a low voice, "While Mr. B. was occupied with writin' his letter for us, Mrs. B. quiet-like dashed off one o' her own and asked me t' make sure you received it. Here it is."

Samuel's hand trembled as he received the folded piece of foolscap. He laid it aside and hugged John. "Be very careful, brother," he said tenderly. "The Holy Spirit be with you." In a few seconds John had departed, and Samuel returned his attention to the unexpected communique.

It was brief. The Blennerhassetts, Margaret wrote, would be temporarily locating in Natchez. As soon as the unpleasant business with the Mississippi officials was completed, Harman intended to travel to Lexington on business, then go on to the island to assess the likelihood of returning there. The letter read in closing:

> John tells me that you may go on to the Bastrop Lands. I wish you God-speed. Please accept my gratitude for your and John's thousand kindnesses, and know that I will always be overjoyed to learn of your good fortune.

There was no signature.

Samuel found himself unashamedly elated over the usage of "I" in place of the less explicit, less personal "we." In the weeks since Margaret's arrival in camp, they had avoided all but the lightest of conversations. There was, though, no mistaking the mutuality and the depth of their feelings. Margaret Blennerhassett without silk dress, flashing jewelry, or cloud of perfume was as attractive as ever to Samuel. And what she carefully chose to say (and not say) in the brief letter spoke joyous volumes to him.

Neither person intended to act further on those feelings. Sharing them tacitly would have to suffice.

Burr did flee the Mississippi Territory. He was soon captured and hustled off to be tried for treason in Richmond, Virginia. Nor did Harman Blennerhassett escape further ignominy. While in Lexington, he was arrested and charged as a co-conspirator and was whisked away to Richmond.

The trial of Burr proved to be a unique exercise, presided over by U.S. Supreme Court Chief Justice John Marshall and further distinguished by one of the great assemblages of legal minds in recorded American history. As an overflow crowd and a jury headed by John Randolph listened intently, the sides battled each other and the sweltering summer heat for more than three months. Jefferson stayed away from Richmond, though he did all he could from afar to seal Burr's doom.

On September 1, 1807, Burr was found not guilty, but the equivocal language of the verdict left the former vice president frustrated and angry. It also left him under a cloud of mistrust he would never fully shake. Burr's immediate anguish, however, could not match that of Jefferson, who depended in vain on the pompous, unconvincing Wilkinson as his star witness. That worthy would later manage a narrow escape from a court-martial called to examine his own activities.

After the president's big fish got away, Blennerhassett was released without having to stand trial. Attempting to recoup his squandered fortune, the Irishman in 1808 purchased a thousand acres north of Natchez near Port Gibson, even as Wilkinson was settling in Natchez. For four years, Blennerhassett successfully grew and ginned cotton on his plantation, named La Cache, but then he fell victim to a suddenly adverse economic climate with the advent of the War of 1812. After eight additional years of financial struggles at La Cache, the family removed to Montreal, Canada, there faring no better while Blennerhassett tried to establish a law practice.

Blennerhassett's Island fell into other, less careful hands. One summer night in 1811, reportedly as a result of the carelessness of slaves, the empty mansion was lost to fire. For years thereafter, the great twin chimneys stood naked, overseeing the burnt, uncleared rubble of the once happy home as it gradually slipped into the viney grasp of Nature.

A story was told for decades by the impressionable inhabitants of Grand Gulf, a small Mississippi River port community serving the plantations above the Natchez district. Each year for many years, around the middle of April, a beautiful lady on horseback would begin making her appearance at the Grand Gulf docks. These visits were often repeated over several days. She arrived at midmorning, well dressed regardless of sunshine or shower, seated side saddle with riding crop and parasol in hand. Following a leisurely survey of the landing, and a short time spent in stretching her legs, she would ride away. Though she spoke with no one, gossip had it that she was the wife of a Port Gibson plantation owner.

After several recurrences of this annual phenomenon, the sages of Grand Gulf came to understand that her appearance portended the eventual arrival of a certain keelboat flotilla from Kentucky. Even though the flotilla seldom loaded or unloaded much of value, it always remained at the landing for most of the day before tying up overnight at the mouth of Bayou Pierre, eight miles downriver.

Residents of Bruinsburg, located on the river just below Bayou Pierre, confirmed for their Grand Gulf neighbors that the captain of the flotilla invariably came ashore for a while before taking the flotilla downstream. This captain was always the same man, slimly built but broad of shoulder, with a riverman's ruddy complexion and black, curly hair. His jaunt afoot took him out of sight for an hour or so among the thick tangles of willows, poplars, and under-brush lining the river.

Once the flotilla had made its appearance at Grand Gulf, the beauty on horseback did not return to the landing until the following spring.

In April of 1815, Grand Gulf was visited for the first time by the *Paragon,* one of the newfangled, noisy, steam-driven vessels that were beginning to compete with the flatboats and keelboats for river trade. It was duly noted that the erstwhile skipper of the Kentucky keelboat flotilla was now the captain of this steamboat. Upon departing the docks, true to tradition, the steamboat nosed into the mouth of Bayou Pierre and was moored there for the night. The next day, the captain took his customary walk into the shadowy woods. The *Paragon* and its captain returned to perform this ritual the next April, and the next, and again the spring following.

The year the mystery rider finally failed to appear in Grand Gulf (a consensus of locals established it as 1819) the *Paragon* came steaming down the river but declined to stop, either at Grand Gulf or at the bayou. Never again did either the lady or that particular steamboat grace the little port with their presence.

In truth, no one from Grand Gulf or Bruinsburg ever claimed to have seen the horse rider and the riverman together, or even within the same vicinity of the tree-shrouded bayou. After all, the oldsters hinted, there were some things best left to the imagination.

Chapter 30

During the three years of his absence from New Ephrata, John Cumings lived the fullest of lives. He returned shortly before the winter of 1809, riding bareback on a little Texas mustang over the autumn glory of discarded Ohio Valley foliage. A gusting north wind was loosing the last dying leaves from their weakened moorings and flinging them, flipping and spiraling, onto the roadway carpet of russet and gold. Man and mount, buffeted and chilled all morning by the penetrating gusts, entered New Ephrata around noon.

Riding slowly through the village, John waved at a couple of familiar figures but did not stop. He made straight for the family home, unsure of what he would find.

Two of his brothers stood under a lean-to in the yard. Stoical Tony, now settled into the unwanted role as the man of the house, was demonstrating to James the artful process of skinning a deer and removing the venison. They glanced without recognition at the brown, buckskin-clad stranger seated Indian-style on the mustang.

"Lord-a-me, James, are those whiskers I spy on your face?" the horseman asked in a bantering tone. "Tony, looks like you need t' teach your younger brother how to skin his-self before botherin' to skin a deer." He slid off his horse with an easy, fluid motion.

"John!" they exclaimed as one. Tony grabbed John's hand and shook it vigorously, and pounded him on the shoulder. John playfully wrapped his left arm around James's blond head and squeezed the youngster against his side.

"Did my letter get here?" John inquired, shouting in order to be heard over the happy yells of James. "I sure hope so. How's Ma and everyone?"

"Yeah, your one an' only letter made it home," Tony quipped. In a more serious tone, he added, "We told the Fenwicks about Tully. They took it pretty hard."

John dropped his head. "So did I," he said softly, the words drowned out by James's noisy exuberance. "Hush, boy, or I'll wring your neck!" he admonished the lad with mock sternness.

"As for Ma," Tony said, grinning, "ask her yourself."

Rebekah Cumings stood in the open doorway of the house.

At fifty-two years of age, a widow for the last three, she looked remarkably fit. The gray in the pulled-back brown hair was definite but unobtrusive, as were the wrinkles around the eyes and under the chin. The trim frame spoke of quiet strength. But as John lowered his mother to her feet following a boisterous hug, he noticed something disconcerting—something that he had never before seen, lurking deep in her green eyes.

There was scant opportunity to reflect on it, as the twin girls, Becky and Sarah, pushed past their mother with attention-demanding squeals. Pale little Robert, now eight, peered with a bashful smile from behind a small fistful of Rebekah's skirt.

John's letter had arrived home in the summer of the year previous. It was short, considering the elapsed time since his departure; travels in Louisiana and Texas were referred to in a paucity of detail. He was, he wrote, living "with friends" in Upper Louisiana. The main news in the epistle was that he was alive and well—and that Tully Fenwick was not.

A couple of days after his homecoming, John told a full gathering of the Cumings clan something of what he did and saw during the years of his absence.

Harman Blennerhassett, in giving John and Tully his bateau for their journey to the Bastrop Lands, had included a map showing the route, annotated in his own hand. Far up the Ouachita River, on the right-hand side, the Irishman had scribbled "Fort Miro." Above this notation was a vast expanse of land, carefully labeled, "Bastrop Lands—Spanish Grant to Baron De Bastrop." Here appeared more scribbling: "Purchased by Burr, 1805."

Winter drizzle gave way to full-blown spring rains while the

Kentuckians struggled against the currents of three consecutive rivers to reach the spot marked Fort Miro. The long, hard journey was made through country as desolate as it was damp. However, when finally they neared their destination, signs of life began to spring up on the Ouachita shores. In some cases, families occupied what were doubtless intended as temporary quarters: tents, over-turned boats, and primitive huts assembled from the wood of boats and wagons. John and Tully surmised that these campers were the recipients of land grants located in the dense forests, from whence came the ring of axes signifying menfolk hard at work on more permanent dwellings.

There appeared on the east bank a pleasant-looking farmstead of considerable age. Vestiges remained of wooden palisades which once may have enclosed the farmhouse and its outbuildings. Thinking this to be Fort Miro, John and Tully brought the bateau to shore and approached the house. They saw no sign of soldiers. In fact, the only person in sight was a sharp-eyed old man who nursed a corncob pipe while propelling his rocking chair slowly and contentedly on the front porch.

The travelers' conversation with him yielded little in the way of comforting news.

Their interviewee was a mustachioed Frenchman named Filhiol, who said he had served as the commandant of Fort Miro for most of the years that Louisiana belonged to Spain. His farmstead, in fact, had been utilized as the fort until the transfer of the territory to the United States. A new post—not very well constructed, the Frenchman opined—could be found upstream on the same bank. Some miles east of this new fort lay the plantation of a Colonel Morhouse. The colonel, Filhiol informed them, dark eyes glittering under bushy brows, was who they needed to call on if they intended to purchase land.

"Those you saw encamped below," he said without enthusiasm, "they are buying land from the colonel." Monsieur Filhiol, it was obvious, did not approve of these new neighbors.

Tully, always the impetuous one, volunteered the information that he and John already held claims to property in the vicinity of Fort Miro. "We received them by virtue of our service to Colonel Aaron Burr, late vice president of the United States," he said importantly.

Filhiol removed his pipe and spat—a purely coincidental act, no doubt. "I do not know this Burr," came the Frenchman's astonishing rejoinder. "Where is his land?"

The young men exchanged glances. "I'll fetch the map, and Mr. Blennerhassett's letter," John offered. In a few moments, the map had been spread open on the porch. Tully pointed to the area labeled Bastrop Lands. "Our property is somewhere within that grant," he said with boyish confidence. "Colonel Burr bought it from the Baron de Bastrop—or, more correctly, he got it from someone who the baron had sold it to."

The retired commandant's laugh was scornful. "Bastrop!" he exclaimed. "The Dutchman who has the French title, who speaks Dutch, French, Spanish, and English, all so beautiful! My boys, my boys! He sold this so-called grant more than once, and I do not believe he ever really owned it."

Seeing the alarm on the faces of his young listeners, Filhiol knew that he had made his point. In a more kindly fashion, he elaborated on the subject of the Bastrop Lands.

The baron, he said, had been very well connected when he first came to the Ouachita Valley a few years before the turn of the century. Carondelet, governor of Spanish Louisiana, granted Bastrop the use of more than a million acres for the purpose of developing a colony. "This colony," Filhiol said pointedly, "was seen as a way to keep the American adventurers and hunters out of Louisiana." Bastrop was empowered by Carondelet to deed up to four hundred acres to every family he brought in, plus a like amount to each male child who achieved majority.

His contract called for Bastrop to settle five hundred families within three years. In return, Filhiol said, the baron received the exclusive right to mill and sell flour to the colonists, as well as to market it to Havana and elsewhere. "I do not know," he emphasized, "that Bastrop was ever deeded the land for his own, or any part of it except where the flour mills were built." Regardless, the Frenchman continued, the baron's plans were undone when Carondelet was promoted to another governmental office and departed New Orleans. His successor, Governor Gayoso, decided that the cost to the government of relocating and grubstaking the colonists (conditions agreed to by Carondelet) was too great, and he terminated the aid. Without this help, Bastrop could not perform his part of the bargain, and Gayoso ultimately declared the contract with Bastrop to be null and void.

This action, Filhiol said, foiled the baron's intended sale of the grant to Morhouse. The baron had borrowed against the property to finance his other business enterprises. Then came the acquisition of Louisiana by the United States, casting at least a temporary cloud over all land contracts made by the Spanish colonials.

"Still, I know that the Baron de Bastrop continued to treat the land as though it belonged to him," the Frenchman noted. "He sold it again, and maybe your Monsieur Burr purchased it from someone else in between. But I am afraid, my boys, you will find it very hard to prove your claims. You tell me you have nothing in writing from this Burr. And the letter from the gentleman with the strange name says much but really proves nothing.

"Morhouse is another who says he owns the Bastrop Lands, or a part of them," the Frenchman continued. "These unfortunates decorating our beautiful river banks, waiting to occupy their dream land, may be doomed to disappointment. At least, my boys, you did not pay good money to get nothing."

John sorted through his thoughts. He and Tully were a long way from home, and he hated the prospect of their hard journey being made for naught.

"Maybe," he ventured, "the Baron de Bastrop can help us. Do you know where we might find him?"

The Frenchman smiled. "After Governor Gayoso canceled the contract for the colony," he said, "the baron still had his flour mills to operate, and he enlisted as his partner a well-to-do merchant in New Orleans who financed him in building and stocking warehouses on the Ouachita. They wanted to control the trade here and with the Indians to the north and west. That failed, and the baron decided to cast his lot again with the Spaniards and moved to Texas. He lives there now."

Resignedly, Tully rolled up Blennerhassett's map while John thanked Filhiol for his time and information. Dejection was written all over them as they stepped from the porch. The Frenchman decided to share a final bit of information.

"Perhaps you should go to Natchitoches," he suggested, "and look up a man named Nancarrow. Summer before last, the baron came back here for a while and tried to get some of his old colonists to move to Texas. He promised them free land if they would go. They had no interest in his proposal, because they have not yet grown unhappy with being back in the United States.

"You might like Texas. I do not know where Bastop lives, but this man Nancarrow has been a business partner of the baron and handles his remaining affairs in the United States.

"I have two fine horses available. For you they will not cost very much, if also you leave me the little bateau."

Despite the warnings about hostile Indians and ruthless highwaymen, the young Kentuckians succumbed to the lure of Texas. Bearing business papers sent by John Nancarrow of Natchitoches to the Baron de Bastrop at Bexar, John and Tully rode the winding Camino Real for more than four hundred miles. They crossed the Sabine, Neches, Trinity, Brazos, Colorado, and Guadalupe rivers. The wooded, rolling hills teemed with game and glistened with April wildflowers. As they made their way west, the travelers were favorably struck by the ever-increasing openness of the terrain.

"Fewer rocks t' dig up than in Kentucky, less timber to clear than in Louisiana," John commented to Tully.

"I could really come t' like this country. Mr. Jefferson thinks we bought it, but the Spaniards claim it still belongs to them. Makes you wonder what kind of folks we're about to meet up with, an' what kind of a place Bexar is."

Chapter 31

*I*t was in May of 1718 that New Spain sent soldiers and churchmen trekking northward into the scrub-brush wilderness of South Texas. Finding a pleasant valley in which to settle, these agents of the Crown established a presidio and a Franciscan mission on the San Antonio River. Their avowed purposes were to convert to Catholicism the roving bands of fierce, pagan Indians and to provide a way station at midpoint between the interior of Mexico and New Spain's most remote missions in East Texas.

Mission San Antonio de Valero, which more than a century afterward achieved shrine status as the Alamo, was situated on the outside of an ox-bow bend in the river. About a mile upstream, on the opposite bank, the military arm of the expedition erected the Presidio San Antonio de Bexar. Four years later, the garrison was relocated directly across the river from the mission.

There was from the outset a civilian adjunct to the presidio. However, it took the arrival of Spanish subjects recruited from the Canary Islands to prompt the official creation and organization of a villa. San Fernando de Bexar, enabled by election in 1731, was the first formal civilian settlement of permanence in Texas.

By the time the Islanders arrived, there were four more missions situated up and down the San Antonio River. Each mission controlled large areas of open range and owned herds of angular longhorn cattle, valued as much for their hides as for their tough flesh.

This outpost, so small, so far from help, and so vulnerable to the hostile whims of the Apache and Comanche, somehow endured. It provided the nucleus for what would become San Antonio.

When the Baron de Bastrop moved there from Louisiana, it was commonly referred to simply as "Bexar."

Felipe Enrique Neri—or so the Baron de Bastrop had introduced himself—apologized to John and Tully for the sparse and humble furnishings of his newly purchased adobe cottage. As though to atone, he produced three fine goblets and a bottle of once-opened wine. "To our future friendship and success in business," the baron offered as a toast.

Thin to the point of gauntness, the middle-aged Neri nevertheless projected an imposing presence. He stood well over six feet. His long hair and lively eyes were complementary hues of gray, and from his chin projected a stiff, neatly trimmed beard of the same color. A curled mustache anchored his long, aristocratic nose—the latter no doubt the baron's finest facial feature.

Bastrop evidently held his personal appearance in higher regard than he did the furnishing of his home. He was clad in a long-tailed coat of bright blue, the waist-high front studded with rows of brass buttons. It was worn open, revealing a form-fitting gray vest and a high-collared shirt with carefully arranged black tie. A yellow cotton sash encircled the baron's slender waist. His gray "stove-pipe" pantaloons ended in stirrups slipped around brass-buckled shoes of polished leather.

After offering profuse thanks for the delivery of the papers from Nancarrow, Neri listened politely while Tully finished explaining the real reason for their visit.

"On the subject of land grants, whether in Louisiana or in Texas, I can no longer be of help," the baron confessed. "I sold my remaining interest in the Ouachita colony some years past, after a disappointing series of experiences. More recently, I failed to meet the requirements under which I could have settled many families in Texas on the Trinity River. Both setbacks, I might add, were due in some part to the unwanted influence of the United States government.

"Even had the Texas colony been successful," Neri added, "the two of you would not have been eligible to receive land or settle there. Spain wants to keep the Americans out, not bring them in. In fact, you do not know how close you were to being ordered out of Bexar, had you not shown the officials my papers as evidence of your business here."

His information caused the Kentuckians to feel weary, reviving the disappointment they had experienced during their interview with Filhiol—only keener at this juncture due to the additional investment in time and travel.

The baron easily read their thoughts. "Gentlemen," he asked, "do you not remember our toast?"

They looked at him blankly.

"I spoke of our future business success," Neri reminded them. "I have a proposal that I wish you to consider. The horses that brought you over the Camino Real are mustangs, yes? Greatly prized in the United States, I believe." After they nodded vaguely, he continued.

"I am petitioning the Spanish colonial authorities for permission to engage in trade with the Indians. These officials cannot help but be interested, because at present Americans are trading illegally with several of the tribes in Texas, and the Indians' pelts and money are leaving the province.

"It will do worse than no good to tell the Indians that they cannot trade with the Americans simply because it is against the laws of New Spain. The only hope of diverting this lost revenue is to match or better the Americans' prices. It will at first be difficult, because what the Indians now pay are New Orleans prices. New Spain cannot compete without enduring initial losses.

"Last year, I proposed to the governor of Texas that I be allowed to trade with the Indians, subsidizing my expected deficit by the export of Texas mustangs out of the province. These wild horses are plentiful, and as you have verified, the market for them in the United States continues to grow.

"I was turned down. My mistake, I believe, was in explaining how I intended to recoup my losses rather than leaving it to the imagination. My present petition before the governor does not speak to the issue of recovering costs."

Neri clasped his hands and leaned forward.

"It has occurred to me that there are two ways to do so. One is to very quietly round up, tame, and sell mustangs to the people of Louisiana and Mississippi. The second is to bring goods into

New Spain without declaring them for tariff. My proposition to you combines these two ideas."

John squirmed uneasily, but said nothing. Tully's eyes were shining with expectation.

"I have mercantile connections in Louisville," the baron continued. "They are interested in shipping trade goods downriver to New Madrid in exchange for mustangs.

"To the west of New Madrid, on the St. Francois River, sits a village of Cherokees. This group is outlawed from other Cherokees and from the United States because of a massacre of whites that happened long ago. Their chief is a half-breed, an intelligent fellow who probably understands English better than he lets on. It is my belief that these Indians can be persuaded to help our enterprise— using their village as a post where the goods and mustangs can be exchanged."

"What is our role?" asked Tully, excitedly.

"I am applying for Spanish citizenship," Neri said, "and cannot afford to be linked to the exporting of horses or the smuggling in of goods. However, one stipulation of my current petition for Indian trade rights is that the government will not inspect my business records to see how and at what prices I obtained the goods I sell.

"Your first responsibility will be to round up mustangs and break them for use. You must then convince the Cherokees on the St. Francois to allow you the use of their village—and further persuade them to construct a warehouse. I pledge to you fifteen percent of my profits, to be divided between you and the Cherokees to the best of your bargaining ability."

Tully appeared ready to jump at the offer. John clapped a restraining hand on his companion's shoulder. "Fifteen percent divides up kind o' funny," John said slowly. "How 'bout twenty? That way we can offer the Indians a firm ten percent from the git-go. After all, it seems t' me our risk is ever' bit equal to your own, and we're doin' all the work."

The curled ends of the baron's mustache rose in a smile. "Very good, my young sir," he murmured. "Very good, indeed. Yes, yes, you have a bargain." He reached for the wine bottle. "Shall we drink on it? Let us get to know one another a little better."

Business behind him, the baron regaled the Kentuckians with

well-rehearsed stories from his past. He was, he said, born in Prussia of noble Dutch parentage. As a young man, he served in the Prussian army under Frederick the Great while that monarch was helping William V of The Netherlands suppress the Dutch revolutionaries. Later, Neri related sorrowfully, he was forced to leave his family and property and flee The Netherlands upon its conquest by France. He chose Spain as his refuge.

There, finding favor with the Crown, he was dispatched on a special mission to Mexico in which he nearly lost his life. The years following were spent in seeking his fortune in the United States and New Spain. "Although I have ever been a loyal subject and valuable ally of Spain, it has never profited me," the baron lamented. Then, rubbing his hands together, he added in a hopeful tone, "Perhaps the time of reward has finally come."

Near the Red River—four hundred miles northeast of Bexar and three hundred from the St. Francois River in Upper Louisiana—the Kentuckians, aided by a pair of mulattoes in the employ of Bastrop, built a corral, pens, and a willow-roofed shed. This locale had been suggested by the baron as being far enough from any Spanish outpost to make detection unlikely. The trade-out, not entirely to the party's liking, was that it lay within Comanche hunting territory.

Experienced trackers and trainers of horses, the mulattoes shared their skills with John and Tully. The first weeks of the humid Texas summer were passed in putting those lessons to use. By July, the pens were bursting with horseflesh. The time had arrived, John decided, to broach a deal with the Cherokees. Leaving Tully at the camp, he struck out on a newly broken bay mount in search of the St. Francois.

Within the week John located the Cherokee village. His entry was made easier than anticipated by the surprising likeness he bore to Chief John Bowles. Both men were tall, auburn-haired and gray-eyed, and the dark skin that was John's ancestral Welsh birthright heightened the similarity. They might well have passed for father and son. Bowles even pointed to John's mustang with some amusement. "Men's hair, horse's hair, all same color," the half-breed observed merrily.

Conducting business proved agreeable despite the limitations in language. The chief's only concern was the distance from the horse pens on the Red River to his village. He argued that it would be difficult for John and only three companions to drive many horses so far. As a solution, he offered to send a number of braves with John. Of course, Bowles noted shrewdly, the added help would necessitate the Cherokee portion of the profit being more than just one in ten.

The chief underscored his bargaining logic with a confident smile. John shrugged and nodded. Without the Cherokees, there could be no profits for anyone.

"Good," Bowles said. "You take Big Mush and five braves. Big Mush know best way to mustang land."

Under the guidance of Big Mush, a young, powerfully built petty chief, John and the Indians rode in a straight line to the Red, then crossed the river and turned west. It took less than a day to locate their destination. However, the camp proved to be silent and devoid of any living thing except a trio of circling vultures.

John stared in horrified disbelief. The scalped corpse of Tully Fenwick, two arrows in his chest, lay sprawled face-up between the corral and the shed. The killers had taken his long rifle, powder horn, and fine leather belt. There was no sign of the mulattoes or any of the horses. As John knelt beside his dead companion, numb with shock and grief, the Cherokees methodically took stock of the situation.

"He not dead more than two day," Big Mush ventured. "This done by Comanche—only three. They take other men to help with horses. They not move fast with so many horses. We go now, catch them tomorrow."

John rose without a word, pointed grimly to the buzzards, and went to find a shovel. The Cherokees helped him bury Tully, then waited impatiently while he fashioned a wooden cross and drove it into the fresh soil of the grave, praying aloud all the while. He mounted the bay and rode with the red men in pursuit of the stolen herd, leaving behind three disappointed carrion crows.

Big Mush proved to be prophetic. The next afternoon, they spotted the cloud of dust signifying the mustang herd being driven over the open, rolling hills by the Comanches and their prisoners. After the pursuers had drawn closer, Big Mush called a temporary halt. "You no fighter," he told John. It was a statement of fact, noted without disdain. "Stay out of way," the chief added. Angered but resigned, the Kentuckian hung back. Three Cherokees began circling to the left of the unsuspecting Comanche herdsmen, three to the right. All carried long rifles.

It was over in a few minutes. Insulated from discovery by the dust, noise, and the attentiveness of their prey to the task at hand, the warriors of Big Mush cut down the three Comanches before any of the latter could return their fire.

John suddenly reflected that the terrified mulattoes likely didn't know one Indian from another. He spurred the bay forward, waving his hat and shouting their names until they recognized him. Then they all joined the Cherokees in attempting to contain the rapidly scattering horses.

That accomplished, John searched the dead Comanches and their mounts until he had collected Tully's plundered belongings. He tried in vain to ignore the bloody blond scalp hanging with others from the belt of one of the slain. But the Cherokees had waited through one burial; they would not have the understanding or patience for a second.

John studied his audience of family members. The narrative had enthralled them.

"We managed t' get the horses to th' St. Francois with no other problems," he resumed. "Within a couple o' months, the trade goods arrived from Louisville. I reckon I did a pretty good job of tradin' because we only gave up about half our horses for all the goods sent us.

"The Baron de Bastrop was s'posed to let us know where an' when to deliver the goods, but we waited and waited without gettin' any word. When it got t' be October, the mulattoes left out for Bexar. I stayed on at the village, in part just to make sure none of the merchandise walked off.

"The winter came an' went without a word from the baron. Finally, a boat workin' its way upriver brought me a letter. It was from Bastrop, sayin' the governor had turned down his proposal and that I could do whatever I saw fit with the goods."

John dropped his eyes. "There wasn't much I needed while livin' in the village, so I mostly traded for whiskey," he said almost in a whisper, then added apologetically: "It was kinda hard, gettin' over Tully."

Clearing his throat, John continued:

"Another year passed, and I don't remember much about it. Finally, I ran low on trade goods, so I had to shake the cravin' for the whiskey. We made a run to Texas—Big Mush and me and some others—and captured and broke lots more horses. Then I took off alone and saw a lot more o' Texas, clear down to the Gulf of Mexico.

"It's fine, fertile country, and someday some o' you might like t' go see it. Lookin' back, I'm a bit surprised I didn't get killed, travelin' alone and all. At the time, I s'pose I didn't care much what happened to me.

"When I got back to th' St. Francois, I just thought it was finally time t' head back home. I sure am glad to see your ugly ol' faces.

"That's just about all. Now, pardon me while I step away for a little fresh air an' a stop at th' well."

Early the next morning, John slipped out of the house and with a determined stride headed up the lane to David Singletary's fine new farmstead.

The Singletary domicile was full to overflowing with the noisy fruit of the patriarch's three consecutive marriages. The latest Mrs. Singletary solemnly informed John that the colony's founder was fasting and meditating alone in his "house of prayer" to the rear of the residence. Undaunted, John searched out the backyard sanctuary and knocked discreetly.

The door swung open. Singletary, rugged strength and vigor evident in disregard of his eighty-plus years, stared down at the unexpected caller. "Come in, young man," he said, civilly enough. "What brings you out so early?"

"Thank you, sir," John said, hat in hand. Stepping inside, he coughed nervously and met the gaze of those light blue eyes so feared by generations of New Ephrata children.

"I'm terribly sorry t' bother you," he began. "But I—I've been through some things, th' past year or so. There's a couple o' questions mighty important to me I'm needin' to ask, and prob'ly no one but you can answer 'em. I'd appreciate it if you'd hear me out.

"You've known me always, sir. In spite o' how it sometimes looked, as a youngster I really did heed th' sermons an' Bible studies an' prayer times. And I understood—at least, I thought I did—about salvation."

Singletary deduced that this interruption of his solitude was going to last longer than a mere moment or two. He seated himself and proffered a rude wooden stool, but John shook his head. "Thanks anyway, sir, I'll stand," he said, and resumed.

"I'm sure you know 'bout Tully Fenwick bein' killed whilst he and I were in Texas. Well, ever since then, I've been livin' in a Cherokee Indian village in Louisiana. I fell into an awful bad drinkin' spell, but later I confessed my sins an' prayed for forgiveness from Jesus Christ, just like we were always taught.

"But I also did somethin' else. I didn't even tell my family 'bout this, and I don't ever plan to. It would just hurt Ma and the others like it already hurts me." John gave Singletary a meaningful glance, and in turn received a curt nod affirming that the confidence would be kept.

The words now came out in an anguished torrent.

"There was this Indian girl, the sister of a young chief. She was sweet, an' awful pretty. She did a lot to help me shake the drinkin' problem. We—we fell in love, and decided there was nothin' for it except to be married. The weddin' ceremony, of course, was done Cherokee style. Now, I gave John 3:16 out loud from memory durin' the weddin' and tried to explain it to anyone who would listen. But my wife never believed in Jesus or Christian salvation. 'You have your god and I have mine,' she'd always say.

"Early in th' fall, she told me we were goin' to have a child. We spent the whole winter countin' each an' every day of her progress. Nothin' else mattered t' either of us.

"But when it came time for th' baby, things went bad wrong. She finally had a little boy . . . but givin' birth took her life. One of th' squaws tried nursin' our son, but a few days later she caught sick and both of 'em died."

John clasped his hands to his face, a picture of misery. There was silence while Singletary framed the inevitable answer to John's unstated question. No one could have been more sympathetic than the patriarch. His first wife, sister to Chief Logan, had shared a terrible fate with her unborn child at the hands of bestial white men. His second wife, a Cherokee, died of complications following childbirth.

But Singletary would not allow himself to shrink from his unenviable duty. God's word must supersede sentimentality.

"Young man," he finally said, "if you are wondering about the salvation of the woman you called your wife, then you have known the proper answer since your childhood. Except they be called to the Father through the Son . . . I am sorry."

John bared his tear-stained face. "I guess I knew that, all along," he said in a broken, trembling voice. "I was just hopin' against hope . . . But tell me—what about our son? Our baby? He did nothin'—he was innocent!"

Singletary heaved a great sigh. The words fell from his lips with the force of a hammer. "You admit that you were not married in a Christian ceremony," he said, carefully and sternly. "It is not possible for a holy God to intervene in such a situation."

This dread pronouncement should have shattered the younger man. Instead, a singular thing occurred.

John heard himself speaking in a calm but strong voice, smoothly quoting scripture he had never memorized:

"Take heed that ye despise not one of these little ones. For I say unto you, that in heaven their angels do always behold the face of my Father which is in heaven. For the Son of man is come to save that which was lost."

In the midst of despair, John was suddenly buoyed by a flood of hope—and not only hope, but reassurance and peace. He dropped to his knees, tears flowing. "Thank you, Jesus," he said, over and over.

The icy blue eyes of the witness widened in wonderment. Well did Singletary know the Gospel of St. Matthew, and he marveled at John's flawless recitation. Struggling to maintain his composure, he placed a giant hand on the bowed head of John and prepared to pray. But this effort proved futile. No force of his will could summon the words. Baffled and more than a little alarmed, Singletary hastily removed the hand and stepped back.

Regaining his feet, John used a sleeve to wipe his eyes. Without a word to Singletary, whose show of impassivity masked a mounting uneasiness, he exited the "house of prayer." He turned homeward with a lightened heart, convinced that a higher source than the patriarch of New Ephrata had revealed divine truth.

Chapter 32

*I*n 1811, a time rife with rumors of war, Nature went berserk in the Ohio Valley. That year, and years after, people argued over whether these mystical events should be cited as omens of biblical prophecy coming to pass. For Rebekah Cumings, they portended more tragedy.

Of the natural occurrences, the most bizarre—and least explainable—involved the common gray squirrel.

Late in April, Rebekah's brother-in-law James came to New Ephrata to visit and see firsthand how the widow and his nephews and nieces were getting along. James and his own large family had been living in Ohio for nearly a decade on land located near the headwaters of Brush Creek. During his stay in New Ephrata, the leading item of topical conversation was the recent, mysterious mass migration of squirrels.

By the tens of thousands, as though responding to some sovereign command they alone could sense, the little woodlanders had initiated a southward movement. This summons proved stronger than the very instinct of life, manifesting its power when wave after wave of the squirrels unhesitatingly plunged to watery deaths wherever the Ohio and other streams blocked their path.

"Durndest thing I ever saw," James volunteered while sipping a hot mug of Rebekah's coffee. "Or heard, neither. You would've thought the woods had turned gray and come alive. One big, furry, flappin' carpet—that's what they looked like, an' not stoppin' to eat or sleep.

"But the really unnervin' thing was the racket they made.

219

When you take one squirrel's chatterin' an' multiply it by a thousand, and fill the woods with it 'til they echo . . . well, it's kinda chillin' to the bones."

"What do you think it means, James?" Rebekah asked.

"Means?" The question surprised him. "Why, I don't rightly know as it means anythin' special." He set the mug down. "Kinda funny you would say that, though. Have you took a look at the night sky lately, Rebekah? Seen anythin' peculiar, off to the west, after the sun sets?"

She nodded. "There's a bright new star," she said. "Not the evening star, either."

Her brother-in-law chimed in, "Yeah, it's different, all right. If you squint real hard, you can see it has a tail. In fact, it looks like maybe the tail is split. But bless me, Rebekah, I sure don't know what any of this means."

A dramatic, unexpected rise in the Ohio River, arriving later than the usual spring freshets, forced James to cut his visit short. Only three days after his arrival, he rode the Cumings Landing ferry through a driving rain across the strengthening river. He advised the ferry operators, who were his nephews, Thomas and William, to "tie up for keeps, until the Ohio lessens" after they returned to the home shore.

It was sound enough advice, except that the water kept rising and gathering its force. The river soon became a roaring torrent, more ferocious than any flood seen before by New Ephrata, throwing awful strength against every manmade improvement within its swollen reach. For five days it raged and foamed like a rabid animal, subsided briefly, and then returned as stout and ugly as before. By the time the floods played out their fury in early May, the wharves, ferry, floating sawmill, and boat yard at Cumings Landing were among the casualties.

As the stream receded into its banks, and warm, sultry air began to blanket the valley, a new and greater peril crept in unheralded. Singletary's colony, safe against Indian attack for half a century, found itself in the silent, deadly grip of a pestilence deposited by the polluted river waters. The young proved especially susceptible to the malady, developing a high fever and a cruel, scarlet rash. In Rebekah's household, the twin girls and little Robert fell victims. Becky and Sarah recovered; the boy, sickly from birth, was no match for the nameless plague. In all, eight youthful villagers succumbed.

The unexplainable death march of the squirrels . . . the appearance of the star with two tails, now glowing brightly in the night sky . . . the unprecedented and destructive floods . . . the terrible, mysterious killer disease. Grief-stricken, Rebekah cried out before God: "What next? Oh, my Lord, what next?"

In that year of 1811, war with New Spain was rumored. War with Great Britain seemed inevitable. War with the Indians became a reality before year's end. In the midst of this unrest, and by all accounts oblivious to it, brash businessman and inventor Nicholas Roosevelt pursued the construction of a steamboat in Pittsburgh.

Roosevelt was an associate of Robert Fulton, who in 1807 built and launched the first steamboat capable of water travel and transportation. Fulton's device cruised the relatively tranquil surface of the Hudson River in New York. Roosevelt intended his vessel, the *New Orleans,* to be the first of its ilk to ply the turbulent, challenging western streams—namely, the Ohio and Mississippi. At forty-three, saddled with debts from earlier business failures, Roosevelt was matching his ingenuity and grit with the financial resources of fellow New Yorkers Fulton and Robert Livingston for one final shot at fame and fortune.

Word of his endeavor trickled out to the river towns, whose skeptical denizens had never seen any device of man master the Ohio. For years, yards in Redstone, Pittsburgh, Marietta, and elsewhere had skillfully crafted large, impressive vessels designed for the open seas. These ships could access the world's oceans by first traversing the Ohio and Mississippi. However, ice in the winter and low water in the summer severely limited the opportunity for such travel on the Ohio. Too, propulsion by sails was impractical in the river's narrow, winding channel. In fact, the rigging was usually packed away, not to be assembled until reaching the Gulf. Such ships were essentially given over to the mercy of the river currents as they headed downstream. Many encountered calamities of one kind or another and never reached New Orleans.

And none, of course, could go upstream.

Now a new invention was being prepared to test the vagaries of the mighty river. Most rivermen, the Cumingses among them, doubted that Roosevelt would be able to tame the Ohio.

New Ephrata was introduced to the steamboat on a hazy October morning. Having put their ferry, floating sawmill, and boat yard back in order following the floods, three of the brothers— Samuel, Thomas, and William—were busily building boats when something drew William's attention to the treeline upriver.

"What's burning over on the Ohio side, I wonder?" the twenty-year-old asked. Samuel and Thomas glanced up from their labors. Thomas whistled. "Man, that smoke is sure black!" he exclaimed. "Looks like it might be somethin's caught fire on the Grimes place."

The three men put down their tools and descended the slope to the water's edge. "Listen!" Samuel said, spreading his arms to ask for quiet. The surface of the river seemed to be giving off a faint but persistent screeching noise. As the eerie, unfamiliar sound grew louder, the brothers sensed, rather than heard, an accompanying steady throb as of a giant, racing heart. The billowing column of smoke was actually moving behind the trees, coming closer as it polluted the hazy atmosphere. Birds up and down the river valley were taking to flight in wholesale numbers. The screech had grown into a roar, the throbbing was now audible.

Other New Ephrata residents, some carrying rifles, began accumulating excitedly along the riverbank. They had to shout at one another to be heard above the mounting, infernal racket. Something uncanny, very large and very loud, was making its way down the river. William quelled an urge to take to his heels and tried to draw reassurance from the calm demeanor of his older brothers.

The blue hull of the *New Orleans* glided into view. "The steamboat!" Samuel shouted, relieved and exultant all at once. "The steamboat they were building in Pittsburgh! It got through Letart's Falls!"

Escaping steam caused the roar; the deep, regular throb came from the engine it drove. Both sounds were new to the western waters. And the craft's appearance was as novel as its noises.

The long rectangle of the hull was basically boat-shaped, though without the graceful lines of the sailing ships that had preceded it down the Ohio. The slender bowsprit and brace of masts seemed ridiculous and out of place on the squatty form of the steamboat. Between the masts rose a ponderous chimney blowing black smoke and sparks. A spinning paddlewheel located amidships (and presumably matched with another wheel on the opposite side) churned the water mightily. Men on deck waved as they cruised by, traveling probably three times the speed of the current.

Samuel's face glowed. He turned excitedly to Thomas. "There goes history in the making," he yelled over the grotesque sounds of Roosevelt's contraption. "We may have just seen the future of river travel! Thomas," he added, eyes dancing, "I'm going to take a horse to Louisville. If that thing can manage its way through the Falls of the Ohio, then our boat yard is going to begin crafting hulls and cabins for steamboats!"

As it turned out, Samuel could have taken a canoe down the river and still had plenty of leisure time in Louisville before the *New Orleans* dared the falls. But a twist of fate made the unexpected wait worthwhile.

The Falls of the Ohio, rock-ribbed rapids forming the river's greatest hazard, were at their worst when the water was low. In November of 1811, the water was very low.

At Louisville, the Ohio began a giant, S-shaped curve and widened to nearly a mile. Spanning the broad expanse were the vestiges of a prehistoric reef, eroded through the ages to the point where the remnant consisted of jagged rocks and low islands. The level of the river dropped more than twenty feet over the two-mile course of the rapids. Low water rendered the falls an impenetrable barrier for all traffic but the flatboats.

The *New Orleans* drew four feet of draught, so she had to wait for higher water just as other vessels did. River veterans like Samuel could tell from the amount of exposed rock that none of the three main channels, or chutes, was running deep enough. Samuel, in fact, was getting close-up looks almost daily as an appointee of the municipal court of Louisville.

For years, inexperienced and foolhardy boatmen had lost ill-advised challenges of the falls. The resulting disasters sometimes blocked the passage of those behind until the wreckage could be cleared. In an attempt to lessen this expensive problem, and to save lives, Louisville and its Indiana Territory neighbor, Jeffersonville, enacted restrictive laws. Now no vessel was allowed to attempt the falls unless the pilot in charge was licensed and appointed by one of the cities. Samuel, counted among a number of licensed pilots who waited impatiently to see the steamboat's encounter with the falls, covered the expenses of his extended stay in this fashion.

Still, the river remained low for much longer than anyone expected. Finally, in early December, there came an almost imperceptible rise. Derelict in his duties back home, Samuel was about to give up his vigil and start for New Ephrata on December 7 when he received a missive from the municipal court.

"You are hereby appointed to represent the City of Louisville as its licensed pilot aboard the '*New Orleans*,'" the notice read. "The owner, Mr. Roosevelt, and the pilot, Mr. Jack, have expressed their intent to attempt passage of the falls on 8 December. Mr. Roosevelt has pledged to cover all expenses of any mishap. Please report to one of these gentlemen and present the accompanying letter of instruction."

Incredulous, Samuel read the message again. Normally, the city stood behind the pilot and acted as surety should any error in the pilot's judgment lead to disaster. Apparently, Roosevelt was desperate enough (or arrogant enough) to assume financial responsibility so that his steamboat could proceed. But Samuel would have the final say on when and if the *New Orleans* tackled the rapids.

On his way to Beargrass Creek, where the steamboat lay in harbor, he checked the day's readings. The deepest channel was Indian Chute, closest to the Indiana shore. He was appalled. The water level of Indian Chute was four feet, five inches: less than half a foot of clearance between the steamboat's hull and the razor-sharp rocks. Had Roosevelt lost his mind?

The urbane New Yorker, nearly ten years Samuel's elder, knew how to stroke men.

When Samuel came on board, trying to hide his excitement, Roosevelt and his own pilot, Andrew Jack, greeted him cordially. They pointed out and explained every detail of the amazing craft. Roosevelt then introduced his wife, Lydia, only twenty years of age, along with their daughter and infant son, the latter born since the steamboat's arrival in Louisville.

Then Roosevelt got down to business.

"I must say, Mr. Cumings," he began, "I am very impressed. You come highly recommended by the best rivermen on the Ohio. Mr. Jack here knows your reputation. In fact, we leaned nearly as heavily on your unpublished notes and charts for our navigational needs as we did those of Mr. Cramer, in Pittsburgh."

Samuel glowed inwardly. He personally thought his work was the equal of that printed by Zadoc Cramer. In fact, he believed Cramer might have availed himself of Samuel's research in producing his popular guide for river pilots.

"Now, sir," the inventor continued, studying him closely, "Mr. Jack and I have checked on today's readings. We all know what a small measurement five inches is. That's not a great deal of clearance. But ponder this.

"We have taken the *New Orleans* this far. We came through Letart's Falls without a problem. We have paddled and pushed our way over sandbars, across the tips of islands, and through underwater forests of planters and sawyers.

"Mr. Cumings, my fortune and the fortunes of men who are my friends are tied up in this enterprise. It will be successful. It must be! Mr. Jack, who has steered this steamboat all the way from Pittsburgh, assures me five inches is enough clearance."

Roosevelt turned his back and strode to the gunwale. There he turned and faced Samuel. "I am a loving husband and father, sir," he resumed. "You have just met my beautiful wife and precious children. Lydia was eight months pregnant when we began this journey, fully expecting to give birth on the river. I am a sane man. Now I ask you: would any sane man endanger his family so needlessly?" He spread his arms wide, palms open.

"As you are already aware, I have pledged to underwrite any costs attendant to miscalculations on navigating the falls. The city of Louisville has no obligations in the event we fail. But in you, Mr. Cumings, we have the best man available for the job. My confidence in you is unflagging. Tomorrow, you and I and this ship will be victorious."

Lydia Roosevelt had joined the little conclave while her husband was speaking. She fixed proud eyes upon Samuel. No fear or apprehension clouded her young, aristocratic features.

"My son Henry will likely be asleep tomorrow when we go over the falls," she said calmly. "Will you gentlemen please make every effort not to wake him?"

Chapter 33

New Ephrata, as Rebekah Cumings had known and loved it, was wilting on the vine. And, judging from the disasters visited on the community during the course of the year, she doubted that the one-time paradise on earth would be restored to its former glory before the return of Christ.

The deaths of husband and youngest child had, of course, dealt Rebekah terrible heartache. Both of the Ellisons were gone now, too. But her sense of emptiness was not confined to the loss of family members and friends. She grieved for the community, whose very soul lay dying. It was as though God, having discerned that He was no longer foremost in the hearts of New Ephrata inhabitants, sorrowfully quenched the divine spark that had set this community apart.

Much of the blame for the spiritual estrangement, Rebekah believed, could be laid at the feet of the colony's patriarch.

David Singletary was defying the way of all flesh. At the advanced age of eighty-six, his seed continued to multiply through the willingness and endurance of the third Mrs. Singletary. Yet these remarkable occasions served more to celebrate the fecundity of the man than to glorify his Creator, and Singletary had fallen into the primal snare of narcism. The word of the Lord remained in him, but when it came forth was dry and dusty.

In an unprecedented experience for New Ephrata, members of the younger generation began departing in search of new lives elsewhere. At the same time, there appeared in the glens of Sycamore and Cabin creeks and Quick's Run new clans who did not hold the standard of Christ as high as the old colonists had. Remarkably—and carelessly, to Rebekah's way of thinking—the move-ins were welcomed into the communal dining halls and their offspring allowed to mingle in the schoolrooms with the children of God's chosen.

Among these recent arrivals was a family named Ayles, whose eldest son Peter took an immediate liking to Becky Cumings.

Peter was sixteen, dark and robust; Becky, not yet thirteen, was sprouting into early womanhood. Tall, supple of movement, she looked and acted years older than her awkward, quiet twin, Sarah. Peter admired Becky's auburn hair, large green eyes, full lips, and coquettish dimples, and also observed with relish the budding figure underneath her homespun dresses.

The roar from the Falls of the Ohio drowned out all other sounds.

In the engine room below the deck of the *New Orleans,* the stoker fed his raging furnace. The churning boiler was taking all the steam it could handle. The escape valve shrieked. The single piston throbbed mightily. But, while Samuel could feel the racing heartbeat of the steam engine against the soles of his boots, he heard nothing but the all-encompassing din of the falls still hundreds of yards away.

The blue-skinned craft was being pushed to outrace the mounting current of the Ohio as her crew tensely prepared for the mad dash into the Indiana channel. If she did not achieve a speed greater than that of the water racing through the chute, she would not be able to answer her helm. Already, those aboard sensed the raw strength of the current as the *New Orleans* drew near the falls. The water, turbulent and foamy, slapped nastily at the churning paddle wheels and splashed over the rail, soaking the deck and those who rode it.

Samuel and Andrew Jack stood in the bow, braced against the buffets, eyeing the course before them and hand-signaling their directions to the helmsman at the wheel. With the exception of the stoker and the engineer below, the rest of the little crew were also on deck.

The pulsating engine spun the paddles faster and faster. As they entered the rocky outcropping of the falls, a great cloud of mist and spray engulfed the boat. The *New Orleans* had reached full speed and was about to pass over the lip of the Indiana chute. Henceforth the pilots' decisions must be lightning-fast—and correct. If they erred, the unforgiving falls would surely crush the brash challenger and scatter its debris and occupants the length of the rapids.

Lydia Roosevelt, wedged in between the stern rail and the cowering hulk of her giant Newfoundland dog, Tiger, had both arms wrapped tightly around the neck of the frightened animal. She insisted on coming along, although the children had been left on shore despite her bravado of the day before. Drenched to the skin underneath her bulky winter apparel, she stared, open-mouthed, at the oncoming rush of jagged black rocks.

Five inches of clearance . . . less than a half-foot of water would separate the wooden hull of the weighty vessel from instant destruction.

The *New Orleans* entered the chute. Irregular, foam-flecked fangs of glistening rock framed the narrow, twisting passageway. Without turning their heads, the pilots flashed a furious succession of signals to the helmsman. From his chosen post amidships, Nicholas Roosevelt abruptly felt helpless. Had the helm maintained command, or were they now in the grip of the murderous maelstrom? He could not tell. Ebon boulders seemed to leap at the *New Orleans* as she sped by, though none touched her.

Suddenly, there was a sickening instant of weightlessness and of falling, followed by the impact of returning to the water's surface. They had plunged into the longest and most treacherous drop in the chute, and were safely through it before anyone except the pilots knew what had happened.

The turbulence lessened. The spray diminished. Then the *New Orleans* emerged from the last eddies of the falls, exultantly belching a column of black smoke. Though the Roosevelts could not hear them, hundreds of spectators cheered the amazing exploit from their vantage point at the Shippingport landing. This little city at the foot of the falls had seen many such efforts end very differently.

Nicholas Roosevelt, wringing wet but flushed with victory, vigorously shook his pilots' hands. "Wonderful job, men! Wonderful job! History has been made here today!" he declared. To Samuel, he added, "You'll have a bonus coming, above your fee. You certainly earned it."

But the court-appointed pilot shook his head. "If you'd be willing, Mr. Roosevelt, sir," he responded, "I'd much prefer the privilege of continuing with you down to Natchez. This is a wonderful machine, and I intend for my family's boat yard to get into the business of building steamboats."

The New Yorker studied the frank, honest face before him. "Mr. Cumings," he said, "you have earned that privilege. You are welcome to remain aboard, sir. In fact, we will talk later about whether our respective plans might not come together."

Samuel glanced at Andrew Jack, wondering how Roosevelt's hand-picked pilot would respond to his continued presence.

Jack stuck out his hand. "I've been wantin' a little relief from my duties," he said cordially as Samuel shook it. "Now I have someone I can trust to spell me. We're goin' to lay over for a couple of days at Shippin'port and take on supplies. If you want, we'll spend some of that time goin' over the charts."

Inspection of the charts proved to hold even more interest for Samuel than he had expected. At first, he was intrigued by what he found. Within a short time, he had grown incredulous.

"Mr. Jack," he asked at last, trying to conceal his agitation, "do you know the source of these charts?"

"Why, of course," came the nonchalant reply. "We took the information out of that book printed by the newspaper in Pittsburgh. Haven't you seen Cramer's book?"

"No, sir," Samuel answered slowly. "But I've seen some of the information on these charts before. I gathered it myself. I know it's my work, because I recognize several mistakes which I have since corrected. I had no idea someone else would take my charts and sell them without my knowledge or permission."

Jack whistled. "Well, I'll be switched!" he exclaimed. "It's good work you've done, an' a real shame you've not made money on it. It's also a good thing for Mr. Roosevelt and myself that you're here to point out those mistakes you're referrin' to."

For a month, including the time the *New Orleans* lay in wait at Louisville for a rise in the river, a dreary stillness had hung in the air. The atmosphere seemed leaden, and a persistent stagnant haze on the horizon turned the sun a bloated red at sunrise and sunset.

The weather remained unseasonably warm and oppressive as the steamboat resumed its journey downstream. On the second evening following the departure from Shippingport, after the *New Orleans* had been moored to the Indiana riverbank for the night, the air struck the travelers as more burdensome than ever. "The sensation of it is a whole lot like things feel just before a big storm," Jack remarked to Samuel, "except in this instance, the storm never comes."

Around two o'clock the next morning, something did come. Something much bigger and stronger, more destructive and more terrifying than anything the weather alone could have produced.

A stupendous jolt, accompanied by a blast of sound Samuel later likened to a hundred simultaneous thunderclaps, bounced him about in his bunk and wrenched him from a heavy sleep with heart pounding. The boat was rocking violently as he jumped out of the bunk and scrambled in the darkness for his coat and boots. He heard a confusing medley of loud noises from outside the cabin, and a strange, nasty odor assailed his nostrils.

Just as the rocking had begun to lessen, a second jolt rattled the craft and tossed its contents to and fro. Instinctively, Samuel cried out, and a couple of shouts from aroused crewmen answered out of the blackness. The cabin door popped open, and Jack's dim, hatless silhouette leaped through it onto the deck.

Within seconds, everyone else was on deck except for the Roosevelt children and their nurse, who remained in their quarters on orders from level-headed Nicholas Roosevelt. There was little to be seen, but strange, alarming sounds came from all directions. Scores of birds on the wing uttered terrified cries as they blindly sought safety somewhere in the dust-filled night sky. Tremendous groanings and poppings issued from the riverbanks and beyond, where trees old and great, young and small, swayed and rocked to the tortured undulations of the earth. Crash followed crash as they were shaken loose at their roots and flung down. A deep, powerful roar, as from the throat of an irate giant, compounded the elements of the din. "An earthquake!" Roosevelt shouted, unnecessarily.

Jack had managed to light a lantern. By its illumination, they could see that the river was swirling, boiling, streaked with foam and mud. In its agitated grip rolled mud-packed trees, apparently thrust to the surface after countless years of captivity far below.

Large bubbles appeared, possibly rising from even greater depths, and burst to release a sulfuric gas. The odor was nauseating.

"It's like the Devil's vomit!" Jack exclaimed.

Roosevelt snatched up the lantern and staggered across the rolling deck to the bow. Holding the light over his head, the New Yorker examined the trees jutting from the steep bank where the ship's cable was strung. The bank itself was in grotesque motion, sloughing off chunks of earth and rock.

"We must pray that these trees hold firm!" Roosevelt bawled out over the din. "I don't wish us to come a-loose in the dark with those dead trees surfacing."

Someone suggested that they cast off from the bank and re-set the anchor. Roosevelt shook his head. "We cannot get to the line with the river like it is," he said. "Even if we could, who's to say there is anything left within reach of our anchor?"

The Cherokees of Chief John Bowles had never experienced anything like it. Even the shaman was too frightened to assume his traditional mantle of arrogance; he pleaded frantically to the Ancient Red, the spirits of Sun and Fire, to save the village from the wrath of the Thunder Man.

They had been awakened in the middle of the night by an awesome sound like a clap of thunder many times magnified, and a shock that leveled half of their flimsily built homes and damaged the remainder. A series of lesser quakes followed. The night air bore thick dust and a terrible smell. No stars were visible; the darkness was total.

A sound as of a strong wind raced through the trees, but the terrified Indians felt no wind. Wooden snappings, creakings, and groanings came from all sides. The ground shook repeatedly. Bowles decided that the "wind" was actually the sound from thousands of limbs and branches shaking as the trees swayed to the vibrations of the earth.

From deep underground came a rumbling, felt as much as heard. The shocks continued.

"Torches!" roared Bowles. "Light the torches!"

His order was obeyed none too soon. As the pine knots flamed and drew the Cherokees close around like moths, the earth writhed again. Ripping and popping, the main path of the village separated into a crevasse six feet wide and belched forth gas and steam. Suddenly deprived of footing, a squaw and her babe in arms plummeted into the quivering fissure. The accompanying quake knocked down the remaining huts along with most of the panicked villagers.

As they regained their feet and retrieved the scattered torches, a new terror announced itself. From the direction of the St. Francois River a series of loud hissing sounds penetrated the inky blackness, each successive hiss seemingly nearer than the one before. The frenzied shaman shrieked that they were hearing the angry breath of a great serpent, released from the riverbed by the Thunder Man. Bowles quickly asserted his courage and leadership, ordering the medicine man to shut up and commanding the others to stand firm instead of fleeing into the night.

The cause of the hissing soon crept into the radius of the Indians' torchlight. It was water from the river, spreading rapidly over the ravaged earth and plunging into the heated fissures with great explosions of steam. Soon it would overrun the village grounds— and, Bowles suddenly realized, would completely blanket the treacherous terrain. The quake had either forced the river out of its banks or lowered the earth. In either case, the result was going to be the same.

"The river comes!" the chief shouted. "We must leave the village, and quickly. But do not run! Stay together! Our torches will show us the way around the holes in the earth."

Chapter 34

For Tecumseh, most magnificent of the Shawnees, the long-awaited rumble of the earthquake came as an empty roar, a hollow reminder of the glory that might have been.

The great warrior and spellbinding personage had invested years in a self-imposed mission to form a confederacy of Indian nations. This native alliance, Tecumseh preached, would purge the red man's land of the invading Americans. He traveled thousands of miles and spent countless hours in charismatic oratory before council fires across the northwest and midwest and to the south. At every stop, to every assemblage of fascinated chieftains, Tecumseh promised a sign by which all Indians should know simultaneously that the time had arrived to unite and drive out the whites. There would come, he foretold, a groaning from deep in the earth and a powerful shaking of its surface. This unmistakable message would be heard and felt and understood by all who were willing to lift the tomahawk and reclaim the land.

No other mortal in America ventured such a bold prediction. There was little basis for expecting a massive earthquake, either within the scientific knowledge of the day or from Indian lore. Yet Tecumseh confidently promised this wondrous event and cited its arrival as the omen that would transform his audacious plan into reality.

As uncanny as the prophecy proved to be, however, Fate decreed that it would not deliver the desired result.

In November 1811, during Tecumseh's absence from the

Shawnee stronghold in Indiana Territory, his brother foolishly precipitated an attack on American soldiers under the command of territorial governor William Henry Harrison. A combined force of braves from several tribes surprised the white eyes in a predawn assault near the junction of the Wabash and Tippecanoe rivers. Harrison's troops withstood early losses, kept their composure, and ultimately won the field.

The embryonic Indian confederacy, so long in the shaping, was demoralized. This ignominious defeat laid waste to nearly a decade of hope and hard work. Returning home and learning of the disaster, an enraged Tecumseh disowned his brother.

Now those Indians remaining faithful to the cause faced a dilemma. They could either resign themselves to being driven ever westward by the relentless white tide, or they could join forces with the despised British. A new war between Great Britain and the United States appeared inevitable, and the British were always generous in supplying arms for use against the Americans.

A student of history, Tecumseh was fully aware of the results of the prior war between these nations, and how the British had abandoned their promises to the Indians who sided with them against the colonists.

It was a repugnant set of choices. But, truthfully, there was only one choice.

"Our lives are in the hands of the Great Spirit," Tecumseh declared. "We are determined to defend our lands, and if it is his will, we wish to leave our bones upon them."

The Battle of Tippecanoe took place on November 7, 1811. The first of the monster earthquakes, Tecumseh's long-anticipated portent of Indian military supremacy, rattled the greater Mississippi Valley thirty-nine days later.

Dawn on the quake-shaken Ohio furnished small relief to the crew and passengers of the *New Orleans*.

As the firmament turned from sooty black to sullen purple, its wan light confirmed that prodigious forces had been at work. The normally uniform stands of trees atop the riverbanks appeared in violent disarray. Many trees were down; others leaned crazily into one another like drunken companions. The clay banks were split and crumbling.

Equally alarming were the changes in the river.

In the four hours since the first big shock, the water had risen between six and seven feet. The current ran more rapidly, and with greater force. It carried trees freshly shaken off upstream banks along with muddy timber monstrosities freed from the muck of the channel bed.

The air, polluted with the stench of sulfur, remained unseasonably warm and oppressive. Occasional tremors vibrated the vessel, ominous reminders that Nature's anger might be rekindled at any moment.

There was no way for the travelers to determine which direction, upstream or down, presented the lesser danger. Either one might inadvertently take the steamboat into the heart of the next disturbance.

But Nicholas Roosevelt did not suffer hesitation. He was determined to deliver the *New Orleans* to her namesake city, and it lay downstream. They reeled in the cable, heated the boiler, and fired up the engine. Snorting and clattering, the steamboat began picking her way through the swirling debris and submerged planters in the direction of Henderson.

The river continued to rise, and along and beyond its diminishing banks signs of the temblor's nocturnal destruction were plentiful. In many places where the bluffs rose vertical, great sections of earth and rock had sloughed off. Without fail the stone chimneys of habitats had collapsed, frequently onto the dwellings they served. Even more pathetic, though, was the occasional sight of overturned boats, pirogues, and bateaux bouncing aimlessly in the stream or caught up by snags—dumb witnesses to the fate which had overtaken sleeping occupants.

A rather small and subdued crowd turned out to greet the *New Orleans* at Henderson. This piqued the proud Roosevelt, though he could plainly see that almost every structure in town had suffered damage. After taking on wood, the steamboat resumed its journey. Roosevelt wanted to utilize every hour of daylight toward reaching the Mississippi, still a day away. He believed that the *New Orleans* would be relatively safe from submerged hazards and crumbling bluffs while plying the broad, deep Father of Waters.

But the next morning, Andrew Jack and Samuel found themselves in serious trouble.

On the lower reaches of the Ohio, the water had escaped the banks and flooded the river valley. It was with increasing difficulty that the pilots maintained their bearings and followed the meanders of the channel and the increasingly sluggish current. They exchanged looks of bewilderment over the cause of this phenomenon. There had been no evidence of rain within the watershed of the Ohio for more than a month, and presumably little or none had fallen within the upper valley of the Mississippi. What mysterious forces were at play, causing the flow of the Ohio to back up?

When the *New Orleans* exited the mouth of the Ohio and swung into the larger river, the answer lay before them. A spasm of panic gripped Samuel. Here, too—on a much grander scale—the water swirled over the banks and reached far into the treelines; entire bluffs had disappeared and islands were missing, either washed away or obscured below the murky surface. It became incredibly hard for even an experienced pilot to find his bearings. The flood had rendered Samuel's charts all but useless, making the voyage riskier than ever. Jack solemnly apprised his superior of the situation.

But Roosevelt was adamant, and the pilots dedicated themselves to playing out the hand dealt them. Navigating the flooded expanse, with its arsenal of hidden hazards, taxed their combined Mississippi lore to the utmost. The steamboat paddled on, stopping only at a sturdy-looking, timbered stretch of bank to allow the cutting and loading of firewood.

Shortly before nightfall, they entered the horseshoe bend at New Madrid.

Hopes were high for the future of this little port town in the early 1790s, when it was founded with the acquiescence of the colonial Spanish government. Situated on the table-like crest of a sturdy clay ledge, some twenty-five feet above the river, New Madrid commanded a view of six miles upstream and ten miles downstream. As secure as the ledge appeared, however, the indomitable Mississippi gradually eroded its base to the point where the village's initial structures had to be abandoned and ultimately fell into the river. New Madrid was forced to retreat almost continuously from the undercut cliff.

Now, as the *New Orleans* approached, Samuel noticed that the swollen surface of the river boiled within fifteen feet of the ledge's crest. The steamboat entered the natural harbor of Bayou St. John east of town. The bloated stream was backed up into the trees that normally marked its banks. Roosevelt's crew made their charge secure amid the deepening shadows of evening, and the New Yorker, along with Lydia, Jack and Samuel, climbed the wooden steps of the landing.

The voyagers found precisely what they had feared. New Madrid had been savagely shaken by the earthquake. No chimney remained erect, although many damaged houses still stood. Drawn by the noise and spectacle attendant to the novel craft's arrival, a few residents trickled through the otherwise empty streets to the landing. Among them, Samuel recognized a former keelboat hand named Chaumette. As they exchanged greetings, the pilot could read in the Frenchman's eyes the terrible spectre of uncertainty haunting the town.

"M'sieur Cumin's!" There was joy in Chaumette's tremulous voice. "What strange boat is this you travel in?" After Samuel had told him, he laughed nervously. "Some of the people, they run and hide from you' boat 'cause they think it's the Devil himself come from a hole in the river bottom. Preacher here is talkin' that we reachin' the 'end time,' and lotsa people done repent of their sin."

"Have you repented, Chaumette?" Samuel asked. His eye twinkled, but he intended the question to be sincere. The Reverend Lewis Craig had long ago convinced him that repentance must precede salvation.

"Damn right!" Chaumette said forcefully. "If Hell gonna be like this, I sure don't want to go! Besides," he added, "we out of whiskey, and all the women are scared to death they gonna get caught by the Devil if they sin anymore."

Samuel didn't know whether to laugh or cry. So, instead of attempting to enhance Chaumette's tenuous grip on theology, he went to another subject. "How bad was the earthquake here?" he inquired.

"Plenty bad," the Frenchman declared. "I don't know of anybody got killed right in New Madrid, but the river shake so hard that it run backwards—*mon Dieu!*—and throw boats outta the water onto dry land! Later on, after daylight come, we seen upsidedown boats driftin' by.

"We been hearin' it was worse, even, down the river and to the west. Little Prairie been hit hard. Every last house there is knocked flat, and they got splits in the ground six feet wide. We been told that miles and miles of ground sank along the St. Francois and it's all bad flooded there. We got high ground here, and it didn't split so bad. But we still get the shakin' and we just waitin' to see if another earthquake gonna come."

He gave Samuel a furtive glance. "Say, M'sieur," he asked, in a wheedling tone, "do you think Chaumette could catch a ride on this steam contraption? If New Orleans ain't sunk into the river, that's where I'm meanin' to go."

"I don't know," Samuel told him honestly. "I'll have to ask Mr. Roosevelt. He's the owner. But Chaumette, the New Orleans women may be as scared of the Devil as they are here."

"Naw," came the response. "That ain't likely. Anyhow, they bound t' have plenty whiskey."

With a sigh, Samuel presented Chaumette's petition to Roosevelt. The latter mulled it over for a surprisingly long time before answering.

"All right, Mr. Cumings," he said, "provided he's a willing worker. My fear, though, is that in taking him aboard we risk causing problems with others in New Madrid who also may want to be rescued. We have neither the space nor the provisions to accommodate very many more."

Samuel thanked him. "Be reassured, sir," he added, "that Chaumette will carry his own weight in work, and he's also a fine marksman. If the game in these parts ever comes out of hiding, he'll provide us with some fine venison."

That night, Chaumette surreptitiously came aboard with only his rifle and the clothes he wore. "It might be a good idee to cast off before the sun come up," he suggested candidly. "That's about when some of the others gonna miss me and figure out where I went."

Chapter 35

*D*espite other quake-created confusion and dangers to be encountered on the river as far south as the Chickasaw Bluffs (later the site of Memphis), Roosevelt's steamboat met with no further adventures except for a small fire on board. The vessel arrived at the Natchez landing on New Year's Eve, executing an exaggerated loop in its approach to demonstrate the superiority of steam power over the mighty currents of the Mississippi. More than a thousand cheering spectators crowded the landing and overflowed onto the steep hillside, provoking a broad smile from Roosevelt. He and Lydia alighted first, and were immediately enveloped by jubilant welcomers.

The entire crew, including Chaumette, received a heroes' greeting. The Frenchman wrested away a jug of whiskey from a celebrant and, placing it between eager lips, downed a couple of long swigs. Samuel wagged his head in disgust. Natchez-under-the-Hill, adjacent to the landing, offered all the sins of the flesh Chaumette could want.

"What a constant demand he makes on God's grace!" Samuel muttered.

Andrew Jack tapped him on the shoulder. "Look over there, Samuel," he said, pointing to a bearded, jaundiced-looking man in the throng surrounding the Roosevelts. "That's Zadoc Cramer. He's the Pittsburgh publisher who took your charts and printed them."

Samuel felt his face turn warm. Without a word to Jack, he stepped quickly toward the man indicated. Jack hesitated at first, then hurried after his co-pilot.

At the same time, Cramer moved forward and managed to tug on the sleeve of Roosevelt. The New Yorker glanced down, and, recognizing the newspaperman, greeted him warmly. Samuel came to a halt, studying the conversationalists through narrowed eyes.

Cramer held a pad of paper and a sharpened piece of lead. However, his attempts to write down Roosevelt's comments were interrupted by spasms of hoarse coughing. At last, he apologetically waved off Roosevelt and turned away, producing a heavy blue scarf and holding it to his mouth. He doubled over with a groan, and coughed deeply and repeatedly. As he wiped his mouth, dark smears appeared on the cloth.

"Consumption," Jack spoke into Samuel's ear. "He left Pittsburgh last summer and came to Natchez, hopin' the climate would help. I'd say that it hasn't."

Samuel dropped his head. A scant moment before, he had been judgmental of Chaumette. Now he was about to confront a dying man in front of friends with an accusation of theft, even while Roosevelt basked in the glory of a great accomplishment.

"Forgive me, Lord," he murmured, deeply ashamed.

Natchez was where Samuel parted company with the riders of the *New Orleans.* He joined a large and well-armed group of travelers headed north up the Trace. The steamboat resumed its triumphant voyage to the Crescent City, proudly displaying a bale of Natchez-grown cotton in the bow. From New Orleans, the Roosevelts journeyed by sea to New York. The hardy little vessel that earned Nicholas Roosevelt his one great moment in history spent the remainder of its days as a packet on the lower Father of Waters, transporting passengers and cargo between Natchez and New Orleans.

Two more gargantuan earthquakes shook the Mississippi Valley in the winter of 1811-1812, strong enough to be felt across nearly one million square miles of the U.S. and Ontario.

The final temblor, which occurred in early February, was the strongest and most vicious of all. Beginning sometime after midnight, just as the first quake had done in December, the February shocks completed the destruction of New Madrid's frame and log habitats and forced residents to erect tents and lean-tos on the periphery of the prostrated village. The turmoil visited upon the waters and bed of the Mississippi was dramatic in the extreme, and the great river once again flowed backwards for several hours.

In Arkansas, Missouri, and Tennessee, the ground was shaken so hard that it rolled and flapped in earthen ripples several feet high. Many square miles of land subsided in some areas and rose in others. Rivers changed their courses. Forests disappeared and were replaced by lakes. Subterranean pressures forced their way into temporary fissures and blew prehistoric matter through them onto the earth's surface.

The tremors were felt in faraway places, including New Ephrata. A terrified Becky Cumings, just turned thirteen years of age, pulled the covers over her head and screamed for a merciful God to forgive her. But when hugged and clasped to the comforting bosom of her alarmed mother, she refused to divulge the reason for her guilt-ridden outburst.

North of New Ephrata, near wandering Brush Creek, the temblor delivered enough force to crumble a certain limestone hillside. This collapse sealed off the final resting place of the Welsh prince Madoc.

Before the War of 1812 drew to a close, it would claim thousands of American lives in combat. An estimated 1,200 of the dead were from the Commonwealth of Kentucky—a staggering toll for any state to pay, and especially one so sparsely populated. And they died fighting in some of the most controversial and poorly conducted campaigns this nation has ever waged.

Great Britain and France had been at war almost continuously since 1793. Early in the nineteenth century, America enjoyed a rich trade with both sides. Then, after the British crushed the naval forces of Napoleon and his ally Spain at Trafalgar in 1805, thwarting France's invasion of England, the combatants engaged in attempts to cut off each other's sea trade.

The United States found itself adversely impacted. Britain and France alike seized American merchant vessels trading with the other side; the British frequently added insult to injury by "impressing" sailors from the captured ships into involuntary service under the Union Jack. Many of the crewmen were indeed native Britons who had deserted from the British navy, but the arrogant practice quickly inflamed American pride.

The seizure of American trading ships and impressment of "American" sailors were offenses frequently cited by anti-British war hawks in Congress. In point of fact, the war hawks mostly consisted of western statesmen who were more concerned with British-supported Indian hostilities and the prospect of forcibly annexing Canada than they were over maritime injustices. Conversely, New England, the region of the country worst hit by Great Britain's actions on the high seas, was strongly against the prospect of war.

Despite this bitter division of national opinion, President Madison asked for and received a congressional declaration of war against Great Britain in June 1812. Napoleon, for one, was delighted; his longtime foe was already bleeding economically and could ill-afford this costly new distraction on a separate continent. Tecumseh, too, found his spirits lifted once again. Now the British would openly supply his confederation with weapons and supplies and treat the Indians as allies and equals.

Three months after the declaration of war, Becky Cumings left home. Her departure, however, had nothing whatsoever to do with the smoking state of international affairs.

She was with child.

Once Rebekah overcame her initial shock and unwillingness to believe the worst, and made an honest pursuit of her growing suspicions, she gently confronted her daughter. Without a word, the anguished adolescent burst into tears and sobs. Sarah, wide-eyed and white-faced, was the only witness to the drama. She had shared in Becky's terrible secret; wisely, Rebekah did not rebuke the twin for her silent sibling loyalty.

Within twenty-four hours, Becky was gone, whisked across the Ohio River under cover of darkness. She would spend the next several months with one of Uncle James's daughters at a farmstead near the head of Brush Creek.

On the traumatic night of her child's departure, Rebekah stormed blindly out into the woods. She wept and wailed, and railed against God over the awfulness of Becky's predicament. "Why, Lord?" she screamed into the darkness. "Why have you forsaken your faithful, and allowed such a thing to happen to my little one?" Her only answers were echoes.

Not thirty feet away, his giant form silently hidden in a thicket, stood the patriarch of New Ephrata. He heard plainly the lament of Rebekah, but was not moved.

Of all the Cumings brothers, Thomas and William were in several respects the most alike. Both were tall and lean, similar as to countenance, and red-headed with tempers to match. Both possessed fighting spirits and the capacity to back them up. William was especially close to his twin sisters, and Rebekah feared his and Thomas's reactions to the plight of Becky.

Which was precisely why she prevailed on them to escort Becky to their cousin's place, taking along a sealed letter of explanation. For their sister's sake, they struggled to remain calm on the trip into Ohio, and the journey back offered them a full day for reflection.

Still, Rebekah greeted them with some apprehension when they returned. Thomas assured her that the relatives had expressed full willingness to take care of Becky until the baby arrived. Then, to further meet the wishes and conditions outlined in Rebekah's petition, a suitable Ohio home would be selected for the child in consideration of ongoing financial support.

"I have to head on home now, Ma," said Thomas, after reporting this favorable news. "But I need to know somethin' before I go. Becky wouldn't say nothin' about who—who the father is. William and me, we didn't press her on it. But we want to know who's responsible for this."

Rebekah looked both sons squarely in the eye. "I don't know," she said steadily. "I honestly don't. Becky didn't offer to tell me. In fact, she wouldn't talk about her condition at all—and anyway, I didn't ask her."

"Well, we know who it is," William said angrily. Thomas nodded slowly in agreement.

"No, you don't!" their mother shot back. "You may think you do. I know what you're thinking. Maybe it is Peter Ayles, and then again, maybe it's not. Becky didn't say."

Green eyes blazing, she shook her finger in their startled faces. "Listen to me!" she barked. "Who it is doesn't matter, not one twit! What matters is that no more sinful behavior come out of this. What matters is that Becky be able to pick up the pieces of her life! What matters is that we—all of us, including you two—be prayerful and vigilant, and be sure Sarah doesn't make the same sort of mistake.

"Who did this? The Devil did it, that's who! That's all you need to know. And don't be thinking of doing some terrible thing to the Ayles boy. First, you can't be sure he's the one who's responsible. Second, two wrongs will never make a right."

For the time being, Rebekah's admonitions worked. Peter Ayles helped matters by keeping his distance, even though the Cumings brothers viewed this behavior as a sure sign of guilt.

In February of 1813, fourteen-year-old Becky gave birth to a boy. In due time, the infant was placed in the home of a childless couple in Adams County, Ohio, and the young mother returned to New Ephrata. To the chagrin of the brother whom she most loved, Becky naively insisted upon her departure that the illegitimate tyke be christened William Cumings.

Chapter 36

To say that the early stages of the War of 1812 went badly for the Americans is a gross understatement. Even among the dark calamities of that first miserable year, though, one blood-drenched event achieved a level of horror all its own.

In January of 1813, American soldiers under the command of Gen. James Winchester (most of them Kentuckians) routed a small British force while capturing Frenchtown on the River Raisin in Michigan Territory. The flush of victory was short-lived. Three days later, a much larger body of redcoats and Indians surprised Winchester with a dawn attack on Frenchtown.

Fifty Americans were slain and scalped within twenty minutes, and Winchester and most of his surviving men were soon taken as prisoners. The humiliated commander was brought before British Maj. Gen. Henry Proctor and told to order the surrender of a Kentuckian contingent still offering stiff resistance within the town. These stalwarts ignored Winchester and fought on until they exacted a personal promise from Proctor that he would not permit the Indians to fall upon helpless prisoners. His promise proved worthless.

The British general took his regular army and the able-bodied prisoners on an all-day march across the frozen Detroit River to Fort Maldin in Ontario. Proctor left the more seriously wounded Americans in Frenchtown under the watch of a single British officer, pledging that the redcoats would return and convey the remainder to Maldin for medical attention. This second promise likewise proved worthless.

Early the next day, it was Indians wearing red and black war paint who returned to Frenchtown. They gleefully set fire to the structures housing the wounded. Many Americans perished inside the burning buildings; the savages tomahawked others as they hobbled or crawled out of the flames.

Acting in the absence of their supreme chief, Tecumseh, the Indians forced the surviving wounded to attempt a march through freezing temperatures to Fort Maldin. The pitiful party set out across the ice and snow. Whenever a prisoner fell, unable to go any further, he was slaughtered and scalped where he lay. The mutilated bodies of the Kentuckians, left for carrion, were strewn over miles of trail where they remained throughout the winter and spring.

Tecumseh, upon learning of the atrocities committed by his warriors, expressed outrage and angrily confronted Proctor for allowing them. The Shawnee's fury, however, was as nothing compared to that which swept Kentucky when the news reached home of what had happened to husbands, brothers, and sons on the frozen banks of the River Raisin.

Even so, six more months passed, marked by further bungling and heavy casualties, while the United States tried to conduct war on a shoestring effort. Finally, the secretary of war authorized William Henry Harrison, commander of the Army of the Northwest, to call up from state and territorial militias the numbers of men he needed. He requested from Kentucky, which had already given sacrificially, between four hundred and two thousand militiamen. The aging Kentucky governor, Isaac Shelby, a beloved hero of the Revolutionary War, promptly published an appeal to the pride of Kentucky militia.

> Fellow-soldiers your government has taken measures to act effectually against the enemy in Upper Canada. Gen. Harrison, under the authority of the President of the United States, has called upon me for a strong body of troops to assist in effecting the grand projects of the campaign . . .
> . . . Believing as I do, that the ardor and patriotism of my countrymen has not abated, and that they have waited with impatience a fair opportunity of avenging the blood of their butchered friends, I have appointed the 31st day of August next, at Newport, for a general rendezvous of KENTUCKY VOLUNTEERS. I will meet you there in person. I will lead you to the field

of battle, and share with you the dangers and honors of the campaign. Our services will not be required more than sixty days after we reach headquarters . . .

Those who have good rifles, and know how to use them will bring them along. Those who have not, will be furnished with muskets at Newport.

This stirring appeal was printed on handbills and carried into every corner of Kentucky including Lewis County, formed in 1807 from Mason County and encompassing the river country around New Ephrata.

Unlike other Commonwealth villages and towns, New Ephrata was not caught up in patriotic fervor or a craving for revenge. David Singletary had always preached allegiance to God first, community second, and family third. Then, he would grudgingly add, render unto Caesar what was Caesar's—provided that Caesar first came and demanded it. In no event did many in New Ephrata believe that they should put their lives on the line for Kentucky or the United States.

In the case of William Cumings, though, extenuating circumstances prevailed.

About the same time that Shelby's handbills were being printed in Frankfort, Peter Ayles had a run-in with young Seth Swearingen. Seth, all of eleven years in age, was inflamed over the gossip he'd heard about Peter and Becky Cumings. Like virtually every boy in the neighborhood, Seth was infatuated with Becky. At his first opportunity to exact justice—a chance meeting with Peter on the road—young Swearingen charged the seventeen-year-old and bowled him over.

Also on the road by chance was William. He witnessed the attack, admiring Seth's pluck and ferocity. When, however, Ayles began to get the better of the fray, William stepped in and halted the proceedings. Embarrassed over the black eye and bruised mouth inflicted on him by a lesser antagonist, Peter spread the story that William had assaulted him after separating the original combatants. Seth's shrill testimony to the contrary did not stop the Ayles family from preferring charges of assault and battery against William.

The Shelby handbill and William's arraignment before the justice of the peace arrived on the same day in the county seat of

Clarksburg. James, having joined brother William on the trip to court, became excited upon witnessing the handbill being nailed to the courthouse door and hearing it read aloud in all its florid intensity. "Hey, William!" the younger Cumings exclaimed. "Let's you an' me sign up with the militia an' go to Newport! You're the crack shot of Lewis County, an' I ain't far behind. We'd show everybody a thing or two!"

William laughed off the notion of joining the militia—at least, so far as it included any joint venture with James.

"Ma would skin us both," he rejoined. "Besides," he added, more seriously, "you know how Tony's health is failin' him. He may get better, and he may not. Even if he gets okay, we're gonna be needed around the place more than ever."

Still, James had planted a seed in William's mind. When it appeared that the judge was taking the Ayleses' complaint seriously, and began talking about a trial date in September, William grew uneasy over the visions of a large fine and a jail sentence. Finally, he blurted out: "I won't be able to make any September trial, your honor. I'm gonna join the militia so I can answer Governor Shelby's call for volunteers at Newport the end of August. We're headed to Canada to lick the British and Injuns!"

James stared at his brother in astonishment. A couple of men awaiting court appearances jumped out of their pews and rushed forward to take William's hand. "That's great, Cumin's!" thundered one of them, a big farmer named Hiram Bennett. "If you're a-goin', I reckon I am, too! I been thinkin' about it ever since they read out what the governor writ on that bill."

In lieu of a gavel, the judge rapped the tabletop with his knuckles. "Order in here!" he bellowed. He peered up at William. "If you're serious, young man," the magistrate said, rubbing his stubbled chin, "see that your commanding officer provides this court with evidence that you have enlisted, and charges will be dismissed." He shot a glance at the Ayles entourage and was met with scowls. "What Mr. Cumings is volunteering to do," the judge said evenly, "is of considerably more importance than the matter complained of. Mr. Cumings, the court's offer stands!"

James berated William on the way back to New Ephrata for omitting him from the pending adventure. William, however, was more concerned about how he was going to break his news to

Rebekah Cumings. Instead of going straight home, he decided to stop at Samuel's house and solicit advice.

Wearing a wan smile, the oldest brother listened to William's account of the day's events. When the little tale was told, the smile disappeared. Samuel stood up and moved to the fireplace. He reached above the mantel and took down the rifle given their father years ago by Grandpa Russel. Samuel handed the weapon to William.

"It's yours, now," Samuel said, with suitable solemnity. "It'll be used in defense of our family. Despite the prevailing sentiment around here, you and I know that we're part of a free state and a free nation. Now, New Ephrata will be sending at least one man to help defend it. Tell Ma I said that, and show her Pa's rifle."

Although he had hoped for a few hundred more men, Governor Shelby wasn't dissatisfied with the response at Newport. Upwards of four thousand volunteers, representing almost every company of militia in the Commonwealth, crowded into the little town across the river and just upstream from Cincinnati. This was twice the number Harrison had requested.

Capt. Aaron Stratton arrived at the head of a company of horsemen from Lewis and Greenup counties, including William and Hiram Bennett. They were smartly attired in knee-length black hunting shirts and gray breeches. Stratton, one of the organizers of Lewis County and a man of means, had personally financed the clothing for his company. Each volunteer brought his own weapons—knives, hatchets, pistols, long rifles, and a scattering of swords—and his own mount.

The sixty-three-year-old Shelby greeted the turnout warmly, and promised them battle and victory. Then began the laborious process of moving the entire force northward to join Harrison's army at Lower Sandusky on Lake Erie.

Accompanying the volunteers from Harrodsburg in central Kentucky was a sow shoat. The Harrodsburg militiamen, just commencing their march to Newport, had halted outside of town to watch a tussle between two pugnacious porkers. Once the loser had been put to squealing flight, the men resumed their march—and the victor joined the procession. At Newport she became known publicly as the governor's pig, in honor of Shelby, and more discreetly as Sue, in honor of Shelby's wife, Susannah.

Sue pleased everyone by choosing to ride one of the barges

crossing the river with men and horses. She trekked tirelessly across Ohio with the army as its mascot and good luck charm.

At Urbana, Shelby and the Kentuckians enlisted an old and valued friend. Big Simon Kenton, just five years younger than the governor but still a robust specimen, came along in unofficial capacity as a scout and adviser on Indian ways. To the delight of William and Hiram Bennett, the giant frontiersman recognized them (or, at least, spotted family resemblances) and cheerily greeted both by the last name.

As the militia continued its northward movement, a bold young Rhode Islander named Oliver Hazard Perry was achieving immortality on Lake Erie.

Perry, in command of nine small warships, took on the highly regarded British Commodore R.H. Barclay and a contingent of six larger, better-armed vessels from the world's mightiest navy. The quicker American fleet was maneuvered into close quarters, and Perry forced Barclay into submission with a devastating mixture of cannon and rifle fire.

Harrison at Lower Sandusky and Proctor at Fort Maldin, on opposite sides of the lake, were aware the battle was taking place but did not immediately know the outcome. Two days later, Harrison received the twenty-eight-year-old Perry's laconic dispatch: "We have met the enemy and they are ours—two ships, two brigs, one schooner and a sloop."

This was stupendous, unexpected news for Harrison. With the control of Lake Erie in American hands, the British could no longer threaten Detroit or safely utilize Fort Maldin as a base of operations. As a result of the two-hour naval engagement, Upper Canada lay exposed and vulnerable from the southwest.

Shelby and his Kentuckians reached Lower Sandusky at about the time Perry was unloading prisoners there. Once Harrison and Shelby sat down to plan strategy, welcoming Perry into their deliberations, it didn't take long to agree on invading Canada and attacking Fort Maldin.

Harrison shared the decision with his and Shelby's men. As promised all along, they were about to invade Canada. But the news was not all good for the Kentuckians. The mounted militia would have to leave its horses at Lower Sandusky in order to be transported across Lake Erie.

The mounts were penned behind a fence made of brush and fallen timbers on a point of land entering the lake between the Portage River and Sandusky Bay. The site, recommended by Harrison, was abandoned farmland, and at the time of Shelby's arrival in mid-September the grass had grown high and thick.

The Kentucky militiamen and Harrison's regulars pitched camp along the outside of the fence. The former spent the evening grousing about the abandonment of their horses. Also on their minds, though not as a topic of discussion, was concern over crossing the lake. Most of them had never seen a body of water approaching its size.

After everyone except the picket had turned in for the night, something panicked the horses and sent them stampeding blindly against the brush fence. A breach was opened, and many of the steeds poured through and galloped into the bivouac of the Kentuckians.

William awakened to the thunder of many hooves as the herd swept down upon the camp. Shouts and screams rang out in the dust-filled darkness. Attempting to gain his feet, William received a stunning blow to the left hip and collapsed in helpless agony. Miraculously, the fleeing beasts passed him by without inflicting further injury.

Other soldiers fared much more poorly, including three who were trampled to death. Groans and curses sounded from all around, part of a general confusion as campfires were hastily rekindled and men tried to locate scattered equipment and supplies. The damaged fence was secured temporarily until the roundup of the runaways could be made in the light of day.

William lay very still, gritting his teeth and sweating despite the chill night air. The pain in his hip was intense. But he had already decided to hide the seriousness of the injury. Otherwise, he would be left behind to help tend the horses while his companions moved on to engage the enemy.

The first stage of crossing Lake Erie began at daybreak. Fortunately for William, the distance to the embarkation point was short. He told Hiram that the painful limp was the result of blisters on his foot.

As the Kentuckians were clambering into several small transport ships, conversation centered around the refusal of a Pennsylvania militia company to cross over into Canada. The officers of this company told Harrison that their men must remain on American soil "on account of their constitutional scruples." Harrison angrily impugned their courage, but did not press the matter, and the Pennsylvanians departed Lower Sandusky in a huff.

Of more personal importance to the Kentuckians was the firm refusal of Sue the sow to cross the lake with them. She could not be cajoled or coerced into one of the transports. The Harrodsburg faction theorized dryly that she was observing "constitutional scruples" barring her from participation in the invasion.

The army spent several days on cramped, slimy Middle Sister Island off the Ohio coast, while Harrison and Perry reconnoitered the Canadian shore from the deck of a schooner. Despite the filth, cold, and small rations of food, William was thankful for the inactivity. The pain in his hip had lessened, and he hoped it would heal before being subjected to more exercise.

Harrison and Perry returned, and in consultation with Shelby reached the decision to land the invasion force not far from Fort Maldin. Resistance was anticipated, prompting the development and issuance of a battle plan. The troops shed their boredom at the prospect of finally facing the enemy.

On the morning of September 27, the army departed Middle Sister Island, and that afternoon the flotilla put ashore at an open field several miles distant from the British fort. Harrison was prepared for a fight, but no sign of the enemy could be found. A brisk march ensued in the direction of Fort Maldin, during which the men sang "Yankee Doodle Dandy" at the top of their lungs.

What they found at the end of their march were the smoldering ruins of Proctor's one-time stronghold. The redcoats and Indians, having torched the fort the afternoon previous, were in full and hasty retreat into Ontario along the River Thames.

Chapter 37

*C*apt. Aaron Stratton's company of Lewis and Greenup militiamen was part of the Third Regiment, Kentucky Volunteers, under the command of Col. John Poage. The day after the Americans invaded Canada, Poage elevated Stratton to the rank of major. Stratton's replacement as company commander, Capt. Richard Soward, promoted William Cumings to fourth corporal.

While proud of his new rank, William understood that there would be less inactive time to rest his aching hip. He now had responsibility for the preparedness of others.

Harrison was elated by the abandonment of Fort Maldin. With the Americans in control of Lake Erie, Proctor apparently decided that the fort had become too vulnerable. Catching the fleeing British and their Indian allies, though, was going to be a tall order. The enemy, with the aid of hundreds of horses, had a day's jump on the pursuers. The latter were without mounts and any immediate prospect of them.

But Col. Richard Johnson's crack regiment of Kentucky horse soldiers, sent around Lake Erie to secure Detroit, soon crossed the Detroit River and arrived at Maldin. Spirits bolstered by Johnson's presence and the renewed prospect of a battle, the infantrymen vowed to do whatever was necessary to overtake the redcoats and Indians. The venerable Shelby clarified the challenge in an oft-repeated message: "If we desire to take the enemy, we must do more than he does by early and forced marches."

With Johnson's mounted regiment leading the way, and the

foot soldiers following at a half-run, the army made twenty-five miles along the shore of Lake St. Clair on the first day of pursuit. By degrees, William grew inured to the pain in his hip, convincing himself to accept it as a fact of life.

At the mouth of the Thames River, the Americans spotted a hovering eagle and took the sighting as an omen of good fortune. More importantly, following the trail of their quarry along the Thames, they became the beneficiaries of the enemy's haste in the way of abandoned food, clothing, and gunpowder. As the gap narrowed between pursuers and pursued, Harrison's army came upon pile after pile of discarded supplies and munitions—and even field pieces.

Nine days after finding the ashes of Fort Maldin, the last four spent in long and difficult marches, Harrison and his forces caught up with the enemy and met them face-to-face eighty miles into Ontario.

Proctor (or, more probably, the brilliant Tecumseh) chose a solidly defensible spot on the Thames at which to turn and fight. Simon Kenton, among the spies sent out in advance of the main body of Americans, reported that the prospective battleground was flanked by a high bank of the river to the east and a large marsh to the west. A smaller, narrow marsh lay between the large one and the road which followed the river. Simon noted that the higher ground, wooded chiefly in large beech trees intermixed with oak, was "tolerably" free of underbrush.

Sometime around four on the afternoon of October 5, with Johnson's regiment in the lead, the American army made its approach up the road. Harrison called a halt when the enemy came into view. Two long, tree-shaded lines of scarlet-clad British regulars were stretched across the road, the first line positioned thirty paces in front of the second. The riverbank lay to their left and the small swamp to their right. The redcoats, seven hundred in number, were aligned in open order, three feet apart, muskets held in readiness. One small cannon, the only artillery Proctor still had available, squatted defiantly in the middle of the road.

In addition, a mixed assemblage of regulars and Indian warriors waited in the high grass on the narrow ridge between the marshes. But Kenton had determined that the great majority of the savages, possibly a thousand strong, were concealed within the large, densely overgrown swamp to the Americans' left.

Making last-minute adjustments to his plan of attack, Harrison split up Johnson's mounted regiment into two battalions. The first battalion, under the command of Johnson's brother James, would charge the two lines of redcoats; the second, under Johnson, was to engage the enemy on the ridge. The infantry stood ready to follow the mounted men into combat at both points.

Poage's regiment, consisting largely of untried volunteers, was part of the rear, or reserve, brigade. As a result, William heard more than he saw of the ensuing battle.

Having formed four columns of two riders abreast, five hundred Kentucky horsemen approached the British lines to draw their fire. Once that occurred, they responded to the bugler's blast and Lt. Col. James Johnson's signal to attack. Spurs dug into the tender flanks of horses, and from five hundred throats came the battle cry: "Remember the Raisin! Remember the Raisin!" The cannon belched once, but its load landed harmlessly between two of the onrushing columns. The screaming riders thundered through both lines of the intimidated redcoats. They wheeled their mounts, swiftly alighted, and delivered a withering fire into the shattered ranks of the unnerved foe.

The British hurled down their weapons and thrust up their hands. This part of the battle was over in a minute's time. Observing the fiasco from a vantage point far to the rear, and deciding all was lost, Proctor took to his waiting carriage. He, too, remembered the River Raisin.

On the far side of the small swamp, the Tecumseh-led Indians were much more determined to fight.

Col. Richard Johnson personally rode with an advance guard of twenty men onto the ridge between the swamps. This courageous action, designed to draw fire and reveal the position of the enemy, would earn the ill-fated little band the nickname of the "Forlorn Hope."

After several tense moments of unnatural quiet, a savage cry split the silence. An instant later, hundreds of rifles rang out almost as one from within the large swamp. Twelve of the twenty members of the "Forlorn Hope" fell from their horses, slain or mortally wounded. Johnson, also wounded, maintained his steed and ordered the rest of the mounted battalion into the swamp before the Indians could reload.

The boggy conditions made this a bad notion. Recognizing his mistake, Johnson hastily bade his men to dismount and engage the enemy on foot. He alone stayed in the saddle as the battle raged, making an attractive target for enemy muskets.

Shelby, seeing the horsemen dismount and disappear into the miry swamp, and hearing the war whoops of the Indians and the staccato discharge of firearms, gave the impatient front line of infantry the order it craved to hear. "Those brave men will be cut to pieces!" he bellowed, and directed the foot soldiers on the run into the marsh.

It was with some difficulty that the officers of the remaining brigades restrained their eager troops from following.

Johnson, weakened by multiple wounds, struggled to stay astraddle his white mare. He happened to glance down just as an Indian broke from the underbrush and raced toward him with upraised war club. The colonel managed to point his pistol and discharge it into the chest of the warrior, who fell dead at the feet of Johnson's horse.

Almost immediately, the ferocity of the Indians abated. As though responding to a silent command, the red men abruptly quit the battle and melted away into the forest in full retreat. Though Johnson did not know it, he had just dispatched the greatest Indian leader of them all—the heart and soul of the red man's confederacy, the one warrior thought to be invincible. Tecumseh was felled, and with him the great Indian vision of a redeemed homeland.

Hearing the battle subside without having seen action, William Cumings didn't quite know how to feel. He had hobbled along for nearly two weeks, hiding his injury and enduring the pain, in order to fight. On the other hand, he hadn't stopped a bullet or felt a tomahawk smash his skull.

For several minutes, Americans continued to take occasional shots at the fleeing Indians. The Battle of the Thames, which proved not to be much of a battle after all, was over. Proctor made good his escape, but he would have a lot to answer for when he faced his superiors. Harrison's men rounded up about seven hundred British prisoners and collected a wealth of munitions and supplies. It wasn't until those things were done, and the wounded located and tended to, that Harrison inquired of his officers whether Tecumseh had escaped or lay among the enemy dead.

Dusk was falling when a small detail, including Simon Kenton, began sifting the corpses of the red warriors. They fanned out, hoping to conclude their search for the chieftain before daylight failed completely. When Kenton came to the body of the Indian shot by Johnson, he carefully studied the shadowy, majestic features. Then he quickly bent over the corpse, gripped one bare, cold shoulder, and rolled it belly-down.

A shout sounded from another part of the battlefield. Kenton and others strode over to where one of Harrison's scouts exultantly stood astraddle a body richly garbed and ornamented. A trampled headdress of many bright feathers lay beside it.

"This is him, ain't it, Simon?" the scout asked, cockily. "This has gotta be him!" Other men gathered around, unsheathing their knives.

Simon glanced down. "Yep," he said, with false enthusiasm. "That's the red butcher hisself."

Quickly, the silver armbands were stripped from stiffening limbs. The necklace of bear claws and silver beads went next. The bloodstained, finely beaded buckskin shirt was ripped into two dozen souvenirs, followed by the moccasins. Finally, they started in on the skin. Kenton had stayed only long enough for them to shove past him in their ghoulish eagerness to strip the corpse. Then he spat on the ground and stalked off, his face twisted in disgust.

The big frontiersman was still scowling when he sat himself down before the campfire next to William.

"Well," the younger man asked, wincing as he shifted his weight off the damaged hip, "did you find the big chief the general wanted to know about, or did he get away?"

Kenton looked at him long and hard. "Nope," he said at last, "he didn't get away. He's out there. But he won't be there in the mornin' time. His braves will come find him an' tote him off to a fine funeral." Noting William's serious look, he added: "Aw, there won't be no more fightin' here. It's just that Tecumseh was a great chief, so they'll risk their necks t' claim his body. They'll hide him where no white man'll ever find him. It's a damn good thing, too."

The big man raised his face to the Canadian night sky, dotted with stars. "Tecumseh mought'a known he was gonna die today," he mused. He looked at William once more. "Can you keep a secret?" he asked abruptly. Reassured by a vigorous nod, Kenton resumed.

"Tecumseh give his chiefly trappin's to another Injun to wear in the battle. He's lyin' out there now, just in plain buckskins. He'll have the last laugh on them damn vultures hackin' away at the wrong Injun."

Early the next morning, Kenton revisited the field of the dead. Tecumseh was gone. So was the mutilated corpse Simon had so willingly misidentified.

The Americans spent the day burying their own fallen in one long trench, wrapped in blankets, and laying the British dead in another. After a second night on the battlefield, they began the long trek toward Detroit. Canoes and flatboats transported the wounded down the Thames. William's hip was getting no better, but he refused to place himself in among those who had received their injuries in combat.

Winter asserted itself, packing snow and ice on the back of a biting wind. Footing grew uncertain. The infantrymen grumbled about not having their horses, still penned at Lower Sandusky across the lake. This time the weather would not permit any crossing of Erie. Instead, they were forced to walk around its perimeter. When the army crossed the Detroit River and regained native soil underfoot, it, too, was frozen.

The Americans straggled into Detroit for the better part of a day. They enjoyed a brief, blessed respite while the various companies re-formed. Then they were off again into the foul elements, headed for Lower Sandusky.

Not far south of Detroit, they broke the ice on a small, shallow creek and began wading across. William, favoring his throbbing hip, tripped on the stones in the creek bottom and went down. Two of his men blundered into him from behind and fell on him, their combined weight pressing his injured hip against the stones. An explosion of pain caused him to lose consciousness.

Seven months later, summer arrived in New Ephrata.

A man and a little girl sat lazily on the front porch of Jonathan Ruggles's split-log home, which doubled as the local cobbler's shop. A warm June breeze slipped through the shin-high weeds in the yard. The man removed his battered hat from its jaunty perch over his eyes and forehead and dropped it next to a stout hickory crutch.

"Tell me again, Uncle William," piped eight-year-old Lucinda Ruggles, blue eyes sparkling, "about Sue the pig!"

"Now, Lucy," the man responded, playfully placing the palm of one large hand over the cotton-haired head of his young interrogator, "I just told you about us Kentucky men leavin' little Sue at Lake Erie when she wouldn't go on to Canada."

The girl wrinkled her brow and stretched her skinny body in frustration, then caught the twinkle in the gray eyes studying her and smiled. "You know what I mean!" she squealed. She plopped herself onto his lap and tugged gently on the auburn beard brushing against her face. "Ma says you're just a big tease to all the girls," she taunted. "Now tell me 'bout when you came back from the war and found Sue the pig."

"What does your ol' ma know, anyway?" he protested in a theatrically loud voice, then cocked his head in anticipation of a response from inside the house.

There appeared in the frame doorway the diminutive form of Elizabeth Ruggles—she whose infantile wail, coupled with the crying of her older sister Mathilda, led to their rescue in the Maryland wilderness thirty-eight years before. Though not blood kin to the Cumingses, and raised in another household, Mathilda and Elizabeth had always been like sisters to the Cumings siblings.

"I mought choose to christen you with my wash water, William Cumin's," Elizabeth bluffed, indicating an unseen bucket within the house, "exceptin' you'd be obliged to draw me another bucketful. You better watch what you say about your betters." She slipped back inside.

Elizabeth's marriage to Jonathan Ruggles was the pairing of orphans found along Nemacolin's Path at separate times, by separate caravans making their way to New Ephrata. Lucinda, the youngest child, had two sisters as well as a slow-witted brother by the name of Moses.

"Well, when the army got back to Ohio, where we'd left our horses," William began the story the child had demanded, "why, there was Sue, fat and sassy as ever in spite o' the winter. You see, the men who stayed with the horses made sure Sue got fed full rations ever' day even if the horses had t' go without."

"What's rations?" queried Lucinda.

"Real bad grub," William answered. "Anyway, the army came

home across Ohio, grousin' and cussin' over not havin' enough food. They even got into fights. But through all of that, we saw to Sue gettin' a daily snootful.

"Once the army crossed the river at Maysville, it was disbanded. Everybody went home." He paused, as though that were all of the story.

"What happened to Sue?" Lucinda demanded on cue, emphasizing her impatience with a yank on the red beard.

"Well, she was left with a farmer in Maysville to rest up for a spell. When she felt fit to travel again, she went to Traveler's Rest, which is where Governor Shelby lives. Sue's a member of the governor's family now. Sits under the dinin' room table at the governor's own feet and roots out the best scraps. Uses a fine linen napkin."

Lucinda laughed, just as she had done numerous times at the same story. She snuggled against William's hunting shirt. "I love you," she said emphatically.

He wrapped one arm around her and issued a squeeze. "That's what all the ladies tell me," he responded loudly, and didn't flinch when Elizabeth's dust cloth smacked him across the back of the head.

"Some cobbler's apprentice you are!" The lady of the house sniffed in mock irritation. "You'd better get busy on those shoes before Master Jonathan gets back here. He'll half your wages!"

"Oh, my pockets couldn't stand that, for sure!" William quipped, reaching for the tools scattered about the porch. Unable to put weight on the permanently damaged hip without extreme pain, he had determined he would try the sedentary trade of shoemaking and repair.

Lucinda watched him adoringly. "I'm gonna marry you someday," she announced.

He glanced at her and laughed. "You're too short," he retorted. "Come see me when you grow up!"

"That's when I'm gonna marry you—when I grow up," she said emphatically.

Part IV

Texas
(1821 - 1874)

Chapter 38

*I*t was apparent to the two gray-haired men seated across the table from him that Antonio Maria Martinez, governor of the Province of Texas in New Spain, had changed his mind.

Short, stout Moses Austin, turning sixty on his next birthday, and the tall, spare Baron de Bastrop, of uncertain age but older than Austin, tried to suppress any premature show of exultation while Martinez pretended to read once again the epistle addressed to him:

"Moses Austin, a native of the state of Connecticut in the United States of America and a resident of Missouri, with due respect, sets forth and declares that, being a vassal of His Catholic Majesty when the Province of Louisiana was turned over to the French nation, and, later sold to the United States—as the credentials I have presented to your Excellency show—saw himself forced to remain there without making an attempt to immigrate so that he might not lose his property and possessions.

"These, added to his love for his family, detained him; but upon learning of the establishment of the political constitution of the Spanish monarchy and because the removal of immigrants was not forbidden, he has come with the purpose of asking the requisite permission to settle in this province under your command in the place best suited for the cultivation of cotton, wheat, sugar cane, corn, etc.—for which reason he needs to select a suitable place from his knowledge of the requisites.

"At the same time, he presents himself as the agent of three hundred families who, with the same purpose in view . . . bind themselves to bring credentials and testimonials proving their good character and conduct. All of them, or the greater part of them, have property. Those without it are industrious. As soon as they are settled, they bind themselves by oath to take up their arms in defense of the Spanish government either against the Indians, filibusters, or any other enemy that may plan hostilities—coming upon call and obeying the orders given them. For this reason, I respectfully ask that you will deign to take whatever action you may think just—in case you have the authority; or, in case you have not, to send it to the proper person with such information as you may think just and may consider necessary. I will appreciate this kindness.

"Bexar, December 26, 1820."

The brown eyes of Martinez smiled.

"I have," he said in Spanish, glancing at Austin, "a much clearer picture of your proposed business with the Crown." Bastrop translated the governor's words into English. Austin's dark eyes glittered expectantly.

"I will see what I can do on your behalf," Martinez added. "I alone do not have sufficient authority. However, your case will be placed before my superiors, along with a favorable recommendation." The governor's demeanor was relaxed, friendly, encouraging—in all ways the opposite of what Austin had encountered just three days previous.

Martinez stood and extended his hand. Austin took it joyously, smiling and bobbing his head. No further words or translations of words were necessary to convey the warm support of the governor.

"What a turnaround! What a Christmas miracle!" Austin said to Bastrop after they left the governor's office and stepped out into the damp, chilled Texas air. "What a wonderful turn of circumstances for myself and my family!" He thumped Bastrop on the shoulder. "Many thanks, my friend," he added more soberly, emotion tugging at his voice. "My debt to you is great, and I pledge that it will be repaid."

The governor might well have smiled again had he caught a glimpse of the departing duo—the gaunt, caped figure of the baron and the stumpy, rotund Austin in his thread-bare traveling clothes. A strange pair they made, these overaged, underfinanced entrepreneurs. Even stranger were the circumstances which led to Martinez's complete about-face.

Bastrop had lived in Bexar for fifteen years following his departure from the Ouachita Valley, years filled with grandiose plans for amassing wealth which never came to fruition. Even so, his steadfast loyalty to the provincial and municipal governments had long since served to dissolve the doubts and rumors aroused by his arrival. He was by 1820 a trusted friend and confidant of the local authorities.

Sharing a bench with other idle conversationalists on the wind-sheltered north side of the main plaza, the baron had watched with interest Austin's arrival on horseback two days before Christmas. After a futile fuss over his mud-spattered clothing, Austin located the governor's office and made as dignified an entry as his soiled garb and travel-stiffened torso would permit.

The governor's visitor looked familiar to the baron. The Dutchman, having just purchased a supply of cigars, had nothing better to do than wait for him to reappear. Within the half-hour, he did, and judging from his clouded visage the meeting with the governor had not gone well. Rank curiosity about the man and his purpose in coming to Bexar moved Bastrop to arise from the bench and intercept him.

"*Señor,*" he said warmly, removing his sombrero, "you and I know one another from some other place, do we not?"

Austin, red-faced and flustered, glanced up at the angular inquisitor. A look of recognition softened his angry expression. "Why, yes," he replied, trying to inject civility into his voice, "I believe so."

"I observed you when you rode into town," Bastrop purred, "and happened to see you leave the governor's office just now. I know that we have met before. If you are not in too much of a hurry, you would do me an honor by stopping at my humble *hacienda* for a meal."

Some of the anger was rekindled in Austin, mixed with embarrassment. "I—I do not have much time," he stammered. "The governor has informed me that he wishes me to depart Bexar—in fact, the Province of Texas—immediately."

Bastrop thumped the ash from his cigar. "I am a longtime acquaintance and supporter of Governor Martinez," he observed. "Once you and I have established that we are old friends, the governor will suffer your presence in Bexar indefinitely."

Austin jumped at the offer extended by this kind stranger. He was exhausted from weeks of horseback travel, exposure to bad weather, and insufficient food; that condition, coupled with the just-suffered defeat of his plans, threatened to overwhelm him. He took Bastrop's proffered hand in gratitude, collected his horse and his slave, Richmond, and accompanied the baron home.

Over a simple, hot supper, the men determined to their mutual satisfaction that they had met nearly twenty years before at a tavern in New Orleans. Then, at the encouragement of his host, and feeling the warm glow from a glass of wine, Austin laid aside his caution and pride and shared the unhappy details leading to the disastrous session with Martinez.

The mining and smelting of lead near Ste. Genevieve, in the portion of Spanish Louisiana which would become Missouri, had brought a measure of wealth to the dynamic Austin. But a series of misfortunes, chief among them the collapse of the Bank of St. Louis during the Panic of 1819, left him in financial disrepair. His vision of developing a colony in Texas, considered once before, was revived as an opportunity for regaining solvency and restoring his good name.

Then, at the conclusion of a grueling and time-consuming trip to Bexar, he had met with refusal in a matter of minutes. The governor, nettled over the unwelcome interruption of scheduled business, would not hear of any colonizing schemes. The fact that the interview was haltingly conducted in French, the one tongue Martinez and Austin knew in common, had not helped matters.

"I have nothing to look forward to but a long return journey and facing up to creditors and a disappointed family," Austin said mournfully. "Frankly, Baron, I am a desperate man. My complete ruin is at hand."

Groping for words of encouragement, Bastrop lit another cigar. "You must remember, *Señor*," he said at last, "that this is *Navidad*—Christmas, the season of miracles. If you are a believer, then believe that your efforts in coming to Bexar have not been in vain. Stay here with me for the holiday! We will attend Mass on Christmas Eve and Christmas Day and petition for divine intervention, and perhaps see Governor Martinez again."

Studying the crestfallen features of his guest, Bastrop added, "In the meantime, let us busy ourselves with writing out your proposal. If it contains certain things—such as proof of your former Spanish citizenship, such as development of the agriculture and economy of Texas—the governor may very well give it his blessing and forward it to the higher authorities. I also believe we can secure the endorsement of the *cabildo* of Bexar, the town council."

Moderately encouraged, and dreading to make the long trip back to Missouri empty-handed, Austin readily agreed to Bastrop's plan of action. Left in the capable hands of the baron, things went even better than expected.

Immediately following the second interview, which was greatly aided by Bastrop's translating back and forth, Martinez wrote to the commandant of the Eastern Interior Provinces, located in Monterrey. His letter enthusiastically supported the proposal of Austin, "a man of some honesty and formality." While Austin was returning to Missouri, Commandant General Joaquin de Arredondo received Martinez's letter, submitted the petition to the provincial legislature for approval, and subsequently wrote Martinez:

> It will be very expedient to grant the permission asked for by Moses Austin for the removal and settlement in the Province of Texas of the three hundred families . . . It would be well also if, in addition to the first and most important conditions of being Catholics or agreeing to become so before they enter Spanish territory, and that of proving their character and good conduct as is offered in the said petition, they would take the required oath to be obedient to the government in all things . . .
>
> Very flattering hopes may then be entertained that the province will receive a noticeable development in the branches of agriculture, industry, and the arts through the new inventions they shall bring with them.

While Austin's request was receiving the best possible reception from Spanish politicos, the Missourian's trip home proved to be rougher than his failing constitution could handle. The treachery of a fellow-traveler left Austin and Richmond without horses or any means of killing game, and there followed a period of several days spent on foot, in cold, damp weather, with nuts and berries their only food.

Back home, Austin was overjoyed with the report from Martinez that his petition had been honored, and that he had been granted 200,000 acres (site unspecified) for the purpose of colonization. However, as he became bedridden and his health worsened over the next six months, he finally faced the bitter fact that he would not personally be able to realize his dream. Two days before Austin's death on June 10, 1821, his wife, Maria, wrote to their oldest son in New Orleans regarding the colonizing venture:

"He called me to his bedside, and with much distress and difficulty of speech begged me to tell you to take his place . . . to go on with the business in the same way he would have done."

So the task of establishing the first formal Anglo colony in Texas fell to twenty-seven-year-old Stephen Fuller Austin.

Chapter 39

*A*s capitalistic endeavors gradually supplanted the old communal system in New Ephrata, few benefited more than did the Cumings clan. Yet, the lure of free land in Texas would ultimately pull apart the family circle.

David Singletary lived on, a great scarecrow of a man, within a few years of attaining his centennial. Still able to evoke sensations of love, fear, and awe, he was, however, no longer the dynamic leader of a remote colony. Events and his great age had diminished him in authority and stature to a kind of neighborhood icon. He had ceased to preach, and in fact was seldom seen in the company of others. When not fasting and praying in the little cabin to the rear of his residence, Singletary stalked the ridges and wooded hollows of the countryside and talked out loud to God.

The elder Anthony Cumings, in honoring the bargain struck upon reaching New Ephrata in 1776, had always seen to the upkeep and operation of the community grist mill and sawmills. Following Anthony's death in 1806, Singletary attempted a number of unsatisfactory arrangements to keep the mills running. Finally, he and Samuel Cumings reached an agreement whereby ownership of the Sycamore Creek mill sites and improvements was conveyed to the widow Rebekah Cumings in exchange for her written pledge to run and repair those mills. Rebekah also kept half of the corn meal and lumber production, and shared the sales income from them with her miller and millwright John and James Cumings.

The floating sawmill at Brush Creek Island was retired from service because it presented a nuisance and a hazard to the ever-increasing steam traffic on the Ohio.

Samuel, Thomas, and William Cumings became partners in the family's boatbuilding enterprise. Hulls for steamboats were assembled at the yard in New Ephrata and floated downstream to Cincinnati, where they became finished products with the installation of steam engines and related mechanical parts.

But river travel remained Samuel's passion. Each spring, he piloted the steamboat *Paragon* with cargoes of freight and passengers down to New Orleans. In the summer and fall, when the water levels were low, he frequently took passage on slow-moving flatboats. This enabled him to more closely observe and take soundings of the Ohio and Mississippi channels for the purpose of updating his beloved charts. He was determined to produce and publish a pilot's guidebook that would be superior to Cramer's.

In October of 1820, Samuel and a nearly destitute French-American named John James Audubon were among the passengers on a flatboat journey from Cincinnati to Natchez. Having no money for his fare, Audubon agreed to earn passage as a hunter. His keen marksmanship kept passengers and crew supplied with fresh meat, primarily fowl. He carried a pocket flute on which he imitated bird calls, in addition to entertaining the dance-prone crew members with lively French tunes at day's close.

Audubon was much more interested in drawing the birds he bagged than in plucking them for the spit. Hard-drinking Capt. Jacob Aumack observed with scornful amusement Audubon's practice of propping up the feathered bodies with wire in order to replicate lifelike stances. The scorn turned into grudging admiration once the artist applied pencil, crayons, and chalk to paper. Magically, Audubon restored the vibrant life of his subjects and returned them to their woodland habitat. Samuel marveled at the Frenchman's drawings, and knew he was witnessing a true genius at work.

Over the course of the long voyage, a friendship developed between Samuel and John James Audubon. Part of the bond sprang from the discovery of a mutual aspiration: each wanted to have his chosen life's work published. Long after parting company in Natchez, they exchanged letters lamenting the difficulties of interesting a publisher in their respective masterpieces.

Almost exactly a year after the trip on Aumack's flatboat, Samuel received a letter from Audubon eagerly suggesting that he contact a Philadelphia publisher with the unlikely name of Eliakim Littell. While Littell did not wish to produce a volume of bird like-nesses, Audubon wrote, he had expressed interest in the French-man's chance mention of Samuel's river charts. As proof of this interest, Audubon enclosed Littell's rejection letter on which the Frenchman added the brusque notation: "BURN When You Have No Further Use Of It."

Arriving at the same time as Audubon's epistle was the Sep-tember 3, 1821, issue of the *Louisiana Advertiser* from New Or-leans. It was only after dashing off a letter to Littell, in which the charts and an accompanying gazetteer were described in glowing terms, that Samuel turned his attention to the newspaper.

His eye was arrested by a headline on an inside page: "Migrate to Texas." According to a subtitle, the account to follow consisted of "Extracts from letters addressed by Stephen F. Austin, Esq., to a gentleman in New Orleans." Recalling the fascination that the Spanish province held for John, Samuel perused the article.

Austin, it appeared, was given authority by officials of New Spain to assume the Texas land grant issued to his late father for the purpose of establishing a colony. Although the younger Austin had not visited the site of the grant, he wrote from Texas on July 20 that an eyewitness described it as "the richest and best watered part of the province. All travellers unite . . . in alleging the climate to be one of the most delightful in this, or any other country."

An extensive survey was to be made of the site, Austin assert-ed, after which he would personally "select the most judicious points for our settlement." He then noted that he was authorized "to introduce and settle on the grant, three hundred families; and they are permitted to carry with them all the property, effects and supplies they think proper . . . Every facility will be given calculat-ed to aid the settlers, and they will be secured in grants of land pro-portionate to the numbers of each family, and the force or means they possess of carrying on useful and agricultural pursuits.

"Liberal grants of land will also be made to mechanics of all descriptions who will become settlers; but no settler will be received, or grants made to any individual, who does not produce satisfactory evidence of a good character and industrious habits; and the settlers will supply themselves with certificates to this effect from some court, magistrate, mayor, justice, notary, or other public officer."

The Austin grant amounted to 200,000 acres. Although the

precise location remained a mystery, seemingly even to the recipient, it was apparently in the vicinity of the gulf coastal plain and near the lower reaches of the Brazos, San Bernard, and Colorado rivers. John quite possibly was familiar with the region, Samuel reflected, and he set aside the newspaper for his brother to read.

John fairly devoured the article, and wasted little time in broaching the subject of Texas to his mother.

"They're givin' away land down there," he told Rebekah. "Samuel has a newspaper from New Orleans, and there's a letter in it talkin' about comin' to Texas and gettin' free land. Those of us who kin go ought t' go."

At that moment, "those of us who kin go" stood for John and James, two of the family's three remaining bachelors. Tony had been stolen from them two years before by consumption, dying slowly and horribly. Samuel and Thomas, both with growing families, were doing well at their boatbuilding enterprise and were unlikely to contemplate a new start elsewhere. William, also a partner in the boat yard, was free from family constraints but faced life with a crippled hip which rendered one leg all but useless. It would be difficult for him to be of much help in clearing virgin land, raising stock, and farming.

John was, in fact, on fire to leave for almost any place, and he knew James felt the same way. They had grown heartily tired of running and repairing the Sycamore Creek mills, and their dissatisfaction was no secret to their mother.

"You know full well that I would never stand in the way of you two boys bettering yourselves," Rebekah told John. "I can find other help for the mills, or I can sell them to old man Catts. Of course, I hate to see you leave home. The Lord has truly blessed us here in New Ephrata." That having been said, a dark look crossed her face as she reflected on the community's current state of decline.

Then came the thought, as if divinely inspired. Without hesitation, Rebekah put it into words. "Maybe the girls and I should come along," she suggested to her astonished son. "That would give you and James a third grant to divide between you. And goodness knows, you'll need help to keep yourselves in a clean house and square meals."

John stared hard at her, not believing she was serious. He shrugged. "If you really want t' go, sure," he replied, "Come on. As you said, it'd mean that much more land."

"But remember, we're lookin' at life in the wilderness. There'll be lots o' hard work, and Becky and Sarah will be doin' without the nice things they've got here. There's liable t' be danger, too, from Indians . . ."

Rebekah cut him off. "No one in this family," she pointed out archly, "has nearly as much experience as I do in dealing with deprivation and danger." She was sixty-four years of age, but robustly healthy except for frequent pain in her wrists and hands—an ailment she dealt with so stoically that no one else even suspected.

In truth, John knew that his mother would be a valuable addition to the enterprise. But at this point in life, he told himself, she should be cozily settled before her stone fireplace, or somehow engaged in further spoiling the grandchildren. And what would her two maiden daughters, on whom she kept such a tight rein, think about their chances of finding acceptable suitors on a foreign frontier? Surely his mother was only joking!

John looked into those indomitable green eyes. "You're right, Ma," he said, keeping a straight face. "None of us has your experience. Why, shucks! We just need t' put you in charge and right up front, and follow you t' Texas."

"Being boiled and skinned alive would be too kind of a fate for you," she shot back, but his laugh forced her into a smile. "No, you boys go on to Texas and get your land," she continued. "Fix up things down there so as to make me comfortable, just in case. I'll pray about maybe joining you later."

But the idea was planted. And Rebekah had a compelling reason to shake the dust of New Ephrata from her feet for all time.

Recognizing the taller of the two white men being led before him, Chief Bowles wrapped his leathery face into a smile. "John Cumin's!" he exclaimed. "You come back to Cherokees."

This assurance of friendship relieved the apprehensions of James Cumings, who did not enjoy being escorted by armed, frowning braves. His brother had cautioned him to show no fear when their attempt to enter the village was met with a show of hostility. John had said something in the Cherokee tongue, and within a few moments they stood before the old chief and his crackling fire.

John and Bowles locked arms in an embrace, and began conversing in the Indian's tongue. While they talked, the chief occasionally smiled at James.

"This yellow-haired one did not grow so tall as my son-in-love John," Bowles rumbled. "Nor does he look so much like you as you looked like me, in the time long past when my scalp had not grown white. Yet, he is strong about the shoulders. He will make a fine brave.

"Both of you, sit and warm yourselves by my fire! Now, tell Old Bowles why you searched out the Cherokees. How many seasons has it been since you lived with us on the St. Francois?"

John thought it over. "Twelve years have gone by," he responded. "My brother and I are on our way to the flat country by the sea, where a man named Austin is giving away land to those who promise to become Spaniards."

"I know of this Austin, and what his father and he were given by the Spanish in San Antonio," Bowles said. "Our council chief, Richard Fields, is there now, to see if the Spanish chief has the same generosity in his heart for the Cherokee. Gatunwali, called in the old days Big Mush, made the journey with him."

"As to why I searched out you and your people," John said warmly, "I can say that it was solely to renew our friendship. I knew that the earthquakes drove you away from your home and that you settled in the western part of the Arkansas Territory. Then, when James and I stopped in Natchitoches on our way to find Austin's grant, we heard you had come to Texas—a day's hard ride west of the Sabine River, among the red hills and green pine trees. It was not difficult to find this village."

Bowles frowned. "According to our shaman, it was the Thunder Man who chased us from the banks of the St. Francois. Old Bowles can tell you that we left the Arkansas Territory because of the growing numbers of white men, and the trouble they always bring with them. We have come to Texas in desperation, hoping against hope that the Spaniards will welcome us and we can remain here in peace. Now the young American Austin and others are bringing in their own kind. This, I fear, does not bode well for the Cherokee."

Chapter 40

*A*s finally determined, the boundaries of Stephen F. Austin's grant enclosed a generous portion of southeast Texas. The southern limit followed a line located ten leagues inland from the Gulf of Mexico and running parallel to the coast. The land below this line was to remain an unsettled buffer strip between the colony and the open gulf.

Above the line, the grant extended northward one hundred and fifty miles or so to the ambitiously named Camino Real, over which John Cumings had ridden in 1807 en route from Natchitoches to Bexar. The colony's northern boundary tracked the winding thoroughfare in a northeast-to-southwest direction.

The western boundary followed the meanders of the Lavaca River; to the east, the colony ended at the San Jacinto River. Roughly, the distance between the two streams averaged one hundred and twenty-five miles.

The major rivers watering the colony were the Colorado and Brazos, flowing south from respective distances of six hundred and eight hundred miles. About halfway across the grant, where they entered the coastal plain, the valleys of these two streams merged with that of the smaller San Bernard River to form an immensely fertile region. It was along the Colorado and Brazos that Austin's earliest colonists settled.

Coastal Texas teemed with life, not all of it friendly.

John and James Cumings arrived at the Brazos River in March of 1822, searching for Stephen F. Austin and some of his well-advertised free land. They were directed instead to one Josiah Bell, and found him at his residence atop a high bluff on the west side of the river. Austin, it seemed, had departed for Mexico City in order to straighten out "legal matters." In his absence, Bell was managing the affairs of the enterprise and welcoming prospective colonists.

John presented Austin's agent with a letter, intended to serve as a certificate of character for both brothers. Composed at "Kinney, Lewis Co., Ky.," and addressed to Austin, it read:

> The bearers of this missive, Msrs. John & James Cumings, were raised in the county of Lewis, on the Ohio River in Kentucky. I take the liberty of recommending them to you as useful men whose family I have known for some years past. Their late father saw service as a commissioner for the adjoining county of Mason, when the neighborhood wherein they reside was part of that municipality. The said John Cumings has served Lewis County as a captain of militia, and a third brother, William, accompanied myself and General William Henry Harrison into Upper Canada during the late war against the British and Indians.
>
> I personally know the said John & James Cumings to be honest men, possessed of considerable industry and enterprise. In addition to those attributes, they are first rate mechanics who have the skills necessary to build and operate water mills. In my estimation, the addition of these men to your enterprise in Texas can only strengthen the chances of its success.
>
> As for myself, my reputation is established. Aside from exploits related to the aforementioned war, I was one of the organizers of the said Lewis County and have since maintained a position of prominence there. You may rest assured that my word as regards the character of men is not given lightly.
>
> I am, Sir,
Hon. Aaron Stratton, Esq.

Bell finished examining the epistle and handed it back to John. "It seems a real shame we can't have Mr. Honorable Stratton hisself jine up," he said dryly. "But I reckon you boys will pass muster. Hold on t' that letter, though, an' present it to Stephen when he gets back."

The applicants, Bell confirmed, were eligible to receive grants of six hundred and forty acres apiece as advertised, and, further, their two tracts could be laid out contiguously. Formal conveyance from the newly formed Mexican government must wait until Austin returned, but Bell urged the brothers to proceed with the research and selection of likely sites. He pointed out that the richest soil lay downstream.

"Stephen give me this location 'cause I asked him fer it," Bell commented. "Had I t' do it over again—and I believe I just may, yet—I'd get myself off this high prairie and find somethin' nearer the coast."

"What about Injuns?" asked James in a voice ripe with concern. "Are they bad here?" His brother pursed his lips to prevent a smile, and glanced aimlessly at the sky.

"Well, young fella," came the rejoinder, "we fer sure got Injuns in Texas, but they ain't been much problem as I know of. 'Course, things kin change—likely will, in truth, when more of us shows up an' starts clutterin' up their huntin' grounds.

"Now, where you're goin' you may run into a few Kronks. Just use your head, an' don't give 'em any chances t' get the advantage of you. I heerd tell they may be cannibals, so fer sure you don't want t' get yourself captured an' invited t' supper."

With this parting advice, Bell wished the brothers good luck and Godspeed.

At John's suggestion, they followed the river to its very mouth in order to make a complete inventory of their choicest options. On the way, they met colonists who were already clearing land. The encounters served to remind them that more competition for the best sites was arriving almost daily. Less than twenty miles into their return journey from the gulf, the brothers located a site they agreed to claim.

The locale, flat and flood-prone, was partly open prairie and partly forested in a fine array of trees bearded with Spanish moss: oak in several species, along with pecan, ash, hackberry, locust, elm, cypress, cottonwood, and sycamore. The most distinctive feature, though, was a proliferation of canebrakes—extensive stands of giant cane grass so thick as to be impenetrable. Bayous, sloughs, marshes, ponds, and lakes, around which willows and palmettos grew in profusion, encumbered the land and helped keep damp the poorly drained clay soil. "As you kin see," John lectured James, "almost anything is gonna grow here. An' there's plenty o' forage for stock the year-round."

They soon learned that game abounded, including an extraordinary number of migratory birds. Wild turkeys were plentiful. There was a tasty selection of water fowl, such as wood ducks, teal, and snipe. The forest also yielded deer, rabbit, and squirrel, while they readily caught catfish (several varieties) and bass in the streams and larger lakes.

Among the less pleasing forms of life, the brothers agreed, were alligators and insect pests. The former, big, ugly, and menacing, occasionally shortened fishing expeditions simply by putting in an appearance. Of the latter, the mosquito, wood tick, and horse fly became the most hated.

John and James persevered, first constructing a one-room cabin and then beginning to clear the land. Battling the mounting heat and humidity, they planted their first corn crop. An entire summer of dry, scorching heat passed without significant rainfall, and the crop shriveled and died.

Tempted though they were to quit the venture and return to Kentucky, the brothers decided to give Texas one more year. But not everyone in the colony felt the same way. A number of men pulled out, declaring that their wives would never agree to undergo such tortures. Even John and James had to admit that it might prove difficult to convince their mother and pampered sisters to stay in the challenging land that John had christened Eden-on-the-Brazos.

Fortunately for James, John was on hand when the younger brother first encountered a Karankawa.

The aroma of cooked turkey, emanating from their campfire, enticed a single "Kronk"—tall, naked, filthy, and equally slothful in movement and wit—to come shuffling out of the woods. James, mouth agape, glanced around hastily to locate the always-loaded Kentucky rifle.

In a quiet voice, John told him to stand still. Then, moving calmly and deliberately, the older brother stepped over to the fire, cut off a drumstick, and tossed it to the ground in the direction of their uninvited caller. The Indian picked up the sizzling morsel and inserted it between crooked rows of yellow teeth, apparently impervious to the scalding juices. He cleaned it to the bone, threw away that remnant, and gave John a wolfish, expectant look. John pointed to the turkey and then to himself and James. The Kronk scowled and jerked an imperious thumb toward his open mouth. John scowled back and made a theatrical move for the rifle.

The intruder uttered a one-syllable grunt, presumably a Karankawan oath, and lumbered back into the woods more quickly than he had emerged. James heaved a sigh of relief.

"That ugly devil's seen a rifle before," John commented with satisfaction. "He won't give us any more problems, less'n he forgets."

During the turbulent years of 1822 and 1823, major political events in Mexico proliferated like rabbits.

Stephen F. Austin arrived in Mexico's capital on April 9, 1822, with precious little money and even less knowledge of the Spanish language. He quickly learned that the chaotic state of government was not conducive to the resolution of minor issues like frontier colonization.

Austin's journey to Mexico City, in fact, was prompted by the emergence of Mexico at the close of 1821 as a nation independent of Spain. The advent of sovereignty threw into question the validity of Moses Austin's pact with the Spanish colonial authorities, transferred to his son just months before the finalization of Mexican independence. In San Antonio, Governor Martinez made it clear that the younger Austin must secure confirmation of his contract from the new nation. In order for this to happen, Martinez added, Austin should be on hand in the capital to personally persuade the new leadership.

Control of the infant nation was being contested by three factions: conservatives, who favored a strong centralist republic and retention of ruling-class status for the clergy and the rich; liberals, who clamored for creation of a federal republic to politically enable the rural *mestizos* and Indians; and General Agustin Iturbide, who had decided he should be the people's choice at the head of a monarchy.

A month after reaching Mexico City, Austin presented his case to the Mexican congress in hopes of a quick resolution. But on the night of May 18, thousands of demonstrators took to the streets in a massive show of support for Agustin I. The intimidated congress conferred upon the usurper Iturbide the title of emperor. Austin was forced to do his work all over again.

In October more of Austin's efforts were voided when Iturbide ordered the congress adjourned and established in its place a *junta,* consisting of forty hand-picked men. Admirably patient, Austin began pursuing his well-polished agenda with the new body politic. His persistence paid off early in 1823 with the passage of a colonization law offering surprisingly liberal grants of land.

It provided each qualifying head of household with a square league, or 4,428 American acres, for raising livestock, and a *labor*, or 177 acres, for farming pursuits. In addition, anyone bringing a special skill or ability (or significant wealth) to a colony could receive a five-league tract known as a *hacienda*. The colonists would be allowed to import on a duty-free basis their own machinery, implements, and household goods. In fact, they would not be assessed government taxes or tithes to the Catholic Church for a period of six years.

The colony organizer, or empresario, would receive three *haciendas*—a staggering 67,000 acres—for every two hundred families he brought into his colony. But, as the empresario Austin would later learn, being land-rich in an environment where land was being given away sounded better than it proved to be.

For the moment, Austin was elated with the new law, and prepared to return to Texas. However, the winds of political change were blowing again, due in part to the activities of a military leader and intriguer named Antonio Lopez de Santa Anna. In March the Mexican congress was returned to power, and the following month it exiled Iturbide. Fortunately for Austin, it also honored the concession given him by Iturbide's *junta*, and in a final stroke of generosity increased to three hundred the number of families an empresario could recruit.

Thirteen months after arriving in Mexico City, the young colonizer departed for Texas having abundantly achieved his goal. He could now legally issue titles to land grants on behalf of the Mexican government.

Among the acquaintances Austin made during his stay in the Mexican capital was Richard Fields, who shared with John Bowles and Big Mush the leadership of the Cherokee tribe occupying land near Nacogdoches. Fields was on essentially the same mission as Austin, seeking a grant of territory in Texas on which his tribe could settle, but he failed to emulate the success of Austin before his money ran out. He returned to East Texas with no formal approval of the Cherokee presence there, other than a vaguely worded letter from the new provincial governor in San Antonio, Jose Felix Trespalacios.

Chapter 41

*T*he first grants in Austin's colony were issued in the summer of 1824—more than thirty months after the arrival of the first settlers. In the interim, many colonists stayed on in spite of isolation, homesickness, an uncertain future, one particularly severe winter, an equally severe summer drought, primitive and unhealthy living conditions, frequent thefts and occasional murders perpetrated by the Indians, and numerous defections from their far-flung ranks.

Austin wrote about what he found upon his return in 1823: "The settlement was nearly broken up, in consequence of (my) long detention in Mexico, and emigration had totally ceased. Many of the first emigrants had returned (home) . . ."

It did not help that the Baron de Bastrop, who issued the titles as land commissioner for the colony, was required to first honor his commitment as a representative of Texas in the provincial congress at Monterrey. This further delayed the distribution of grants for nearly a year following Austin's return, and the settlers' mounting impatience grew audible.

Finally, though, the great occasion arrived. Prospective grantees were summoned to San Felipe de Austin, the newly established seat of government for the colony, where Bastop and Austin set about the business of dispensing land.

John Cumings was among the riders who streamed into San Felipe, a dusty village situated on the west side of the Brazos River at the Atascosito Road crossing. John had learned that Bastrop was involved in the process, and wondered whether the enterprising baron would recall their dealings of seventeen years before. It would be good to renew his acquaintance, John thought.

But there was a more pressing piece of business to pursue. As soon as he had tethered his horse, John located Josiah Bell and reintroduced himself.

"You'll no doubt remember, Mr. Bell," John began, "tellin' me an' my brother James that each of us was eligible t' receive a grant apiece."

Slowly and cautiously, with a quizzical stare, Bell agreed that he had "prob'ly" made such a statement.

"My point, sir," John continued, "is the Mexicans has come up with some new rules. One is that the grants we're s'posed to get are gonna be bigger than first promised. That's good. But another rule is that a man either has to be a head o' household to be eligible, or else he has to partner up with another fella. James an' me are not heads o' households, but we want a grant each, like you promised back then—not just one between us."

Bell rubbed his chin reflectively. "I reckon as how that's only fair," he concluded, "since there wasn't no sich rule to begin with, prohibitin' single men from gettin' grants. It might cause a bit of a fuss, but I'll let Stephen and th' baron know so they'll understand when you go before 'em. Still got that letter of reference you showed me?"

John nodded. "That brings up the other thing I was wantin' to see you about, Mr. Bell," he said. "My brother William, my ma an' two sisters in Kentucky are all comin' to Texas soon, and they want t' settle nearby James an' me. William was mentioned in this letter from Major Stratton, so I reckon his character is also vouched for. Now, you know a man couldn't say much n'cept good about his own ma. Can't James and me vouch for her?"

Bell blinked, then smiled crookedly. "You're hopin' to mow th' whole durned hayfield, ain'cha? Well, you'll have to run all that stuff 'bout your brother an' ma past them two," he answered, jerking his thumb toward the crowd-encircled table where Austin and Bastrop were conducting business. "Like I said, I think I kin clear it with 'em so's you an' James will each be gettin' grants. The rest is gonna be up t' you."

John took his place in the long line of aspiring landowners and studied the men seated behind the table. Bastrop, in well-worn but genteel attire, looked aged and unhealthily thin. But his friendly, animated manner was standing him in good stead with the anxious and impatient pioneers. In contrast, the smaller, much younger Austin appeared to be uncomfortable with the proceedings. His dark eyes seemed to look straight through the petitioners standing before him.

John watched closely while Bell leaned in between the empresario and the land commissioner and briefly engaged them in conversation. Bastrop nodded, almost imperceptibly, but Austin maintained his frown and gave no response.

It was a hot July day. Men who had eked out wilderness existences over the past two years were expecting the empresario to be quick and generous with the grants. Occasionally, an applicant turned irate and raised his voice in heated argument with the two officials. Twice, to John's surprise, men cut short their apparently unsuccessful appeals by storming off. For the most part, though, the process went smoothly.

When his turn came in front of the table, John smiled broadly at the baron. Bastrop stood, shook John's hand vigorously, and introduced him to Austin in glowing terms. The smaller man nodded soberly and, without leaving his seat, gave John a brief handshake. John presented Stratton's letter. Both men read it through before Austin rolled it up and placed it with a stack of similar documents.

"We understand your concerns, *señor*," the baron said smoothly, "regarding the understanding you and you brother had with Mr. Bell when you joined this colony. Mr. Austin and I"—here he glanced at the empresario—"are in full agreement that you each should receive a league of land." The last words effectively hushed the idle conversations among those settlers standing closest to the table. Others were now listening. Austin studied the table top, the hint of a smile tugging at the corner of his mouth.

They conducted the preliminary paperwork for John's grant, and gave John a note of instruction for the absent James, who was participating in a punitive foray against the pesky Karankawas.

"Your brother must appear in person to receive his grant," Austin said.

John's spirits sank. If that were going to be the case, would they even listen to his petition on behalf of William and his mother? Quickly, he explained that he desired two more leagues: one for his brother William, also mentioned in Stratton's letter, and one for his mother as a head of household.

Austin shook his head. "I regret, sir," he said, "that we cannot issue grants to absentee applicants."

The baron touched the arm of the empresario and leaned over to say something in his ear. Then he looked up at John and said gently, "Please do not be in a hurry to leave San Felipe. When the chance presents itself, perhaps we can talk over old times."

Apprehensive but clinging to hope, John thanked both men and moved away. He waited as patiently as he could for Bastrop to be free from his duties. Finally, all in the long line of men had been heard and given a response. After further conversation with Austin, Bastrop sought out John and invited him to take a walk along the banks of the Brazos, away from the other settlers.

"My friend," the baron said, "many years ago, when we went into business together, it cost you a close companion—a fine young man named Fenwick." John nodded, marveling at the Dutchman's keen recall. "During that episode, you retrieved the horses stolen by the Comanches and saved the lives of my two *mestizos.* You were also faithful to conduct the exchange of goods as planned, and to maintain custody of the merchandise until I released you from that responsibility.

"The young Mr. Austin and I have just now talked about these things. He was, of course, impressed with your valor and trustworthiness. Among his paperwork, to be retained by him until your mother and brother arrive from Kentucky, are grants of one league to each of them, issued with today's date. Their grants will adjoin those of yours and your other brother."

John was incredulous. Bastrop laughed, then added:

"There is one provision that I could not get around. Stephen Austin acknowledges your mother to be the head of a household— and, in fact, agreed to grant her two *labors* for your two sisters as well. But he insists that the current rule must apply to your brother William. That brother will have to be the head of a household before he can claim his league."

Joyously, John wrung the baron's hand. "Praise th' Lord!" he exclaimed. "Thanks, Baron, for all of your help! It's a great day!" In a more subdued tone of voice, he added, "We'll just have to see 'bout William, I reckon."

Bastrop pursed his lips. "Something else occurs to me, my friend," he said meditatively. "In the letter you presented today, there was mention of you and James as mechanics, as builders of water mills."

John nodded, smiling wryly. "It's true enough," he admitted. "But that's one reason we come to Texas—t' get away from millin' for our ma."

The baron shrugged. "Maybe for five more leagues of land, you can like it again, eh?" He laughed at John's expression. "Are you not aware," he asked, "that Stephen Austin will give a *hacienda*—five leagues—to colonists who can offer special skills and abilities for the common good? Milling is very much in demand here! Not only would you be eligible for a *hacienda*, you would grow rich from grinding meal and cutting boards. I urge you: when brother James comes to claim his league, have him apply for a *hacienda* in exchange for erecting and operating a grist mill and sawmill."

John later found to his surprise that the league he had been granted was located across the San Bernard River from the land he and James were working. However, it proved to be equally fertile and somewhat more open.

Within the month, James went before Austin and Bastrop with his petition. He received one league of land where the brothers had their farm and stock, a generous portion of it fronting the San Bernard River opposite John's league. In addition, he was awarded a *hacienda* straddling Palmetto Creek a few miles north of San Felipe. According to the language in the instrument conveying the five-league grant, James also received "the use of all the water of said Palmetto Creek." James stood "informed of his obligation to build a water mill to grind corn and another to make planks on said Palmetto Creek within said *hacienda*."

One evening, as John sat painfully composing a letter to tell Rebekah Cumings of the good fortune God had delivered, he began to laugh. He and James had traveled more than a thousand miles to get away from running and maintaining mills. Now they were faced with not only those same despised duties, but with having to assemble the contraptions as well. "I suppose," he wrote, "that you mite call this turn of events the pruf of a Divine sens of Humor."

John's letter reached New Ephrata in September. After reading it, Rebekah sighed deeply.

Truthfully, she did not want to go to Texas. However, this confirmation of family ownership of free land there—the sign she prayerfully sought from God—had been provided, and in staggering abundance. Forty thousand acres! The dew-dampened fleece laid out by Gideon hardly compared to such a sign as this, she acknowledged. There could be no backing down now.

After all, moving to Texas meant finally escaping New Ephrata and the long shadow of decay and evil it lay under. Two sons were already in Texas; Thomas had moved away to Indiana some years before. The relocation of herself, the twin girls (now actually young women, twenty-five years of age), and William would leave only Samuel in New Ephrata. And Rebekah believed that Samuel, whose oldest female offspring was about to co-mingle blood with that of a Singletary, would be safe enough.

But what of William? John's letter made it clear that the empresario Austin would issue no more land titles to single men. William might, of course, go to Texas anyway. Due to his damaged hip, though, he could perform only limited labor. And no Cumings, least of all William, would tolerate being dependent upon anyone else. A land grant of his own would give him a certain amount of independence. Yes, Rebekah decided, William must have a wife.

William, it so happened, was away visiting the family of his uncle, Robert Russel, in the Blue Ridge Mountains of Virginia. He could still ride a horse as well as anyone, and in fact exhibited a greater than normal endurance for going long distances in a single stretch. In all likelihood, he would not be back until October. By that time, Rebekah planned on her household being packed and ready for a steamboat trip to Texas. William, she told herself, simply had to convince some giddy young female of what a grand thing it would be to accompany an invalid to a faraway frontier. But he must do it in short order.

When he did return, William was surprised to find his mother and sisters nearly ready to start down the river on one of Samuel's packets. Becky and Sarah were none too happy, but did not have the collective spunk to stand up to their domineering parent on any issue. William's surprise turned to incredulity when Rebekah told him of the prize awaiting him in Texas—and of the condition he must first fulfill.

"You can't be serious! Don't expect me to do that!" William angrily blurted out. "Besides," he added with bitterness, "who is gonna want a cripple for a husband if they can get a whole man?"

The green eyes blazed. "You are my son, the seed of your father," Rebekah declared, her voice choking with fury, "and a child of the Most High! You are as much a man as your brothers—as much a man as any other man in New Ephrata, or anywhere in Kentucky. It is an offense to me and an offense to God Almighty for you to talk so!"

William had no reply except to turn his back. Red-faced, hickory crutch thumping angrily against the wooden floor, he limped quickly out of his mother's house.

It was a fine autumn evening. The setting sun had gilded the underside of the clouds. A light north breeze, bearing an agreeable chill, cooled William's flushed cheeks. He found his way through drifts of dead leaves to a mammoth sycamore near the bank of the Ohio, seated himself under it, and stared sullenly as the shadows gathered across willow-laced Brush Creek Island.

A familiar, cheery voice dispersed his gloom.

"Oh, Uncle William!" cried out eighteen-year-old Lucinda Ruggles, blue eyes shining as she hurried toward the sycamore. "I didn't know you were home! What did you bring me from Virginia?"

Chapter 42

The Mexican Constitution of 1824 joined the provinces of Texas and Coahuila into a single state. In the fall of that year, the venerable Baron de Bastrop went to represent Texas in the new congress meeting at faraway Saltillo. But the baron had not abandoned the inclinations of a lifetime; while he was thus embroiled in the affairs of government, his business manager John Nancarrow of Natchitoches put together Bastrop's partnership offer to the Cumings brothers at Palmetto Creek.

To John's way of thinking, the baron's proposal was a good deal for everyone. Bastrop had helped orchestrate the great windfall of the *hacienda* grant, asking nothing in return. Now John and James were strapped for money and still owed Stephen Austin's surveying charge of twelve and a half cents an acre—times forty thousand. They had no means of acquiring the burrstones, saw blades, and other equipment needed to equip the mills. Neither, as was usual, did Bastrop have cash to spare. His credit, though, remained good, and he offered to extend it to the brothers in exchange for a share of the milling profits.

Of more immediate concern was the raising of a house at Palmetto Creek, suitable for the womenfolk coming from Kentucky. John and James had determined that the terrain around the creek, rolling and more accessible to fresh breezes than was their flat farmland downstream, offered a relatively healthy and agreeable place to live. Prompted by a letter from their mother, they worked long hours to complete the new quarters in time for her projected arrival.

Late in October, Rebekah Cumings and her daughters left New Ephrata aboard one of Samuel's steam packets. The moment of departure was a poignant one for the matriarch. True to the custom of the erstwhile colony, the bones of her husband and two sons lay in the cool earth under the flooring of the family home. She was also abandoning a half-dozen grandchildren, the fruit of Samuel's union with Nancy. The trip to Texas would be briefly interrupted by a visit in Indiana with Thomas and another tribe of next-generation Cumingses. Afterward, though, Rebekah could be reasonably certain that she would never again see most of the faces of her Ohio Valley brood.

Still, she believed this decision to be ordained by God. It was best for herself, for Becky—and this way she would not be cornered into witnessing the January wedding of her oldest granddaughter to a Singletary.

Her face set like flint, green eyes glittering with purpose, Rebekah refused to take a final glance at the shore when the boat pulled away from Cumings Landing.

As the packet steamed downriver, Becky and Sarah were agog over the passing panorama on the Ohio—especially the sparkling cities of Cincinnati and Louisville. At the latter port of call, the passengers disembarked. They and the cargo were taken by wagon to Shippingport while the steamboat successfully ran the deep-seated nearer chute of the Falls of the Ohio. Two days later, in fledgling Evansville, they were reunited with Thomas, Mary, and their children.

Beyond Evansville, there remained for Rebekah's daughters the anticipation of experiencing firsthand the heralded mystique of Natchez and New Orleans. However, it also began to dawn on the twins that their ultimate destination was a primitive, foreign, and perhaps hostile frontier.

Passing the tip of Illinois, the steamboat entered the Mississippi River and exposed its stern to the raw north wind ushering in November. Shivering, the sisters watched the mouth of the Ohio recede, and stared in awe at the surrounding expanse of brown, churning water.

There existed between them the stout bond which twins so frequently seem to possess; in addition to this rare biological link, they shared like gender, environment, and upbringing. And for several years now, they had smarted in common under the inflexible rule of a domineering mother. They would turn twenty-six on their next birthday, and prospects of independence after reaching Texas appeared cloudy at best.

Besides the normal parental advantage in such relationships, Rebekah utilized the guilt-plagued episode of Becky's thirteenth year to help maintain control over both daughters. Sarah had been almost as anguished as her twin over the latter's pregnancy, beginning in its early stages as a horrid secret whose discovery was inevitable, and concluding with the girls' painful separation while Becky had her baby.

Now they stood in the stern of Samuel's packet, auburn head and dark close together. Gazing at the gray bluffs rising above the river, Sarah once again posed to Becky the question which seemed always to be on their minds: "Do you think it will be any different with us and Ma when we get to Texas?" There was no real hope in her voice.

Becky sighed. "Someday there will come a change," she responded with bitterness. "There just has to be. Even if Ma—"

Even if Ma has to die first. Neither sibling would utter the unthinkable, but it haunted their thoughts just the same.

William and Lucinda were married two days before Christmas at the Ruggles home on Quick's Run, with Jonathan Ruggles acting as bondsman for his minor child. Justice of the Peace W. B. "Red Buck" Parker officiated. Thomas, the groom's first choice for best man, could not attend. His replacement was Seth Swearingen, who handled the role with pride even while continuing to pine over the loss of Becky. The newlyweds took as their abode the vacated Cumings family home, next to the substantial grounds of Samuel's large house.

But the season's most anticipated social event in New Ephrata was the wedding of Samuel's oldest daughter, Sarah, and Richard Singletary. Despite David Singletary's diminished status to little more than an incredible relic (he would turn one hundred in the spring), the family name still commanded homage. And Capt. Samuel Cumings was the richest man in the village. Under the captain's critical eye, workers were battling the winter weather to construct his wedding gift to Sarah—a fine new house across the river.

The big day arrived; the ceremony took place in Samuel's

home. Mrs. David Singletary overpowered her husband's penchant for woodland wanderings long enough to clean him up, dress him tolerably, and drag him to the wedding. Wisely, she did not insist that he sit up front. Instead, with giant, skeletal frame lolling on a settee to the rear of the assemblage, the one-time patriarch carried on a disjointed soliloquy about Solomon's downfall. Those seated near him ignored his ramblings as best they could while a leather-lung Baptist preacher from Maysville performed the ceremony.

It was an especially heady time for Samuel. Besides the excitement of his daughter's nuptials, he was elated over a new contract with a Cincinnati publisher that would fetch much better money than before for his river charts and gazetteer. At the close of the wedding proper, he offered wine to the celebrants and proposed a toast.

"To the houses of Singletary and Cumings!" he shouted euphorically, flushed with pride. "To the historic occasion of their union through this blessed event!"

Standing behind William and Lucinda, the widowed mother of Tully Fenwick made a strange snorting noise. "Not like t'were th' first time," she muttered, as though to herself. William felt the blood rushing to his face, but managed to remain still. Feeling a sudden tightening of his hand about her own, Lucinda glanced at him curiously. The elder Singletary, with a mumbled warning against strange women, separated himself from the crowd and slipped out of the house.

Festivities over, the happy couple and many of their well-wishers braved the elements and crossed the frozen Ohio to the freshly completed wedding nest. Richard carried the blushing bride over the threshold and, with a parting wave, shut the door. By dusk, the last of the guests, plied with venison and turkey and blackberry cobbler, were ambling homeward through a light snowfall. It was then that William rather sternly asked Samuel to give him a few private minutes in the captain's study.

"What is it, brother?" asked Samuel as William closed the door. "You've rather a long face for such a happy occasion."

William stared out the window at the falling snowflakes, glittering against the gathering dusk. "I need to ask you 'bout some things, Samuel," he said methodically. "Mainly 'bout Becky's son. My namesake," he added, with no hint of humor in his voice.

Samuel sat down, his good humor ebbing. "Go ahead," he said quietly.

"I believe you've been seein' to it, an' very rightly so," William resumed, "that our family is helpin' them that's raisin' Becky's boy, over in Ohio. Tell me truthful, Samuel—truthful, I say! Have you laid eyes on the lad?"

There was a brief, uneasy silence. Samuel did not care for the impertinent phrasing of the question. Neither did he like where the conversation was headed.

"Yes," he said finally, "I have seen and visited with the boy. Several times, in fact."

William pursued the topic, his voice softer but laced with menace. "Does this young fella—I reckon he must be ten or eleven, by now—does he look anything like a whelp fathered by Peter Ayles should look? After all, it's Peter who we figgered all along was t' blame. Isn't that so?"

Samuel bowed his head and stared at the floor. "No, William," he responded dully. "The boy does not favor Peter."

He glanced up. William stood directly in front of him, his hand clinching the hickory crutch far tighter than was necessary, his face almost purple. Samuel jumped up in alarm.

"Wait a minute, brother," he began weakly. But the other man interrupted him, eyes blazing.

"Tomorrow, ice or no ice, I'm crossin' th' river," William said hoarsely. "I'm goin' t' take a good, close look for myself at Becky's boy." He pushed away Samuel's outstretched arm. "Don't say nothin' further, 'less you want to tell me now what I kin expeck t' see tomorrow!"

Samuel's arm dropped to his side. He turned away without a word as William, crutch thumping, stormed out of the study.

Despite the heaviness of the recent snowfall, the founder of New Ephrata wrapped himself in a ragged, patchwork mantle and resumed his rustic ramblings. A man of normal size would have struggled to get through the deep drifts; David Singletary's giant strides carried him with minimal effort into the forested hills south of the village. Hooded head bobbing, he hummed with quavering voice a melodious hymn learned long ago at the Camp of the Solitary.

"David Singletary!" a voice called out. The old man stopped, almost in midstep, cadaverous form swaying back and forth. He turned his eyes in several directions, fighting the dazzling brightness of the sunlight on the snow, but saw no one.

"This is your call t' repentance, David Singletary!" the voice roared.

This time, the old man picked up the direction from whence the speaker addressed him. He spotted a man astride a horse, in a stationary position among a clump of cedars. The rider's hat was pulled low over the eyes and a comforter was wrapped around the lower part of the face.

Singletary also saw the gleaming gun barrel pointed in his direction.

"Hear me good, David Singletary! 'Less you repent of your sins, here an' now, you'll be in mortal danger of meetin' your Maker without bein' prepared!"

The speaker's quarry was not daunted. Defiance flamed in the faded blue eyes of the ancient. He laughed wildly, derisively, until the woods mimicked his scorn. Then, simultaneously with the discharge of the long rifle, the laughter stopped. There was only the rolling echo of the gunshot.

Night came without the return of David Singletary. Mrs. Singletary began to worry immediately, because her husband had never become so confused that he couldn't find his way home. Within a short time, she enlisted a party of men to conduct a lamp-lighted search of the woods. Samuel was among them; William was not. After several hours, alarmed by their lack of success, the searchers returned to New Ephrata to refill lanterns and warm themselves. They also turned out the remainder of the men in the village to help.

This call added Jonathan Ruggles to the effort. When Samuel asked Ruggles if he knew William's whereabouts, Lucinda's father stared at him in amazement.

"Tarnation, Cap'n!" Ruggles exclaimed. "Surely, you know they've gone! Didn't William stop by to tell you? They left today, in spite o' the weather, headed to Texas where your ma an' brothers are! You mean, with your place sittin' right next to theirs, you didn't even see 'em leave? Don't that beat all!"

As the renewed push to find Singletary wore on, Samuel's sense of dread mounted. It was late morning when the searchers finally succeeded.

Men, hats in hand, gathered to stare in disbelief at the great, stilled form. Before them lay the being they had known all of their lives and, for the most part, both revered and feared—the larger-than-life leader who boasted that he would participate in the Second Coming at the right hand of Jesus. Someone had directed a bullet through his massive chest.

Having confirmed that which he feared, Samuel left the scene of the slaying and returned hastily to New Ephrata without a word to anyone. Furtively, he approached the outbuildings of the old family home.

The slave hut was empty; the horses and wagon were missing from the barn. Samuel climbed the steps to the back door of the main house and found it unsecured. He needed only a couple of minutes to ascertain that the house was no longer occupied. The personal belongings of the vanished couple had been removed.

Samuel opened the front door and shut it behind him as he stepped out on the porch, nervously running fingers through his salt-and-pepper curls. A flapping movement caught the tail of his eye and he turned around. Affixed with wax to the door was a large piece of paper, folded once. Samuel snatched the paper from the feeble hold of the wax and opened it. The scrawled message inside was exceedingly brief: "G.T.T. William & Lucinda."

Chapter 43

Seldom had the world seen a more favorable set of circumstances for colonists than those enjoyed by Stephen Austin's settlers in Texas.

The liberality of the Mexican colonization policy achieved what the designers had in mind: it attracted foreigners to settle the remote, empty northern borderlands and provide a buffer against Indian attacks on the more populous interior. Still, the terms offered were remarkable. Ordinary Mexican citizens had to pay the going price for land, were liable to be pressed into military service, and must satisfy the levies of taxes, duty on imports, and church tithes. By contrast, the Austin colonists received large amounts of free land, performed very few public duties, and were to pay no form of taxes for the first ten years.

Of course, the colony caused no financial burden for either the central or state government. What few public services the empresario and his people deemed necessary, such as military protection, they themselves provided. For all practical purposes, the colony was self-sufficient, a virtual commonwealth of social equals who were not dependent upon (nor particularly concerned about) the Mexican bureaucracy.

To be sure, the American expatriates—Texians, they would soon style themselves—had sworn allegiance to Mexico and ostensibly became members of the Catholic Church. Contained in the Constitution of 1824, the document so reverently cited by the rebels when war clouds gathered years later, was a law which declared illegal the practice of slavery. Within a short time, though, and for the remainder of its identifiable existence, Austin's colony contained far more enslaved blacks than bona fide Catholics. After all, slaves were considered an indispensable commodity in a frontier agrarian society.

Despite the early years of drought, famine, pestilence, and Indian depredations, the colonists persevered because they knew they were unlikely to stumble onto another opportunity as sweet as this one. And, despite the almost constant demands placed upon him as the sole leader of the colony, Austin could hardly have hoped for a better situation.

It would not last.

From the moment William laid eyes on James, he grew fearful that his brother was dangerously ill.

William and Lucinda and three slaves—a thirtyish woman, her half-grown daughter and little boy—reached the Cumings place at Palmetto Creek on a gray and windy February day. Their arrival gave John and James the perfect excuse to climb off the scaffolding surrounding the half-finished mill. Out of the house poured Becky and Sarah, with their mother close behind.

"Just in time, William!" quipped John. "My hammerin' arm was beginnin' to play out." He helped Lucinda down from the wagon bench, then gave William a hearty handshake. James also extended a greeting hand; with a sinking heart, William realized how his little brother's strength had ebbed. The face beneath the tangled locks of yellow hair was ominously thin and drawn. There could be no denying the chilling parallel in the declines of James and Tony during the latter's final months.

The unpacking done, William used the pretext of viewing the mill machinery to corner John alone. "James," the other confirmed sadly, "isn't goin' to last the year. Maybe not the summer. It's th' damn consumption, same as got Tony. Privately, he has already had me t' help him make out his will. Ma an' me haven't talked about James, but she's aware how fast he's losin' ground. Mothers just know them things.

"I kin tell you somethin' about Ma, too," John added. "She is a tough one, nowadays. You'll never catch her at a weak time. And th' way she handles those girls! William, you recollect how she kept th' men shooed away from 'em in New Ephrata? Well, they've come all th' way to Texas with her, an' now she's sayin' there's just papists and heathens here—nobody for them t' be equally yoked to! She's given James an' me the same lecture, only o' course we're not lookin' for anyone.

"Everythin' considered," he concluded, "it's been a mite cloudy hereabouts. I'm glad you an' that little wife of yours have joined up. Maybe it'll be more cheerful around th' place. Among all us brothers, you know, the girls always seemed partial t' you."

William grinned crookedly and tapped his bad hip with the hickory crutch. "If there's any truth to what you say about the girls bein' partial to me, this here's the reason," he contended. "All the rest of you were out, runnin' around; me, I stuck close t' the house most of the time and had to entertain the girls."

"Well," rejoined John, "little Lucinda is sure a ray o' sunshine. She'll be great for what's ailin' us. And since she's from New Ephrata, Ma oughtn't have a problem with her bein' a part of th' family."

John's prognostication of human chemistry missed the mark in one respect. The sisters, especially the mercurial Becky, acted coolly toward Lucinda. Their behavior was not so obvious as to attract the notice of other family members, but the twins made Lucinda aware that they did not accept her as part of the clan.

Had either sister been confronted with the question of why, she might have been at a loss to explain. The simple truth was that, isolated from outside male company, Becky and Sarah had eagerly awaited the arrival of the bantering, teasing William. However, the man who showed up was freshly married and deeply in love. He spent far more time with his wife than with his sisters. Young Lucinda, radiant with the glow of happy conjugal relations, unwittingly flaunted her enviable status right under the raised noses of her jealous sisters-in-law.

Even so, the first real strain on the new marriage did not result solely from family relationships. It grew more out of Austin's policy regarding service in the colony's militia.

One of the empresario's edicts was that grantees faced a month of such service for every half-league of land given them. In the case of the Cumings clan, even though the *hacienda* grant was exempted from the tally, this totaled eight months out of every year. William, more able to ride a horse than to do most forms of labor, found a renewed sense of self-worth in service with the militia. His willingness to take on extra shares of this family obligation came as a relief to John and the ailing James. But his absences distressed Lucinda. During those times, she enjoyed little companionship from the aloof sisters and their increasingly taciturn mother.

William happened to be away on an expedition to deal with the unfriendly Waco tribe when a letter from Kentucky arrived at Palmetto Creek. Penned by Samuel, whose major news proved to be the murder of David Singletary, it read in part:

> I thought you might not have heard of this shocking & despicable deed, tho it is of course the talk of the entire Valley here. It appears to have taken place on the very day William & Lucinda departed New Ephrata (and I learned by way of Jonathan Ruggles, who is freshly in receipt of a letter from his daughter, that they arrived safely in Texas).
>
> On the whole, the Singletary tragedy is as inexplicable as it is terrible; while suspicions might normally attach to a passing vagabond on the river, the Ohio of course has been frozen & impassable for the most of several weeks. Too, the spot where the deed was perpetrated, on the backside of the Frizzel place, approaches two miles' distance from the river . . .

Rebekah was the first to read the letter. On the heels of her surprise came an undeniable and profound sense of relief. She went into the bedroom she shared with her daughters, knelt at her bed, and prayed in silence. Then she regained her feet and her composure and called Becky into the bedroom. At a sign from her mother, Becky shut the only interior door of the house.

Studying the beautiful, inquisitive face before her, Rebekah said in a matter-of-fact tone, "David Singletary is dead."

Becky gasped. Her hands flew to her cheeks.

"It is all over, child," Rebekah said. "You may tell me everything now. No possible harm can come to you."

Sobbing, Becky knelt at her mother's knees and threw her arms around them. Rebekah smiled wanly; almost all of her children, when very young, had in times of trouble done just as Becky now did in search of sanctuary.

"Oh, Momma, he threatened me!" Becky, one cheek pressed against her mother's knee, told her story between gasps. "He told me if I ever said a word to anyone . . . that he would call upon God to come like He did for the firstborns in Egypt and take . . . take everyone in our house! Oh, Momma! Is it really, truly over? Can he not . . . come back? He always said he would, you know!"

Rebekah took her daughter's tear-stained face in her work-worn, arthritic hands. "No, child," she said, tenderly running a finger under each glistening eye to divert the saline streams. "He cannot, he will not come back. I promise you that. Besides, God is on the side of the righteous and the repentant, and David Singletary in his latter years was neither of those things. Satan snared him with the lure of aggrandizement and he became the tool of Satan, just as he had been used mightily of the Lord for so many years before."

Then she pulled Becky to her feet. "There is something more you must yet tell me," the older woman said, her voice the slightest bit stern. "How did he first . . . persuade you?"

Becky's face, already reddened from crying, turned a deep scarlet. Again, she hid behind her hands. Finally, she said, in a small, whimpering voice, "He came upon . . . Peter and me, in the woods, like the Lord did Adam and Eve. We both jumped up and ran off, but he—he called me back." She began sobbing anew.

"I see, I see," Rebekah said, and hugged her daughter tightly to her. "He threatened to tell me, or maybe even the whole village, about what he had caught you in . . . unless you did with him what you were doing with Peter. Is that not right?" The auburn head pressed against her tear-dampened breast nodded vehemently.

"And when you had done what he wanted, he threatened you again. This time, he said God would surely strike your entire family dead if ever you told on him!" Again came the nod, and a series of agonized groans.

"It's as much my fault as yours, child," Rebekah said dully. "I rebuffed his vile advances in a manner he found offensive, and he blustered that he would not be mocked. So he took it out on you! Ah, how Satan can use pride to delude a man!"

Becky finally dared to look into her mother's face. "You knew the whole time who . . . who it was, didn't you, Momma?" she asked, sniffling.

"No, not the whole time," came the reply. "Not for years. But finally, I couldn't leave things well enough alone. I did that which I forbade you to ever do. I went across the river to West Union to see your son. He is, after all, my own grandson. Poor creature! God have mercy on him, he more resembles a Singletary than do most of the other dozen sons!"

Rebekah looked into her daughter's tear-filled eyes—green, after her own. "We must forgive each other," she said, "for what has been said and done in the past about this matter; you and I, and tender Sarah, too. What's more, and much harder, we must find a way to forgive David Singletary. After all, it is Satan who is truly to blame."

It required a big boost from hired help, but the Cumings brothers finished the assembly of the sawmill and gristmill in May. Finally out from under that burden, James took to his bed and was never again to leave it. Like Tony before him, he suffered intense pain during the final stages of the illness. His eternal release from agony came in early July as an answer to his family's prayers.

Soon afterwards, William acquiesced to the quiet but insistent urging of Lucinda and saw to the raising of a small cabin they could call their own. However, Lucinda could not dissuade him from continuing to defray his family's obligation to the militia.

Chief Richard Fields, frustrated by years of barren efforts to secure a land grant for his Cherokees in East Texas, became a willing listener to plotters who proposed to declare Texas independent from Mexico.

The success of Austin's enterprise had prompted others to try for grants of Mexican land. Among these were the Edwards brothers, who proved incapable of handling the responsibility entrusted to them.

Haden Edwards proposed to attract eight hundred families and settle them in the red hills and piney woods between Austin's colony and the Sabine River. What he received from Mexico in April of 1825 was a substantial grant in the desired area that chanced to include the long-established village of Nacogdoches. Unlike Austin, whose grant had consisted of essentially unsettled territory, Edwards encountered numerous individuals living within the boundaries of his proposed colony who either were squatters or had themselves been granted land. Neither Haden Edwards nor his brother, Benjamin, exhibited much tact in their dealings with these longtime residents. The Edwardses summarily ordered them to prove up ownership or move. There could be no remedy for the distress this caused the squatters. However, the Mexican government had clearly instructed Haden Edwards to honor the claims of the Spanish grantees, and the complaints of this outraged group soon reached the ears of Mexican authorities.

Haden Edwards also botched an effort to seat his son-in-law as *alcalde* for the Nacogdoches district. In addition, by raising and commanding a militia, he exceeded the authority given him. An exasperated Austin wrote to Edwards in 1826, "The truth is, you do not understand the nature of the authority with which you are vested by the government, and it is my candid opinion that a continuance of the imprudent course you have commenced will totally ruin you, and materially injure all the new settlements." Austin noted his remarks were "made in perfect friendship . . ."

But the friendship would not long endure. The Edwards brothers' inability or unwillingness to recognize and give due respect to Mexican governance at last resulted in the declared forfeiture of Haden Edwards's colonization grant.

Thus it was that in the closing months of 1826, the brothers and selected friends plotted rebellion against the government and dreamed of creating the Republic of Fredonia. They sought as allies the various Indian tribes in the vicinity, principally the Cherokees. In exchange for the red man's support of the rebellion, the Edwards coalition promised, the portion of Texas lying north and west of the Camino Real would forever be the domain of the Indians.

Chief Fields was ripe for such an enterprise. He had grown disgusted with his own fruitless attempts and those of others to obtain a land grant for the tribe. John Dunn Hunter, a peculiar white man who lived with the Cherokees and claimed to have been raised by Indians, also favored radical action. Fields and Hunter were attracted to the ideas of the conspirators. However, the tribe's war chiefs, Bowles and Big Mush, remained lukewarm.

Word of the devious doings around Nacogdoches reached Austin's colony in autumn. Then, in December, it was rumored that the Cherokees were about to strike an agreement with the Edwards group on behalf of not only themselves, but neighboring tribes as well. Indian participation in the pending rebellion made the matter much more serious; the longtime settlers of the Nacogdoches district, who had stood up to the Edwards faction almost to a man, now fearfully began uprooting themselves and heading east to the Sabine. Meanwhile, the Edwardses hoped for a counterflow across the river of rifle-toting Americans with blood in their eyes and fire in their bellies.

Placed classically on the spot was Stephen Austin, who along with his colonists had sworn allegiance to Mexico. Now came the first true test of that professed fealty. Could Austin maintain control of his people to the point that they took up arms on behalf of their adopted country against other expatriated Americans? Worried Mexican officials organized a military expedition and sent it north toward Nacogdoches—by way of San Felipe. Austin was expected to join it and swell its ranks with men from his colony.

Benjamin Edwards wrote Austin, pleading for his support in the coming fray. He also sent inflammatory dispatches for public consumption to various points in the Austin colony. Austin countered this tactic with stern instructions to ignore "the madmen" in East Texas, reminding his settlers where their loyalty and duty must lie.

The Mexican forces arrived in San Felipe in January 1827. By then, the news was out that Benjamin Edwards had led a small armed force into Nacogdoches in mid-December, parading under a flag which bore the words "Independence, Liberty, and Justice." This band of insurgents took over the venerable governmental structure known as the Old Stone Fort, and declared that Texas was now the free Republic of Fredonia.

Bad weather kept the Mexican army mired in San Felipe for most of January. This extended presence allowed Austin and his militia leaders to add four hundred colonists to the effort by the time the road to Nacogdoches had once again become passable. William Cumings was among them.

During this time, Austin sent word to Palmetto Creek that he had need of John Cumings and Cumings's neighbor, William Robbins. Reluctantly, John saddled his horse, and he and Robbins made the eight-mile trip to San Felipe. John could easily guess what the empresario wanted; the year before, Austin had dispatched John and another colonist with Cherokee ties to recruit the tribe as an ally against the Wacos.

Austin greeted John and Robbins in his usual sober fashion, and wasted no time in broaching the business at hand.

"We have received word directly from Haden Edwards," he said, "that the Cherokee chief Fields signed a treaty of alliance with the Edwards men, as did the chiefs of several other tribes. Mr. Cumings, you have always maintained that the other leaders of the tribe, the war chiefs Bowles and Big Mush, do not want conflict. Do you still believe this to be so?"

John nodded. Smiling slightly, Austin rubbed his hands together. "Good! On that premise, I have already written a letter to those chiefs, which you and Mr. Robbins are to deliver—and, probably, will have to read to them. Here it is; familiarize yourself as to its contents."

The gray skies outside gave poor illumination through the windows of Austin's small office. John had to use the glow of the empresario's table lamp to study the lengthy epistle. He did not altogether like what he read.

Austin's message cited a recent attempt by Mexican emissaries to deliver important letters from the governor of Coahuila and Texas to the Indians. "I fear," Austin wrote, "that John D. Hunter has concealed the letters and the truth from you, for he and Edwards would not suffer those men to talk to the Indians. I therefore now send you copies of the same letters that were sent by the Governor and delivered to Hunter which he promised to send to you immediately—by these letters you will see the Government has never had any intention to break the promises made to you and that they are ready to comply with them provided you do your duty as good men.

"My brothers, I fear you have been deceived by bad men who wish to make use of you to fight their battles. They will ruin you and your people if you follow their counsel."

John glanced up from the letter and looked its author in the eye. "Colonel Austin," he said, "I've always held th' trust of Chief Bowles. Now, it's certainly possible he may ask me, point-blank, if I really think the Cherokees'll get their land grant by stayin' out o' this Edwards mess. If he does, what do I say?"

Austin did not smile. "You perhaps need to pray, John," he responded, "that either the question not be asked, or that you answer it in the fashion which best serves your country."

With a scowl, John handed the letter back to Austin, who rolled it up, secured it with a ribbon, and returned it to the intended bearers along with copies of the government letters referenced.

"I 'spose you understand, Colonel," John said bluntly, in parting, "your letter is purty much Hunter's death warrant, and maybe as much of one for Richard Fields."

As John moved toward the door, with Robbins close behind, Austin stood. "My conscience is clear," the empresario told them. "Those two gentlemen have been undone by their own hand—as have the Edwards brothers." The wan smile returned. "Among the North American savages," he reflected, "there is no known tradition of killing the mere bearers of bad news. The pair of you, at least, should be safe enough."

Chapter 44

William Robbins comprehended just enough of the Cherokee language to marvel at the fluency exhibited by John Cumings.

Robbins, a respected acquaintance of the Cherokees from prior interactions in the Arkansas Territory, sat as silent witness to the three-way conversation conducted in the red man's tongue among John, Chief Bowles, and Big Mush. They talked as they huddled, wrapped in blankets, around a crackling pine-knot fire. January's north wind whistled through the tall evergreen forest surrounding the Indian village, and its gusts pummeled the animal skin coverings of the scattered lean-tos and huts.

From the outset, Robbins perceived the warm feelings the two chieftains held for John, as compared to the polite recognition he himself had been given. Too, he noticed that there was more than a passing physical resemblance between John and Bowles, and he heard the latter's repeated references to John as "my son."

"We know this man who travels with you, who you call your brother and neighbor," Bowles said to John, as though Robbins were not present. "He has always conducted himself honorably and well in his dealings with the Cherokee. But tell me, my son, where is your blood brother of the yellow hair and big shoulders? Does he yet distrust the Indian?"

John dropped his eyes. "The brother you speak of," he answered somberly, "hunts the catamount among the clouds. He was taken by sickness two summers past."

Bowles grunted, leaned forward, and squeezed John's arm. "I

305

hurt for you," he said simply. Then, settling back, he demanded: "Tell Big Mush and Bowles why you have come."

John rubbed his chin. "If I may," he replied, "let me first ask you—who is this white man John Dunn Hunter, and why does your respected Chief Fields place such confidence in him?"

Bowles and Big Mush exchanged glances. "Chief Fields," ventured Big Mush, "knows the passing of many seasons. He has endured heartache after heartache in his quest for land for the Cherokee. His eye grows dim, and he no longer has the patience to be the stalker of game. He wants to believe that the man who calls himself Hunter has the right answers."

Bowles nodded. "John Dunn Hunter," he said, "came here a season ago to live with the Cherokee. He has said many things about himself, and we do not know what to believe. He said that he was adopted by Indians, yet allowed to go to the white man's schools. He can read and write the white man's tongue, and says he wrote a story about himself which made him famous on both sides of the great water.

"He claims to have lived for a time in the land of the British, and was very famous there. According to him, the British squaws, who compete with one another for attention, insisted that he come to each of their homes.

"It is the belief of Hunter that the Indian must assume the ways of the white man in order to survive. He has said many times that his mission in life is to save the Indian by making him over to be like the whites. This idea the Cherokees do not like. Now he advocates taking the warpath against the Mexicans—they who control the land we live on—in brotherhood with the renegade whites at Nacogdoches. This thing the Cherokees will not do!"

John produced the letters Austin had given him, opening those from the governor of Texas and Coahuila. "According to my chief, Colonel Austin," he said, "copies of these letters from the great man in Saltillo were intended for the eyes of the Cherokee and other tribes in East Texas. The man Hunter, it is said, refused to let the Mexican messengers deliver them to the tribal leaders, but promised to do so himself."

The face of Big Mush darkened. Bowles studied the epistles for a moment. "We have seen no such letters," Bowles said. "What do they say?" John began to read and translate from the top letter, but

Bowles stopped him with an impatient wave of the hand. "Tell us in your own words what is written to us."

"They are flattering," John responded carefully. "They talk about how great the Cherokee warriors are, and how important your tribe is to Mexico. They contain new promises to consider your request for tribal land if you refuse to ally yourselves with the Edwards brothers."

Big Mush expectorated into the fire. Bowles snorted in derision. "Should the Cherokee put his trust in these letters?" Bowles asked, eyes glittering. "The Mexicans have sent their agent Bean among the lesser tribes, and he is telling them the same things. Do you believe it will finally be as Bean and these letters say?"

Although Robbins had not entirely kept up with the conversation, he inferred Bowles was asking the very question that had been discussed in Austin's headquarters. He listened intently as John replied.

"You may put as much faith in the word of the Mexican leaders today as you always have, and for the same reasons. These things do not change."

Big Mush came to his feet. "Then why," he rumbled angrily, "do we not consider following the wishes of Chief Fields and join forces with the white men in Nacogdoches? Are their promises of land for the Cherokee any emptier than the promises of the Mexicans?"

Still seated, John raised his eyes. "You have given yourself the answer," he commented. "I believe there is no truth in the white men who implore you to fight. They have lied to their own kind, to those of us in the Austin villages. And even if they had honest intent, they cannot possibly deliver on promises of land.

"As we talk, an army made up of Mexican soldiers and men from the Austin villages is moving on Nacogdoches. You will learn of them when they cross the Neches. Their numbers are more than your braves and the Nacogdoches whites combined. One of my blood brothers rides with them. Hunter and Fields have long been warned of this."

"Whites against whites!" Bowles said, marveling. "Mexicans and whites riding together against other white men! If it were not you telling me this, John Cumings, I would not believe it." His face grew hard. "How can Chief Fields urge us to fight, knowing of such a thing? If, as you say, he was told in advance about this large army, why has he hidden this from us while talking of the warpath?"

"It is Hunter!" growled Big Mush, who had seated himself. "Hunter is like a shaman! He has put a spell over Fields, and Fields can no longer think for himself. Both of them must be dealt with before they push the Cherokee into war."

Bowles studied John in silence. "You have told us the truth, or surely what you believe to be the truth," he said at last. "It is well that Colonel Austin chose you to come here, for we would not have listened to another."

He arose, and Big Mush and the white men did likewise. "You will stay the night with us, out of the cold," Bowles said by way of invitation. John, though, shook his head.

"My neighbor and I must leave at once for home," he responded, clapping his hand on Robbins's shoulder. "With my one brother dead, and the other brother riding to Nacogdoches, our families are unprotected. Not all Indians are honorable in their ways with the women and children of those whom they regard as enemies. The Tonkawa is treacherous and may try to do harm in our absence."

A few days later, John Dunn Hunter stopped at a pine-shadowed creek and broke the light coating of ice to allow himself and his mount a drink.

Unfortunately for him, the Fredonians had further injured their cause in the eyes of the Indians with a drunken brawl in Nacogdoches. The Cherokees, following the advice of the irate Bowles and Big Mush, rejected the urgings of Hunter and Fields to form an alliance with the rebel whites. Thus rebuffed, Hunter declared he would concentrate on persuading some of the lesser tribes in the region to take up arms on the side of the Edwardses. In this effort, he was traveling alone.

As Hunter's horse guzzled the chilled water, a Cherokee brave rode up from the direction of his village. Hunter recognized him and nodded familiarly. He then turned to mount his horse. He felt no sensation of peril, even when he heard the brave's rifle being cocked. If in fact anything occurred to him, it was probably that the other man had spotted game. Then came the explosion of the rifle and, simultaneously, the tearing of the ball into Hunter's back.

He fell forward into the icy stream, and tried feebly to raise himself up on one arm. Reluctantly, the brave drew his tomahawk, waded into the creek, and stood over Hunter to complete the task assigned him.

At the same hour, in the same vicinity, Chief Fields met his fate in roughly the same fashion.

The outcome of the Fredonian rebellion reminded William Cumings of his experience in the Canadian campaign. Once again, he had traveled a long way and built up his expectations, only to miss out on the excitement. The major difference was that, in this instance, a true battle never developed.

By the time he and the main body of the expedition arrived at Nacogdoches, most of the Fredonians were nowhere to be seen. They had already cleared out in disarray, chased toward the Sabine by an advance detachment of the Mexican army. The slowest ones found themselves once again inside the Old Stone Fort, this time as prisoners rather than as self-proclaimed liberators. Their fanciful flag had been appropriated.

There was at first the very real possibility that the captured adventurers would be executed in cold blood as examples to other enemies of Mexico. Austin, however, quietly intervened. Taking his counsel, the commander Ahumada agreed that the rebels might accomplish in martyrdom what they had fallen woefully short of doing in the flesh: to incite the greater number of Anglo inhabitants to revolt.

All in all, it was quite a victory for Austin. He and his colonists had passed muster as faithful Mexican citizens, rallying in a time of crisis against their former countrymen. The Indians, whom the Mexicans most feared all along, were kept neutral. And very little blood was shed.

Once the returning army moved to within two days' march of San Felipe, William received permission to strike out on his own for home. He rode the ferry across the Brazos at the Atascosito crossing and turned north toward Palmetto Creek, now becoming known as Mill Creek.

Spotting his cabin at last, William observed a strange horse tethered in front. Apprehensive, he urged his tired steed into a light gallop and gritted his teeth at the flashes of pain in his hip. When he had drawn closer, he recognized the horse as one belonging to William Robbins.

Polly Robbins met him at the door. She was smiling. "Welcome home, neighbor!" came her robust greeting. "Everything's fine an' dandy! Seems your Lucinda is just now findin' out what it's like to be carryin' a child!"

Chapter 45

The advent of September in 1828 only brought a continuation of the summer-long heat and humidity. Conditions were stifling inside the cabin where William Cumings spent his final days, languishing on a sweat-soaked sickbed which consisted of a canvas mat stuffed with corn husks and Spanish moss.

The weather was not the only element torturing the stricken pioneer. Infection of an open wound on William's bad leg, which he foolishly tried to ignore rather than treat, was soon having its deadly way as family members stood by helplessly. The wounded area had turned a gangrenous black, from which red streaks of inflammation ran up into his abdomen. The fever was incessant and the pain intense, and no home remedy available in this frontier without doctors could provide relief.

Rebekah Cumings, having already witnessed the passing of a husband and three sons despite her dedicated nursing and prayers, once again sensed impending death. "Lord!" she cried out. "I can't abide any more losses! Why are you allowing this poor, wretched mother to suffer more than she can bear?" For a time, she yielded to despair over the coming separation from yet another loved one. Then, of a sudden, the uncertainty of William's salvation came to mind, and the resulting flash of fear moved her to act.

"Your brother is near to dying," Rebekah said tersely to John, who nodded glumly. "What you must do now," she ordered, voice trembling, "is to make sure his immortal soul is saved."

John took the family Bible and went to William's bedside,

where Lucinda and Polly Robbins were seated. When she saw the Bible, Lucinda shook her head wildly and uttered a moan that turned into a howl. She flailed her arms in a kind of frantic, pathetic denial. Gently but firmly, the older woman removed Lucinda from the room.

Washcloth in hand, John reached into the wooden bucket at the side of William's bed. It still contained an inch or so of well water. John hesitated. In his mind's eye appeared the sweating, twisting, slender form of a young Indian woman, her newborn baby boy just taken away. From outside the hut in which she lay came the crying of women mingled with the shaman's maddening chant. Though twenty years had passed, John saw and heard—and felt—those memories as if they were from yesterday.

He mopped the fevered face of his brother. "William," he called. Eyes shut, William tossed his head back and forth. John called again. The eyes opened, stared straight ahead, then shifted and found him. Recognition warmed their gaze.

"William," John continued, "you need t' hear me. Can you?" There came a slight nod. "Good," John said. "Now listen real close. You may be 'bout to reach your appointed hour with th' Lord. Understand me?"

A hurt expression flashed across William's face, but he nodded again. "Yes," he added aloud.

John licked his lips and cleared his throat. "William," he asked, "d' you know Jesus as your lord an' savior?" Once more came an affirmative nod, the dying man displaying neither fear nor hesitation. John heaved a sigh of relief. Then he inquired, "Is there anything—anything at all—you need t' confess before you're called?"

William shut his eyes and jerked his head in pain, and for half a minute did not answer. John thought to himself, *That's all right, brother. Whatever you may have to confess, the Lord is sure to forgive you.* But William opened his eyes again and looked intently, almost urgently, at John.

"It really was . . . an accident," he said, in a rasping whisper. "What I wanted was t' make him crawl an' beg me for mercy . . . for Becky's sake. I never should o' . . . pointed th' rifle at him. When he laughed that awful laugh, I just saw red and my finger jerked th' trigger. God knows . . . that's th' truth."

John's eyes widened in amazement at this staggering revelation. Then, recovering, he responded carefully. "But, William, it's still a sin t' take another man's life, even in anger. Even if you didn't mean to. Are you confessin' your sin an' askin' forgiveness?"

"Yes," William said, and closed his eyes. "Lucinda never had a 'spicion, I don't believe," he whispered. "She won't have to know, will she? Nor Ma an' the girls? I 'magine brother Samuel figgered things out, but I guess maybe . . . nobody else in New Ephrata ever did."

John squeezed his brother's hand. "No one else has t' know, William," he said tenderly, "'cept me, an' you, an' Jesus."

Standing in the dog run just outside the bedroom, Lucinda placed both arms against the wall of rough-hewn logs and buried her face in her sleeves. She sobbed brokenly. Polly Robbins, for once feeling inadequate to better the situation, decided she would cross the meadow to her own home and see how her oldest daughter was caring for thirteen-month-old Samuel Anthony Cumings.

Raphael Washington Thompson, known to the world as "Rafe," buried his wife in frigid February of 1829. Her loss left the Thompson household with two small children and Rafe's widowed mother-in-law, Nancy Owen.

Rafe, by trade a carpenter, lived at Poplar Flat, a Kentucky hamlet located ten miles south of the Ohio River. When the Grim Reaper struck, Thompson had been considering a move to Concord, a newly surveyed townsite right on the river near the mouth of Sycamore Creek. Rafe fashioned his helpmeet's casket, shedding tears all the while, thawed out an appropriate patch of ground, and secured the services of the Baptist preacher for the last rites. Then he packed up his belongings and the remainder of the family and headed to Concord, which lay in the heart of the fast-fading New Ephrata community.

The Thompsons' new house was almost completed when Lucinda Cumings, her baby Sam, and three slaves arrived at nearby Quick's Run in the company of her father. Jonathan Ruggles had received word about William in October, followed by horror-filled newspaper accounts of a fever epidemic ravaging Texas. But bad weather prevented the rescue of his daughter and grandson until well after the first of the year.

Rafe was a man of few words, and usually a bit shy around the ladies. These drawbacks notwithstanding, his introduction to Lucinda at a harvest dance struck a spark of mutual interest. In December 1829, five years almost to the day since marrying William, Lucinda became Mrs. Raphael Thompson.

Lot sales in Concord lagged miserably. Realizing he had made an unwise choice of towns, and willing to correct the error, Rafe in 1830 relocated his enlarged household to neighboring Mason County and the vibrant river port of Maysville. There, at the corner of Limestone and Fifth streets, young Sam Cumings would spend the next ten years of his life. But Texas—to Sam a mysterious name and place, about which he retained no memories—always seemed to beckon.

After all, the land representing the bulk of his father's estate lay in Texas, waiting to be claimed as soon as Sam achieved manhood.

The Ruggles rescue party had been gone from Mill Creek only a short while when Becky and Sarah observed ("celebrated" was hardly the proper word) their joint birthday. Thirty years old ... By all standards of society and self-respect, they had long since eclipsed the age of eligibility.

Seth Swearingen and his younger sister Abigail, their family having recently arrived at Austin's Colony, were invited to a "get-together" hosted by Rebekah Cumings in honor of her daughters. Seth was now twenty-seven, with evidence of more than ordinary strength in his towering frame. Thrilled at the prospect of seeing Becky again, he found it all too easy to fan the flame of his previously unrequited love.

Seth and Abigail decided to bring along George Dennett, a cooper who had accompanied the Swearingens from Kentucky. En route to Mill Creek, Dennett learned that Seth considered Becky spoken for—on this occasion, at least—but that her sister Sarah was unclaimed. When Dennett first viewed the twins, his heart skipped a beat. How, he wondered, had either of these beauties avoided marriage?

A sixth sense warned the newcomer to be discreet in his attentions to Sarah. The sharp-eyed matriarch of the house kept a rein on her daughters as though they were fifteen instead of thirty. Dennett struck up a conversation with John, an encounter which led to John offering him a job at the mill and residence in William's abandoned cabin. The offer was eagerly accepted.

After the guests departed, Rebekah remonstrated angrily with her son over proffering the cabin to "a perfect stranger." John, however, stood firm, and Dennett moved onto the property within the week.

Sarah was thrilled. Dennett had managed to communicate his interest during the birthday social, and she returned it in full. He was mature, thoughtful, reasonably handsome, and completely available.

Romance, nourished by clandestine, nocturnal meetings on the creek, blossomed quickly. Within six weeks, Sarah convinced Dennett to join her in front of a magistrate—without even asking her mother's approval. "She won't give it," Sarah argued, "because you're not from New Ephrata. Truly, Becky and I think she'll never let go of us, regardless of where anyone we meet is from. This is the only way I'll ever be married."

Alcalde Joseph White performed a civil ceremony in San Felipe. But he insisted that the Roman Catholic priest from San Antonio who visited the colony on occasion must someday conduct a "proper Mexican weddin' to make it all legal."

Rebekah's outrage at this act of independence was noted in a letter from Stephen Austin to David Burnet in Cincinnati: "Miss Sarah Cummins married Mr. Dennet a short time since in defiance of the old woman her mother, who is very wrathy. You know she has made a rule to discard every child who marries, right or wrong. Sarah did right, as I think."

Even John could not long withstand his mother's fury. With great reluctance, he told Dennett he could no longer work at the mill nor live in the cabin. Secretly, though, John loaned money and extended credit to the newlyweds so that they could buy land and materials for a house in San Felipe. He also formed a business partnership with Dennett for the manufacture and sale of furniture, crates, barrels, and coffins.

In the forced absence of her twin sister and confidante, Becky soon found her own existence becoming a living hell. Sarah was not allowed to visit, nor should her name be brought up in conversation. In addition, Becky was forbidden to have male company; even Seth, thanks to his role in bringing Dennett to Mill Creek, found himself no longer welcome.

The weeks stretched into months, and the months into years, and still Rebekah remained unbending in her attitude toward Sarah. One of Becky's rare outbursts occurred on her thirty-first birthday, when her mother behaved as though there had never been but one child born on that date. "If you can't acknowledge my sister, even on her birthday," Becky complained bitterly, "then I shan't have any more birthdays, either."

Sarah had lost a child in midterm during her second year of marriage, and friends were at first apprehensive when she announced she was again pregnant in the fall of 1831. As the months passed without trouble, their fears diminished. But, close to the time of delivery, Sarah suffered a massive hemorrhage. Neither she nor the child survived.

It fell John's lot to tell his mother and sister. "I know we are not to bring up Sarah's name in this home," he announced, in a voice shaking with shock and anger, "but she and her unborn baby have just died without any of us being at her side."

Becky flung herself into John's arms, crying hysterically. Rebekah's stiffened lips collapsed and she, too, wept like a child. But she repulsed attempts by her forgiving son and daughter to embrace and comfort her. "Sarah, if you can hear me," she wailed, eyes lifted toward Heaven and arms outstretched, "please forgive your mother!" Turning a seamed, tear-stained face to John and Becky, she said brokenly, "You can only help me by leaving me to God and His judgment."

Rebekah spent the entirety of that night alone in the recesses of the mill, praying aloud. John slept fitfully; once, when he awoke, he heard his mother's voice but failed to make out the words. They did not seem to be English, or Spanish, or any Indian dialect known to John. From where he lay, her utterances sounded like total gibberish.

The distraught Dennett would not hear of burying his wife and child at Mill Creek, so the double funeral was held in San Felipe. To her children's surprise and resentment, Rebekah refused to attend. "I'll mourn them in my own way," she insisted. Reluctantly, John and Becky left without her.

When they returned home late in the afternoon, Rebekah was not there. Laid out on the kitchen table were their mother's will, composed and witnessed in 1825, and a couple of short letters apparently just written. Together, they read the first of the letters, painfully penned in Rebekah's arthritic hand:

> Loved Ones —
> Where I go you cannot follow. I ask all my children living & dead to forgive me. Things were never the same after your father died. I loved him so very much and still do. Sometimes I was head-strong in doing what I thot was the will of God for my family. I know now that I did not honor the simple message of His grace & mercy. We will all be reunited one day—you dear children & Anthony & I.

Becky looked at her brother with frightened eyes. "Where's Ma gone, John?" she asked in a voice already hoarse from hours of lamentation. "We never should have left her!"

John shrugged wordlessly and fought back a feeling of dread. Leaving the second letter untouched, they quickly stepped outside. Rebekah did not answer their repeated calls.

Well-trained by the Cherokees, John examined the ground for traces of the elderly woman's departure. "I can follow you, Ma," he declared aloud while he searched. "I wouldn't be much of an adopted Injun if I let a seventy-five-year-old white lady give me th' slip."

He soon picked up what he believed to be her trail. It first led along the creek, then turned into the woods.

They found Rebekah shortly before dusk. She was seated with her back against the base of a big sycamore, her head tilted to one side, eyes closed, a soft, peaceful smile on the wrinkled face. The sun's fading rays touched a few stray strands of hair, alternately brown and gray, curling from underneath the faded blue bonnet. Worn hands clasped the family Bible where it lay closed in her lap.

Even before they dared extend trembling fingers to touch her, John and Becky knew that she was dead. Becky took her mother's cool hands in her own and held them to her lips. Having just returned from twin funerals, she had no tears left to give.

Tears, though, welled up anew in John's eyes. "I reckon Ma was right," he said huskily. "Where she's gone, we can't follow. Leastways not just yet."

Chapter 46

*A*fter nearly a decade of burying its collective head in the sand, Mexican federal officialdom finally decided that something must be done to slow the flow of Anglo-Americans into Texas. And so there emerged a combustible little piece of legislation known in history by its birthdate: the Law of April 6, 1830.

At this time, the population of former U.S. residents in Texas was anyone's guess. Austin had fulfilled two colonial contracts and was busy with a third. Other empresarios—among them Green DeWitt, Sterling Robertson, Martin De Leon, and the partnerships of McMullen-McGloin and Power-Hewetson—had either begun their projects or were in the midst of preparation. In addition to the legal Mexican citizens holding grants and pledged to the Roman Catholic Church, there were many craftsmen, merchants, speculators, itinerant drifters, and fugitives from American justice and debts adding themselves to the mix.

From the Nueces River eastward, and more especially to the east of the Guadalupe, southeast Texas had taken on much more the appearance of a North American frontier than an extension of Mexico. Except for a number of residents in Bexar and La Bahia (Goliad), which lay at either end of the old Spanish cattle ranching empire, the inhabitants of Texas felt little ethnic or practical kinship with their fellow citizens in the distant Mexican interior. They had received no help from the central government in fighting Indians or in making peace with them. Too, the natural trade links for Texas were with New Orleans and other relatively close U.S. ports.

The United States had thrice offered token amounts of cash for Texas, with borders variously defined, and had thrice been indignantly rebuffed or ignored by Mexico. It didn't take much imagination on the part of the infant nation's leaders to conjecture that their land-grabbing northern neighbor was deliberately pumping Anglos into the desired territory for the purpose of revolution.

After certain officials repeatedly aired their fears in writing, the Mexican government adopted and began to enforce the 1830 decree. Its provisions included the prohibition of further immigration into Mexico by North Americans; the military occupation of Texas, marked by the establishment of garrisons in major towns; and the imposition of duties on U.S. imports by customshouses located in the seaports of Galveston, Anahuac, Velasco, and Matamoros.

To the Anglo-Texians, all of this sounded ominously like the dictates of the British Crown prior to the American Revolution. Many of them were just a couple of generations removed from that struggle, so gloriously remembered.

The enactment of the Law of April 6, 1830, split colonial Texas into two political factions: the worried but conservative peace party, headed by Austin and made up of longtime settlers reluctant to put their life's work at risk; and the war party, consisting of younger men and new arrivals whose tolerance of anything resembling "tyranny" was essentially nil. Among the ablest spokesmen for the latter group were two attorneys who hadn't even set foot in Texas when the Law of April 6, 1830, was circulated: veteran soldier and politician Sam Houston and aspiring soldier and politician William Barret Travis.

Luck was simply not a staple of Seth Swearingen's love life.

To be fair, Seth had his chances. In fact, under the rules of eligibility dictated by Becky's mother, Seth as a product of New Ephrata was the only known male in all of Texas qualified to court Becky. Unwittingly, though, he forfeited the advantage of that exclusive pedigree by introducing George Dennett to Sarah.

After the devastating deaths of Sarah, her baby, and the widow Cumings early in 1832, Seth felt compelled out of respect for Becky's grief to cool his ardor some six months. Then, ever optimistic, he resumed his trips to Mill Creek, conducting an earnest but bumbling courtship that touched John Cumings's heart more than his sister's.

Seth was in fact pretty much a man's man. Well over six feet tall, he had huge hands and biceps to match, and was a wonder to behold at house-raisings and horse-breakings and other occasions showcasing physical prowess. His long face was rugged but not unpleasant to look at, and it wore an engaging smile whenever he ran into an acquaintance.

Being around Becky, however, reduced Seth to warm taffy. He became clumsy in speech and movement, was constantly apologetic, and hovered over her in trying to anticipate her every want. "Durn it, Seth," an exasperated John once advised him, "you're too dadgum nice to her."

John, who for a season had savored a truly passionate relationship, observed an absence of such emotion in Becky. He pitied Seth, yet he could not blame his sister's reluctance to discourage the persevering suitor. In the physical prime of life at thirty-three, and quite striking, Becky had received precious little in the way of proper male attention. At least, John reflected, she was doubtless safe in all respects while in Seth's company.

Having found themselves alone in a rather large house, John and Becky in late 1832 ended weeks of speculative discussions by opening the residence to the public as a "house of entertainment"— an inn offering rooms and meals. Their location on the road between San Felipe and Washington-on-the-Brazos already attracted tired, hungry travelers. The paid announcement in the newspaper simply formalized the venture.

The spring of 1833 brought with it a series of rainstorms. Abrupt, heavy rainfall in the shallow Mill Creek watershed tended to flush the little tributary out of its channel. The Cumings mill and inn, located on the high north bank, were safe from flooding. But from the creek southward, water spread over the undulating lowlands for dozens of square miles and severed contact with San Felipe.

One of those storms, coming up suddenly in the late afternoon, halted a solitary rider in his journey south and drove him to the door of the inn.

John answered the knock, and stepped back to admit a tall young man whose elegant clothes were soaked under his tardily donned cloak.

"Quite a sudden rain," the stranger commented, then stuck out

a hastily dried hand. "My name is Travis—William Travis," he continued, in modulated tones of a distinctly Southern flavor.

John returned the courtesy of introduction, then stepped past
the other man onto the porch and cupped his hands around his
mouth. "Henry!" he bellowed, and repeated the summons. A black
lad of about ten came scurrying barefoot through the rain from the
direction of the stables. "Take Mr. Travis's horse, an' see that you
rub him down well an' feed him," John instructed the youngster.
"Then bring in the gentleman's blanket and saddlebags."

Travis hesitated, watching intently while the boy led the horse
away. "Your horse'll be well taken care of," John assured him.
"Henry's ever' bit as conscientious as any stable hand, boy or man,
an' a lot smarter than most of 'em. Let me get a fire goin' for you."

While John tended to the kindling of the fire, he noticed with
amused eye Travis, hat removed, rearranging disheveled red locks,
straightening his collar, and even using a bandanna to remove mud
from his new-looking riding boots. Soon, a stout blaze in the fireplace was radiating heat and the promise of drier garments. Henry
arrived with the visitor's blanket and saddlebags, and spread the
former out on the hearth. John bade the youth stay by the fire until
he, too, became warm and dry.

The rain increased in intensity, drumming against the pitched
roof of the story-and-a-half structure. Travis raised an eyebrow as
he listened. "It would seem," he said, turning to John, "that I may
have need of a bed tonight. As I understand it, your creek doesn't
take too much water before it overflows."

His host nodded. "By now, our crossin' has prob'ly widened
from thirty feet to a half-mile," John observed. "Since it's gettin' on
towards dark, you'd be less than wise to try t' go on, even should
the rain stop. By stayin' put," he added genially, "you'll be able t'
testify t' others about our cookin' abilities at Mill Crick."

Becky entered the room, unaware that the inn had received a
guest. She stopped just inside the doorway and glanced at the new
arrival. "Mr. Travis," John intonated, "my sister, Miss Cumings.
Becky, this is Mr. William Travis, who's found himself at th' mercy
of Mill Crick, unable t' go on to San Felipe tonight."

The gloom of the storm had darkened the room except for the
flickering light from the fire. Travis stood in front of the fireplace,
a slim, six-foot silhouette. He bowed deeply at the introduction.

"My pleasure, Miss Cumings." The youthful voice was suave, very pleasant. Its owner, Becky decided, was quite sure of himself. She did not step forward to offer her hand, but instead curtsied and welcomed him to the inn. Then she turned and lighted a lamp.

The added illumination allowed a much better examination of the visitor, a study she would not soon forget.

His face, framed by jaw-length sideburns and a head of curly hair redder than her own, could have belonged to a Roman god. Noble was the only word to describe the high, smooth forehead and distinctive brow. The steel-gray eyes spoke of arrogance and ambition; yet warmth and goodwill abided there alongside the baser emotions. A long but finely fashioned nose connected the brow and a full, sensuous mouth marred by its hint of weakness. From the terminus of each sideburn, the clean-shaven jaw ran in a determined line to a prominent, dimpled chin.

The visitor returned her gaze, eyes boldly speaking admiration, and a calm awareness of being admired.

Becky recovered herself. "Shall I tell Hannah to add a place for supper?" she asked. John and Travis both nodded, and she departed for the kitchen.

The two men took seats in front of the fire, enjoying cigars Travis had retrieved from an oilcloth pouch in his saddlebags. The younger man volunteered that he was an attorney in practice at San Felipe, having moved in a few months before from Anahuac. John idly asked if he had brought family with him, commenting that his failure to reach home as intended might be a cause for alarm. "I am a single man, sir," Travis replied shortly. Then, turning the discussion away from himself, he began a dissertation on the warring topics being examined throughout Texas: promotion to full Mexican statehood versus out-and-out independence.

As he talked, it dawned on John that this man was one of the hotheads who had brought Texas to the brink of conflict a year earlier on Galveston Bay. He and other young troublemakers had agitated the commander of the Mexican garrison at Anahuac, finally goading him into arresting them. True, this commander—Bradburn by name, Kentucky-born, and despised by the Anglo Texians as a "turncoat"—took some unnecessary actions that smacked of hostility and high-handedness. And when word spread (valid or not) that he intended to execute the prisoners, colonists from Brazoria and other communities quickly formed rescue parties.

Before it was over, shots were fired and blood shed in a skir-mish between Texians and Mexican soldiers at Velasco, and the pris-oners at Anahuac were freed upon the demands of an armed mob. Mexican President Anastacio Bustamante would most surely have taken direct and ruthless steps to punish the province, except that simultaneously he was fighting an insurrection led by the popular army officer Antonio Lopez de Santa Anna. In John's opinion, the only good sense the Texian participants had shown was to adopt and circulate resolutions citing support for Santa Anna, a heavy favorite in the current struggle, and defending their actions as directed solely against the despotic regime of Bustamante.

John listened in feigned agreement as Travis rattled on about the importance of the convention held last fall in San Felipe. At that gathering, delegates from all over the province drew up a list of de-sired legal reforms regarding immigration, tariffs, and local govern-ment. They also called for the creation of Texas as a state separate from Coahuila.

"Bustamante is out," Travis continued. "Santa Anna has now won control of Mexico. There will be another convention in April to review our petitions for the purpose of submitting them to the new government in Mexico City." He paused, and then looked keenly at John.

"Mr. Cumings," he asked, politely enough, "do you share the dream of a free and independent Texas?"

John exhaled the last smoke that could be safely drawn from his spent cheroot. He tapped the cigar out against the sole of his brogan, then glanced at his guest.

"How long have you lived in Texas, Mr. Travis?" he queried.

"Going on two years, sir," came the reply. "However, I can as-sure you that I have been very observant during that period."

John stood up and visited the fireplace, stirring the glowing ashes in search of a final burst of heat. He considered his next state-ment while Travis sat in silence.

"I've been here since 1822," John said at last. "Most o' those years, we've had peace an' quiet—mainly because the Mexicans were busy tendin' to other things. Now, I don't like some o' what we're havin' t' put up with any more than the next man. I do hap-pen t' think we dodged a bullet, by the kindness o' God alone, over what you an' your amigos got into at Anahuac. But I don't put much stock in any one Mexican *presidente* over another, an' continuin' t' call the attention of this Santa Anna fella to ourselves may not be th' smartest thing for us to do."

Eager to forestall a debate, John abruptly announced, "Come, Mr. Travis, to th' supper table. I believe our cook Hannah has a fine meal ready."

Becky heard little of the conversation over supper, and participated even less. It took a constant effort for her to study her food rather than the virile young man seated across from her. But, as Travis and John chatted, she was aware from time to time of the gray eyes darting her way. On those occasions, she felt the blood flow warmly to her cheeks.

After their meal, John directed Travis to one of the bedrooms in the "loft," the half-story upper section of the house. The lawyer lighted a candle and read a chapter out of Sir Walter Scott's *Rob Roy*. After extinguishing the flame, he lay awake for some time, reflecting on the beauty of the woman sleeping somewhere below.

William "Buck" Travis was accustomed to having his way with the fairer sex, and even entered in his diary the number of each successive "adventure." As a rule, the older women proved especially grateful for his attentions; but he did not quite know how to assess the charming spinster of Mill Creek.

Chapter 47

*F*or the people of Mexico, the latest change in political leadership would prove to be yet another case of hugging a viper to their bosoms. The name of this particular reptile was Antonio Lopez de Santa Anna.

But in the spring of 1833, and for a while to come, Santa Anna was proclaimed a hero and deliverer in all corners of the struggling nation, including the province of Texas. A declared federalist and defender of the liberal Constitution of 1824, the charismatic army officer easily won the presidential election in March. Then, professing a need to regain his spent health, Santa Anna enigmatically sidestepped active duty as chief executive and installed as functional head of state his idealistic vice president, Valentin Gomez Farias.

Fortuitously, the Texians had declared for Santa Anna as a way of explaining the rash actions taken at Velasco and Anahuac against soldiers representing the "despotic Bustamante regime." Now, emboldened by the ascension of what they perceived as a sympathetic administration, the colonists in April conducted a second convention at San Felipe. It was just as illegal as the one held the October previous, official sanction never having been elicited for either.

The stated goal of the delegates was separation from Coahuila in favor of Texas statehood. By the close of the convention, a proposed state constitution had been drawn up. It was heavily influenced by the new delegate from Nacogdoches, the lawyer Sam Houston. Producing such a document was simply a time-honored part of the process followed by U.S. territories aspiring to statehood. That this might appear presumptuous (and even audacious) in the eyes of Mexican officials did not occur to the delegates—or, at least, did not deter them.

Stephen Austin, already forced into the role of apologist over the unlawful assemblies, was chosen to journey to Mexico City and place the petition for statehood before Gomez Farias. Even though Austin disagreed with some of what took place at both conventions, he, at least, could speak Spanish.

Austin departed on his mission in April. It was the last he saw of his adopted homeland for more than two years. In the interim, he suffered unjust imprisonment and was witness to the chameleon Santa Anna transforming himself from people's president to ensanguined dictator.

Buck Travis did a little snooping around San Felipe and learned that Becky Cumings already had a dedicated, well-regarded, and muscular suitor. It was whispered, though, that Becky's allegiance to the relationship might well crumble under the proper competition.

Still, Travis maintained his patience. It wasn't that Swearingen's imposing physical presence intimidated the newcomer. Well might Travis be guilty of multiple weaknesses, but cowardice wasn't among them. However, an attorney just beginning to build a practice didn't need to be creating enemies.

In the meantime, in a community reputed to be virtually devoid of female companionship, Travis managed to unearth a surprising number of temporary companions (including slaves, servant girls, and prostitutes) whose morals didn't get in the way of their fun. Dutifully noting and numbering those so-called "adventures" in his diary, the twenty-four-year-old Travis had run the sum well into the fifties.

All of these things notwithstanding, Travis retained a yearning to again glimpse the lady of the green eyes and russet hair. So, twice that summer he finagled appearances at the inn on Mill Creek. On the second occasion, Travis persuaded John Cumings to turn over to him the unfinished business of the Bastrop milling partnership. The baron had died in Saltillo in 1827, so penniless that fellow representatives in the state assembly took up a collection for his burial. John was long since square with the estate, but had never dissolved the partnership.

During the business discussion, Travis idly commented on

Seth Swearingen's well-known ardor for Becky, and how she doubtless returned it in full measure. "Oh, I wouldn't go so far as t' say
that," John replied, carelessly. "Just th' same, he's a fine young man.
She could do lots worse in this neighborhood."

Inwardly, Travis smiled—partly over his success in securing a
response to the random question, and partly over the favorableness
of the answer. While John's opinion of Seth was significant, that of
Becky was much more so. The lawyer's next challenge was to bridle
his well-known impetuosity until the time was right.

In October, Travis received assistance from an unexpected
source in his clandestine pursuit of Becky: Lucinda Thompson,
one-time widow of William Cumings.

William's estate included the one-league grant on the Brazos
River below Brazoria, a distance of two to three days' hard riding
from San Felipe. When Lucinda left Texas, she arranged for an
adjoining landowner to maintain the property in exchange for grazing rights. Another neighbor had recently written her to say that
the land was in a badly neglected condition, and to express an interest in utilizing it himself.

Lucinda conveyed this in a letter to John, closing with a plea
for his help. John chose to discuss the problem with Swearingen, a
childhood friend of Lucinda. Seth agreed to go to Brazoria at once
and investigate the matter. So, when the Townsend clan announced
the hosting of a dance for that coming Saturday, Travis was confident Becky Cumings had no prospect of an escort.

As there was insufficient time for correspondence, the young
attorney made a personal visit to Mill Creek. Finding herself the
sole object of the handsome caller's attention, Becky hesitated only
briefly before accepting his invitation.

After Travis rode away, she excitedly sought out John and
found him at the mill. He sat astride a log being fed slowly to the
ribbon saw, entering figures in an account book.

"Oh, John!" his sister said, eyes dancing. "Mr. Travis was just
by here, and guess what he wanted!"

John glanced up vacantly from his work. "Dunno, Sis," he responded. Then he noticed the glow in her cheeks. "He must've
invited you out somewheres," he ventured sagely.

"To the Townsends' ball!" she said eagerly. "He rode all the
way up from San Felipe just to ask me!"

"Why, goodness knows you're worth th' time," John responded, brushing wood particles off the pages of his journal. He added, "I reckon you told him you'd go?"

Becky nodded, but her countenance clouded. "Should I not have?" she asked.

John pondered for just a moment. "You need t' do what suits you," he answered. "I was just thinkin' o' Seth." That was in part a lie. He was thinking more about the stories he'd heard of Travis and his nightly gambling escapades, and more so the gossip about his penchant for loose women.

Becky sighed. "I know," she said. "But I have never made any commitment to Seth Swearingen."

John nodded, and tried to be reassuring. "He'll just have t' understand," he said. "After all, it's your life, too."

He attempted to get back to his bookkeeping, but Becky had something else on her mind. "John," she asked, pensively, "how old do you reckon Mr. Travis to be?"

John smiled. "He is likely 'bout twenty-five or so," he estimated. "Whatever his age, he'll be proud as a peacock t' be escortin' th' prettiest woman there."

The Townsends had timed their shindig to correspond to the appearance of the full moon. Should a clear night be in the offing, as was hoped for, the moonlight would help the partygoers find their way home. The sphere did not disappoint, rising goblin orange over the treetops well after dark.

Lunar illumination augmented that of lanterns hanging from tree limbs near every corner of the outdoor dance floor. The floor consisted of wooden flats from packing crates, laid over a solid foundation of hewn logs. About half of the merrymakers could dance on it at once, though they had to be cautious while cavorting across the uneven surface.

There were two fiddles available, not in tune with each other, and musicians of varying talent and energy took turns coaxing upbeat tunes out of them. The percussion needs were met through the incessant beating of a triangle iron, more or less in rhythm with the fiddlers.

John had prophesied correctly. His sister and Buck Travis made the handsomest couple at the dance, the latter decked out in red pantaloons, hose, and new pumps. Becky was resplendent in her best full-length cotton dress, green ribbons tied in her hair.

There was, of course, some murmuring about Becky being out with someone other than Seth, especially when that someone was the flashy young dandy with the spotty reputation. The comments grew less guarded when the objects of their barbs withdrew from the dance floor for a walk through the heavy shadows of the surrounding woods.

Travis, though, would have no luck this night in pressing for physical attention. Holding hands was the extent of what Becky encouraged. Otherwise, they made light chit-chat and admired each other in the moonlight.

When at last the dance was over, and he returned Becky to the door of the inn, Buck Travis leaned forward in anticipation of a goodnight kiss. Instead, he received a playful but cautioning finger against his lips, and with a radiant smile Becky thanked him for the evening and bade him good-night. Travis quickly took hold of the teasing finger and succeeded in pressing a lengthy kiss on the back of her hand.

"May I call on you again, Miss Cumings?" he asked, in that mesmerizing Southern voice. Even shadowed from the moonlight, his eyes glistened with expectance.

She nodded, gave him a barely audible "yes," and withdrew her hand. The young man opened the door to the inn, and Becky stepped quickly inside and threw the bolt.

Perhaps Austin had simply tired of his own conciliatory posturing. Perhaps he was in bad health or weary from the long journey to Mexico City, either of which could have contributed to an exercise of poor judgment. Whatever the provocation, he made to acting Mexican president Gomez Farias a less than pleasing presentation of the Texian petition.

Essentially, Austin told Santa Anna's puppet that Texas wanted and expected statehood and would not suffer further delay. The interview ended without resolution, its participants mutually angry and discouraged.

At this juncture, Austin unwisely wrote a letter critical of the attitude of the national government and sent it to the *ayuntamiento* of San Antonio. Aware that the Hispanic leadership there was in favor of statehood, and believing them to be in better standing with Mexico City than the Texians, he urged them to take the lead in getting Texas separated from Coahuila.

While Austin yet remained in the capital, Santa Anna diminished Gomez Farias and assumed the role of president. The empresario visited Santa Anna several times in meetings which were more cordial than had been the interview with Gomez Farias. Although the president denied the application for statehood, pointing out that Texas was far shy of the required 80,000 citizens, he agreed to several reforms: removal of the ban on immigration, better mail service, and nullification of the tariff. These measures would later become law.

With some sense of accomplishment, then, Austin in December 1833, set out for Texas. He got as far as Saltillo, where he was arrested, returned to the Mexican capital, and thrown into a small, windowless cell in the old Inquisition prison. Denied bail and not informed of the charges against him, Austin remained in solitary confinement for three months. Later he was relocated to slightly better environs at a city jail. Only then did he learn the cause of his ill treatment.

Some members of the San Antonio *ayuntamiento,* obviously not acting in Austin's best interests, had caused his imprudent letter to be forwarded to higher authorities. The missive wound up in the hands of Gomez Farias, who recalled Austin's earlier attitude and read into the letter the threat of a revolution. It was he who ordered Austin's arrest.

Word of the empresario's imprisonment did not reach Texas until February. When it did, Austin and his friends back home intuitively reached the same conclusion: in the present instance, discretion was the better part of valor. Austin urged in his correspondence that the Texians avoid rash actions or provocative steps. Similarly, the Texians feared that incautious reactions to this outrageous treatment of their delegate might actually place Austin's life in jeopardy. While Austin awaited the onerously slow movement of the Mexican judicial system to process his case, Texas officials tried to work within the system to bring the prisoner relief.

Despite the outward show of caution, the resentment caused by Austin's plight helped swing sentiment within the province toward the radical viewpoint. Among those verbally rattling their sabers was William Travis; soon, as once before, he would find at Anahuac the opportunity to do more than talk.

Chapter 48

*I*t would not be accurate to characterize Seth Swearingen as a good loser. Seth had too much pride to simply shrug his shoulders in philosophical acceptance of defeat by another suitor for the heart of the Mill Creek maiden. At the same time, there lived within the Kentuckian's soul a sense of fair play. If left alone to work his way through the anger and heartache, Swearingen might have at least achieved the status of a dignified loser.

However, others in San Felipe had no intention of letting the situation stand.

There was no mistaking the fact that Buck Travis enjoyed a sweeping victory at Mill Creek. The early entries in his diary regarding this new romantic interest spoke carefully of "Miss Cummins," but in later notations she succinctly and intimately became "R—." The young attorney seemed intuitively to know that the object of his pursuit preferred being called her formal name rather than its childhood diminutive. After all, differentiating between mother and daughter was no longer necessary.

These were times of euphoria for Rebecca Cumings. At long last, she felt as if she were truly her own person. Due largely to the attentions of Travis, her self-esteem soared to new heights. However, one rogue element among this giddying swirl of emotions actually frightened her.

After twenty years of guilt-driven suppression, the nearly forgotten fire of physical passion was rekindled. A simple glance or casual touch from Travis was enough to fan the coals. As an adolescent, Rebecca had indulged such feelings with tragic results. Her unrestrained response to the advances of Peter Ayles led unexpectedly to the diabolical, soul-searing experience with David Singletary —and pregnancy. The succession of ordeals inflicted emotional and physical scars, and neither set had ever quite healed. In fact, the crimson stripes still marring Rebecca's lower abdomen were, of themselves, eloquent reminders of a dark and shameful secret. Somewhere in the Ohio Valley there lived a man, now twenty-one years of age, sired by Singletary but bearing the last name of Cumings.

Travis, skilled far beyond his years in issues of sexuality, well knew how to exploit them. And yet, in this new and potentially passionate relationship, he held back. Perhaps, despite his many carnal episodes, Travis was sufficiently influenced by the popular literature of the day to play the self-denying role of the gallant gentleman. Perhaps, too, the very naiveness and vulnerability of Rebecca (in truth, not an inconsiderable segment of her overall charm) dissuaded him from pressing any advantage. And most importantly, the careful reader of his diary might well discern an attitude toward the Mill Creek maiden which approached reverence.

In spite of a growing caseload, the lawyer managed to find time for a weekly trip over the eight miles separating San Felipe and the Cumings inn. One stormy evening, the prairie flooded by rain and the resulting overflow from the creek, Travis stubbornly saddled his horse and started to the inn. The hostile elements and impending darkness forced common sense to take charge over an uncommonly strong will. "Set out for Mill Creek," he ruefully recorded in his diary that night. "Waters all swimming & prairie so boggy—could not go—the first time I ever turned back in my life."

For the most part, though, the weather proved an asset. Springtime transformed southeast Texas into a paradise for courtship, tossing out a green mat of young grass shoots under the arching, moss-draped limbs of ancient oak and pecan. Across this mat, and thicker in the open fields, sprouted myriad flowers clothed in every conceivable color and hue. The fresh northerly breezes had not yet succumbed to summer's sultry, prevailing gulf breeze. When twilight deepened into night, there arrived along with the stars a delicious little chill to the air.

Travis found Rebecca especially receptive to outdoor pursuits such as fishing, picnics, and horseback rides. There remained in parts of the colony the remote prospect of unfriendly Tonkawas lurking in the woods, so some measure of vigilance was required. This led Travis to instruct Rebecca in the use of a pistol. Her brothers, William chief among them, had taught her how to load and shoot a rifle; but, like many other frontiersmen, the Cumingses disdained the smaller firearm to the point that none among them even owned one. The small pistol used by their mother to dispatch the renegade Abbott more than a half-century before had long since succumbed to corrosion, and was valueless for any role other than that of heirloom.

It was also the intent of Travis to improve Rebecca's reading ability and to instill in her some of his own love of literature. Together they read Sir Walter Scott's ballads out of borrowed books, as well as the poetry of Lord Byron, reprinted in the San Felipe newspaper. These sessions often took place at a pretty spot overlooking the confluence of Mill Creek and the Brazos River.

One afternoon they were at that location, Scott's "Lady of the Lake" furnishing the material for the day's reading. To pique Rebecca's interest, Travis offered a short dissertation on the history and customs of the Scottish Highlands. After he had finished, and was leafing through the pages for a favorite passage to read aloud, Rebecca chose to change the subject.

"Who is this handsome and generous young man," she asked, smiling sweetly, "that chooses to spend so much of his valuable time with an unread country spinster?"

The question surprised Travis into a blank stare. He plucked a blade of grass to mark the spot from which he intended to read, then closed the book and laid it down. "What on earth do you mean?" he responded, a bit guardedly.

"The gentleman has the lady at a disadvantage," Rebecca said with a playful pout. "What little you don't already know about me, you can easily guess." The lie slipped past unchallenged. "I surely don't present much of a mystery to you. On the other hand, I only know that you're an accomplished lawyer at a young age, that you came to San Felipe from Anahuac, and lived in Alabama before that.

"I know nothing about your family, where you studied law— even whether any of your family came to Texas with you. And, honestly, I can't begin to imagine what brought you all the way to Texas, anyway."

It was Travis's turn to smile. "Ah, the fatal curiosity of the female!" he mocked. "Well, I arrived in Texas as I am now, a single man. As to my training in law, I studied and worked under a judge who possessed one of the finest legal minds in Alabama.

"As far as Texas is concerned, it offers a great challenge and much opportunity. Rebecca, it is my firm belief that the Americans, who are the real inhabitants of note, will not long endure the tyranny and injustices being heaped on them so arrogantly by their adopted country. Just look at how poor Austin is being treated. Kept in jail! The Mexicans haven't the decency to allow him bail or his day in court! These people of ours will one day fight for independence, and they will win. And the men who are willing to risk all in that effort also stand to profit handsomely in the outcome— a new nation, or a new state in the United States of the North, whichever they create."

The proud rhetoric thrilled Rebecca, and she admired the determination reflected in the steely gaze and jutting chin of her companion. It wasn't until after they parted company, late in the day, that she realized he had said nothing about his family.

Robert Williamson, master storyteller and one of the outspoken advocates of independence for Texas, sat in a corner of the little chamber that served as the law office of William Barret Travis. Williamson's cane leaned against the wall next to him. The room, located at the front of Travis's modest residence on the south end of San Felipe, was also occupied by its renter and by a fourteen-year-old youth, Hampton Kuykendall, who functioned as a law clerk.

A childhood illness had left Williamson's right leg severely drawn back below the knee. Not one to allow any dilution of life, the lawyer wore a wooden peg leg attached at the knee. He even had his pants modified to cover both the real and artificial appendages, and so suffered without rancor the moniker "Three-Legged Willie."

As he and Travis were palavering about politics, and Kuykendall sat busily transcribing legal papers, there erupted a demanding flurry of knocking at the door. Kuykendall answered it and stepped back to admit Seth Swearingen.

The big man ducked his head to avoid the door frame as he

entered. He ignored the young clerk, nodded brusquely to William-son, and glared at Travis. The latter, sensing that the unsolicited visit was not intended as a social call, rose from his chair.

"I've come, Mr. Travis," Swearingen said, fairly spitting out the Alabaman's name in distaste, "to warn you that your masquerade is over an' done with."

Swearingen took several steps toward Travis. The latter drew himself to his full height, still giving up a good three inches to his erstwhile rival. Williamson, poker-faced except for a lively gleam in his eyes, casually took his cane in hand but remained seated.

"It's soon t' be all over th' colony, sir," the accuser continued, "that you abandoned a wife an' children back where you come from, and left considerable debts owin' as well."

The face of the accused turned crimson. His hands balled into fists, but he kept them at his side. "What is the meaning of this in-trusion, sir?" he demanded, voice quivering with anger.

Swearingen came a pace closer. "The meanin' o' this here intru-sion," he mimicked, "is t' tell you that you are through at Mill Crick. Miss Becky knows all about your past, and she don't ever wish t' see you 'round there again. She knows you for what ever'-body else in Texas is gonna know you—as a cowardly liar and a cheat!"

In a flash, Travis seized his riding quirt, simultaneously leaning across the table. With a vicious flick of the braided leather lash, he cut open Swearingen's cheek. The Kentuckian bellowed in fury. At this juncture, Kuykendall flung his youthful frame onto Swear-ingen's back with the intent of bringing him to the floor. Seth went to one knee, twisting his great arms behind him to seize the law clerk. Travis, eyes smoldering, quickly stepped around the table.

The explosive crack of Three-Legged Willie's cane, slammed with great force across the table top, arrested further action. Wil-liamson stood and held up both arms as a plea to halt the budding melee. "Please, please, kind sirs!" he cried out. "This is no way for civilized men to settle their differences!

"What we have witnessed here is a slur—actually, two or three slurs—against the character of Mr. Travis, and his resultant chal-lenge of Mr. Swearingen to give him satisfaction in a duel."

Swearingen shook off Kuykendall and lurched to his feet, rub-bing the stinging cheek with a massive hand. Travis flung his quirt to the floor. "That's right, Swearingen," he said through clenched teeth. "Which will it be? Swords or pistols?"

The big man looked first at Travis, then at Williamson, not totally comprehending. "You must admit, sir," Williamson said to him, "that you initiated this fractious encounter and assailed the character of Mr. Travis in front of witnesses. Mr. Travis has called on you to meet him on the field of honor."

"Swords or pistols?" Travis again demanded to know.

"Tut, tut, Mr. Travis," Williamson interjected, with light admonition. "You have hurled the gauntlet. The choices of weapons, time, and place belong to Mr. Swearingen."

"I don't have no sword or pistol," grumbled Seth. Then a crooked smile lighted his face and caused the cheek to bleed anew. "If it's really my choice o' weapons," he said, craftily, "then I choose huntin' knives! Huntin' knives it'll be! We'll meet at the big sandbar on the Brazos, below Allen's place. How 'bout seven o'clock in the mornin'?"

Williamson examined his cane, which had been cracked by its impact with the table. Pursing his lips, he looked first at Travis, then at Swearingen. Neither man displayed a glimmer of hesitation. "Very well, sir," he said to Seth. "Hunting knives, the sandbar below Allen's, seven sharp. I will serve as Mr. Travis's second, and will arrange for a doctor to be present. Choose you a second—you know, man, a close friend who will accompany you—and have him notify me in writing by nightfall, confirming our arrangements.

"Now, sirs, we must keep the general populace unapprised of tomorrow's plans. Do what you must to leave your affairs in order, but say nothing to anyone other than your intimates. Should word get out, there won't be room for the two of you on the sandbar for all the gawkers. And, Buck, please send young Kuykendall to Mr. Dennett with my cane, and instructions to find a suitable set of brass fittings to clamp it together until I can locate another."

Chapter 49

*D*awn's initial sunrays strove to dissipate the thick Brazos bottomland fog, with only marginal success. Through the clinging moisture rode Travis and Williamson. After passing by the Allen place, they began their search for a large sandbar situated somewhere at the base of the mist-shrouded riverbank.

Travis was due to rendezvous with his opponent a half-hour earlier than the time first named by Swearingen. Three-Legged Willie, upon reaching his quarters at Peyton's hotel the night before, had found awaiting him a brief, anonymous note, presumably from Swearingen's unnamed second. It reinforced the arrangements already in place for the duel, with a single exception: "To take place at half past the hour of Six O'Clock in the Morning, rather than at Seven O'Clock sharp, expect busy day to-morrow."

Thus, Williamson returned to Travis's house well before daybreak, waking the Alabaman with the news of the change in time. Taking seriously the advice of Three-Legged Willie to set his affairs in order, Travis had worked at his table late into the night. The prospect of a showdown with pistols, or even swords, would not have troubled him unduly; but, while wanting nothing in the commodity of courage, he soberly conceded that the brutish Swearingen held the advantage in close combat with hunting knives.

Among the epistles the young lawyer penned was a lengthy one to Rebecca. He sealed it and notated, as he had done with the others, that it be opened only in the event of his death.

Now, as the neophyte duelist and his second probed the misty grayness along the river's edge, the latter recalled the note and wondered aloud who Swearingen's second might be. "If your adversary composed that missive himself," Williamson remarked dryly, "he appears confident of prevailing in your contest and moving blithely on to his day's labors."

They plunged their mounts through high, sodden grass to a line of cottonwood trees marking the riverbank. There they found a lone horse tethered to a limb. Travis groaned. He recognized the big roan as belonging to John Cumings.

"Well," Williamson observed, "presuming this is the spot, we have beaten Dr. Phelps here. Surely he received my message about the change in time . . . And, apparently, we have preceded your opponent as well. Unless, of course, he borrowed Cumings's horse and it is he who awaits us on the bar."

A glance into the eddying white fog below discerned little except a gray, shadowy mass that was presumably a stand of willows. The friends dismounted, secured their steeds, and, with Travis assisting the much less agile Williamson, slowly clambered down to the sandbar. The mist was even thicker there. "This is surely the spot, eh?" Williamson wondered aloud between heavy breaths.

"You've found th' right place, gentlemen," the unmistakable voice of John Cumings assured them. John stepped out of the fog and rather formally shook their hands. He wore no shirt. His torso, glistening with moisture, was that of a man who, though nearing fifty, remained strong and fit. A blanket was rolled and tied snugly around his left forearm. Tucked in his leather waistbelt was a Bowie knife.

"This is sure an honor," John said, his tone of voice belying the words. "Here we have th' *alcalde,* Mr. Williamson, and th' secretary of th' *ayuntamiento,* Mr. Travis. The leadin' men in San Felipe! What a strange business t' be conductin' this mornin'! Well, shall we get started?"

The question nettled Travis. "First of all, we're waiting on Dr. Phelps," he pointed out testily, "and I haven't seen any sign of Swearingen, either. I conclude he's not here yet. So how can we begin now?"

But Williamson saw the situation clearly. "It was your note I received last night, wasn't it?" he asked John. Without waiting for a reply, he added, "I suspect Mr. Swearingen is still under the impression that the duel is to commence at seven o'clock." John nodded slowly. "Well, then," Williamson concluded, "it appears that you are proposing to take the field on his behalf."

"Nope, not exactly," John replied. Looking the astonished Travis in the eye, he added coldly, "I aim to take th' field on behalf o' myself an' my sister. The time for seekin' satisfaction has arrived, young fellow, so, doctor or no doctor, you'd best be makin' yourself ready."

While Williamson produced a bone-handled hunting knife and gingerly ran his thumb along the blade, Travis reluctantly began to remove his shirt. The shift in opponents had him flustered. Then he angrily hurled his hat to the sand. Engaging Rebecca's brother in a duel would never do!

"My fight, sir, is not with you," he protested heatedly. "It wasn't you who burst into my home and insulted me in front of my friend and my young employee."

John offered no reply except to jerk the ugly-looking Bowie knife from his belt. He balanced the handle in the palm of his hand and carefully gripped it, aligning the thumb and tip of the index finger against the hilt. The cutting edge of the monstrous, hump-backed blade ran parallel with his knuckles. Then, using left hand and teeth, he tied a rawhide thong around the right hand and knife.

Meanwhile, Travis stubbornly refused to accept the weapon urged on him by Williamson. Instead, he picked up his hat, brushed the damp sand from it, and returned it to his head.

Having knotted the thong, John looked up. "I didn't come here t' waste my time, Mr. Travis," he said gravely. "This affair needs settlin' one way or t'other."

"I will not fight you, sir," Travis replied doggedly. "I'll wait for the one who slandered me."

John raised an eyebrow. "Are you sayin' that Seth was lyin' when he called you—whatever it was he called you?" he asked pointedly. "Quick, man," he demanded, his voice suddenly harsh, "answer me! Be truthful, or defend yourself against this Bowie knife!" John lifted both arms and assumed a fighting crouch.

The Alabaman's face turned crimson. He knew better than anyone how solidly Seth's accusations were grounded in fact. Travis literally choked on his first response, an attempt to frame a denial. He finally managed to answer, in a low, hoarse voice, "Some of what he said . . . was right."

John abandoned the crouch and dropped his arms. "Buck," he

said, matter-of-factly, "I remember th' day you first dropped by th' inn, durin' that rainstorm. You said then you was single. Did you lie t' me?"

Travis shook his head vehemently. "In my mind, John, it was not a lie," he contended. "In my mind, it wasn't a lie, either, when I declared on the application for my land grant that I was divorced. There is a woman in Alabama that I once called my wife, but so far as I am concerned she is no longer anything to me."

A bull-like bellow cut short John's further interrogations.

"Is ever'body down there?" roared the voice of Swearingen from the top of the riverbank. "I can't see a blessed thing!"

"Come on down, Seth," John called to him. "An' if Dr. Phelps is up there anywhere, tell him he kin head back home." With those words, John began loosening the string binding hand and knife.

Williamson briskly rubbed his hands together. "Capital!" he exclaimed. "Due to the timely intervention of Mr. Swearingen's second, we have averted the needless shedding of blood." He gave Travis a penetrating stare. "Because Mr. Swearingen's accusations were sincere, and apparently had some element of truth to them," he advised his friend, "you would be wise to close the matter by offering him an apology, your quirt, and an uncontested swing at your cheek." Travis bit his lip but made no reply.

A heavy crunching of earth and crackling of brush signaled the descent of the big Kentuckian. In a moment, he had joined the gathering on the sandbar, and Williamson explained the situation to him. Seth was initially vexed over John's deception, and appeared genuinely disappointed at the prospect of the duel being canceled. He finally accepted Travis's subdued apology, but spurned the offer of the quirt. "I don't care nothin' about that," he rumbled. "Just be sure you don't go 'round Mill Creek anymore!"

Travis vigorously refused to honor any such edict, and for a moment it appeared that the duel might be fought after all. Then John spoke up.

"Friend," he said to Swearingen, "I'm grateful t' you for stickin' up for Becky, an' I was honored you asked me t' be your second. But I have t' say, it's gonna rest with Becky t' decide who she'll see or not see. Whatever she wants to do, it's neither my call nor yours."

The big man grunted in irritation. "I ain't too sure," he remarked, "that Becky, or any woman for that matter, is capable o' decidin' what they want. But I guess what you say is fair enough. Anyway," he sneered, "I'm thinkin' it's highly unlikely she'll want t' see th' likes of Mr. Travis ever again."

For one long, anguish-filled week, Travis tended to believe Seth's prediction might be right. He sent Rebecca the letter he had written to her the night before the duel; it was returned, to all appearances unopened. Then he composed and dispatched a briefer epistle, begging her to hear him out. Two days dragged by without a response. Travis had tentatively decided to risk all by making an uninvited appearance at Mill Creek when the Cumingses' young slave, Henry, came riding up to his house.

The brief note he delivered simply asked Travis to be at "the reading place on the creek" the next afternoon. There was no signature or initial affixed, but the young lawyer was elated. He knew the location to be Rebecca's favorite. "Tell your mistress I'll be there without fail!" he jubilantly instructed Henry, flipping him a coin. The boy's nod and broad grin indicated that Travis had at least one ally at Mill Creek.

Still, not unexpectedly, the reception was very formal and equally chilly. Rebecca would not let the penitent suitor get within arm's length of her. "Say whatever it is you have to say," she commanded, in her sternest manner, "and see to it that you tell me only the truth. I should warn you that others have not been as reluctant as you to share the details of your past."

Travis did as instructed. He told Rebecca how, as a beginning schoolteacher in Alabama, he met and married one of his pupils, Rosanna Cato. They had a son, Charles Edward, and the little household seemed happy and complete. Then, he said, rumors began circulating about town that Rosanna was unfaithful.

"At long last," said Travis, his face hardening, "I determined beyond doubt that the stories were true. Privately, I went to the man involved and demanded that he either leave town or give me satisfaction. He promised he would leave town. I said nothing of this to Rosanna, although I am sure that he told her."

The narrator glanced at Rebecca. She quickly averted her gaze, but Travis glimpsed what he had hoped to see.

"Soon," he continued, "Rosanna told me we were going to have another baby. I knew in my heart it could not be ours. The other man had not yet left town. Under the cover of darkness, I went to call on him. We chanced to meet in the alley, at the back door to his business house.

"We argued, fought and . . . I killed him."

A small gasp came from Rebecca.

"To the best of my knowledge," Travis continued, "there were no witnesses. Now, as luck would have it, a Negro belonging to Judge Dellett first came across the body and reported the crime. He was immediately accused of doing the deed, because there had passed between him and the dead man some things he had good reason to resent.

"Judge Dellett was who I studied law under, and later helped with his practice. I became afraid that an innocent slave was going to be hanged over the death of a man who deserved what he had gotten. Late one night, I went to the judge's house and told him the entire story.

"Even though killing a man for the reason I did is viewed as justifiable in Alabama as it is in other states, it is not part of the written criminal code. Too, any public airing of what preceded and provoked the incident would have held my family up to censure. For my wife alone, I would not have cared; but in the best interests of my son, Charles, and of my wife's kin, who are fine, God-fearing people, I decided it was best that I simply leave Alabama.

"That is my story, Rebecca. How many times have I reproached myself for not telling you! But it is painful to recount, and I lacked the courage to follow through. Besides, as you say, others have not been bashful to spread talk about me. I trust that what you have just heard are the same things you have already been told by Swearingen."

Rebecca's eyes flashed. "Oh, Seth is the least of them!" she exclaimed angrily. "Poor, simple man, he was just upset on my behalf. But oh, Buck! There are others who want your reputation ruined. All they told Seth is that you abandoned your wife and children to run away from your debts. And, no! Don't demand of Seth that he tell you who told him. He'll never do that."

She stepped close to Travis. A hint of tears shone in her wide, green eyes. "Anyway," she continued, her voice soft and warm, "it doesn't matter to me who they are, or what accusations they make." She lifted her face toward his.

Travis took her in his arms.

Chapter 50

*H*eavy, recurring rains plagued Austin's colony for the better part of two weeks. The downpours were evidently just as prevalent far to the north, from whence the Brazos flowed; the river took on the appearance of liquid red clay, and the peril of the swift and bloated current forced the suspension of many routine activities along its course.

The waters of Mill Creek also moved—laterally, that is, for they had nowhere to go but out of the banks. The little stream rose well above the millrace at the Cumings mill, and spread its added load across the prairie to the south. Such overflows were not uncommon, but this was the first time John had seen the Brazos rushing so hard and high that it backed up Mill Creek at the mouth.

Finally, the deluge ceased, and a blue sky replaced the dark rain clouds of days past. At long last given the opportunity, Travis soon headed to Mill Creek, his black Spanish mare picking her way gingerly along the mushy trail. John did not especially relish the reinstatement of the young attorney in Rebecca's social circle, but he was bound by his own speech at the sandbar to honor her wishes. So when the Alabaman arrived at the inn, the two men exchanged cordial greetings and Travis shortly launched into a recitation of the latest news.

Actually, there was not very much to report. Residents in the coastal villages of Velasco and Brazoria were deeply concerned about the standing water from the rains, fearing it would stagnate and bring on a return of last summer's deadly outbreaks of malaria and cholera. Meantime, writing from his prison cell in Mexico City, Austin continued to urge the applications of caution and patience in dealing with the state and national authorities. Again, the prospect of putting Austin into even worse straits was enough to stay any outward show of rebellion on the part of the Texians.

"It remains my opinion, sir," Travis pontificated, "that Colonel Austin is dead wrong in his long-standing conciliatory attitude toward this ill-fated nation and her incompetent leadership. Once he has been extricated from his perilous position, hopefully through movement at last by the courts, Texas likewise must free herself from affiliation with Mexico."

John heaved a sigh. He did not wish to be quarrelsome. "Is it so easy t' do—end our affiliation with Mexico?" he asked with a faint touch of sarcasm.

The gray eyes of the visitor flashed. "When free men stand to their feet, determined to assert their liberty, then their oppressors need beware!" he declared. John winced inwardly at the melodramatic statement.

Rebecca entered the room, and to her brother's relief the political rhetoric faded. Soon Travis and his lady were strolling along the muddy bank of the creek while John went to the mill, where Henry was employed in mopping up the rainwater that had blown inside.

A half-hour later, the miller was halted in his cleanup effort by the excited call of his sister. "John! Oh, John!" she trumpeted, bursting into the mill on the run. The green eyes were shining, the full lips parted in a joyous smile. As she rushed up to him, one slender hand fondled a heart-shaped silver brooch pinned to her collar.

"Isn't it beautiful, brother?" she exclaimed. John's heart sank, and he averted his eyes.

"Yes'm," he said faintly, "it's sure nice." The absence of enthusiasm in his voice caused the green eyes to cloud, and the lips to push themselves into a pucker of disappointment. Before she could utter a word, though, he recovered himself, smiled, examined the pin, and gave her a hug.

"You're sure one for surprisin' your poor brother," he said lamely. Easily reassured, Rebecca raced on to a related topic. "John," she said, blushing, "I'd really like for Buck to see Ma's letter. You know, the one we found . . . afterwards, on the table."

John could taste the ashes in his mouth. "Why, sure, sis," he replied gamely. "There's no harm in it. An' I b'lieve I can guess what's put it in your pretty head."

Rebecca's smile deepened, and then her radiant face (somehow too radiant for her own good, John thought) disappeared as she turned and quickly left the mill.

Travis stood in contemplation of the eddying creek as Rebecca approached. "What did John have to say?" he asked, without turning his head. She did not reply, instead holding out to him a rolled sheet of paper bound with ribbon. Her left hand was hidden in the folds of her dress. "Please, Buck," she said. "I wish for you to read this."

He carefully untied the ribbon and flattened the paper to study its painfully scrawled contents.

> My dear Becky,
>   You & Sarah were made to suffer by a well-meaning Mother. Altho you must always keep Jesus first in your life, I pray that someday you meet a man like your father. When that should happen, and you know beyond doubt that he is the man for you, then if you wish you may give him your father's ring. God bless & keep you—He loves you even more than I.

Travis blinked as he lowered the paper and tenderly rolled it up. His hands trembled when he attempted to re-tie the ribbon, and he gave the letter over to Rebecca to secure. He had been genuinely moved.

Rebecca extended her clenched left hand and opened it. In the work-hardened palm lay a man's ring of hammered gold. The single stone was dark and smoky.

"Take this, Buck," she said. "It was Pa's, although I never saw it on his hand. The place where we lived in Kentucky, they didn't believe in sporting fancy things like jewelry."

Travis placed the ring on the proper finger of his left hand. He admired it, then looked into the beaming green eyes.

"Are you sure, Rebecca?" he asked, his voice almost a whisper, the words imbued with an uncharacteristic anxiety.

She nodded. "Yes, love," came the answer, "I'm sure."

Although the late afternoon sky was blue, a low grumble of thunder reached their ears. Rebecca glanced northward through the trees and spotted the gray horns of a thunderhead.

"I suppose we are in for another round of rain," she said to Travis. "I should not like for you to get caught out in it on your way home. Would you consider staying the night?"

He would.

When the lovers returned to the inn, they encountered a solemn John Cumings awaiting them. "Please have a seat," he said, in a manner soft yet imperative. "I believe we might have th' need for a chat."

Vaguely apprehensive, they followed his bidding.

"You've both made a decision, I see," John began. "I kin say without hesitation, even though no one's asked me, that I want for you both all th' happiness in th' world. But"—he held up a warning finger—"th' seriousness of what you're plannin' begs for a little more discussion. A little airin' out, if you will. As th' last family member remainin' in Texas t' look after Becky, there's somethin' I need t' know."

Gray eyes and green stared at him in mystification. Satisfied that he held their attention, John continued.

"Buck, we found out not too long ago (an' initially, not from you) that you left a wife an' children back in Alabama. Sure, I know you've been sayin' things to th' effect that, as far as you're concerned, she's no longer your wife. Now, a sharp lawyer like yourself knows what it takes t' fix that up legally."

With some difficulty, Buck met John's gaze. "Certainly, I understand what you're driving at, and I applaud you for attending to your family duty," he responded. "And, no, I have not yet sought a writ of divorcement. Before proceeding with that, I must first settle certain issues of property on behalf of my son."

John's eyes narrowed. "Forgive me for seemin' simple," he quipped. "I thought you had more'n just one child."

"It is my belief, sir," the reply came coldly, "that my wife's second child, a girl, is not my own. This is, in fact, the specific issue with which I must wrestle and find a resolution to before I focus on the writ."

"So," John pursued, "then there's other legal things t' consider." He looked first at Rebecca, who was twisting her hands in her lap, then back at Travis. "All o' this effort could take some time, huh, Buck?"

Travis nodded.

John scratched his head. "Becky," he said, slowly, "I do want you t' be as gloriously happy—*always*—as you seem t' be right this minute. At the same time, I've a responsibility t' fulfill." He sighed, then resumed. "I'm goin' to plead with the both of you t' let me reason with you. 'Til Buck gets that writ in hand, he's legally a married man. Becky, now try t' understand me. Hear me out.

"It's plain t' me that you two really are in love. I wouldn't even think o' tryin' t' stop you from seein' each other. Easier to make th' Brazos run upriver! But, Becky, I am goin' t' ask for you an' your intended t' let me keep th' brooch an' th' ring while th' legal work is bein' taken care of in Alabama." He looked intently at Travis. "Do you have any problem, sir, with what I'm askin' or why I'm askin' it?"

The attorney's face reddened, but he shook his head. "No, sir. I fully understand and respect your position."

John studied his sister. Rebecca bit her lip and remained silent. John smiled. "All right, Sis," he said in a kindly tone. "Go ahead an' wear that breastpin for a week or so. It really is a fine-lookin' pin. And then you keep it in your room, if you want." However, he accepted his father's ring from Travis. "I consider this yours," John told the Alabaman gravely. "My sister gave it t' you with the permission of her dead mother. I'm just goin' t' safeguard it for a spell."

Three-Legged Willie felt no zeal for broaching the real reason he had "dropped by" to see Travis. When, however, the law intern Kuykendall left for the day, he removed Williamson's final excuse for delaying what promised to be a distasteful discussion.

"Mr. Travis," the crippled attorney began, in his usual pompous fashion, "there has recently emerged as a topic among the vulgar in this community a matter which concerns me gravely—concerns me, I might add, on your behalf."

His host, who had just dipped his quill into homemade ink and was about to attack a blank sheet of paper, instead returned the pen to its resting place. Travis leaned back in his chair and honored Williamson with his attention.

"This is an awkward topic for me, one which under other circumstances I should consider none of my business," the caller said with an apologetic air. "However, the perception of the public is always something that must be considered."

Travis gestured impatiently. "Let's hear all about it, sir," he commanded.

"Well, sir," Three-Legged Willie resumed, "it concerns your

alleged—alleged, I say—dalliances with some of the lower sort of women in the community. There, now, I've said it."

Travis, arms folded, sat very still. "Is this one simple subject," he asked steadily, "all that brought you here? And how would you like for me to respond?"

The other man grew flustered. "Well, for one, I should have hoped you would deny it!" he exclaimed. "To hear the idle gossips talk, you have developed the habits of a reckless libertine! I needn't remind you, I suppose, that if word of this real or fancied behavior were to reach Mill Creek—"

"I should trust that it has not and will not!" Travis barked. Then he resumed his calm manner. "Prayerfully, in any event, it would not be given the first crumb of credibility. Thank you, friend Willie, for your concern. I admit it is a bad habit I am indulging, however much it is a necessary one."

"Necessary!" Williamson, astounded, flung his arms wide and sent his cane clattering into a corner. "How on earth can you deem behavior of this ilk *necessary*? You are flirting with romantic disaster—or perhaps worse, should it be brother John who hears of such things."

Travis defiantly propped his feet on the table. "I have taken a sacred pledge," he countered, "to conduct myself as only a gentleman should while in the company of Miss Rebecca. Though you may be a year or so older, sir, surely you must be aware of what damage the suppression of natural passions can wreak on one's physical self. This reckless behavior, as you style it, is my way of siphoning off some of that passion."

Williamson rolled his eyes. "Very well, sir," he conceded. "All I may ask of you, then, is to be the soul of discretion in those pursuits. There is some indication that this aspect of your . . . activities . . . could stand improvement."

The friends' conversation passed on to other topics. Williamson at last excused himself and left.

Travis remained seated behind the table for some time. Then, scowling, he pulled from a leather bag of toiletries a vial of liquid mercury.

Later that evening, he posted in his diary a terse entry in colloquial Spanish. Translated, it read, "Venereal disease bad."

Chapter 51

On Christmas Day of 1834 in Mexico City, Stephen Austin received a fine present. Thanks to the efforts of Peter Grayson and Spencer Jack, two of his colonists who were also lawyers, and to the season-inspired magnanimity of President Santa Anna, Austin stepped forth from prison—under bond—in time to celebrate *Navidad*.

Grayson and Jack made the grueling trek to the Mexican capital with the intent of securing Austin's full freedom. They brought with them a half-dozen resolutions in support of his release, issued by the Anglo-dominated *ayuntamientos* in their home province. The attorneys were only partly successful, for Austin was still bound to stay within the capital until his case went to trial. Still, the empresario enjoyed a relative sense of freedom by escaping the vile atmosphere of his cell.

Austin also experienced release of a different kind.

For the past decade, despite seemingly endless setbacks, fears, and mutual suspicions, he had consistently exuded an attitude of loyalty toward the Mexican government and its liberal Constitution of 1824. This stance came with a cost, for almost invariably it engendered criticism on the part of recalcitrant colonists. While the infant nation boiled with political upheaval, the Texians watching with contempt as their adopted country repeatedly shot itself in the foot, Austin labored to reach the high road and stay there.

Finally, he came to realize that the high road led to nowhere.

Santa Anna was rapidly destroying the fabric of federal government in a no-holds-barred effort to centralize all authority and power. In one ominous instance, the dictator viewed as contrary to his interests the existence of state-maintained militias. He ordained that no state could have a militia with a strength greater than one member to every five hundred residents, thus reducing these forces to the point of impotence. In another glaring departure from the path to democracy, the body of men acting as Congress proved to be a servile entity with no mind of its own. Still styling himself *El Presidente*, Santa Anna sensed (perhaps accurately) that, despite all the commotion about freedom, the people of Mexico were actually happiest when placed under absolute rule.

But Austin recognized that nothing could be further from the truth where American expatriates were concerned. Although a majority of the longtime Anglo residents wanted nothing more than separate and equal Mexican statehood for Texas, they would not willingly suffer a centralization of government under which local controls were lost. Under Santa Anna, the only peaceful hope for Anglo Texas lay in the possibility, however remote, that Mexico would finally agree to terms of a U.S. purchase and relinquish its northernmost province. A more likely occurrence, Austin knew, was outright armed rebellion.

El Presidente soon enjoyed an occasion to illustrate, in a sufficiently bloody fashion, his intolerance for states' rights and a total disregard for lives.

The inhabitants of Zacatecas, a state situated to the immediate south of Coahuila y Texas, resisted the edict to reduce their militia. Santa Anna led his centralist army into the region and, brilliantly enough, routed a Zacatecan force of superior numbers in a matter of a few hours. Then—or so the rumors insisted—he turned loose his troops to slaughter prisoners and unarmed civilians. The final death toll among these defenseless targets reportedly exceeded two thousand. It was further avowed that looting and raping raged unchecked.

The atrocities reputedly perpetrated on Zacatecas offered an object lesson to anyone in Mexico who might consider exalting himself against the president. The Texians, though, would prove to be a brash lot, and maybe too obtuse for proper intimidation.

John Cumings, suspecting nothing out of the ordinary, answered the knock at the door of the inn.

Standing on the front step was a short, full-bodied young woman whose plain face and long black hair peeked out from underneath a red bonnet. Behind her stood a splendid open carriage containing two small children. The rig appeared to have been driven by a huge black man, who, reins in hand, stood alongside the dusty horse.

John did not know any of these people, but he recognized the carriage and the charcoal mare pulling it. They were the property of fellow colonist Jared Groce, who with his sons operated a sprawling plantation a dozen or more miles above Mill Creek on the opposite side of the Brazos River.

"Are you Mr. Cumin's?" the woman asked, her voice bespeaking a deep South heritage. When John nodded and stepped back to admit her, she smiled, extended a hand, and said, "I am Mrs. Travis, of Claiborne, Alabama."

The innkeeper blinked at the information. *A Travis from Alabama. Could this be a relative of Buck's?*

"The Groce family, up the river yonder," she continued, "has been of great assistance to me and my children. It happens that they also have Alabama connections. The younger Mr. Groce—Mr. Leonard Groce, of Bernardo Plantation—lent me his carriage and saw me across the river on his ferry. It was his suggestion that I avail myself of your kind hospitality.

"The fact is, Mr. Cumin's, we have come all this way from home to see my husband, who is practicin' law in Saint Phillip. Do you by chance know of Mr. William B. Travis?"

John's tongue grew thick. At first, he could only nod. "Fetch your children, Mrs. Travis," he managed to say at last, "and come in." Regaining his wits, he innocently inquired, "Is Mr. Travis expectin' t' meet you here, at our inn? Or do we need t' notify him that you've arrived?"

"No and yes, Mr. Cumin's." The traveler was full of surprises. "No, he's not expectin' us. I am certain he is unaware, even, that we are in Texas. But, yes, I would be very grateful if you could send word to him that we're here."

"Yes'm. Sure will," John responded, as the woman retreated to the carriage for the children. Turning, he started in surprise to find young Henry at his elbow. The boy's eyes were wide with the understanding of what he had heard. "Go help with th' horse," John ordered, irritated, and then added in a low voice, "And mind you, not a word o' this to Miss Becky 'fore I catch up with her an' tell her myself."

That self-assigned, miserable chore took only a few moments. His sister's initial disbelief was at first followed by a burst of tears, then by a predictable attempt at rationalization.

"Why, she's surely come to Texas so Buck's children can see him," Rebecca theorized between sniffs. "As to why she happens to be lodging here, who knows? She certainly couldn't know anything about Buck and me. She's just staying away from San Felipe so as not to embarrass him, and the Groces suggested our place. I guess they don't know about Buck and me, either."

John shook his head. "It don't make sense t' me that she'd bring those children all this way t' see their daddy without lettin' him know ahead o' time," he said. "Maybe the rest o' what you say is true. One thing's for sure: I'll wager Buck didn't ever expect t' come see her at Mill Crick." His voice hardened. "I thought all this was goin' t' be handled in an Alabama court months back—th' writ o' divorcement, I mean."

"Maybe it has been, and she's trying to save face in front of strangers," Rebecca offered. Her voice, though, did not ring with confidence.

"Well," John said, "in any event, I'm sendin' Henry t' San Felipe an' let Buck know what's up. No offense, Sis," he added with a smirk, "but I'd almost like t' be there an' see th' look on his face when he learns where she's lodgin'!"

Rebecca was not amused. "I can't stand to be here for any of this!" she wailed. "Where can I go? Oh, John, help me! Where can I get away to?"

"How 'bout over t' Swearingen's, an' stay with Seth's sister an' ma?" John suggested. "In spite o' all that's happened, they're still your friends. Henry can go there with you 'fore he takes Buck the message 'bout his family. In fact," he growled, "have Henry tell Buck where you're stayin' as well. It'll serve him right!"

Buck Travis certainly had a load of disturbing information to sort through on his way to Mill Creek. He reached the inn shortly before dark, still nettled over where Rebecca had gone—though he also felt relieved that she and his wife would not be under the same roof.

It was a glowering John who met him at the door. "Tell me th' meanin' o' this," the proprietor demanded.

Travis denied knowing his family was coming to Texas. "I'm every bit as surprised as you are," he said, unwisely.

"I doubt that," John snapped. "Anyway, it has sure upset Becky no end, havin' a woman who calls herself your wife droppin' in like this."

The lawyer shrugged helplessly. "These legal things take time," he pleaded. "Please believe me when I say that I no longer harbor any feelings for Rosanna. We're finished. And, as for the little girl, it is my belief that she is not my own."

John gave him a hard stare. "Well, when you see her," he commented, "I b'lieve you'll have t' change your mind."

Travis ducked past John and climbed the short staircase to the upper room where his family awaited him. He had decided to tackle this unforeseen problem head-on.

Whatever took place during the Travis family reunion did so quietly and behind a closed door. John was about to turn in for the night when the young lawyer came downstairs and requested a room of his own. The next morning, he left before dawn without taking breakfast. His wife and children descended shortly thereafter, ate quietly, and were soon whisked away in the Groce carriage, presumably starting back to Alabama via Bernardo Plantation. To be sure, Rosanna Travis gave the appearance of having slept little and worried much.

John sent Henry to Swearingen's with word that all of the Travises had departed Mill Creek. From what John observed upon Rebecca's return, his sister's sleep had been no sounder than that of the estranged Mrs. Travis.

Meanwhile, Travis was finding it impossible to concentrate on the details of his law practice. He finally began a letter to Rebecca. Once completed, it went straightaway to Mill Creek in the custody of the clerk Kuykendall. When that young worthy returned, Travis immediately demanded to know whether Rebecca had accepted the missive. "I didn't see her, but her brother took it," came the unsatisfactory reply.

After much fuming and indecision, Rebecca did, of course, open the letter. It read, in part:

You must understand that I care nothing for R. Travis & intend to pursue writ of divorcement with all diligence. It can now proceed smoothly. She was fighting it until we should meet face to face one last time—and for a good reason in part, as it has turned out. By this I mean that I have come to accept Susan Isabella as my own child. There can be no doubt she is mine. I therefore have an obligation to do a father's duty by her as well as by my boy, Charles Edward.

They are all gone back to Alabama, altho I have told R. Travis that I wish Charles Edward to join me in Texas when I can properly arrange for his care and education.

My darling Rebecca, the hours will pass slowly & painfully until I hear from you. Please release me from the anguish of further uncertainty and let me know when I may again delight myself by being in your company.

Su enamo,
W.B.T.

Late into the night, Rebecca was still reviewing the contents of the letter with a troubled heart. As an artful effort to allay her concerns, the composition fell short in a couple of crucial areas.

First, Travis unwittingly suggested that Rosanna had more than her daughter's welfare in mind by fighting the divorce. John had been right after all, Rebecca told herself. It did not make sense for Rosanna to attempt such a lengthy, uncomfortable, expensive, and dangerous journey with two small children solely for the purpose of showing Travis his daughter. In all likelihood, Rosanna Travis did not want a divorce. Her trip to Texas had doubtless been fueled by the hope of salvaging their marriage. How, then, could Buck be so sure that she would no longer resist the legal process? Was he, in fact, being totally honest about his feelings toward Rosanna?

Second, the very fact that Travis now accepted Susan Isabella as his own offspring weakened his stated case for leaving her mother. Faced with this new evidence to the contrary, did he still believe so strongly that Rosanna had been unfaithful?

Rebecca decided that both she and Travis would have to endure the anguish of uncertainty for some time to come. Before seeing him again, she needed to invest further thought and prayer toward resolving those disturbing issues.

It would not be easy.

Chapter 52

*P*ico de Orizaba, Mexico's tallest mountain, towers over the many lesser projections of the spectacular Sierra Madre Oriental. In the midst of this breathtaking locale, sixty miles north of Vera Cruz, the city of Jalapa clings to the tiered slopes of Macuiltepetl Hill. To the east lies Lencero, a historic *hacienda* which once served as headquarters for the plantation of Santa Anna. In that day, Lencero boasted populous herds of cattle and abundant stands of sugar cane. *El Presidente* had been born in Jalapa to a landowning Creole family, and the hills of home beckoned to him whenever he needed a respite from the immense pressures of single-handedly running a nation.

Santa Anna retreated to Jalapa in July 1835 to escape the dust and confusion of the capital and to contemplate what might lie ahead. The month previous, he had published his plan to formally abolish the Mexican states and reduce them to the status of provinces. The plan served to announce the burial of the federalist Constitution of 1824 with its commitment to strong statehood. All real power was thus transferred to one man, who then took a vacation.

One day shortly before the advent of August, the master of Lencero received a visitor.

Stephen Austin, who had never been granted a day in court since his arrest in January 1834, was finally freed from custody along with a flood of other detainees as the result of a general amnesty. The release came with a condition, however: he must personally seek and receive final dispensation from Santa Anna. Hence his involuntary appearance in Jalapa.

Austin was presentably attired; the authorities made sure of that, out of nervous deference to the man whose goodwill he sought. Santa Anna received him with cordiality, rather than as a suspected seditionist just recently given his liberty. Austin, a cultured and prudent man, tendered the respect due *El Presidente*. He did not, though, overdo it.

The two men, similar in age, physique, and coloring (though Austin's skin retained the pallor incurred by his incarceration), took facing seats in an ornately appointed drawing room. A set of French windows, facing east, was thrown open to reveal the black volcanic peaks of the sierra and to receive the afternoon breeze. The conversants spoke in Spanish, essentially because Santa Anna had but feeble command of English.

"You are to be commended, Colonel Austin," the dictator purred, "for the way in which your people have conducted themselves during your . . . absence. These are momentous times for Mexico, and as you are aware, not everyone has accepted our reforms as gracefully as has Texas."

"To be candid, *Presidente*, you likely have more current information regarding Texas than do I," Austin remarked. Santa Anna could not repress a fleeting smirk at this. "I am therefore overjoyed to hear such a good report," the caller added.

Santa Anna placed the tips of his fingers together. "It is my sincere wish," he said pointedly, "that more such reports reach me in the coming months. I intend to visit Texas in the spring. I have not been in that country in more than twenty years, since I was a military cadet in the service of Spain."

He glanced out the French windows. "The unfortunate business at that time involved an insurrection, conducted by Mexican rebels who encouraged the assistance of certain *norteamericanos*. Their army, so called, was tracked down and crushed among the oaks and sand hills south of Bexar."

The dictator's casual reference to the wholesale slaughter conducted by the victorious royalists, in which numerous Americans met their deaths, sent a thrill of anger through Austin. Would *El Presidente* exhibit the same blase attitude, Austin wondered, if called upon to describe the recent butchery carried out under his orders in Zacatecas?

But the Texian did not let his feelings show. "I trust that his excellency's upcoming journey to Texas will be a peaceful one," he said. Then, upon reflection, he added, "Even during my absence, Excellency, I have received some limited communications from Texas. The citizens there are aware of certain actions taken by *El Presidente* whenever he has deemed it necessary to enforce his policies of reform. They, quite naturally being cognizant of differences in language, customs, and attitudes between our peoples, have concerns about the potential for misunderstanding. It would be well, Excellency, for you and your advisors to consider carefully before making any show of force that might be misconstrued as a threat."

Santa Anna raised an eyebrow. "A threat?" he asked carefully. "A threat to what?"

"I ask you to remember, Excellency," Austin replied, "that, from the beginning, the colonists in Texas have clung to the ideals of the Constitution of 1824. It is true that in the past weeks you have announced your plan to centralize the power of government, and that the constitution is now obsolete. Please be aware, though, that this comes as distressing news to men whose prior experiences with government were as citizens of the United States of the North."

The dark eyes of the dictator narrowed, and his jaw stiffened. "What I am putting in place, Colonel Austin, is the method of governance preferred by my people," Santa Anna replied in an ominous tone. "I suggest that the Texians find a way to become comfortable with the will of Mexico." He then appeared to check his mounting emotion, and lowered the intensity of his speech. "Of course," he resumed, "I do appreciate that there are indeed differences. It is my belief that, given the time, we—you and I—can work through those differences to the satisfaction of all parties."

Santa Anna rose to his feet. "And now, *señor*," he said, "I grant your petition to be allowed to return to Texas." He clasped his hands behind him. "You will sail from Vera Cruz to New Orleans with the compliments of *El Presidente*. I am very desirous of receiving continued good reports from Texas."

Austin bowed, and left the room. Neither man could know that, thanks to actions already committed by Buck Travis, the next report regarding Texas would be anything but pleasing.

History repeated itself at Anahuac in the summer of 1835.

The little port on Galveston Bay had been the first Texas residence of Travis in 1832, and the site of his initial disagreement with Mexican officialdom. The dispute centered around the enforced taxation of imported goods, a practice from which the colonists had been exempt since their arrival. The dispute escalated to the point where Travis and others were jailed and threatened with a firing squad, and a band of Texians from Brazoria rode to their rescue and ousted the Mexican garrison. Only the fact that then-President Bustamante was busy fighting the forces of Santa Anna prevented some kind of punitive response from the Mexican authorities.

In 1835, after a hiatus of two years, the customshouses at Anahuac and Velasco (the latter located at the mouth of the Brazos River) were reactivated. A friend and former client of Travis at Anahuac, planter Andrew Briscoe, grew demonstrative at the resumption of the practice and soon found himself in the calaboose. He wrote Travis for succor.

Briscoe's letter reached San Felipe at a time when many Texians were already agitated about the June takeover and occupation of Saltillo by centralist troops. There, the state government of Coahuila y Texas was summarily abolished by order of the military commander: Gen. Martin Perfecto de Cos, Santa Anna's brother-in-law. The fact that the takeover was provoked by exhibitions of corruption, incompetence, and foolhardy defiance on the part of the legislators and governor did not make the army's action any easier to swallow. The governor was thrown into prison at Monclova, as were several Texians visiting that city on business.

Still, Saltillo lay several hundred miles into the interior. A majority of the colonists rejected the idea of challenging Cos and his army on behalf of a state government that only nominally represented Texas interests. However, Anahuac was close by, the Mexican force there small in number, and Anglo acquaintances were calling for help. At a secret meeting of the more hawkish Texians, Travis was commissioned "to collect a force and expel the garrison at Anahuac before the coming of (Mexican) reinforcements."

The reference to reinforcements was not idle rhetoric. In a rather high-handed act, several colonists had intercepted and purloined a dispatch sent by Col. Domingo de Ugartechea and intended for Capt. Antonio Tenorio at Anahuac. Ugartechea, in writing Tenorio for information about the terrain of southeastern

Texas, explained, "In a very short time, the affairs of Texas will be definitely settled, for which purpose the Government has ordered to take up the line of march, a strong division composed of the troops which were in Zacatecas and are now in Saltillo . . . These Revolutionists will be ground down, and it appears to me that we will very soon see each other, since the Government takes their matters in hand."

Travis easily raised a contingent of two dozen men and the use of a sloop. Armed with a brass six-pounder, the rescue party found its way into Galveston Bay. They suffered the indignity of running aground before reaching the landing at Anahuac, but were taken ashore by residents supportive of the mission. Despite the objections of the local *alcalde,* Travis marched his little band straight to the Mexican barracks, towing the cannon on a sawmill truck. The garrison, though, was gone. Despite having a superior number of men, Tenorio had discreetly ordered them into the nearby woods to avoid confrontation.

Buck Travis would not be denied. He finally forced Tenorio to meet with him face to face, and demanded the release of Briscoe, the removal of all troops from Anahuac, and the surrender of their arms. Tenorio, finding himself deep in what logically could be considered hostile territory, capitulated. The Mexicans departed Anahuac, armed with a few firearms for protection against the Indians. No blood had been shed. The grateful planter Briscoe made a present to Travis of his prize slave, Joe.

But if the young lawyer anticipated a hero's welcome on the journey back to San Felipe, he was badly mistaken. Many Texians, especially those who had invested the best years of their lives in building up family fortunes as citizens of Mexico, angrily condemned Travis and his expedition as idiotic and provocative. They believed Santa Anna would promptly send troops into Texas to teach its citizens the same lesson he had taught Zacatecans. The conservatives, clearly in the majority, drew up and issued formal statements censuring the Anahuac adventure and proclaiming the unswerving loyalty of Texas to the centralist government. Several "peace commissioners" were elected at a meeting in San Felipe and given instructions to confer with Cos in a conciliatory fashion.

Cos, however, overplayed his hand. Angered by the ouster of Tenorio, he ordered that Travis, Three-Legged Willie Williamson, and others identified as agitators against the government be arrested and turned over to him. This must be done, he added, before there could be any conferences held with penitent Texians.

A majority of the same colonists who had denounced the Anahuac expedition now spoke out just as heatedly against the edict of Cos. They understood Mexican justice, especially as it might be applied to those still considered foreigners. Delivering up the accused men to the authorities could mean consigning them to the attention of a firing squad. Such a thing could not—would not—be allowed to happen.

Buck Travis maintained exceedingly high spirits for the entirety of his journey to Mill Creek. Rebecca, notified of his pending arrival by the ever-alert Henry, watched through a window of the inn while the tall, handsome rider dismounted and tossed the young slave his mare's reins along with a silver coin. Travis whistled exuberantly as he mounted the steps and delivered a vigorous rap on the door.

It was immediately flung open. Rebecca stood within, the large green eyes clouded with concern, the full lips forming a worried pout. To Travis she had never looked lovelier. The lawyer, noting her frank anxiety and guessing its cause, felt a swelling in his chest. *She has heard about the order for my arrest,* he thought, *and she's worried sick!*

As usual where women were concerned, his intuition was on target. "Buck, I'm so glad you've come! I've been so upset!" she said unashamedly, wringing her hands. "John told me about the Mexicans wanting to arrest you! Have they arrested anyone yet?"

Smiling broadly, Buck took her hands in his. "No, my dear," he responded, in a soothing voice. "No one has been arrested. And," he added vociferously, "no one is going to be arrested! It's marvelous what's going on, Becky!" In his enthusiasm, he lapsed into using the diminutive of her name.

Surprised and irritated over his apparent lack of concern, Rebecca pulled her hands away and stepped back. "That's a rather strange thing for you say under the circumstances, it seems to me," she said coldly, suffering sudden embarrassment over being so transparent about her feelings.

Travis removed his hat and stepped across the threshold. The gray eyes were dancing.

"At long last," he exclaimed, "the people of Texas are becoming united against the tyrant! They have forgiven me for the episode at Anahuac, an act I would repeat tomorrow! Now, most of them stand shoulder to shoulder in agreement with me, that we must win our independence from Mexico!"

The green eyes clouded again. "Does this mean war?" Rebecca asked soberly.

"It means," the young firebrand replied, "that there will be no rest until we have driven the despot from our land! The people are finally aroused, and I believe will be of one mind."

He clapped his hands over Rebecca's shoulders. "And I have other news, more meaningful in its own way to us," he added. "I have dispatched the last of the paperwork necessary to secure a writ of divorcement by action of the General Assembly of Alabama. They meet in November, and it will be among the items of business they consider. By January, I will be a free man!"

Her full lips parted in a smile, but Rebecca also felt a pang of guilt. *Why*, she asked herself, *must my good fortune be another woman's loss?*

For once, Travis was too keyed up to notice this tell-tale nuance in his lover's attitude. "There is even more to tell you," he resumed. "My kinsman and good friend James Bonham is coming to Texas. As young boys in South Carolina, before my family moved to Alabama, we were the closest of companions. James is now in Alabama himself, practicing law. He is coming here, and he will bring my boy Charles Edward with him!

"I am determined to train my son in the way he should go! He will board with the Ayers family at Montford, and shall be schooled in all the proper disciplines."

Chapter 53

For Travis to say that the residents of Texas stood unified in seeking independence from Mexico was, at the time he said it, a gross exaggeration. Many did harbor a strong resentment toward the centralist government, some to the point of defiance and even to the consideration of war. But the larger issue of whether the province should actually break away from Mexico remained a divisive one.

There was no longer any doubt in the mind of Stephen Austin about what to do, although upon his return to Texas in September he did not fully divulge his feelings to the public.

In a personal letter to David Burnet, Austin confided that he was through equivocating. "No more doubts," he wrote. "No more submission. I hope to see Texas forever free from Mexican domination of any kind." And yet, Austin added in that same letter, "we must arrive at it by steps and not all at one jump."

So the one-time empresario and current political icon electrified listeners by boldly declaring that the province's "only recourse" against Santa Anna was open warfare. At the same time, he couched his argument in terms of fighting as Mexican citizens for rights granted in the Constitution of 1824 and subsequently abolished by the despot. His hope was that the ethnic Mexicans in the province, the *Tejanos*, would join in resisting the centralist regime. For the most part, he would be disappointed.

Travis, Three-Legged Willie Williamson, and the other war hawks were ecstatic over Austin's surprise pronouncement. The erstwhile darling of the conservatives had dramatically swung his weight to the side of the radicals. And what an ally to have! No other man's opinion carried nearly as much clout with Anglo residents, who numbered nearly 30,000 at this juncture. Too, he enjoyed the trust of leading federalists among the ethnic Mexicans such as Lorenzo de Zavala and Juan Seguin.

The die was cast: there would be war, and soon.

However, the Texians felt a need to formalize the decision. Delegates from the various municipalities would meet as a body and decide the fate of Texas. Since the time for harvest had arrived upon the face of the land, an October date was established for the meeting, or "Consultation." For the site, San Felipe won out over Washington-on-the-Brazos.

While the Texians repaired to their fields of ripe crops, the Mexican military began a movement of its own. Cos joined his considerable forces with those of Ugartechea at San Antonio. From there, they could strike quickly into Anglo Texas.

Sam Houston and Jim Bowie shared more traits than just a dependence on liquor. They both lusted after Texas and its opportunities for personal gain. And, as their bitterest enemies would be forced to admit if held to the truth, both possessed an abundance of personal courage.

Houston, eight months older than Stephen Austin, owned the second-biggest name in Texas as the storm clouds gathered. During the War of 1812, serving under Andrew Jackson, the twenty-year-old Houston fought with distinction against the Creeks. The power-playing Jackson became Houston's political benefactor; in 1823 he helped Houston win a U.S. House seat, and in 1827 aided his election to the governorship of Tennessee.

This promising protégé of "Old Hickory" was perhaps on his way to even bigger things when in 1829 he married teenaged Eliza Allen. They parted under a cloud of mystery only eleven weeks later, and Houston resigned the governor's office and took up a drink-fogged residency in Indian Territory with his boyhood friends of the Cherokee tribe.

Nearly four years later, Houston abandoned his common-law Cherokee wife and crossed the Red River into Texas. He opened a law practice in Nacogdoches and jumped head-first into provincial politics on the side of the war faction. Houston never revealed the reasons behind his failed first marriage or his decision to go to Texas. The latter may have been suggested or even orchestrated by Jackson, who by this time occupied the White House and entertained a fixation on adding Texas to the United States.

Like other war hawks, Houston reacted with glee to Austin's September 1835 call to arms. He immediately set his course. Within a month, he was named commander of the volunteer troops for the Department of Nacogdoches. On November 12 the province's brand-new provisional government conferred on Houston the rank of major general of the as-yet unassembled regular Texas army.

By then, undisciplined Texian volunteers had already claimed victories in early engagements with trained Mexican soldiers.

Jim Bowie was truly a legend in his own time. Raised in Louisiana, he and his brothers made a fortune by participating in the slave trade activities of the pirate Jean Lafitte. Bowie moved comfortably in the best social circles money could buy, but the public knew him best by his reputation as a rough-and-tumble rowdy whose distinctive knife bore the family name. Copies of this murderous weapon were popular, worn and flashed by countless adventurers. These men, though, seldom measured up to the owner of the original in terms of tenacity, animal strength, fighting skill, and gambler's nerve.

By 1830 Bowie had become deeply involved in land speculation in Texas. He also became intimate with the family of wealthy San Antonian Juan Martin de Veramendi, soon to be vice governor of Coahuila y Texas. The following year Bowie married the Veramendis' attractive daughter, Ursula.

Money from his in-laws helped Bowie launch an unsuccessful effort to find a fabled "lost" silver mine northwest of San Antonio. The expedition did serve to magnify Bowie's fame as a fighter, for during the journey he and ten other men repulsed an attack by a much larger Comanche war party.

Tragedy struck in the fall of 1833, while Bowie lay wracked with yellow fever in Natchez. A cholera epidemic sweeping northern Mexico claimed the lives of Ursula and her parents. This multiple loss delivered a stunning blow not only to Bowie's heart, but to his lifestyle as well; a weakness for big-stakes gambling seemed to keep him in debt, and suddenly he no longer had access to the Veramendi fortune.

Bowie's renewed efforts to gain wealth through land speculation ended abruptly in the spring of 1835, when the centralists abolished the Coahuila y Texas state government and its liberal land
laws. Austin's public stand against the regime of Santa Anna suited
Bowie. His circle of Anglo and *Tejano* acquaintances included many
declared enemies of *El Presidente,* and, regardless, he always stood
ready for a brawl.

In October, shots were exchanged near Gonzales between centralist soldiers and Texian militiamen. The Mexicans, concerned
over growing unrest in the province, had demanded the return of a
cannon loaned to Gonzales years before for protection against Indians. The Texians defiantly paraded the six-pounder and dared the
soldiers to "come and take it." The men of Gonzales prevailed, and
the war was on.

As badly as Travis had wanted the war, circumstances robbed
him of participating in its initial battles. In late September, having
enlisted in the volunteer army, he fell ill and was forced to recuper-
ate in San Felipe while the Gonzales skirmish took place. By this
time, the long-awaited assembly of Texian delegates to the Consultation was close to convening. And any day now Travis expected
the arrival of his cousin James Butler Bonham, who had promised
to bring little Charles Edward Travis with him from Alabama.

However, the Consultation initially failed to attract enough
delegates to hold a proper meeting. Austin himself was in Gonzales,
where he had just been elected commander-in-chief of the volunteer army gathering there. Travis, recovered from his illness and
afraid he would miss more action, impatiently decided he could wait
no longer to go to Gonzales. Wisely, he first hastened to Mill Creek.

Rebecca did not like the news.

"I don't understand, Buck," she said, her voice shrill with concern. "You said it was more important for you to be here for the
Consultation than to join the army. That the future of Texas lay
more in the hands of the delegates than with the soldiers."

"No, my dear," Travis replied, with what he believed to be
admirable tact. "What I said was that I felt the responsibilities of the
delegates were equal to those of our men in arms. I still feel that
way. But the Consultation may not take place now until November,
and General Austin has called for reinforcements and for military

men trained in forming and shaping a proper army. I have decided that my first responsibility lies in answering the general's summons."

The green eyes flashed. Travis sighed. He had hoped for a passionate soldier's farewell, and instead was being drawn into an argument neither side could win.

"Your responsibility?" Rebecca covered the phrase with a generous coat of sarcasm. "I would think, sir, you might consider Charles Edward your responsibility. Not only are you going off to fight without first seeing after him in person, but the very idea of bringing a child into Texas in such perilous times seems to me like a terrible misjudgment!"

"There will be no peril here, not in the heart of our settlements," Travis said in his most reassuring manner. "We will drive Cos and Urgartechea from San Antonio and chase them out of Texas! When we have made ourselves ready, the Mexicans will prove to be no match for Americans! New volunteers are pouring in by the hundreds, armed to the teeth and ready for a fight!

"As for Charles Edward," he added, "you know that I have arranged for a proper Christian home and education for him with the Ayers family."

Rebecca was familiar with the sprawling Ayers plantation. Marked by a large stone manor house, it lay in the vicinity of Washington-on-the-Brazos, many miles upriver from Mill Creek.

"Since you have mentioned the boy," Travis continued, smiling bravely into the stormy countenance before him, "there is a favor I would seek. As you have pointed out, I'll be away when cousin James and Charles Edward reach the Brazos. With your permission, I intend to leave word in San Felipe for James to bring the boy to Mill Creek. When they arrive, I wish you to notify Mr. Ayers to come and get Charles Edward.

"Now," he asked softly, "will you do this for me?"

Rebecca turned her back to him. "Yes," she said in a low voice. "Now, go to your glorious war and leave me be." But she did not move away. Just as she hoped he would, Travis encircled her from behind with strong arms, gently pulled her to him, and dropped his chin on her shoulder so that their cheeks touched. Unable to stifle a sob, she whirled about and slid into his embrace, burying a damp face in his fine linen shirt.

The next battle Travis missed took place at the Mission Concepcion outside San Antonio. The outcome of the encounter was vintage Jim Bowie.

In the afterglow of the victory at Gonzales, the mob of four hundred Texas volunteers, now including Travis, moved toward San Antonio. There, Cos—with superior artillery and some seven hundred and fifty trained men, many of them combat veterans—unaccountably took a defensive stance, fortifying the town's two plazas as well as the Alamo mission across the San Antonio River.

Although Austin's presence provided the influence necessary to unify the volunteers and give them a singleness of purpose, the former empresario was admittedly not a man of war. As a result, the independent spirits of experienced fighters like Bowie caused them to take the commander's orders with a grain of salt. In the instance of the Mission Concepcion incident, though, the logic behind Austin's orders was sound: don't allow our forces to be divided. Carelessly, Bowie, in charge of a detachment of ninety men including Andrew Briscoe and James Fannin, did just that.

They had been instructed to locate a protected position close to town, and to leave themselves enough daylight to find their way back to camp. With darkness approaching, Bowie chose to spend the night at the abandoned mission rather than to follow Austin's orders. He did send a courier to enlighten the general, who justifiably grew wroth. When the main camp awakened the next morning to the sound of distant gunfire, Austin knew that his worst fears were realized.

Cos, learning of the enemy's presence at Concepcion, had sent out Ugartechea with a force of almost three hundred soldiers and two cannon. The greatly outnumbered Texians had their backs to the river. Bowie's fighting luck, however, had not yet run out. Ugartechea spurned tactical considerations and simply assaulted one flank of the rebel force. The superior range of Texian long-rifle fire proved to be the difference in this encounter. By the time rebel reinforcements approached, the Mexicans were beating a disheartened retreat to Bexar.

Buck Travis, now a lieutenant entrusted with a brand-new company of cavalry, was at the vanguard of the would-be rescuers. Although ordered by Austin to delay any attack until the infantry could arrive, Travis and his riders found Ugartechea's plight irresistible. They enlivened the Mexicans' departure with a spirited attack. This insubordinate action drew inevitable censure from the exasperated Texian commander-in-chief.

Ugartechea had suffered fifty men killed or wounded and lost one cannon. A single Texian was killed, a second wounded.

Jubilant though they were, the rebels knew that storming San Antonio with a relatively small force and virtually no artillery would prove disastrous. The veterans among them suggested a siege. Austin agreed, and November found the Texians attempting to maintain morale while playing the waiting game outside Bexar.

Meanwhile, the Consultation had finally taken place in San Felipe and a provisional government formed. This body, having named Houston commander of a nonexistent regular army, recalled Austin from the field and dispatched him to the United States in pursuit of financial and military aid. The volunteer army selected Edward Burleson as its new commander-in-chief.

Dwindling supplies, winter weather, and inaction all worked against the success of a long-term siege. When Burleson began consulting with his officers about calling off the campaign and withdrawing to Goliad for the winter, Travis decided that it was time to head back to San Felipe—and Mill Creek. The timing of his departure cost him yet another opportunity for glory.

Burleson had already given the order to break camp when, on December 4, Benjamin Rush Milam gained immortality by convincing the general to let him poll the men for volunteers to attack Bexar. "Who will go with old Ben Milam to San Antonio?" he asked repeatedly, and soon an eager group of three hundred assembled. Burleson capitulated, and the next day the battle began.

One detachment of Texians created a diversion by feinting an attack on the Alamo. At the same time, Milam and Frank Johnson led their force into the streets of San Antonio. A mean, house-to-house struggle began. As day after day passed, the Texians slowly but surely captured new sectors, and on December 9, Cos surrendered. He and his disarmed forces were released under an agreement to leave Texas and not return. Milam, another officer, and two other rebels were killed. The Mexicans sustained an estimated one hundred and fifty killed and wounded. It was by every measurement a resounding victory.

The more naive observers in Texas arrogantly concluded that

the defeat and departure of Cos signaled the successful end to a very brief war, one which if weighed in terms of Texian casualties had been unbelievably cheap. The once-feared Mexican soldiers proved to be no match for American fighting spirit. Mexico, so many Texians believed, had been taught a lesson!

Stephen Austin, for one, knew better; so did Sam Houston, who did not yet have an army to command. They were sure that Santa Anna would move sometime during the coming spring to strike down Texas as he had Zacatecas. But even they weren't prepared for the self-styled Napoleon of the West to be crossing the Rio Grande in February at the head of an army of thousands.

Chapter 54

*J*ohn Cumings opened the front door of the inn. On the step stood a tall, well-built young man, jauntily dressed in a military fashion, and holding the hand of a small boy.

"Good evening, sir," began the man in a warm Southern voice, releasing the boy's hand to extend his own. "Allow me to introduce the both of us and explain our errand.

"I'm James Butler Bonham, a proud relative of the Travis family, and this here's little Charles Edward Travis. I'm following through on his father's request to bring him to Texas and deliver him up to a Miss Cumings at the inn on Mill Creek."

John smiled and took the man's hand. "You've come to th' right place, sir," he replied, introducing himself as he stepped back to admit the pair.

Bonham nudged the boy forward and doffed a wide-brimmed planter's hat as he entered, revealing a full head of black, wavy hair surrounding dark and strikingly handsome features. John, who fancied himself a good judge of men, at once liked the look in the sensitive brown eyes. Here was a man of character, confident in himself, whose aristocratic bearing and dress were offset by the absence of vanity or arrogance. The prominent jaw and chin spoke of strength and determination, but were the only features of the caller that reminded John of Buck Travis other than their approximate sameness of age.

If they were indeed related, the innkeeper concluded, the man standing before him might have inherited or otherwise acquired more of the intangibles that contribute to greatness.

Charles Edward, puffy-faced and pouting, stared at the wooden floor. "Come, young man," John addressed him kindly. "Let's find you somethin' t' eat. You've visited us before, you know, and I'm wagerin' you'll remember Hannah's good cookin' soon as you get some more of it. This way, Mr. Bonham, if you please. Henry will tend t' your rig an' belongin's."

Bonham was introduced to Rebecca as they gathered for supper. Her beauty took his breath away. *So, Buck,* he thought, *this is what has kept you in Texas, away from your wife and children. I wouldn't blame a lesser man . . . and she is so wickedly beautiful, it's even hard to blame you.*

The male-dominated conversation at the table stuck largely to one topic: the war. Even as they ate and chatted at Mill Creek, Ben Milam, General Burleson, and others were huddled in a tent outside San Antonio, feverishly detailing plans for the morrow: the diversionary sham assault on the Alamo mission and the simultaneous, naked storming of Bexar.

"It appears Texas has at last set its own course," Bonham remarked. "Besides the safe delivery of young Charles Edward, my other reason for coming here was to help in any way that I can to deliver this country from the oppressor. I am by trade a lawyer, and by nature, I suppose, a rebel.

"It is my intent to leave in the morning and ride straight to Bexar, where I understand Buck is among the men who are waiting out the Mexican army. There I will offer my services to the commander-in-chief, hopefully armed with a good introduction from my kinsman."

John cleared his throat. Instinctively, he felt comfortable in expressing himself to the impressive young man at his table. "Mr. Bonham," he said, "there's some bits o' history an' philosophy I'm inclined to share with you. You may find 'em helpful in understandin' th' politics in Texas. They're kinda hard to put into words, but I'll try." With an encouraging sign from his guest, he warmed to his topic.

"Those of us who've lived in Texas since th' beginnin' o' Austin's colony came in as willin' Mexican citizens. As such, we've been slow t' entertain thoughts o' anything different. We invested considerable time an' effort—an' lives. My sister here, an' me, we're the only ones left out of a family o' six that cleared this place. When you go to talkin' about a revolution, you face riskin' all o' that in addition t' your own life."

The visitor was listening with obvious interest. John licked his lips, then continued.

"The past few years, we've had many a young firebrand, such as Buck Travis, come from th' United States into Texas an' immediately begin t' tell everybody how we should throw off th' yoke o' tyranny an' so forth. T' be honest with you, for the longest time I hadn't been overly patient with all o' their talk. Didn't really think much about anything other than runnin' this inn, and grindin' corn, and cuttin' planks, an' raisin' crops an' livestock. I have two brothers an' our ma buried on this property, an' it's become real important t' me."

Bonham's eyes narrowed the tiniest bit. Otherwise, he had shown no reaction to John's narrative.

"Now, then," John resumed, "along comes this Santa Anna, who we all think at first is gonna be a pretty good fella. But, soon enough, he shows his true colors. Colonel Austin is slapped into prison in Mexico without a reason, and left in there for two years. When we finally get th' colonel back, just a couple o' months past, he tells th' people in Brazoria an' San Felipe that war with Santa Anna is our only recourse.

"I can tell you, Mr. Bonham, that I'm not as big a backer o' Colonel Austin as some others are. But, when he of all people says we have t' have war, I guess there is prob'ly no choice. On th' one hand, war has nothin' about it that I like. On th' other, I'm not goin' to shirk my duty. Things appear t' have come down t' an all-or-nothin' proposition."

Bonham noticed that Rebecca was monitoring her brother's words with ever-increasing concern. The full lips puckered, the delicate brow wrinkled. Evidently, she had been unaware of John's current feelings about the situation.

"What I'm sayin' t' you, Mr. Bonham," John concluded, "is that I'm convinced enough about where my duty lies, now, t' take that old flintlock down off th' wall an' join you an' Buck Travis an' th' others at Bexar."

"No, John!" Rebecca exclaimed. Her hand flew to her mouth. "I-I'm sorry," she murmured. Then resolve swept over her face, and her shoulders straightened. "No, I'm not sorry, either!" she declared. "Forgive me, Mr. Bonham, but I've had quite enough of this manly talk about war! I'm sure you both will excuse me!" She flung down her napkin, scooted her chair back, and fled from the room. The two men stared at each other in surprise while Charles Edward unconcernedly finished cleaning a turkey drumstick.

"My apologies, sir," John said finally. "I s'pose I really can't blame her. If I go t' Bexar, it means she'll have t' run th' place herself with only half-a-dozen slaves—not another white person around. I can see now that I need t' talk all o' this over with her before I go runnin' off."

Although the visitor nodded sympathetically, John did not have his undivided attention. A part of Bonham was reproaching himself for dwelling on the captivating loveliness of his relative's fiancée.

Bonham left the next morning for San Felipe with the intent of continuing on to San Antonio. Before departing, he reassured Charles Edward that the six-year-old would enjoy staying at the inn, and instructed him to "mind Miss Rebecca and Mr. John" until Ayers or his emissary arrived.

Buck Travis had been on the road six days since leaving Burleson's camp and was but a few hours away from San Felipe. Then, yielding to his impetuous, self-indulging nature, the lawyer turned his horse due north and started on a straight line to Mill Creek. He was curious as to whether Charles Edward had arrived, and he didn't want another day to go by without seeing Rebecca. Matters in San Felipe, he reasoned happily, could wait a while longer.

If it was a joyful, tumultuous greeting that he sought, Travis was not disappointed. Rebecca unashamedly flung herself into his arms, wrapping her own around his dusty waistjacket. They exchanged kisses before, eyes shining, she led him over to the creek. They seated themselves on a wooden beam that was part of the millrace structure.

"Little Charles Edward is here, Buck," Rebecca began chattering, "but he is asleep just now. Mr. Ayers is being notified that he's arrived, and should be coming for him later in the week. Your relative Mr. Bonham is the nicest man! He left only this morning, and was hoping to find you at Bexar. And here you are, instead! I would think you might have met him on the road." Privately, she thought it strange how frequently her thoughts seemed to return to Bonham.

Travis began to tell her about the Texian campaign and the siege of Bexar, which as far as he knew was shortly to be discontinued. But Rebecca put a dainty pair of fingers to his lips. "Don't, Buck," she said, sweetly. "I just want to enjoy you being with me. I've missed you terribly, even though I ought never to admit it."

"And why should you not admit it?" The question, prompted by conceit, was earnest rather than bantering.

"Foolish boy!" she shot back. "I don't wish for you to be even more confident than you already are." She kissed him on the cheek, then jumped up to run away. Lightning-quick, Travis reached out and detained her. His gray eyes grew soft and serious, and caused her to cease her playful struggling.

"Rebecca," he said in a tender manner, "I think it's time we followed through with our feelings."

She resumed her seat, staring at him. She moved her lips, but no sound came forth. Then she cupped her hands over her mouth. The green eyes were wide.

"Yes, love," he continued, putting an arm around her and drawing her nearer. "You do wish to marry me, don't you?"

Still, she made no response.

"I expect when I get back to San Felipe," Travis continued, "I'll find in my mail some evidence of what the Alabama Assembly is doing on our . . . my . . . behalf. Perhaps that will be enough to ease your mind." Puzzled and a bit concerned, he leaned over and peered into her eyes. A tear had escaped from one, and was trickling unarrested down her cheek.

"Becky," he asked anxiously, "are you all right?" She managed to nod. "Did you hear what I asked you?" A note of petulance entered his voice. She nodded again, coughed into her hands, and wiped away the trailing tear just as he thought of doing so.

"Yes, Buck, I heard you," she said at last. "Of course, I still want to marry you . . . more than ever."

"Then what's the problem?" he demanded brusquely, speaking out of piqued pride.

She shook her head and looked away, and evaded the hand that sought to turn her face back toward him. "There's no problem," she replied softly. "It was just so—unexpected. Why now, Buck, all of a sudden?" It was her turn to be anxious. "What has happened for you to bring this up today?"

Buck studied his choice of answers. Then, mean-spirited though it was, he picked the one he most wanted to give. "There's a war on," he said, with a touch of drama.

The ploy backfired. "Stop it, Buck!" Rebecca cried. "You know I can't stand the thought of . . . of losing anyone else!" Angrily, she jumped up. "Anyway, Mr. Travis," she added, suddenly becoming composed and cool, "that of itself is no reason for hurrying a wedding. We have always talked about next spring, after we knew that everything was settled."

Travis understood his woman, and so knew that it was useless at present to pursue the subject. *The devil take her!* he said to himself. *Surely she wants me as badly as I want her! How long do we continue like this?*

He went into the inn and greeted John, promising to fill him in momentarily on the progress of the war. Then he climbed the stairs to where Charles Edward lay napping.

James Bonham arrived at San Antonio in time to witness the departure of Cos, Ugartechea, and the rest of the disarmed Mexican forces. The talk among many of the victorious volunteers was about how the fight had been taken out of the enemy and the war was essentially at an end. Failing to find Travis, Bonham was gratified at the arrival in camp of familiar faces among the Mobile Greys. He had personally spent money to help equip the thirty-man outfit, which formed at Mobile, Alabama, in response to dramatic pleas heard in that city to come to the aid of Texas.

"Do not believe what you hear about hostilities being over," he told the officers of the Greys. "The Mexicans will likely be back in the spring, and Bexar and other strategic points will have to be defended. You'll see action, lads."

Having heard that Sam Houston was attempting to assemble a regular army, Bonham called on the general. He had already written Houston a letter in which he volunteered his services as an artilleryman without rank or pay. The young lawyer was cordially received. He found Houston to be a physically imposing specimen and a natural leader. In turn, the general speedily became impressed with the potential value of Bonham, and—as John had been—was moved to be candid in his presence.

"We are at a critical point in the revolution," Houston expounded, his speech punctuated by habitual profanity, "for it is hard to say, right now, who we'll be able to recruit.

"The volunteers you have just seen in San Antonio are not the same ones who marched in from Gonzales two months ago. The army at first consisted mostly of Texians who laid down their farm implements and took up weapons. Due to the length and the inactivity of the siege, many of them went home to their families and their fields. New arrivals to Texas—a few nobly responding to their fellow Americans' call for help, such as yourself, many more simply looking for a fight or a fortune—have steadily replaced the original volunteers so that the makeup of the men available has changed.

"On the whole, I'm afraid, it's a change that has not been for the better. Present company and that of the Mobile Greys excepted, of course," Houston added with a smile.

Bonham's dark features remained serious, and he acknowledged the compliment with only a quick nod. "You must be concerned, General," he ventured. "I cannot believe that Santa Anna will fail to try and preserve Texas as an important province. Can you rely on the men now in Bexar to become your army?"

Houston disgustedly shook his head. "They cannot be relied upon to do much of anything, except to resist all discipline and to conduct themselves as fools. Theirs is a militia mentality, electing their own officers and expecting to come and go when they please.

"Worse, they are spoilers. Had the Anglos in Texas ever hoped to enlist the *Tejanos* in this cause, these rowdies have ruined that prospect with their shameful behavior toward them. They act as though all Mexicans are the enemy."

The general scratched his massive chin. "And I'm not so sure the recruiting will go very well among the Anglo settlers, either. There is an apathy on their part that I cannot fathom. They number many thousands, but we will do well to enlist one man of them out of every ten.

"And the problem does not end there. The Consultation produced an interim government, made up of a governor and a council. The governor, Henry Smith, and members of the council can agree on nothing except by coincidence. The proven leaders of this province are off to the United States, soliciting money and supplies. Meanwhile, the government here has no consensus and no funds."

Houston put his hands together in his lap. "As you can see, Mr. Bonham, assembling a functioning army won't be easy. I sometimes battle a sense of hopelessness, as I have only today. Then, just like my friend Jim Bowie did before you, along you came, with all the ability and high mindedness in the world, to throw your lot in with us.

"Thank you, Mr. Bonham. I can assure you that you have a place in this army, whenever and wherever it collects itself. Please stay in touch."

Chapter 55

When a couple of house slaves from the Ayers plantation arrived at Mill Creek for Charles Edward, the elder Travis was still on the premises. Buck Travis elected to accompany his son to Montford, and spent several pleasant days in the company of David Ayers and his wife, Ann. There he also met Lydia Ann McHenry, who along with Ann Ayers taught school in the manor house. While Miss McHenry expressed herself in far too direct a fashion to suit Travis, she did help him feel good about his son's prospects for a strong education under her tutelage.

Word reached the plantation about the capture of San Antonio and the exodus of the Mexican forces from Texas. David Ayers, whose strong religious bent made armed conflict abhorrent to him, asked Travis if the victory at Bexar signaled the end of hostilities. "Like a ring around the moon," Travis responded, "it only presages the storm." However, he added, there was little doubt that Texas would win independence.

Travis took leave of Charles Edward early on New Year's Eve. Mill Creek lay on the route from Montford to San Felipe, and the attorney did not deny himself the opportunity for a second extended visit with Rebecca. New Year's Day, chilly and rainy, found him in front of the main fireplace of the inn along with John and Rebecca, absorbing the warmth of a crackling blaze and awaiting a holiday dinner.

Rebecca listened with genuine interest as Travis talked happily about the situation in which Charles Edward had been placed. John,

378

perhaps in observance of the advent of 1836, was enjoying a rare pipeful of tobacco.

"There is not a finer Christian couple in Texas than Mr. and Mrs. Ayers," Travis declared. "The teacher they employ, a spinster, is certainly dedicated to the children. She, by the way, is from Kentucky, where her father was a preacher. She and the Ayerses are all devoted Methodists."

Despite Rebecca's wish to avoid it, the talk finally turned to the war. This time it was John who had the most recent information, gleaned from a guest two days previous. There existed a split within the appointed leadership of Texas, he related, in part because the governor and council hadn't been empowered by the Consultation to do much. Their commander-in-chief, Houston, was having trouble recruiting a regular army from among the independent souls who had made up the victorious volunteer force at Bexar. A convention was scheduled to open on March 1 at Washington-on-the-Brazos, and it was hoped that the division and confusion would be replaced by a common and cohesive spirit.

Rebecca silently endured John's diatribe, awaiting an opportunity to redirect the conversation. Before she could seize it, there came a rapid knocking at the door.

The arrival was Travis's rainsoaked slave, Joe, dispatched from San Felipe with a letter for his master from Governor Smith. Travis parted the wax seal and seated himself before the fire, where he read the epistle by the flickering light. His face grew stern as he absorbed Smith's message. Rebecca felt something cold and unpleasant forming in the pit of her stomach.

Travis slowly folded the letter and squeezed the seal. "God help Texas!" he declared dramatically. After glancing at John, whose features behind the tobacco haze suddenly reflected alarm, he summarized the letter.

"The governor and the General Council are at each other's throats," the attorney said. "The council backs the announced intent of Frank Johnson and others to take an expedition to the Rio Grande and capture Matamoros. Governor Smith and General Houston are against it, but the men of the army say that, because they are volunteers, they answer to Colonel Johnson or to Dr. James Grant, but in no event to General Houston. And they are eager to attack and pillage Matamoros.

"Governor Smith says that such an expedition is doomed to disaster, and he does not think he can count on anyone returning alive. General Houston is going to attempt to dissuade such men as will listen to him from going. Meanwhile, the governor has requested that I assume the duties of recruiting officer at San Felipe, enlisting men in the regular army to serve under General Houston. Now, there's a hard and thankless assignment."

He began to pace back and forth before the fireplace.

"Surely, Buck," John commented, "you can stay for dinner before respondin' to th' governor's summons."

Travis nodded. "I shall want as much sustenance from Hannah's kitchen as I may absorb, and a good night's sleep as well," he replied, "before riding off across that wet prairie."

Following the meal, John discreetly found things to do at the mill. This left Rebecca and Buck alone before the fire. The attorney seized the opportunity to return to the topic he had broached on his last visit.

"I want to marry you, love, and soon," he said firmly. "I desire that above all else in the world. I have never wanted anything as much as I want you. Yet, I am sensing that something has come between us."

Anxiously, Rebecca shook her head. "Oh, no, Buck!" she protested. "I wish this for us every bit as much as you do. Just please don't press me to set a date, right now."

Stubbornly, he persisted, but his brief browbeating failed to elicit any motive for her reluctance. It did, though, extract a promise.

"Darling," she said, almost in tears, "we should not—cannot—have any secrets from each other. Please believe me when I say that I do not intend to keep anything from you! But leave me in peace, for the moment, about our wedding plans. Allow me to compose my thoughts on paper, and I pledge to write you within the week."

Sullenly, Travis agreed, and she took his hand in both of hers and immediately steered the talk to lighter topics.

The lawyer and his slave departed Mill Creek next morning. As they began slogging their way across the muddy prairie, Joe told Travis that a Mr. Bonham was in San Felipe and had, in fact, made himself at home in Travis's humble abode. "He say y'all is cousins, an' dat y'all has been bes' frien's since you wuz li'l fellas," Joe recounted.

"In some ways, Joe, we have been like brothers," Travis reflected. "We've not laid eyes on one another for years, but we were tight as lads, and we have corresponded since. James Bonham is completely fearless, and a man of rare principle. He's loyal, as well—a great one to have on your side, I can tell you."

Back at Mill Creek, Rebecca kept to her room after bidding Travis good-bye. John did not notice this unusual behavior of his own accord, but Hannah pointed it out later in the day. Concerned, he went to Rebecca's door and knocked. She opened the door partway and leaned her head against it, not offering him an entrance. Her eyes were swollen, but whether from tears, fatigue, or recent sleep he could not tell.

"Is ever'thing all right, Sis?" John asked tenderly. "Hannah says you came out just long 'nough for a bit o' food, didn't eat much, an' went back to your room."

"I'm fine," she said, a tiny tremor in her voice. "It's just that I promised Buck a letter, and I'm having a hard time putting down just what I want to say. I'm okay, really." Flashing a rather forced smile, she started to shut the door. Then she fixed her eyes on her brother and asked, "John, you don't really intend to go off and fight, do you?"

The question surprised John. He thought it over for a moment. "I can sure understand your concern, Sis," he finally replied. "But, yes, there's prob'ly a chance of it if Santa Anna brings an army into Texas in th' spring. For now, though, you don't fret 'bout it. We're still a ways off from me havin' to make that decision."

This time there was no smile on Rebecca's face as she shut her door.

Travis and Bonham decided to celebrate their reunion, the first one they could observe as grown men, with a steak dinner at Peyton's Tavern. Travis invited Three-Legged Willie to join them.

"You must appreciate and show due respect, Mr. Bonham," Williamson quipped, "on the occasion of supping with a lieutenant colonel of cavalry. The governor and council commissioned our Mr. Travis in order to give him weight as a recruiter for the regular army. And this, mind you, even after he turned down a commission as a major of artillery."

Bonham smiled at Williamson's ribbing of Travis. "Actually," he responded, "I have written General Houston, expressing my own interest in the artillery."

Three-Legged Willie grinned. "Ah, yes! The general who was no men, also has no artillery!"

"But we do have a corps of rangers," Travis interrupted, eager to return Williamson's digs. "And you and I, James, are in the presence of their duly commissioned leader. May I present to you Major Williamson!"

"Rangers? What are they charged with doing?" Bonham asked. Noting the sincerity of the question, Williamson gave a serious answer. "Our primary responsibility is to deal with the threat of Indian depredations, especially from the Comanches and Apaches, during the present state of hostilities with Mexico," he said. "We cannot afford to let our red friends attack us from the rear while we are preoccupied with Mexico. Let me assure you, Buck," he added, turning to Travis, "that it is every bit as difficult recruiting men for ranger duty as it is to enlist them in the army. In both cases, they are eager enough to fight, but do not wish to follow orders or suffer training."

Besides the Indians, Williamson said, the rangers had another element to keep an eye on: renegade Anglos.

"With all the Americans pouring into Texas to fight Mexico," he elaborated, "there has come a certain outlaw element seeking to prey on their own people. Just as the Indians are prone to do, these white men take advantage of the absence of farmers who are off soldiering. They steal livestock and any slaves they can capture, and generally plunder the farmstead, sometimes even doing harm to the defenseless family. We have uncovered more and more instances of these despicable acts, not only in remote areas but in the local vicinity as well.

"It is a sad commentary on the human race, and an odious confirmation of the Scriptures' admonition on the fall and decay of natural man."

Travis happened to be gone—off to the lower Brazos country in search of recruits for Houston—when Rebecca arrived in San Felipe to personally deliver her promised letter. Fearful of anyone seeing the contents, she had ruled out the prospect of trusting other hands with it. She sat apprehensively in the carriage in front of

Travis's modest house while Henry rapped on the door. The knock summoned Bonham rather than the anticipated occupant, and it would be hard to say whether the house guest or the callers were more surprised when the door opened.

Bonham smiled at the young slave, and then at his mistress. "I'm afraid, if you are looking for my cousin," he informed them, "that he's out of town recruiting at the present time."

Henry was disappointed, having looked forward to catching the inevitable silver coin tossed by the hand of Travis. Rebecca, though, actually felt relieved that Buck was gone. She was also pleased to see Bonham, and smiled accordingly.

"I have something for Buck . . . a letter. May I leave it with you?" she asked, a bit uncertainly.

Bonham stepped over to the carriage. "Miss Cumings," he said, "if you've just ridden all the way from Mill Creek, you certainly should step inside and rest for a bit. I'm sure Buck would want me to make that offer. And, too," he added tactfully, "you can leave the letter on his desk yourself."

Rebecca nodded, and Bonham helped her from the carriage. Neither was eager to release the assisting handclasp. However, once she had placed her letter amid the jumble of paperwork on Travis's table, Rebecca told Bonham that she should begin her return journey at once. "It will be dark before we reach home, even if we leave right now," she said with some reluctance.

No sooner had the carriage departed than Bonham recalled Williamson's informed remarks about local renegades and their dark deeds. A fine horse, a young male slave, and a beautiful woman would be on the road well after dark, virtually inviting trouble.

"At the very least, I should have warned her," Bonham chastised himself, then realized that perhaps he still might.

He jotted a note of explanation to Travis, then went swiftly, rifle in hand, to the stable. Within an hour, he had overtaken Rebecca's carriage—and had formulated a better idea. "I hope you won't think me forward," he said apologetically, "but I'd like to ride along in case of any . . . chance meetings on your way home."

Openly pleased and appreciative, Rebecca protested only weakly before consenting. Bonham hitched his horse to the rear of the carriage. He then took the reins from Henry, who, mindful of unseen dangers lurking along the darkening road, readily climbed into the back seat and sank down against the floorboard.

As Bonham chatted with Rebecca, he remained guarded on the topic of Travis. He did not approve of his kinsman's behavior in seeing another woman while his divorce was pending, but that was not his business. What Bonham did not guard against were rapidly growing feelings for the woman beside him. She was very animated, and displayed quaint and charming mixtures of adult and child, sophisticate and naive. Too, it soon became plain to Bonham that, as deeply in love with Travis as Rebecca might be, she was finding the present company enjoyable.

The day had been free of the chilling drizzle so prevalent in January. A dry, cold north wind played across the faces of the travelers. At sunset, the gray wintry clouds began to break up and reveal patches of blue and gold. The moon, two-thirds full, had already climbed into the eastern sky. Soon Bonham grew dependent on the moonlight to give detail to the road, and cautiously slowed the pace of their travel. But he did not mind. Rebecca, a scarf protecting her mouth and nose, was huddled up next to him underneath an overcoat. Within the shadow of its hood, her large, luminous eyes sparkled as she talked. A slender gloved hand occasionally clutched his arm.

Finally, they rattled and splashed through the crossing of the creek, and—too quickly, Bonham thought—saw the lights of the inn. Rebecca suspected that John, worried about her by this time, would be stepping outside as soon as he heard their approach. Without saying a word, she leaned over and lowered her scarf long enough to kiss the startled Bonham on the cheek. Then she snuggled back in the seat. Sure enough, John, lantern in hand, met them as they pulled up to the inn.

"I'm so sorry to be late, John," Rebecca apologized. "Mr. Bonham actually rode out after us and volunteered to escort us home. Wasn't that gallant of him? Poor thing, he didn't even bring a coat. I'm sure he's chilled, through and through. You'd better get him in front of the fire."

To be sure, Bonham's hands and face were numb from the cold. But his heart was on fire.

Chapter 56

Travis and his steed all the way from Mill Creek to San Felipe.
When he finally reached the residence of Travis, the shivering
Bonham found to his relief that the governor's recruiting officer
had not returned. The proof of this was Rebecca's letter, still unopened and occupying a conspicuous spot on the lawyer's work
table.

Bonham quickly made a fire, and shortly thereafter reclaimed
the note he had left Travis and tossed it into the flames. He felt
guilty—not for having chosen to escort his cousin's betrothed safely home, but for the strong and disturbing feelings she aroused. It
would be best, Bonham figured, if the topic of Rebecca simply did
not come up.

Fate, however, decreed otherwise.

Travis arrived late in the day. "How fares the search for
recruits?" Bonham asked cheerily after his cousin had shut the door
behind him and, blowing into cupped hands, hustled to the fireside.
Travis shook his head in the negative as Bonham handed him a
cloth-wrapped cup of boiling coffee.

"Not so well, James," Travis replied, his voice quivering from
the cold. "I'm supposed to raise a hundred men or more, by order
of Governor Smith, and at present barely have a fourth of them. I'm
dismayed at the misplaced confidence, so prevalent among our people, that the Mexicans have turned tail for good."

While Travis warmed himself inside and out, Bonham reflected on the conversation he'd had with John Cumings the previous night. John had hinted again that he intended to join the army, which again caused Rebecca great (though unexpressed) distress. Prompted by a sudden inspiration, Bonham had argued persuasively that the miller could be of much more service to Texas and its defenders by producing barrelfuls of corn meal for their use. When John acknowledged the logic of this premise, Rebecca's face had beamed in silent gratitude.

So, Bonham mused silently, *there's one less rifle for you, Buck, and I'm to blame.*

The slave Joe had accompanied his master on the recruiting trip. Having taken care of their horses, Joe entered the house and discreetly stationed himself at one end of the fireplace. Bonham indicated the coffee pot, and Joe gratefully used an old tin cup to help himself.

Travis sauntered over to his work table. He noticed Rebecca's letter and quickly picked it up. Turning to Bonham, he asked tersely, "When did this arrive?"

Bonham made a quick decision not to offer any surplus information. "Yesterday," he said casually.

"Brought by the boy Henry, I suppose," Travis mused aloud, carefully parting the wax seal. Bonham grunted assent, while trying to conjure up a suitable reason to leave the house. The letter might well prompt Travis to open a dialogue about his and Rebecca's relationship, and Bonham did not wish to be drawn into it. The adverse weather, though, kept him from coming up with a plausible excuse for exiting.

As Travis read the letter, he began to turn red in the face. His eyes widened in surprise bordering on disbelief, and then they narrowed angrily. Veins stood out on his forehead, and the jaw muscles rolled as he ground his teeth. Having apparently finished the epistle, he crushed it into a ball. A string of oaths gushed from his lips.

"The whore!" he blurted out, almost in a scream. "How could it be? How could she? Oh, the pretentious, deceitful slut!" He lashed out with one foot and kicked a wooden stool as hard as he could. It ricocheted viciously off the wall.

Travis glared at Bonham, who was struck dumb with astonishment even as he felt a fury of his own building inside. "And all of this time," Travis snarled, "I took her to be a lady! The purest of virgins! Oh, all the nights I could have had her, and held back—restrained myself, like a chivalrous fool! Came calling instead on the diseased harlots of San Felipe!"

Incredibly, Bonham maintained his self-control. However much the words of Travis shocked and stung him, he had the presence of mind to know that he owned no right of protest. Instead, he turned his back on his kinsman's rage. Joe chose a more expedient solution: he bolted the room for his cold but peaceful quarters at the rear of the house.

Travis waved his arms wildly. "Two years, Bonham!" he ranted. "Two years I poured out my heart—for this! Who would have believed it? Can you believe it, James?"

Bonham felt compelled to make some sort of response. "What has happened, Buck?" he asked, hating his own words. "I can't make heads or tails out of what's gotten into you. Does she not now wish marriage?"

"Marriage!" the distraught man bellowed. "Marriage to that . . . that . . . trollop? I wouldn't have her under any circumstances! She is polluted!" Shaking his fist, the offending letter still squeezed in its grip, he added, "She freely admits everything to me, right here!"

Through clenched teeth, Bonham replied, "Actually, Buck, it seems to me that she made a rather brave choice in attempting to be honest with you."

Travis snorted. "Oh, yes, she made a choice!" he shouted scornfully. "At the age of thirteen, she admits, she bore a son out of wedlock! Don't you imagine that the bastard child left his damnable marks upon her when he came into the world?" Then he looked askance at Bonham. "Are you trying to defend her, James? Why would you defend her?" he demanded.

Bonham gave Travis a severe look, and squared his shoulders. He had lost all patience with himself and his cousin. Before he could reply, though, the other man dropped his head and waved one hand apologetically. "Forgive me, James," he said, in a pathetic sort of tone. "I shouldn't have said anything like that. I know you're just trying to look for the silver lining. Well, in this case there is none. Things cannot go on any longer. It's all over between that woman and me."

Travis retrieved the stool he had just abused, placed it at the work table, and sat down heavily. With a dramatic flair, he reached underneath the table and pulled out a demijohn. "Come, Jamey," he urged, using a nickname Bonham had not heard since childhood. "Let's have a drink. I'll need this much, and more, to mend my broken heart."

Bonham condescended to drink with him, but only pretended to match swallow for swallow.

Around dawn, Bonham aroused himself from an unsatisfactory sleep and quietly collected his belongings while Travis remained in heavy slumber. He left his host a note:

> I regret the unhappy turn your romance has taken. In my estimation, Miss Cumings is a remarkable lady, whose courageous decision to be candid with you has proven disastrous. I should reconsider if I were you.
>
> San Felipe seems to me rather too full of attorneys for yet another practice. I am removing to Brazoria to see what the supply may be in that locality. Thank you for your hospitality. Will see you again soon. J.B.B.

As Bonham started out of the house, he happened to spot the crumpled ball of Rebecca's letter lying in front of the cold fireplace. He took the poker and managed to raise a flicker of flame from the ashes. Then he consigned the letter to the fire and watched it blacken.

Santa Anna relentlessly drove his newly formed army over the rugged terrain of northern Mexico in the dead of winter, through blowing snow and record cold. His target was Texas. The Army of Operations, six thousand strong, would be crossing the Rio Grande in early February.

The dictator's first goal was the retaking of San Antonio, so humiliatingly surrendered by his brother-in-law, Cos. From that stronghold he intended to move east toward the Sabine as part of a double-pronged campaign of destruction. Santa Anna would personally lead the main army through the heart of Anglo Texas, while to the south, a smaller force under the command of the capable Gen. Jose de Urrea would sweep the Gulf Coast with the intent of capturing strategic Goliad.

The fleetest insurgents might escape across the border into the United States, but the slow and resistant would be put to the sword without exception. Freshly enacted law sanctioned the execution of foreigners who bore arms against Mexico. So far as Santa Anna was concerned, all Anglos—no matter their length of residency, or their pretensions as to nationality—were to be classified as foreigners.

While the Mexican army trudged steadily northward, the Texians remained in disarray.

Due in some measure to Sam Houston's subtle sabotage, the Matamoros adventure of Johnson and Grant fell apart. But, for all practical purposes, so did the Texas provisional government, under the combined weight of strife and incompetence.

Houston, casting about in desperation for someone he could depend upon, found the redoubtable Jim Bowie at Goliad. He ordered Bowie to take volunteers and provide relief to the ill-equipped force occupying the Alamo at Bexar. There, under the command of Col. James Neill, one hundred half-starved men—far too few to properly defend the entire city—were ensconced behind fortifications put in place and then abandoned by Cos only two months previous. Houston wanted Bowie to oversee the evacuation of these troops and the destruction of the mission.

Among those who rode into the Alamo behind Bowie on January 19 was James Bonham. He had relocated to Brazoria, as he wrote Travis that he would do, but stayed only long enough to advertise in the local newspaper his intent to practice law. After a few days spent trying not to think of Rebecca, and in pondering the fate of his Mobile Greys, he saddled up and rode to Goliad in search of the latter. When Bowie called for volunteers to go with him to Bexar, Bonham and a number of the Greys responded.

Meanwhile, Travis doggedly continued his efforts at recruiting up and down the Brazos. Rebecca likewise was on his mind, but in a far different context than the dreams of Bonham. On three occasions, he began letters with the intent of expressing his outrage and formally severing their engagement. None was ever completed. Nor did he receive any additional word from Mill Creek.

Then Henry Smith, who still considered himself governor in spite of being impeached by the General Council, ordered Travis to round up the men he had recruited and join Bowie and Neill at San Antonio. Contrary to the orders Houston had given Bowie, Smith indicated to Travis his belief that the Alamo should remain occupied.

Smith apparently had been encouraged in this regard by a letter from one of Neill's subordinates. Green Jameson, an engineer, bragged about how his installation on the mission walls of twenty pieces of forfeited Mexican artillery had rendered the Alamo virtually impregnable.

So, in late January, on a cold and drizzly day, Colonel Travis and his slave Joe departed San Felipe for Bexar with a body of some thirty cavalrymen. There would be plenty of time while in San Antonio, Travis decided, to devise the scathing letter he wanted to send Rebecca.

Word soon reached Mill Creek that Bonham had gone to Brazoria and Travis to Bexar. Rebecca became despondent beyond anyone's ability to cheer her. John, aware of no details except that Travis had not contacted his sister before leaving, found the depth of her gloom hard to fathom. He finally gave up the attempt, at least temporarily, having received something new to think about.

It was a letter from Sam Houston, in which the general sought John's assistance in reaching an assurance of peace with the Texas Cherokees of Chief Bowles. Houston noted that he had held discussions with representatives of the Cherokees and allied East Texas tribes in November, but nothing had been settled. Bowles, in fact, had not attended the sessions. "It was told to me," Houston wrote, "that Duwali, or Chief Bowles, holds you in the highest estimation. I myself am an adopted member of his tribe, and am reasonably hopeful of a successful conclusion to this matter. Your attendance at another meeting, planned for next month in Nacogdoches, would doubtless be very helpful in this regard. We know that Santa Anna's agents are actively trying to stir up the Indians against us. Texas must not be caught in a vise, squeezed by the Mexicans on one side and hostile Indians on the other."

The letter urged an immediate reply.

John did not feel that he should discuss the matter with Rebecca in her present state of mind. There was no one to wrestle with over the question but himself. Two days after receiving the communique, John penned a reply. In it, he noted:

> It is my sincere wish to aid the Texas cause in either or both of two ways. I stand ready to clean my cribs of every last ear of corn & grind them into barrels of meal for your Army at no cost to the provisional gov't. I also am willing to risk my life & join

the ranks of said Army, happily meeting whatever Fate that God has ordained.

I will not, tho, have a part in any dealings with the Cherokee where the promise is once again made to give them title to their land. Such a promise, I am sure, will have to be a condition in any agreement they consider. They have repeatedly been lied to by the Mexican gov't & I beg your pardon, but in my heart I do not believe Americans will treat them any better should we win. While I do not doubt your sincerity, I do not think you can ever deliver on that promise.

The ink was still drying on John's letter when big Seth Swearingen appeared at the inn.

"I've come t' ask you, John," Swearingen began, "t' help my neighbors look after my ma and sister while I'm away. Will you do that for me?" Seeing John's nodded assent and inquiring glance, he added, "I'm meetin' some Kentucky kinfolk who're arrivin' shortly at th' mouth of th' Brazos. They're chompin' at th' bit t' take part in this great Texas adventure . . . seems like th' whole U.S. is stirred up over it."

Seth paused and looked sheepishly at his feet.

"An' I guess, John, if they've come all th' way from Kentucky to help fight our fight, th' least I kin do is join 'em. So I don't know how long I'll be gone, or when I'll be back. Ma ain't none too happy 'bout me goin' away, but she understands. Leastways, she says she does."

As he started to leave he inquired, as though it were an afterthought, about Rebecca. John gave him a noncommittal response, then remembered his just-completed letter. "Hold on a minute, Seth," he said. "I've got somethin' t' post for General Houston, if you don't mind takin' it."

Chapter 57

*J*im Bowie was ordered to Bexar by Houston to remove fortifications within the village, reinforce the Texian garrison at the Alamo nearby, and await further instruction. Bowie expected the general's next orders to be the destruction of the little fort and the removal or spiking of cannon. It only made sense; even now, the men of the Alamo were too few and too poorly equipped to effectively defend the venerable mission.

But Bowie began to rethink things shortly after leading his volunteer force into the convent yard. And James Bonham, eyes shining as he took in the engineer Jameson's placement of ordnance along the adobe walls, quite possibly influenced Bowie's growing temptation to try and hold San Antonio.

Within a couple of days, Bowie had been convinced by Colonel Neill that Bexar was too strategic to abandon. He also seemed persuaded of the Alamo's virtues as a fortress, despite the fact that ten times the available number of men were needed to properly defend its extensive walls. Bonham reinforced the confidence expressed by Jameson in the formidableness of the twenty bristling cannon.

And so, when Travis and his cavalrymen arrived on February 2, they found the garrison busily strengthening the Alamo. To the young lieutenant colonel's delight, he also spotted Bonham. They greeted each other warmly; as if by unspoken agreement, neither mentioned Rebecca or alluded to the unhappy state of Travis's relationship with her.

A week later, one of the biggest names in North America joined the Alamo occupants: former congressman and living folk hero Davy Crockett, riding at the head of a dozen colorful back-woods cohorts. Crockett, at forty-nine, retained a commanding presence. His oratorical magic captivated the entire San Antonio community at a *fandango* thrown in his honor in one of the town plazas. He had come to Texas, he said, with no personal agenda except "to aid you all I can in your noble cause." Crockett asserted that he sought nothing except to defend, in the role of a "high private," the "liberties of our common country."

Bowie and Neill appeared to have built a harmonious working relationship. So it came as a surprise when the latter—announcing on February 11 that he must leave in order to care for his critically ill family as well as search out supplies for the garrison—named Travis as acting commander in his absence. Neill later explained that Travis, the ranking officer of the regulars at the Alamo, had to be selected over Bowie, a volunteer.

But Travis, ruefully observing that Neill's choice of him provoked resentment and hostility in many of the men, ordered an election in an effort to resolve the unrest. A majority of the garrison voted for the popular Bowie, who at Concepcion had reinforced his reputation as a fighter. They bestowed upon him the rank of full colonel. Bitter though the pill was, Travis might have swallowed it with grace had not the victor become rip-roaring drunk.

Bonham had viewed this act before, and knew what it portended. Having already chosen sides by voting for Travis, he quietly transferred his service from Bowie's volunteers to the San Felipe cavalrymen. "It's going to get ugly, Colonel," he warned Travis.

Indeed it did. All the worst of Bowie came out, terrorizing San Antonio in the process. He stumbled about in a drunken show of power, and many of his troops followed his example. He demanded the release of civilian and military prisoners alike. When on one occasion magistrate Juan Seguin stood up to Bowie and remanded a prisoner to jail, armed members of the garrison marched threateningly around the city until Bowie got his way.

Entering the second day of the uproar and debauchery, Travis disgustedly removed his cavalrymen from Bexar. They camped a few miles away on the Medina River, where Travis penned a letter to the governor about Bowie's conduct. "I am unwilling to be responsible for the drunken irregularities of any man," he wrote.

Travis sought out Bonham for advice about Bowie. What he

learned was that, once Bowie's boozing had run its course, the man usually became reasonable and even contrite. "At least," Bonham commented, "I'm told that the Mexicans here have known Jim Bowie for years. Apparently he's almost one of them. They remember his wife and in-laws and how he lost them to the plague. So they may not feel as insulted as they would if some other American went crazy drunk and pushed them around."

Bonham then switched topics. "Colonel," he asked, "have you been noticing the number of ox-carts leaving town? What appears to me to be entire families, with their prized belongings, have been moving out steadily, now, for several days."

Travis sniffed. "Yes, I've seen them," he replied, disdain in his voice. "Our loutish Colonel Bowie has even tried to have some of them arrested. Drunk as he is, their departure seems to upset him."

"Well, that's because he knows why it's happening. It's not him they're scared of. They started leaving even before the garrison voted."

This observation drew a stare from Travis. "Santa Anna!" he exclaimed. "That's who you think they're running from!"

Bonham nodded. "We've been telling ourselves that the Mexican army couldn't get here before Arpil—the middle of March, at the earliest," he said. "And it's just now the middle of February. But I'd put greater faith in their intuition (or outright knowledge) than in our scouts. Even Seguin's scouts. I trust Seguin, but can he trust his own men?"

The following morning, Travis received a politely worded request from Bowie to meet with him. Apprehensive, the young officer nevertheless sent back a response that he would.

As Bonham had speculated, it was a quiet, tacitly apologetic man with bloodshot eyes and blotched face who welcomed Travis into his quarters.

"I want t' commend you, Colonel," Bowie said in a dry, croaking voice. "You didn't have t' call that election after Colonel Neill left you in charge. But you saw th' wisdom in doin' it, so you went ahead, even though it meant you might lose. And when th' result came in, you acted th' gentleman.

"I didn't. I let you and th' garrison down. Hell, I let the whole o' Bexar down with my shenanigans. I want you t' know that I regret my behavior of th' past two days."

Travis nodded. It was as close as Bowie was going to come to an outright apology, and the younger man willingly accepted it.

"Now, then," Bowie continued, "let's see if we can't work everything out 'tween us until Neill gets back here." He proposed that he retain command of the volunteers already in Bexar when Travis arrived; Travis would be in charge of his cavalrymen and the regulars, which included Crockett's contingent. They would jointly issue general orders and sign correspondence pending Neill's return.

Bowie's was a fair offer. Travis extended his hand in acceptance. As they shook, he observed for the first time a crusted smear of blood across one corner of the other man's mouth. Apparently, someone had gotten a bellyful of Bowie and smashed him in the jaw. Considering the reputation of the duelist and the knife he always wore, Travis judged that whoever hit him had either been drunk or very foolish.

When told about the blood on Bowie's mouth, Bonham shook his head. "No man could strike Jim Bowie like that and live," he said, "and we haven't heard that he's killed anybody. I think what you saw is blood he coughed up. He's a sick man, Colonel, and he's growing sicker. Those close to him have known it for some time. But don't ever confuse sickness with weakness where Bowie is concerned."

Texian governmental leadership and military operations were in an absolute shambles as Mexico's Army of Operations bore down on Bexar.

The General Council had removed Henry Smith as governor and replaced him with the lieutenant governor, James Robinson. But Smith continued to behave as though still in power, thereby creating new heights of confusion. His choice as commander of the Texas army, Sam Houston, was in East Texas treating with the Cherokees. Meanwhile, Robinson was offering complete authority to James Fannin as commander-in-chief. Houston had no army; Fannin crouched behind the crumbling walls of an old presidio in Goliad with a force approaching five hundred men.

The core of Fannin's assemblage consisted of dropouts from the Matamoros expedition, dissuaded from that adventure by Houston's ominous rhetoric. Two other fragments of the erstwhile expedition were floundering around under confused commanders at San Patricio and Agua Dulce Creek, respectively. The itinerary of Mexican General Urrea and his army, soon to be sweeping along the Gulf Coast, would bring them to San Patricio, Agua Dulce Creek, and Goliad.

In Bexar, the trickle of departing *Tejanos* increased. Rumors abounded of the Mexican army's imminent arrival. While Travis continued to doubt the stories, believing that the hour of combat was still a month away, he knew reinforcements were sorely needed prior to any showdown. The only real prospect of getting them was to bestir the enigmatic Fannin, holed up seventy miles to the southeast in Goliad with three times the number of men garrisoned at Bexar.

If anyone could persuade the moody West Point dropout to leave his stronghold for San Antonio, Travis decided, it was Bonham. Dashing, charismatic, articulate, straight-arrow Bonham, everyone's favorite, was easily the best choice. A superior horseman to boot, he could quickly cover the ground between Bexar and Goliad.

Bowie, at one of the few consultations he held with his co-commander, enthusiastically endorsed both the message and the messenger. They collaborated to put their plea in writing. Later in the day, Travis broached the plan to his kinsman. Bonham, tired of inaction, accepted the assignment eagerly and left at dawn with the dispatch.

The ensuing six days were marked by repeated claims that a massive Mexican army was nearing San Antonio. By Travis's own logic, this was not possible, and he discounted the stories largely because they all came from the same source: Mexicans. Even the account of Blas Herrera, cousin to Juan Seguin, was received with skepticism by the garrison's brain trust.

Herrera reported to Seguin that he had witnessed a portion of Santa Anna's army crossing the Rio Grande on February 18. He said that he managed to enter into conversation with some of the soldiers. Risking his life, Herrera wheedled enough information to conclude that the size of the army was five thousand or greater. An advance detachment of fifteen hundred men was conducting a forced march toward Bexar, its intent a surprise assault.

At a meeting in Travis's quarters, the Texian leaders first heard

the report from Seguin, who stoutly vouched for Herrera's depend-
ability and integrity, and then from Herrera himself. Surprisingly,
even Bowie appeared unconvinced. Herrera, after completing his
story and studying the Anglo faces gathered around him, angrily
stalked out of the meeting.

The skepticism was shattered on the morning of February 23,
as the garrison awoke to a great commotion in the city. The *Tejano*
exodus had become a flood, with wagons, carts, and pedestrians
scrambling eastward across the river. Their haste bespoke fear bordering on panic. A Texian sentinel in the bell tower of the venerable San Fernando Church, studying the western hills, caught a
glimpse of approaching horsemen and what he thought were lances
glittering in the morning sun. He rang the bell excitedly, and Travis
and Dr. John Sutherland came running to have a look for themselves. Neither man could confirm the lookout's claim, but realized
that a significant force could be hidden within the rolling terrain. It
had rained the two days previous, so even a large number of horses
might not be raising much dust.

Sutherland and John Smith immediately rode west in search of
the enemy. The doctor had told Travis that if they discovered the
presence of Mexican troops, the scouts would be returning at a hard
and fast pace. Within a matter of minutes, the two riders crested a
hill—and suddenly reined in their steeds. Less than two hundred
yards away, they saw large numbers of mounted, well-armed soldiers, clad in bright blue and red, rallied around an officer who was
exhorting them with sword in hand.

The sentry had observed accurately, including the lances.

Retreating down the hill, Sutherland and Smith urged their
horses into a full gallop. The doctor's horse stumbled and pitched
forward, throwing its rider to the ground. The stunned animal
rolled onto Sutherland's leg and lay there momentarily before
regaining its feet. Smith helped the injured man back onto his dazed
mount, and they continued as swiftly as they could back into Bexar.

Chapter 58

The Ohio River was frozen solid, from bank to bank. Wielding an alpenstock to help keep his footing on the treacherous surface, a tall man wrapped in furs carefully made his way over to the Kentucky side.

Having crossed, he ascended the bank by the ice-encrusted wooden steps of a boat landing. This brought him to the snow-heaped yard of a fine, two-story frame home whose twin chimneys discharged smoke into the darkly overcast winter sky.

Inside, Samuel Cumings was seated at a table in his study. Before him were spread a number of large, well-worn maps depicting the meanderings of the Ohio and lower Missouri and Mississippi rivers. Smaller sheets of paper labeled "gazetteer changes" lay stacked at one end of the table. The heat of a crackling fire warmed Samuel's back while he used the relatively steady glow from an oil lamp to study and make notations on the charts. The old captain, glasses perched on the end of his nose, sighed in acknowledgment that he had grown mighty tired of the task before him: the annual revision of his popular guide to navigation of the western waters.

Most of Samuel's firsthand river wandering lay behind him. At age fifty-nine, he now depended on others—chiefly his oldest son, Will, whom he proudly labeled a better pilot than himself—to record the changes in channel depths and direction, the nomadic relocation of sandbars and submerged trees, the sunken wrecks of unlucky river traffic, the fluctuating populations and leading industries of the river towns, and so forth. Now he was forced to enjoy his river lore vicariously.

There came the distinctive knock of his aging manservant at the door. "What is it, Absalom?" Samuel called out, impatient at the interruption.

"Suh, a gen'man heah from de Ohio side, say his name William Cumin's. He ax tuh speak wit'chu."

William Cumings! Samuel flung his glasses onto the table in irritation and rubbed his itching nose. What on earth could his sister's whore-son, named for the favorite brother of the adolescent Becky, want from him in the dead of winter? The payments of support to the foster parents in West Union had long since ceased, for the boy they raised was now a twenty-three-year-old man uncomplainingly making his own way.

"Show him in," Samuel responded, and rose from the chair to greet his illegitimate nephew.

The blond, blue-eyed product of David Singletary's loins resembled his father more closely than did any of the dark halfbreeds borne by Singletary's Indian wives. He stood well over six feet, and the giant hands he now rubbed together for warmth were uncannily like those of his sire.

"Come over by the fire, William, and toast yourself a bit," Samuel invited, and sent Absalom after a hot pot of tea. Despite Samuel's irritation over the unforetold invasion of his work time, he genuinely liked the young man. This William Cumings had been fully aware of his second-class citizenship for most of his life, yet had evidenced no bitterness.

After the visitor had taken his fill of tea, Samuel asked in a kindly manner what his business might be. There was a period of silence, during which William seemed to be carefully framing his petition.

"I've come," he said at last, "to find out a bit more about myself. I know most of the facts, of course, but not all." He blushed momentarily. "You see, I'm about to be married, and I believe I owe it to my bride-to-be, and our children to come, to learn all that I can."

Samuel puffed out his cheeks with an exhalation. "That's certainly a fair request, William," he admitted, "but I daresay there is really very little left on which to shed light."

The young giant folded his arms and politely met Samuel's gaze. "I understand," he said, "that my father was David Singletary, the founder and for years the spiritual leader of New Ephrata. My mother was a Cumings. I am aware that I was born without benefit of wedlock, and as a result no inheritance awaits me from either family." The last observation was stated without rancor.

"Sometimes, when I stand on the Ohio side and look across the river at the Cumings boat yard and shipping activities, I feel like the hairy man in the Bible who sold his birthright. And yet, unlike him, I didn't even have a choice.

"Please understand," he added hastily, "I'm aware and very grateful that you provided a regular sum to the family that raised me. It provided no end of benefits to us. For one thing, I'm among the few young men from my station in life who can read and write."

William stood and clasped his hands behind his back. "What I don't know for sure," he said earnestly, "is who my mother was, and if she's still alive. I've been told that both of your sisters went with your mother to live in Mexico. One of them would almost certainly have to be my mother." His face colored again. "I promise you," he added, "it is not ever going to be my intent to embarrass her by trying to find her. But it's very important to me for you to tell me about her—as much as you see fit."

It crossed Samuel's mind to name the dead twin Sarah as the object of William's inquiry, but he quickly dismissed the idea. After all, the couple in West Union knew who gave birth to William. It impressed him that they evidently had kept their word never to tell anyone, including their foster son.

"All right, William," he said. "I believe you have the right to know what little I can add.

"Your mother is Rebecca, who will shortly turn thirty-seven years of age."

William winced.

"She is well, I believe," Samuel resumed, "and is still living in Texas with our brother, John. You would like me to describe her to you? Very well. The Rebecca I recall was a soft-spoken, well-mannered child, drilled in education beyond the norm for her sex. She was a beautiful young woman when she left New Ephrata a dozen or so years past, and I daresay she has very likely retained her fine looks. Dark red hair, green eyes, a charming smile. There was a twin, Sarah, almost as beautiful in her own right. Sarah died in childbirth four years ago.

"To my uncertain knowledge, Rebecca has never married."

Samuel took a breath. "Now, William," he directed, "mark my words. In spite of the circumstances of your birth, Rebecca is a Christian woman. A lovely person inside and out, really, with a giving heart and a sprightly personality. That, in a moment's summation, is your mother."

William blinked, trying to absorb it all. Then he stuck out a huge hand. "Thanks, Mr. Cumings," he said, warmth in his voice and grip alike. "You've been a great help. What you've told me will make my life easier. I always believed that my mother was just as you describe her, a truly good person. My first daughter will be named Rebecca."

When the visitor had departed, Samuel eased back into his chair. But he did not resume the perusal of the charts. *Like the hairy man in the Bible,* he mused, and rubbed his eyes. Glancing at the fireplace chimney, above the mantel where for years the now-empty hooks had supported his father's rifle, he ran nervous fingers through his salt-and-pepper curls. "At least," Samuel told himself, with a sense of relief, "young William did not choose to inquire about the murder of David Singletary. I'm not sure how I would have answered that one."

Fannin was unwilling to reinforce Bexar.

"Bowie and Travis need to level the Alamo and withdraw from San Antonio, as I should think General Houston would want done," he told an unbelieving James Bonham, scant minutes after the courier had ridden into Goliad and delivered the message for help. "It would make far greater sense for that little garrison at Bexar to join me here at La Bahia."

His flat refusal appeared to bother Fannin not at all, and he gave no further attention to the urgent dispatch signed by the co-commanders of the Alamo. Instead, he moved to other topics, all dealing with the current disastrous situation in Texas as he saw it. He pointed out with bitterness the paucity of longtime Texas citizens found among the ranks of his men ("Are they not willing to take up arms and defend their own homes?") and complained about the indecisiveness of Texian leadership as well as its lack of funds.

Bonham, while frustrated over Fannin's insistence on remaining behind the walls of the presidio, did accept the commander's offer to share his quarters for the night. The next morning, in spite of threatening weather, he began the return ride to Bexar. Bonham considered making a side journey to Gonzales in search of reinforcements, but reluctantly decided against it. Travis had charged him with delivering the plea for help to Fannin and nothing more.

Cold, gusting rain became an unwelcome companion for most of that day and the next, slowing Bonham's progress as he followed the winding San Antonio River. He did not draw near to Bexar until the following morning. By this time, the rainclouds had disappeared in favor of blue skies and a soft breeze out of the north.

Within a few miles of San Antonio, the courier encountered a familiar horseman headed in the opposite direction. Young Johnson was the bearer of bad news. The Mexicans were invading Bexar! A vanguard of Santa Anna's army, ten times the strength of the insurgents, had marched into the city that very morning. The Texians hastily abandoned the city and regrouped across the river within the Alamo. Johnson was under orders from Travis to ride hard for Goliad and deliver a new message to Fannin, beseeching his immediate help.

"I doubt it will do much good, Johnson, but go ahead—you have your instructions," Bonham commented. "You might have done better to ride to Gonzales." To this, Johnson replied that Dr. Sutherland and John Smith had been sent that very direction early in the day. Bonham touched the brim of his hat and wished Johnson Godspeed.

There suddenly came, from the direction of San Antonio, the echoing boom of a cannon. Johnson's eyes widened, and he dug his spurs into the flanks of his horse. Bonham watched him depart, then turned his own mount toward Bexar.

Within the hour, he was cautiously approaching the Alamo from the elevated terrain to the southeast. Hurried activity could be seen atop the adobe walls of the old mission. Waving his hat to attract the favorable attention of the defenders, Bonham urged his steed into a gallop and headed for the main gate. Its twin doors yawned, and as he passed between them welcoming shouts were lifted.

Inside the compound, men hastily went about the business of preparing to meet an assault. Bonham spotted Buck Travis on the west wall, which faced Bexar, and made his way briskly to the side of his commander and kinsman. As Travis turned to him, Bonham could see that the lieutenant colonel was seething with both energy and anger. After they exchanged salutes, Bonham reported matter-of-factly that Fannin and his forces would not be coming.

"I begin to understand," Travis snapped, "why Colonel Fannin washed out of West Point. Well, Lieutenant Bonham, the situation has become much more grave since you were dispatched to Goliad."

Bonham nodded. "Yes, sir," he responded. "I met Johnson on the road this morning. He informed me of the enemy's arrival and of the dispatch he is carrying to Goliad. If I may say so, sir, I have my doubts that the extremity of our situation will make any difference to Colonel Fannin."

Travis scowled but made no reply. "Sir," Bonham inquired, "if I may ask, why was our eighteen-pounder set off this past hour?"

Travis smiled grimly in spite of his agitation. "You are indeed an artilleryman, sir," he complimented Bonham, "if you can tell one cannon from another upon hearing it fired from miles away. As for why I had it discharged," he added heatedly, his face reddening, "I was alerting Santa Anna to the fact that there is someone in command of this fortress besides a common drunk!"

He smote his open palm with a clenched fist. "Disgraceful! Absolutely disgraceful! Colonel Bowie—without consulting me, for he knew full well what my response would be—sent out his aide under a white flag to parley with the Mexicans. Well, of course their response was that the entire garrison must lay down arms and surrender at the discretion of the despot. In short, no considerations promised!

"As soon as the results of this spineless gesture were reported to me, I ordered the eighteen-pounder fired in an appropriate response. We will not surrender nor retreat! I have told my men that, with or without the dubious assistance of Colonel Bowie, we shall taste either victory or death!"

Bonham scratched his forehead in puzzlement. "Surely, sir," he ventured, "Colonel Bowie had his reasons for what he did. With all due respect, sir, I must insist that he is no craven."

There was a dangerous light in Travis's eyes for an instant. Then, in a voice trembling with emotion, he said, "The colonel claimed to receive a report that the Mexicans themselves had first shown a parley flag, and he wanted to know what they had to say.

Then, at the negotiations, the Mexican officer said no white flag had been displayed by his side, and gave us the conditions for surrender—which are no conditions.

"It was mortifying to me and to every fighting man in the fortress. We will not budge an inch!"

Then the Alabaman lowered his voice. "All the same, Lieutenant," he disclosed worriedly, "we must have reinforcements and additional supplies if we are to hold out. Let us pray that Colonel Fannin comes out of his fog of indecision and marches to our aid immediately."

While they spoke, Travis had been using a field glass in a futile attempt to glimpse the Mexican army. Despite the severity of the winter by Texas standards, foliage lined the San Antonio River and screened from view whatever was taking place across the river in Main Plaza. But Travis abruptly spotted something which shocked him out of his military formality.

"There it is, James!" he said dramatically. "The Mexicans are unfurling the flag which signals no quarter! They have declared us to be rebels, and as such we will be shown no mercy if captured."

He offered Bonham the field glass, but the latter had no difficulty in seeing with unaided eye the crimson symbol of Santa Anna's ruthlessness. From the bell tower of San Fernando Church, rising clearly visible above the trees, hung a blood-red pennant.

Chapter 59

At first, Santa Anna was in no hurry to attack the Alamo.

The best plan, he and his subordinates agreed, was to lay siege to the fortress and commence a bombardment with the artillery on hand. They would await the arrival of the slower-moving components of the army, most especially the heavy field pieces. Then it would be a matter of which collapsed first: the old mission walls under large-scale shelling, or the Texian garrison after running out of ammunition and food.

The day following the enemy's arrival, Jim Bowie found out that even the most lion-hearted of men can become too ill to serve. He collapsed in the courtyard while trying to help with the placement of a cannon and was carried to his quarters. There, from his cot, he sent for Crockett.

The legendary Tennessean found Bowie several swallows deep into his demijohn. The front of the sick man's shirt was spattered with vomit and fresh blood, and the room reeked of the former mixed with the odor of whiskey. Bowie trembled from weakness as he propped himself up on one elbow, but his eyes had not lost their fire. He waved a feeble salutation as Crockett, hat in hand, neared his bedside.

"Thanks for comin' so quick, Colonel," Bowie said in a wheezing voice. Crockett once held that rank in the Tennessee militia, and it had become a permanent prefix to his name after appearing in numerous accounts glamorizing the frontier hero.

"I'm always happy to come alongside ol' Jim Bowie," Crockett replied heartily, "and to be of service any way I can."

Bowie inclined his head of matted hair. "Good, good," he muttered. He looked up and fixed his gaze on Crockett. "I know I'm pretty close to cashin' in my chips, Colonel," he said calmly. "I haven't been partic'larly eager to face up to it, but there's no more denyin' that my time's short. I won't ever be leavin' this bed alive."

The Louisianian groaned and stiffened in pain. Then his body relaxed and he collapsed on the cot, sweating profusely. "What I'm askin' of you, Colonel," he resumed, ragged of breath, "is t' assume my command."

Crockett said nothing, nor did any change of expression mark his kindly, attentive manner. Disappointed over the lack of a response, Bowie went on.

"I know you said you just wanted t' be a high private, Colonel . . . didn't want t' be given any rank. Well, my men don't cotton t' young Travis an' his ways. He's never been in a fight like we're facin' now, and he's a fool to boot. You served with Andy Jackson agin' th' Injuns and th' British, and everyone in this godforsaken fort looks up t' you—properly so. We'll need a cool and wise man to get out o' the fix we're in."

Crockett slowly shook his head. "As bad as I hate to disappoint you, Colonel Bowie," he said, "I reckon I'll have to decline. I've no intention of takin' this command. Colonel Travis is the first in line, and that's the way I see it."

Bowie groaned again, gritted his teeth, and tossed a hand weakly in helpless anger. Crockett leaned over and smiled at him. "I'll promise you one thing, Colonel," the Tennessean added. "My men and me, we ain't pullin' out early. Whatever happens, whoever's in charge, we'll dance the whole damn fandango."

He stood up, then said as an afterthought, "Besides, you just may be missin' the mark 'bout Travis and your men. Now, I know full well why you agreed to that parley, even though it turns out nothin' was gained. But when our dandy young colonel touched off the eighteen-pounder, I think he gained some new respect from the rest of us."

Crockett looked down at the stricken man. "Now, Colonel," he asked gently, "would you like me to see that Colonel Travis is fetched here?"

Disgust and resignation chased one another across the perspiring features of the fallen commander. He nodded sullenly and closed trembling eyelids.

Later that day, Wednesday, February 24, the Alamo's sole able-bodied commander penned a dispatch intended for officials of the provisional rebel government, but addressed "to the People of Texas and all Americans in the World":

> Fellow citizens & compatriots —
> I am besieged, by a thousand or more of the Mexicans under Santa Anna—I have sustained a continual Bombardment & cannonade for 24 hours & have not lost a man—The enemy has demanded a surrender at discretion, otherwise, the garrison are to be put to the sword, if the fort is taken—I have answered the demand with a cannon shot, & our flag still waves proudly from the walls—I will never surrender or retreat. Then, I call on you in the name of Liberty, of patriotism & everything dear to the American character, to come to our aid, with all dispatch—The enemy is receiving reinforcements daily & will no doubt increase to three or four thousand in four or five days. If this call is neglected, I am determined to sustain myself as long as possible & die like a soldier who never forgets what is due to his own honor & that of his country —
> VICTORY OR DEATH
> William Barret Travis
> Lt. Col. Comdt.
> P.S. The Lord is on our side—when the enemy appeared in sight we had not three bushels of corn—we have since found in deserted houses 80 or 90 bushels & got into the walls 20 or 30 head of beeves —
> Travis

Entrusted with this letter, courier Albert Martin rode out of the fortress at dark and headed for his hometown of Gonzales.

While Mexican artillerymen cautiously advanced their ordnance closer and closer to the Alamo, Santa Anna found a pretty little *señorita* to occupy his nights. The generalissimo even ordered his own mock marriage to the unlucky girl, whom he eventually tired of and sent away.

The artillerymen had drawn the tougher assignment. They learned the hard way that Texians armed with long rifles could pick them off at distances approaching two hundred yards. As the larger field pieces had not yet arrived, the Mexicans were forced to wheel their light cannon well within rifle range to establish effective batteries. After suffering numerous casualties, they finally resorted to digging trenches at night in order to properly place the weapons.

Place them they did, in an ever tightening circle, and from the second day of the siege forward the Texians fell under an unrelenting bombardment. Actual damage was light, but the constant noise and agitation wore on the defenders' nerves. Crockett, who played a lively fiddle and loved to entertain with his countless tall tales, took it upon himself to relieve the tension as best he could.

Meanwhile, Travis fired off a series of dispatches in a continuous campaign to drum up reinforcements and supplies. He wrote to General Houston, to Governor Smith, even to the leadership of the constitutional convention due to convene on March 1 at Washington-on-the-Brazos. Courier after courier braved the Mexican pickets to deliver the dramatic messages.

Eventually, it became James Bonham's turn once again. On the evening of February 27, Bonham was summoned to Travis's rooms. The redheaded Alabaman was in a despondent mood.

"Johnson's been gone five days—more than ample time to reach Goliad with our last express to Colonel Fannin," Travis noted dourly. "It could be that some foul fate overtook him on the trail, or perhaps that message, too, has been disregarded by the recipient.

"On the other hand, Colonel Fannin and his men may even now be marching to our assistance. It is also possible that General Houston has raised an army and is on his way as well. Not having received any dispatches from the outside, we don't know the extent to which aid is coming—if at all."

Travis shoved out his jaw. "I must be able to tell my men," he said, "what the chances are that this garrison will be receiving reinforcements and supplies. They deserve to know." Momentarily, he studied the ramrod-straight Bonham and was pleased with what he saw.

"Lieutenant," Travis instructed, "you will leave tonight for Gonzales. Once there, hopefully, you can determine the extent to which we may expect help. Having gathered this intelligence, see that it is forwarded to me forthwith. Time is of the essence! I have no dispatch for you to carry tonight. By now, the world is surely aware of our straits."

Bonham understood the message Travis had slipped into his orders. The commander was not only giving his kinsman an opportunity, however dangerous, to escape the Alamo and its fate; there was also a hint that he was not expected back.

"You may depend on me, sir," Bonham responded crisply. "Is there anything else, sir?"

For a brief moment, secure in the privacy of his quarters, Travis stepped out of character. With no one else to see, he abruptly gave Bonham an embrace. Only reluctantly did he unwrap his arms and take a step back. The redhead's eyes grew troubled as he studied the dutiful expression on the darkly handsome face before him.

"Do you remember, Jamey," Travis asked in a boyish voice, "when your daddy told us that fear and cowardice were two different things? That it was okay to be scared, but never okay to run?" His Adam's apple bobbed, and he wiped his nose.

Compassion radiated from the brown eyes of Bonham, who nodded slowly. This was an admission Travis would have made to no other man. And Bonham knew that the young commander felt, in addition to the growing prospect of his own death, the weight of responsibility for the one hundred and fifty Alamo defenders. While Travis had bitterly resented the inaction of Fannin, Bonham reflected, he might now have a better understanding of the other's agony.

Travis regained his composure. "That's all, Lieutenant," he snapped. The boyhood friends took a final, last-second look at each other. Then the courier saluted and, receiving a responding salute, strode proudly from the room.

As soon as the gray, wintry light of day had given up the ghost, a horse and rider slipped out through the east wall of the fortress. They stealthily avoided the bantering, inattentive enemy pickets and soon found the Gonzales road.

Fannin had indeed received the Alamo co-commanders' new message from the hand of the courier Johnson. He did not long ignore it; he could not, in good conscience. Shamed by the impassioned rhetoric, Fannin on February 26 reluctantly ordered most of his army to prepare for a march to Bexar. He sent Johnson on to Gonzales with word that he and three hundred men were proceeding to the aid of the besieged Alamo garrison. One hundred more would remain in the presidio to defend it against the expected arrival of General Urrea.

From the outset, Fannin's army was critically short of food and ammunition. Then, at the crossing of the San Antonio River on the outskirts of Goliad, three of the four supply wagons collapsed under their burdens. While men toiled over the unloading and repairs, the commander gathered his officers to rethink their plans.

The prevalent opinion was to abandon the march. It was argued, with even more truth than could have been known, that Santa Anna expected such an attempt on Fannin's part and that an ambush doubtless awaited the Texians somewhere east of Bexar. Loyalist *Tejanos* had surely observed the departure of the would-be rescuers and were riding hard to alert *El Presidente.*

There was also the threat of Urrea, whose army was coming from the southwest. Should Urrea learn of the expedition, he almost certainly would try to intercept and engage Fannin in open terrain. Thus, the exposed Texian force might well encounter Mexican bullets and lances on two fronts.

If there had ever been an opportune moment to ride to the rescue of the Alamo, the council decided, that time had passed. Readily persuaded, Fannin ordered his army back to the presidio. Once behind the walls of the venerable structure he had named Fort Defiance, he composed a new message to the council of safety at Gonzales. The terse epistle updated the status of the rescue mission. It was aborted; James Fannin's army had gotten as close to San Antonio as it ever would.

The fiercely cold, blowing norther of the past two days had abated. In its place on Sunday, February 28, came gray skies and a chilly drizzle. Bonham, wrapped in a poncho, kept his horse at a brisk trot. He intended to reach Gonzales by nightfall.

As he rode into a densely wooded creek crossing, the figure of a man stepped out of the brush before him. Both arms were raised and waving, in part to show that neither hand held a weapon. Bonham recognized the man as Albert Martin, the rider Travis had sent to Gonzales with the "Victory or Death" dispatch four days previous.

"Lieutenant Bonham!" Martin greeted him with a rather slipshod salute. "We just wanted t' make sure whoever was comin' was friendly!" As Bonham reined in his horse alongside Martin, more than two dozen Texians began emerging from their brushy hiding places. One of them handed Martin his rifle. They bombarded the horseman with questions about the Alamo.

"We've remained under almost constant bombardment since early Wednesday, and still haven't lost anyone," Bonham reported. But he cut short the cheers with an upraised hand. "The enemy's large cannons are not yet in position. It's our belief that they are still on the road west of the city. When they are finally available to Santa Anna, the Alamo will not long stand."

Martin made a defiant gesture. "Me an' the boys here," he said doggedly, "are a-goin' to th' relief of them that you an' me have left behind." Bonham did not like the way Martin phrased his comment, but he gave no sign of it. Instead, he asked what the prospects were for more volunteers, food, and munitions.

"We ain't waitin' on all that," Martin retorted. "They'se men a-plenty comin' from th' States, but right now everythin's kindly disorganized an' in a hubbub. We can't wait no longer, or th' only help for Travis an' them is gonna be prayer."

Martin noted that the officer currently in charge at Gonzales was Major Williamson of the Rangers. "His headquarters is in my store," the merchant added.

Bonham thanked him, then looked him in the eye. "Save me a spot next to the eighteen-pounder," he said pointedly. "I intend to be back." He saluted the others. "Godspeed, men!" he shouted. "Texas and liberty!"

"Texas and liberty!" they bellowed, as he urged his horse into a trot. The men in Martin's party, all from Gonzales, numbered thirty-two. Every one knew full well that, barring a miracle, their heroic gesture was only going to swell Santa Anna's body count.

Chapter 60

Dusk and James Bonham reached Gonzales at the same hour. The latter had no trouble in locating Martin's general store, which doubled as the local headquarters for the Texian resistance. Upon entering, Bonham was recognized by Williamson, who was seated behind a ramshackle desk.

"Mr. Bonham!" Three-Legged Willie jumped out of his chair and hobbled around the desk, his booted but useless right foot bobbing. There was no charade of military formality as the crippled ranger fairly fell on Bonham in an embrace.

"What's happened, lad? What brings you out of the Alamo? Tell me everything!" exclaimed Williamson. "We've heard nothing new since Martin arrived three days ago. By the way, he and John Smith are on their way back to Bexar with a company of rash souls calling themselves the Gonzales Ranging Company of Mounted Volunteers, or some such thing. Oh, you saw them? Well, talk to me! How are my friend Travis and Bowie and their men holding up?"

The garrison's most pressing needs, Bonham replied, were clothing and ammunition. The ragtag defenders did possess sufficient food at present, he noted, but were resolutely preserving their modest supplies of gunpowder and bullets and had to improvise for cannon shot. At the time of his departure, no Texian had been lost to the ongoing cannonade. Crockett, the born entertainer, continued to do wonders for the men's morale.

Still, Bonham warned, whenever the day of battle arrived, they knew they were not going to be a match for the army amassed at Bexar. "The one thing that will truly lift their spirits," he pointed out, "is the certain knowledge that a sufficiency of reinforcements is on the way.

"Now, Major, if I may be so bold: please enlighten me as to the chances for help. My orders are to determine those prospects as accurately as I can, and relay them immediately to my commander. He says his men deserve to know the truth."

Williamson was silent, his lips pursed, searching for a suitable reply.

"With all due respect, sir," Bonham pressed him, "I'm simply asking the major if the Alamo can expect to receive armed men and supplies in enough numbers to turn the situation around. The Gonzales Mounted Volunteers likely will not, by themselves, make a difference in the outcome."

A spark of anger illumined Williamson's eyes for a heartbeat. But he well understood that James Bonham was no one's fool. "Yes, yes," he insisted, "there are enough—more than enough—men and supplies on their way." The major shrugged, then added, "The vital question becomes, will they be arriving timely? Tonight, I cannot tell you. However, we are no more than a day away, or perhaps two at the most, from knowing the answer."

Williamson told Bonham to take a chair, and resumed his own seat behind the paper-strewn desktop. "General Houston," he said, "has doubtless struck a treaty with the Indians by now, and is due to attend the convention which starts Tuesday at Washington-on-the-Brazos. Ideally, that august body will declare Texas independent of Mexico and move to prescribe a suitable government, all in short order, and send the general on his way to this place.

"But, even prior to his arrival, we should very soon be greeting several hundreds of armed volunteers under the leadership of Colonel Wharton. Equally of importance is our last report received from Goliad—that Colonel Fannin and three hundred of his men have taken up the march to Bexar."

Bonham's open astonishment at this unlikely news prompted a smile from Williamson. "A young man named Johnson, who I believe was first dispatched from the Alamo to Goliad, brought us this welcome intelligence just yesterday," the major asserted.

"Now, Lieutenant," he said, signaling a close to their interview, "if you will be so good as to tarry in Gonzales for the next twenty-four or thirty-six hours, you may have joyous tidings indeed to carry back to colonels Travis and Bowie! I suggest that you avail yourself of some sustenance—beefsteak, perhaps—and then find a place to nap."

The major stood to offer a dismissing handshake, then abruptly stopped himself. "Oh, I nearly forgot, Lieutenant," he said, with a glint in his eye. "Besides yourself, another unexpected caller arrived earlier today and I daresay would like to see you. I have yielded my own sleeping quarters in deference to this visitor, who shall remain nameless."

Bonham stared, mystified, while Williamson summoned an orderly. A boy of about twelve responded, assuming a posture of attentive importance in front of the desk. "Zeke, show the lieutenant to my tent," Williamson ordered the youth. Then, exchanging salutes with the puzzled Bonham, the major bade him a good evening.

Night had fallen. Despite a continuing drizzle, the muggy air was the warmest it had been in a week. Bonham, leading his fatigued mount, fell in behind the barefooted Zeke. They slogged along the muddy street, passing by poorly lit habitations until they reached its terminus at town's edge, then plunged into a shadowy cluster of tents and lean-tos. The orderly pointed to the silhouette of a square-framed canvas hut. "That's it, sir!" he piped proudly. "Major Williamson's quarters!" A light glowed within the translucent cloth walls.

After receiving a coin for his pains, Zeke disappeared, leaving Bonham uncertain as to whether he should enter the tent or first hail the mystery occupant. From out of the darkness there abruptly arose a slim, blanket-wrapped figure bearing a rifle. "Who dat?" the figure demanded tremulously, the voice that of a young black man. "Who go dar?"

"Lieutenant James Butler Bonham," the South Carolinian answered testily. His interrogator breathed an audible sigh of relief and lowered the rifle. "I'm here by invitation of Major Williamson, to—to call on whoever he's given his tent over to," Bonham finished lamely.

"What's going on, Henry? Is something wrong?" The voice emanating from the tent was distinctly feminine and distinctly familiar. Bonham gasped.

The light within glided toward the door of the tent. The

heightened illumination allowed Bonham to distinguish the features of the sentinel. The armed confronter was none other than John Cumings's slave, Henry. "Massa Bonham!" this worthy was clamoring. "You s'pos ter be in de Alamo along wid Massa Travis!"

The flaps of the tent parted. Between them, holding a lantern before her, stood Rebecca Cumings. Even in that uncertain light, her sudden pallor upon recognizing Bonham was evident. One small hand flew to her mouth, and she swayed. Henry hastily rescued the lantern. Bonham stepped forward, slipping a supporting arm around her waist.

"James," Rebecca said, almost in a whisper. She took a long, quavering breath, then cried out, "Praise be to God! I have prayed and prayed that I would get to see at least one of you!"

Her words both thrilled and bewildered Bonham. He briefly savored elation at the inference that he held a place in her heart. But she doubtless also referred to Travis. Was she not aware of Travis's bitter reaction to her soul-baring letter? Had he not let her know his feelings, or was her own love so unwavering that she still clung to hope?

As Rebecca regained her steadiness and composure, Bonham reluctantly withdrew his arm. "How wonderful to see you!" she declared, color returning to her face. Bonham stood in entranced silence. The beauty of the Mill Creek maid seemed to increase each time he saw her.

"Please come in, at least for a few moments! You will, won't you?" she urged. Taking his acquiescence for granted, she turned to Henry. "You may hand the gun to Mr. Bonham," she instructed, "and put his saddle and gear in the major's tent. Then see that his horse is fed and penned up with the others."

After Henry led away the exhausted steed, Rebecca retreated to a cot at the rear of the tent. Bonham partially undid his bedroll and took a seat just inside the flaps, leaning an elbow against his saddle. The flickering lantern sat on the grassy floor between them. The continuous sounds of camp life, oftimes raucous, penetrated the canvas walls.

"I suppose it's not a wise thing to do—entrust a slave with a gun, even in these dreadful times," Rebecca conceded, studying her hands as they lay clasped in her lap. "But Henry was the only one available to come with me. John's been sick with the flu." She paused, then added defensively, "I did assure myself that he was recovering before I left."

The woman looked up at her visitor, and flashed a dimpled smile. The green eyes twinkled. "In all honesty, of course," she confessed, "had John been healthy he would not have allowed me to come here. I didn't exactly ask his permission."

Bonham grinned back. "You may be in for a hard time of it upon your return home, Miss Cumings," he said.

She looked distressed. "Oh, please!" Rebecca protested. "Please call me Rebecca. You are James to me!"

"Very well . . . Rebecca," Bohnam said, savoring the sound of that name in his own voice. "Tell me why you've come to Gonzales. This is a terribly dangerous place for a lady."

Rebecca blushed, as if the question had not been expected. Then, resolute, she produced a small cloth pouch closed with a drawstring. She extended it at arm's length toward Bonham. "The reason for my trip is in here," she answered candidly—almost defiantly. "Would you like to see what it is?"

He arose and accepted the bag. Crouching at her feet, he loosened the string and turned the bag upside-down. Into his cupped hand dropped a man's gold ring, the stone dark and cloudy.

"This appears," Bonham said, upon examining the ring, "to be new." He glanced up at Rebecca, who was again blushing.

"It is new," she said softly. "I purchased it in San Felipe because it reminded me of—of my father's ring, which John has in safekeeping." She came to her feet and stepped past Bonham to the front of the tent. Parting the flaps, she pretended to look out at the drizzling rain.

"This is difficult for me to say," Rebecca began, her back still toward Bonham. "For the past three months, the both of you—you and Buck—have constantly been on my mind. I wrote each of you a half-dozen times, only to tear up what I wrote."

Bonham, eager to hear more, studied the ruddy highlights the lantern flame was finding in her long hair. He watched her shoulders flex as she heaved a sigh and continued.

"You will remember . . . I hope you remember . . . the day that I brought a letter for Buck and you were at his house. I was so worried about—the letter, and you were very kind and attentive and even saw me home that evening. I'll always remember what a wonderful evening it was!"

Bonham's heart leaped.

"I know Buck must have read the letter," she went on. "The reason I am sure"—her voice trembled—"is that I never afterward saw him or heard from him, to this day."

The listener clenched his fists in anger.

"I gave Buck my father's ring as a token of betrothal," Rebecca resumed, sightlessly staring at the rain. "It was in exchange for a silver pin he gave me when . . . when he proposed. My poor mother, in her very last letter, suggested that I make a gift of the ring to my future husband." The pain of recollection was evident in her voice.

"Brother John, who proved to be much wiser than I thought him at the time, acted in the kindest way to put everything on hold. He retrieved our father's ring from Buck, saying that Buck should clear up his affairs in Alabama first. I kept the brooch, but have not worn it since."

Rebecca finally turned and faced Bonham. Her cheeks were streaked with tears.

"I guess I have lost Buck," she said slowly, "because of what happened to me—what I did—years and years ago. I've asked the Lord for forgiveness many, many times. Surely He has forgiven me! But I had to tell Buck. I had to!"

In anguish, Bonham blurted out: "The scriptures say God is faithful to forgive if we confess our sins and repent! In His eyes you are again made pure! What does Buck's opinion, or anyone else's, matter alongside that?"

He instantly regretted his outburst. A look of horror distorted Rebecca's face. "What do you mean? What do you know about me?" she cried.

Bonham threw up his hands. "I did not read your letter," he said hastily, "although admittedly I was present when Buck did. He alone studied it; I myself threw it into the fire afterward!

"I only know this, Rebecca: you are the sweetest, loveliest, most wonderful lady I have ever met, and no mistakes you may ever have made matter to me in the least!"

Rebecca burst into tears. Bonham instinctively gathered her in his arms and gently pressed the auburn head against his shoulder. Sob upon sob wracked the slender body. Her comforter held her close and murmured soothingly in her ear. At this juncture, Henry happened to return. He stuck his dripping, poncho-framed face in between the tent flaps, took a quick glance, and vanished.

The sobbing faded, and Bonham loosed his arms. Rebecca turned away, wiping her face. "I'm sorry," she murmured. Then, before Bonham could offer any consoling words, she whirled around. "James," she said, sniffling, "I have a very large favor to ask of you."

He spread his arms and a gentle smile tugged at his lips, as if to say, "Just name it." Rebecca reached for his right hand, which still clutched the gold ring, and took it from him.

"I must know, beyond a doubt," she said slowly, "how Buck feels about me and about our betrothal. I'm sure he behaved rather badly when he read the letter; I expected nothing else. But until I hear otherwise from him, I must presume that we're still engaged. I know you must think I'm chasing after a lost dream, but really, it's not that at all. I need to know whether I am a free woman."

The green eyes met his, and their message was unmistakable. Never had Bonham wanted to kiss a woman so badly. But she had not finished framing her request.

"If Buck should come out of the Alamo alive," Rebecca said calmly, "I would like for you to present this ring to him and tell him it is from me. If he accepts it, then I am obligated to him. I will not be the one to break off our engagement.

"But should he reject it . . ." She did not finish the sentence. Her eyes narrowed, and her full red lips parted slightly.

This time Bonham did not resist the urge. She met him halfway.

A cold front blew in during the small hours of the night, driving away the rain. At dawn, with its promise of clear skies, Bonham saw Rebecca and Henry off. There was a bittersweet ache in his chest as he watched their carriage bounce along toward the sunrise until it disappeared. Then he went to find Williamson. Bonham intended to present the ring to Travis as requested, but he was not about to wait until the fate of the Alamo had been decided.

Chapter 61

*T*ravis's "Victory or Death" missive didn't immediately produce an army, but it did engender a lot of similarly colored prose. On February 27 a certain gathering of Texians was collectively energized to issue the following:

TO OUR FELLOW CITIZENS

The undersigned a committee appointed by a meeting held in the town of San Felipe, on this day, present you with the accompanying letter from the commandant of Bejar. You must read and act in the same moment, or Texas is lost. You must rise from your lethargy, and march without a moment's delay to the field of war, or the next western breeze that sweeps out your habitations, will bring with it the shrieks and wailings of women and children of Guadalupe and Colorado; and the last agonized shriek of liberty will follow. Citizens of the Colorado and Brazos, your country is invaded—your homes are about to be pillaged, your families destroyed, yourselves to be enslaved; and you must one and all repair to the field of war, or prepare to abandon your country. Ere this information shall be generally circulated, the blood of many of our citizens will have crimsoned the soil; and the soul of many a devoted patriot flown to Heaven.

Inhabitants of the east, your fellow citizens of the west are in danger. Of themselves, they cannot resist the foe; we appeal to your magnanimity; we implore you for succor, and we earnestly entreat that your succor might be speedy. Unless it is, Texas and her citizens, and her liberties, and her homes, are forever gone.

As for ourselves, we will abandon the contest only with our lives, and then earnestly appeal to all, every one to do his duty to his country, and leave the consequence to God . . .

On Thursday, March 3, at about eleven in the morning, James Bonham once again entered the hastily opened gates of the Alamo. Though certainly observed, horse and rider did not draw any fire during their dash past the Mexican pickets. Perhaps the enemy saw little harm in allowing one more Texian to enter the doomed fortress.

The rider bore two dispatches for Travis, messages from Williamson and the interim governor Robinson. Both promised all kinds of succor if only the besieged garrison could sustain itself a while longer. But of solid information on which to build real hope, the expresses contained very little.

Travis actually learned all that was important by studying the face of Bonham as the latter came up and saluted. "Dispatches from Major Williamson in Gonzales, sir," the courier reported.

The colonel took them, then invited Bonham to accompany him to his quarters. When they entered, the slave Joe jumped up as though to leave. "That's all right, Joe," his master said kindly. "There will be no secrets from you. You're in this just like the rest of us."

Bonham was impressed. The man whose presence he now found himself in was not the same Buck Travis he had left five days before—not, in truth, the same Buck Travis with whom he had been raised. There was a somber light in the Alabaman's gray eyes, but Bonham also detected a new strength and clarity of purpose. Maturity apparently had arrived all in a rush, and Travis was the greater for it.

Not that his jaw had lost its determined jut. The commander of the Alamo would concede nothing to the inevitable. The Mexicans would have to earn their victory.

A smile flickered across the lips of Travis as he read the emotional message from his longtime friend Williamson. The latter wrote that Fannin was on his way to Bexar with three hundred men, and that as many more Americans would soon be in Gonzales. "For God's sake, hold out until we can help you," the major pleaded in his postscript.

Having read them twice, the second time out loud, Travis folded the dispatches and stuck them in his jacket pocket. "Poor Willie," he murmured. "All he could send to help us were his words." He looked at Bonham. "I don't suppose, James, that Fannin has actually left La Bahia," he said, more as a statement than as a question. "How likely are we to actually see reinforcements from either Goliad or Gonzales, or from anyplace else?"

"Major Williamson has tried his best to be reassuring, sir," came the respectful, matter-of-fact reply. "If you're asking my opinion, sir, I really hold out no hope. There are men gathering in Gonzales, but not nearly enough, and they're not organized or trained. Everyone seems to be waiting on General Houston.

"As for Colonel Fannin, when I left Gonzales I took a southwesterly tack until I reached the La Bahia road. There were no signs of his army or any other along the road. That's all I have to report, sir."

"Drop the 'sir' stuff, James, while we're in my quarters," Travis said bluntly. "Life is going to be far too short for any more of that between us. And, by the way, why the hell are you here? I thought I made it clear enough I didn't want you back in this death trap."

"Beggin' the colonel's pardon," Bonham replied, one corner of his mouth tilting in a sly smile, "but there wasn't anyone else I trusted to bring you word." The smile faded. "You deserved to know the truth, Buck, and Willie was afraid to write it. Someone owed it to these men. Besides, I told Martin to save me a place alongside the eighteen-pounder."

Travis swallowed, ducked his head, and slapped Bonham fondly on the shoulder. Then he looked his kinsman in the eyes. "While you were gone," he said slowly, "I kind of found myself in the pit. That's where a man has to go, sometimes, to sort out what's really important.

"I've made my peace with the Lord, James, and death holds no fear for me. I only regret it for the men—most especially Captain Dickinson, because of his wife and baby girl being here with him. And yet, in a way, maybe he's lucky. The rest of them won't see their loved ones again on this side of Paradise."

Bonham took that comment as a divinely directed prompt. Fishing in his pocket, he pulled out a small cloth bag. He offered the pouch to Travis, who studied it questioningly. "This was waiting for you at Gonzales," Bonham announced.

As Travis loosened the neck of the bag, Bonham explained, "Miss Cumings was there. She asked that this be delivered to you." He held his breath.

No reaction could have surprised Bonham more than the one he witnessed. Upon the mention of Rebecca, Travis's eyes flashed lightning-quick at the speaker. Just as quickly, they were averted. Then he took a rather melancholy look at the gold ring cupped in his palm. His expression hinted at something—regret? disappointment?—which Bonham could not decipher. But there was no display of temper. No angry arrogance, no piqued pride animated him.

Neither, though, did Travis place the ring on his hand. Instead, he pocketed it without a word. Baffled, and also nettled by an unwonted throb of dismay, Bonham made his excuses and left the room.

The commander went over to his desk, seated himself, and prepared to write. "Joe," he instructed, "go find John Smith and tell him I'm sending him out tonight with expresses from me, as well as any the garrison might have. We'll notify him when mine are ready."

Within the hour, there came a knock at Travis's doorway. "Come in!" barked the Alabaman, laying down his quill pen and glancing over his shoulder.

The caller was Bonham. "Word has gotten around," he said, "that you're sending Smith out tonight, and that he will carry letters for any who wish him to."

Bonham produced a single sheet of paper, folded and sealed. "I wrote this while on the trail, coming back from Gonzales," he said. "Now may be the last opportunity to send it on its way." He tossed the letter onto the desk in front of his kinsman.

It struck Travis as odd that Bonham would bring the letter to him, rather than simply hand it to Smith. Then he noticed the address: "R. Cumings, Mill Creek."

His mouth opened in surprise, and he quickly turned his head. Bonham was already passing through the doorway. Speechless, Travis watched him go. For a long time, he stared at the blob of red wax bearing the imprint of Bonham's signet ring.

Finally, Travis picked up the pen again and started a lengthy missive to Jesse Grimes, a client and friend who lived above Mill Creek. "Do me the favor," he wrote, "to send the enclosed to its proper destination instantly . . ."

Eyes straining in the wan, flickering illumination from a single candle, he completed the letter to Grimes. Promptly, he took up another piece of paper for one last note. This was addressed to David Ayers at Montville.

"Take care of my little boy," he wrote. "If the country should be saved, I may make for him a splendid fortune; but if the country be lost and I should perish, he will have nothing but the proud recollection that he is the son of a man who died for his country."

Early on the morning of March 5, Gen. Antonio Lopez de Santa Anna held council with his officers. It was time, His Excellency argued, to attack the Alamo. Customarily, his arguments carried the weight of an edict.

For the most part, the officers—better soldiers and tacticians than he—were dismayed. A couple of the small field pieces had finally been worked close enough to the old mission for their shelling to take effect. The weak north wall would soon collapse. In two days they expected to have the big cannon available to pound the other walls into rubble from a safe distance. The Texians were running low on food. They ultimately must capitulate or starve, eliminating any necessity for storming the fortress.

El Presidente, though, sought glory. That took bloodshed, a victory earned in battle. Santa Anna issued orders placing nearly two thousand of the Mexican army's crack troops on readiness for a predawn attack on the morrow.

Late in the afternoon, a lull occurred in the ceaseless bombardment of the Alamo. Perhaps sensing the calm before the final storm, Travis chose this time to assemble his motley force in the plaza. The dozen men bedridden by sickness, including the terminal Bowie, were brought on their cots into the open air. The young commander aligned the hundred and seventy or so able-bodied defenders shoulder to shoulder in a long, single rank and then faced them.

Travis at first seemed to be wrestling with his emotions. Finally, he summoned his control and oratorical skill.

"My brave companions," he began, "I wish there to be no further doubts. Our fate is sealed." All eyes were on the Alabaman as he flourished the dispatches from Williamson and Robinson. "I have deceived you at length by the promise that help was on the way. In doing so, I have also been deceiving myself, having first been deceived by others."

He held up the folded messages and shook them. "I have received the strongest assurances of help from our friends—assurances that our people were ready, willing, and anxious to come to our relief. In the honest and simple confidence of my heart, I have been relaying to you these promises and my own hopes. But the promised help has not come and our hopes are not to be realized."

To the extent any of those assembled felt dismay, they kept it well hidden. Rather, Travis saw in the eyes of his men only a simple gratitude for this honest confirmation of what they had already concluded.

He stuffed the dispatches into his jacket and continued. "I placed too much confidence in the promises of our friends. But let us not judge them too harshly. They intended to be ready for the invader when he was expected, later in the spring. The invader struck much earlier than anyone anticipated, and surprised us. Our friends did not learn of our situation in time to save us.

"There will be no help, for no force of the size we could reasonably expect would be able to cut its way through the strong ranks of the despot's army. We dare not surrender, for the despot has announced that we are rebels to be put to the sword. Any attempt to fight our way out would only result in our lives being sold far too cheaply. Nothing else makes sense, then, but to stay within the fort and fight to the last man."

The gray eyes blazed. The Roman nostrils flared. The chin became like granite.

"Our choice is not of life or death, but rather the manner of our death. My own choice is to remain within this fort, to resist every assault, and to sell my life as dearly as possible.

"But I leave every man to his own choice. Should any man prefer to surrender, or attempt an escape, he is at liberty to do so. As long as breath remains in my body, I will stand and fight—even if you leave me alone. Do as you think best, though every man who stays to die with me will afford me comfort at the moment of death."

As Travis paused, the silence in the mission plaza grew so profound that the distant careless laughter of Mexican pickets floated in on the evening air. The young commander stepped briskly to one end of the row of soldiers, drew his sword, and with the point pierced the packed caliche of the plaza floor. He slowly dragged the tip through the dirt, tracing a line before one hundred and seventy pairs of feet—many of them bare.

Returning his sword to its sheath, Travis resumed his former position in front of his men. "Every man who is determined to die with me," he declared, "must step over the line!"

In the space of a heartbeat, Tapley Holland stepped forward. The son of one of Austin's first colonists, young Holland unknowingly answered Fannin's accusation that the old guard would not spill its blood for Texas.

The other able-bodied men swiftly followed, with a single exception. Frenchman Moses Rose, a companion of Bowie from Nacogdoches, sank to his knees in apparent prayer. Then he stood and turned away from the line. Bowie, not far distant, called out to Rose from his cot.

"I am not ready to die," Rose said to him, "and will not do so if I can help it." Bowie lowered his head, either in disappointment or in pain, and a couple of men lifted his cot across the line. After dark, Rose bagged his simple belongings and exited the mission through a window.

Travis felt a burden lifted from him. He had shared the brutal truth with the men of his commend, and they had chosen to stay with him and fight to the death. True, surrender was certainly no option; attempted escape offered only the slenderest of hopes, though the dark-complexioned, Spanish-speaking Rose might have a better chance than most. Still, the resolve of the garrison had been demonstrated almost to the last man.

After seeing to it that the pickets were on duty, Travis went to his quarters. Then, in a fit of restlessness, he reentered the plaza and wandered over to the chapel. Within this spiritual and physical refuge huddled a handful of noncombatants: women and children, including Almaron Dickinson's fifteen-year-old wife, Susanna, and fifteen-month-old daughter, Angelina.

Little Angelina was making a tired toddler's unhappy noises. Her cries touched Travis, resurrecting as they did warm memories, suddenly grown poignant, of Charles Edward at that same age. On impulse, he retrieved the gold ring from his pocket, slipped a piece of string through it, and tied the ends together. He placed the makeshift toy around the neck of the child, whose fussiness evaporated in favor of a drooling grin as she clutched the ring with one small, grimy fist. The commander watched with satisfaction for a moment or two, then strolled away, leaving his gift. Susanna Dickinson called out a belated thank-you as he departed the chapel.

During the night, the enemy assembled in four large columns. In the early morning hours, they moved as quietly as possible to take positions on every side of the retangular mission compound. The bone-tired Texian pickets proved to be easy prey for their dagger-wielding stalkers. The slumbering garrison would have no advance warning of the Mexican attack.

A spectral, cloud-shrouded moon hung in the western sky, aiding Santa Anna's forces as they stealthily closed in on the Alamo in the final hour before dawn. Inside, adjutant John Baugh, the only man awake and on duty, was routinely making his rounds. Suddenly, there came to his startled ears the shouts of Mexican soldiers prematurely breaking their silence with fervent cries of *"Viva!"* Infuriated by this gross stupidity, Santa Anna ordered the assault to commence.

With mounted lancers in readiness behind them, fifteen hundred foot soldiers charged the mission walls. As bugles blared literally from all directions, Baugh raced across the plaza, shouting an alarm at the top of his lungs. Travis awoke instantly and grabbed a shotgun and his sword. Followed by Joe, who was armed with a pistol, the commander made for the strategically vital north wall. "Come on, boys!" Travis bellowed as the defenders abruptly stirred. "The Mexicans are upon us! Let's give 'em hell!"

Bonham came to his feet, bleary-eyed, and lurched into the cold, predawn air of the courtyard. His boots crunched against the packed earth as he ran through ghostly moonlight toward the massive, black shape of the eighteen-pound cannon squatting at one corner of the plaza. The compound had come alive with men rushing to their posts, desperate fighters determined to resist every assault that they could and sell their lives "as dearly as possible."

Chapter 62

On March 2, 1836, the Texian convention at Washington-on-the-Brazos voted in favor of declaring independence from Mexico. Four days later, on the morning the Alamo fell, Sam Houston departed the convention for Gonzales. He had been equipped with all the paper authority he needed to command the regular army and volunteers alike.

The task facing Houston was a daunting one, which could have been the reason it took him five days to get to his destination. The rumor later circulated that he stopped for a couple of days at a remote trading post, where he became drunk and indulged himself in a denial of the Alamo's plight.

Reality asserted itself shortly after the commander-in-chief finally reached Gonzales. Texian scout Erastus "Deaf" Smith encountered the forlorn contingent of Alamo survivors on the Bexar road and escorted them into Houston's presence. There, Susanna Dickinson and Travis's slave, Joe, gave accounts of the garrison's annihilation and repeated Santa Anna's vow to purge Texas of all "foreign" presence.

Because at least one in every four Texians slain at the Alamo had come from the vicinity of Gonzales, the town's inhabitants were thrown into mourning and despair. Panic, too, quickly set in. Was the bloodthirsty tyrant already en route to plunder the village and exterminate its people?

Among the men gathered in Gonzales for the purpose of fighting, the prevailing emotion was rage rather than fear. But Houston had already decided that the elements ostensibly under his command were far too raw and undisciplined for a major confrontation. After helping the townspeople with their exodus, the Tennessean directed his reluctant army on an easterly retreat to the Colorado River. Houston sent a message to Fannin, informing him of the Alamo's fall and ordering him to abandon Goliad and fall back eastward to Victoria.

Fannin, though, once again allowed circumstances to stymie him. Instead of immediately following orders, he chose to wait for the return of two detachments sent earlier to Refugio. But they would not be back. Those men, like the ill-fated Texians at San Patricio and Agua Dulce Creek before them, ran afoul of the advancing army of General Urrea and were routed with heavy losses.

Belatedly, Fannin and his four hundred men withdrew from the presidio and headed toward Victoria. The star-crossed colonel was soon caught by Urrea in the open prairie, where—all things considered—the rebels offered a good account of themselves. But they were effectively pinned down with no avenue of escape, and their situation became exacerbated due to lack of water. Fannin surrendered under what he believed (or chose to believe) were terms of mercy from Urrea, and his men returned to Goliad as prisoners of war. The West Point dropout could not know that Urrea, in his sweep of the Gulf Coast, had been executing Texian prisoners as ordered by *El Presidente.*

Among the new captives was Seth Swearingen.

Since January, Seth had been expecting to meet up with the Kentucky cousins who were so intent on adding their rifles to the Texian cause. Logic dictated that they would land at Copano Bay, below Goliad, as had a number of adventurers from the United States. It was equally plausible, then, that Goliad would be their next stop.

So Swearingen joined the garrison at Goliad and began a fruitless wait. His kinfolk still had not shown themselves as of March 19, when he participated in the short-lived march toward Victoria and subsequent encounter with Urrea's army.

All during the week following their surrender, Fannin's men talked among themselves of imminent release: of being placed on American-bound ships at Copano, or marched to the Sabine River. Early on Palm Sunday, March 27, the able-bodied prisoners were roused and escorted out of their former fortress under heavy guard.

They appeared to be headed south toward Copano, and some began rejoicing openly with song.

Then, methodically, the four hundred of them were split up into three groups of roughly equal numbers and herded off the road in different directions.

Seth had casually noted, as the Texians were being removed from the presidio, the sorrowful faces of the Mexican women they passed. When the separation of the prisoners took place, he grew curious but not yet alarmed. Shortly, however, the rebels' high hopes turned into consternation; each group was halted some distance from the presidio and ordered to kneel.

Seth happened to be on the periphery of his group. He heard and understood the order to kneel; he concluded, of a sudden, that the captives' fate had been decided. A quick study of the agitated features of the little soldier nearest him supported this terrible conclusion.

In unison, the Mexicans stepped away from the cluster of suddenly clamoring prisoners, none of whom had knelt. As the *soldados* turned about and took aim with their muskets, awaiting the order to fire, a few of the captives who at last understood did sink to their knees. Seth and many others took action born of desperation.

The big man moved with the speed and urgency required of the moment. He took two bounding strides and lunged, grabbing the closest musket barrel and wresting it from the grasp of the stunned holder. With head lowered, Swearingen charged bull-like through the line of *soldados* in the direction of the nearby San Antonio River. Simultaneously, there came the deafening roar of many guns fired at once, followed by the screams and groans of Seth's comrades. Several others also dashed through the wall of executioners and ran pell-mell down the brushy slope toward the river.

A mounted lancer, musket raised, stood between them and the beckoning stream; the man's hesitation over which fleeing Texian to shoot proved unfortunate for him. Like lightning, Seth threw his seized weapon to his shoulder and fired. The lancer reeled, grabbed at his chest, and slumped against the neck of his horse. Seth yanked him out of the saddle, scooped up the undischarged musket, and vaulted onto the mustang.

Only then, and very briefly, did he steal a glimpse at the terrible sight behind him. What he witnessed, partially obscured by a thick cloud of expended gunpowder, would stay with him for a lifetime. The prone bodies of the massacred prisoners lay intertwined; some of their executioners were reloading while others moved among the fallen, finishing off with thrusts of bayonet and knife those not slain outright. A scattering of fleeing Texians were being pursued in a match of their foot speed against that of the Mexican mounts.

Swearingen assumed that the same butchery was being played out simultaneously at two other sites. He gritted his teeth and blotted out the thought, keenly aware that any hope of survival depended on quick, clear thinking. He punched the mustang viciously with his bare heels, gained the road to Copano and turned south, crouching low to offer as small a target of his huge body as possible.

"I'll never understand," Swearingen would say, years later, "why God allowed so many t' die that day an' yet He spared me." He earnestly credited his escape to divine intervention.

Fully a hundred pounds heavier than almost any man in the Mexican army, Swearingen gloomily figured that his steed could not long outrun those of the lancers. Shots were fired at him as he galloped away, but the confusion immediately following the slaughter did not allow for any organized pursuit and permitted him to disappear into the brush and live oaks of a creek bottom.

There he momentarily reined in, frantically trying to decide which direction to take, and whether to continue his flight on horseback or on foot. A new volley of gunshots erupted from the direction of the presidio. Swearingen could only surmise that one of the three mass executions had been slow to take place. He did not learn until much later that this last round of shooting represented the murders of the sick and wounded Texians still within the presidio.

Two men, one white and one black, stood in a cold, misty rain on the front step of the inn at Mill Creek. The white man, whose right leg was grotesquely bent back at the knee, knocked impatiently with the head of his walking cane. The black man waited a step further away from the door, his hatless head bowed in accustomed subservience.

"Hold on, Major!" cried the voice of John Cumings from

within. The callers heard the sound of a bar being withdrawn, and the door was flung open.

"Step youself in, Major Williamson," John invited. "I had t' take a peek through th' window to see who it was," he added, apologetically. "Can't be too careful, nowadays."

Williamson beckoned to the black man to follow him in. Turning to John, he said, "This is—was—Colonel Travis's boy, Joe. He was with his master at the Alamo, and stepped up and conducted himself like a man on the final day. He's alive only because Santa Anna entertains a notion of inciting the Texas Negroes against their masters on the promise of freedom."

John took them before a robust fire. "You're certainly prudent, Mr. Cumings, to be wary of travelers," Williamson concurred, accepting a steaming mug of coffee. "The truth is, you are the first person we've found at home since leaving San Felipe this morning. The people, most especially in the lower country, have packed up their belongings and are headed in haste for the Sabine, fearing else that they will fall prey to the blood lust of the Mexican tyrant. We were delighted to see the smoke from your chimney."

As he handed Joe a helping of coffee, Cumings asked for the latest war news. By way of a response, Three-Legged Willie explained that he bore expresses from General Houston to David Burnet, ad interim president of the newly declared republic. He expected, he said, to find Burnet and members of the cabinet upriver at Groce's plantation, temporarily ensconced there while on the way from Washington-on-the-Brazos to greater safety at Harrisburg.

"I suppose I am relegated to being General Houston's messenger boy," Williamson added ruefully. "I cannot agree with his headlong retreat, and in expressing that opinion I have fallen from favor.

"The Texas army is soon to reach the Colorado at Beeson's Crossing, and I pray that the general will find the fortitude to turn and fight at that most advantageous position. Otherwise, should he continue his present tactic, the most populated portions of the republic will be left unprotected from the tyrant's mercies—that is, those remnants of the populace who have not already fled.

"Joe, here, was not only an eyewitness to the fall of the Alamo, but was also treated by Santa Anna to a parade of the Mexican military might. This was done in order to impress upon him, and there-fore upon others of us, His Excellency's omnipotence. Joe will tes-tify before the president and the cabinet as to all that he observed in Bexar before his release."

The major glanced at the slave, who nursed his coffee in silence. "Joe saw some terrible things the morning the Alamo was stormed," Williamson said solemnly. "He stood shoulder to shoul-der with his master on the wall, pistol in hand, as the enemy with the aid of scaling ladders attempted to swarm over. He saw his mas-ter take a fatal bullet to the head, in the first moments of the attack. At that point, perhaps feeling a little lost as to what to do next, he reloaded his master's pistol and retreated inside the barracks."

Williamson beat the brass tip of his cane against the wooden floor. "Our men gave a most heroic account of themselves," he declared, "and reliable reports indicate that the enemy lost three or four men to every one of ours."

The major's brow clouded. "After it was all over," he resumed, "Joe saw what had happened to Colonel Bowie and the other sick and wounded in the infirmary. They were murdered in their beds. That same day, he saw the Mexicans strip our dead of all belongings and toss their stiffening bodies onto heaps of firewood, and set them afire. Joe insists he will never forget the odor from those funeral pyres."

John absorbed this information, most of which was either new to him or, at least, not previously verified. Then he inquired as to the whereabouts of Fannin's army. He was aware from talking to Swearingen's sister that Seth had joined the garrison at Goliad.

"Colonel Fannin was ordered to abandon Fort Defiance at La Bahia and fall back to Victoria," the major answered. "I can only suppose he is on the march. However, I have been grievously wrong about him before. He is, I fear, notorious for his indecision."

Conversation lulled for a time, each man reflecting on the gloomy situation. Then Williamson took up a different subject.

"How's your health, John?" he inquired. "You appear robust enough . . . you must be recovering. I saw Miss Rebecca when she was in Gonzales," he added, by way of explanation, "and she said you had contracted the flu."

"That's true, I was pretty sick," John replied with an edge to his voice. "Otherwise, you wouldn't a-seen her. The little scamp took Henry an' made off without me knowin' it. At present, though," he added worriedly, lowering his voice, "I'm doin' lots better than she is."

Williamson raised an eyebrow.

"As you might well expect," John elaborated, "she took th' news about th' Alamo hard—real hard. She's in bed now. She's been there awhile, runnin' a fever off an' on, and eatin' very little. All our doctors are off with th' army, an' Hannah an' I are just doin' the best we can by her."

The major started to express his sympathy and concern when he saw that his host was struggling with an urge to say something more, presumably about his stricken sister. What emerged, though, seemed to be an entirely irrelevant question.

"Tell me, Major," John asked, "is it for certain that James Bonham was killed in the Alamo along with the others? That's the story, but is there anyone who can say?"

Solemnly, Williamson nodded at the slave. "You saw his body shortly after the battle, Joe, isn't that right?"

Joe nodded. "Yes suh," he responded, matter-of-factly. "I seen Mastah Bonham layin' by de big cannon at de wall."

John hung his head and sighed. "Well," he muttered, "that's one more forlorn hope she can't entertain anymore."

Chapter 63

*A*lthough battle at first seemed imminent, Sam Houston finally chose not to fight at the crossing on the Colorado. The Texians were encamped on the east side of the river when an advance force of the Mexican army arrived from the west. Spring rains had swollen and quickened the stream, prohibiting passage. The opposing camps thus stayed close but separated for a week, the rebel troops almost hourly anticipating orders to attack the foe despite the perilous condition of the river.

Then Houston learned of Fannin's aborted retreat and surrender, and the general—aware that his army had become the sole hope of Anglo Texas—ordered a march eastward to San Felipe. "This army has but one fight in it," he wrote an acquaintance, "and the time and place of that fight must be carefully chosen." Houston also believed that the closer to the Sabine he could entice Santa Anna, the greater were the chances of receiving either official or unofficial U.S. military help.

Disgruntled, most of the men nevertheless obeyed his command; however, deserters began trickling away. If Houston wasn't going to fight, they reasoned, they might as well go home and see to the protection of families and property.

The ragged army soon reached San Felipe on the west bank of the Brazos, the one-time colonial capital now all but deserted by its fleeing citizenry. Murmuring among subordinate officers soon erupted into open disdain—even defiance.

This was because the general again refused to make a stand. Although the Mexican army was still checked at the Colorado (and would be for another week), Houston after a single night in San Felipe ordered his army to move north toward Mill Creek. Captains Moseley Baker and Wyly Martin flatly refused to accompany him further. With a shrug, Houston instructed Baker and his company to hold the San Felipe crossing against enemy use and sent Martin south to Thompson's Crossing at Fort Bend for the same purpose.

A torrential rain fell as the army struggled through the flood-prone bottomlands below Mill Creek. Once across the creek, Houston established camp for the night. He sent men to Cumings's mill, three miles distant, for whatever foodstuffs might be available. This request yielded three dozen bags of corn meal.

Meanwhile, Baker aided the evacuation of a few straggling families out of San Felipe, then ferried his small band across the river and, despite an extended downpour, began felling trees and digging trenches on the east bank.

The rain abated overnight, and the next day dawned clear. That afternoon, from Mill Creek, John Cumings saw black clouds collecting against the southern sky. He knew that such massive amounts of smoke could represent nothing other than the torching of San Felipe. The soldiers from Houston's camp, come to collect the corn meal, had told John that the Mexicans were still crouched on the far side of the flooded Colorado. What, then, had prompted the burning of Austin's town? The former empresario, currently touring the United States in search of financial support for the rebellion, would certainly be heartbroken by the loss.

For three days, while the currents of the Brazos raged and Mill Creek spread itself out for miles, John could only speculate as to the reason for—and extent of—the fire. Finally, the creek subsided enough to cross. Arming himself with rifle and Bowie knife, he saddled his horse and set out to satisfy his curiosity.

When John reached San Felipe, only the burnt-out shells of its numerous frame buildings still stood. The hotels, the dry goods stores, the blacksmith shop—all were in ashes. As he rode in saddened bewilderment through the black, skeletal remains, the buzz of voices amid sounds of general activity came drifting over the river.

John approached the ferry landing with caution. He saw, on the far shore, some forty men laboring to strengthen the rude breastworks already in place. They were Texians. He cupped his hands and hallooed; sentinels had already spotted him, and the ferry was soon being reeled over to the town side by mule power.

"Nice o' you t' get us a ride, John," boomed a familiar voice from behind. With a start, Cumings twisted around in the saddle and found himself face to face with Swearingen.

"Seth!" John exclaimed, and stuck out his hand. "Man, it's good t' see you!" His brow wrinkled. "Weren't you with Colonel Fannin at La Bahia?" he asked. "I thought Fannin's army had surrendered to th' Mexicans. How come you t' be here?"

As John spoke, he ran his eyes over the man and his mount. The latter was a mustang; judging from the saddle and bridle, and from the styling of mane and tail, the beast had seen service in the Mexican army. Swearingen, appearing far too large for the horse, was barefoot and hatless. His hair and beard were long and tangled, his eyes bloodshot, and his clothes in tatters. He was carrying a Mexican musket.

"It's a long story, John," rumbled Seth. "No offense, but I don't feel like tellin' it more'n once. So let's save it 'til we get 'crost the river and find th' commandin' officer."

Within the hour, John heard Seth's horrific story as narrated to Moseley Baker and his subalterns. He fully understood why the big man did not want to retell it. When Seth's narrative reached the events of Palm Sunday morning, his voice cracked and he angrily wiped his teary eyes with a huge, hairy hand.

The effect on the audience was profound. Baker turned red in the face and began clenching his fists. Others swore sharply and shook their heads in disbelief. They knew, of course, about Fannin's surrender, but Seth was the first to bring them word of its cruel sequel.

"It's like I've been tellin' you, men," Baker declared. "We're in a war of extermination—them or us. The only difference is, we'll never do prisoners of war that way. Never!"

"Well, then," one of his officers sneered, "the answer t' that is, just don't bother t' take no prisoners."

Baker did not respond. Instead, he turned to Seth. "Go ahead with your story, Mr. Swearingen," he instructed.

There was not much left to tell. Once free of pursuit, the Kentuckian had ridden from one protective island of trees to another, methodically working his way north and east. He had been extremely lucky not to encounter the enemy. His bedraggled appearance and his steed's rigging would have left little to the imagination.

"I hadn't rid into San Felipe maybe twenty minutes before old John here showed up," Seth concluded. "I was a bit more bashful than him 'bout callin' attention to myself 'til I knowed for sure just who was who."

"By the way, Captain," John interjected politely, "I came down from Mill Creek t' find out why San Felipe was set afire."

Baker barked an oath. "Yeah, that there across th' river is a beautiful sight, ain't it?" he asked sarcastically. "I don't know who to blame th' most for that, General Houston or our durned skittish scouts.

"When Cap'n Martin an' I wouldn't follow him anymore, the general ordered me to protect this crossin' and sent Martin down to Fort Bend. He also left word t' burn th' town as soon as th' enemy was at hand. Well, just after we got all th' civilians out, two of my scouts came ridin' in, yellin' that th' Meskins were within a few miles of here. Naturally, we burned everything to th' ground. And we haven't seen hide nor hair of those brown-skinned devils yet."

Something between a moan and a roar rumbled deep within Seth's throat. The sound chilled John's blood. Woe be to any Santanista, he thought, who might happen to fall into Swearingen's clutches.

Leaving Mill Creek, Sam Houston led his men north on a grueling trek through swampy country to a secluded spot on the river opposite Groce's landing. There, for a fortnight, the big Tennessean proceeded to shape his charges into the semblance of an army. "I'll have each one of you ready and able to whip ten Mexicans," he promised them.

But dissension continued to boil. Toward the close of this boot camp, there came reverberating up the Brazos the faint but unmistakable sound of cannon fire. The men knew that the ordnance had to belong to the enemy, and was doubtless trained on Baker's rear guard twenty miles below. Houston's officers repeatedly urged him to send reinforcements, but he refused.

John and Seth were still in Baker's camp when the Mexican army finally did arrive at San Felipe. Thoughtfully, the rebels had removed all of the boats to their side of the river. The enemy's small cannon soon began peppering the rebel fortifications with grape-shot, but the Texians suffered only one fatality and otherwise minor injuries. Neither side ventured within accurate rifle range of the other, except when the Santanistas briefly attempted to construct rafts at the river's edge. Hot Texian gunfire soon halted the project.

The Mexicans, with His Excellency at their head, were stymied. Baker refused to budge, and they could not find a nearby spot up or down the swirling river suitable for fording. Finally, the impatient Santa Anna led seven hundred men downstream, all the way to Fort Bend. There a party of them managed to cross the Brazos in a boat and surprise and chase off Martin's small force.

While pausing at Fort Bend in order to regroup, *El Presidente* learned of the hasty retreat being conducted by the leadership of the rebel republic—including his old antagonist Lorenzo de Zavala, now vice president of Texas. The insurgent officials were reportedly moving in the direction of Harrisburg.

Eagerly, Santa Anna dismissed for the moment the problem of Houston's motley band and initiated a hurried march toward Harrisburg. He planned to intercept, capture, and hang de Zavala, President Burnet, and the others. Then the Napoleon of the West would gather up the centralist forces amassing at Fort Bend and search out and exterminate the so-called Texian army.

Once the last of the enemy had abandoned San Felipe at the summons of Santa Anna, Baker claimed a victory and likewise withdrew. Despite his differences with Houston, he next took his company upstream to rejoin the main army.

John and Seth headed for Mill Creek. They figured correctly that, once across the Brazos, Santa Anna would continue moving toward Harrisburg (and away from Mill Creek) in pursuit of the Texian cabinet. Swearingen was going to collect his mother and sister and leave them at the inn with John. Then Seth intended to cast his lot with Houston—or, as he quipped, "whoever is leadin' th' army when they finally turn an' fight."

John felt duty-bound to remain at home because of Rebecca's illness, and he welcomed the prospect of the Swearingen women being on hand to help nurse her. To him, packing up Rebecca and sending her to the Sabine in the care of slaves was not an option. The weather continued cold and wet, and the rigors of overland travel in such adverse elements could prove fatal to one already so ill.

As John and Seth drew near the inn, they spotted Henry moving about in the family graveyard. It quickly became apparent that the young slave was in the process of erecting two large, wooden crosses where no graves existed. In consternation, John rushed up to him and demanded to know what he was doing.

"Miz Becky ast me ter make 'em fer her," responded Henry, reluctant to elaborate. John gruffly pressed him for more information. "She tol' me ter put 'em up in de grabeyahd," Henry continued, "right heah wif yo' mama an' brudduhs." He swallowed and added: "She say dey fo' Mastuh Buck and Mastuh James, who wuz kil' at de Alamo. Miz Becky, she not doin' so good, Mastuh John."

Swearingen turned an anguished face toward the inn, eyeing the bedroom window he knew to be Rebecca's. The woman he still loved lay within, her mind wandering, her body emaciated from fever and lack of food. And there was absolutely nothing he could do to help.

Pondering the motivation behind the crosses, Seth suddenly suffered sour thoughts. A memorial for Travis he could grudgingly understand. But, inexplicably, the newcomer James Bonham had likewise reached out from the grave to claim a share of Rebecca's heart. Unbidden, the question invaded Seth's mind: how many other men may have tasted her love?

If I am killed in this revolution, Seth wondered bitterly, *will she turn her thoughts to me as well? Will there be yet another cross planted in the graveyard?*

Spanish moss hung in long, gray strands from the stately pecan and oak trees, deepening the shadows of afternoon within the grove where the Texian army was encamped. Three-quarters of a mile away, on the opposite side of the marshy, humpbacked plain of San Jacinto, Santa Anna and his troops were resting themselves for an anticipated battle with the rebels on the morrow.

Buffalo Bayou ran behind the Texians' wooded campsite and then joined the San Jacinto River to form a wide peninsula upon which the adversaries squatted. Retreat would present severe difficulties for either army; neither side, however, was considering any eventuality except combat.

In his zeal to apprehend de Zavala, Burnet, and their cohorts, Santa Anna had foolishly rushed away from the main body of his army with only seven hundred men. It proved to be a fruitless effort, too, except for the lukewarm satisfaction of burning down the Anglo settlements of Harrisburg and New Washington. The rebel officials had made good their escape from the mainland to Galveston Island.

Approaching the ashes of Harrisburg from the north, Houston's army suddenly found itself following Santa Anna into the treacherous coastal marsh country. The Mexicans soon became aware of the Texian presence. On April 20 both armies came to a halt at San Jacinto and prepared for battle. In fact, they conducted an inconclusive skirmish that afternoon involving cavalry and artillery.

Houston had fewer than nine hundred able-bodied men, yet initially held the numerical edge. That advantage evaporated with the morning mists on April 21, when His Excellency's brother-in-law Cos and more than five hundred soldiers arrived as the result of a forced march. This swelled the enemy's numbers to between 1,200 and 1,300.

But the centralists were fatigued. Cos had driven his men without rest to reach San Jacinto. Santa Anna, fearing a predawn or early morning attack by the Texians, worked his men through the night to assemble flimsy breastworks consisting of saddles, packs, brush, and dirt.

The rebel assault did not materialize, and Santa Anna came to believe once again that the backwoods drunkard Houston was short on nerve. After the arrival of Cos, giving them decidedly superior numbers, the weary Santanistas grew amazingly complacent and careless. By midafternoon, most of them were either relaxing or sound asleep, apparently without having distributed scouts or pickets.

For weeks, the Texians had followed their enigmatic commander in apparent flight from the hated and despised Mexican army. They trained hard for a fortnight in a pestilential swamp, then crossed the Brazos and grumblingly resumed the march eastward. But, at a point not far from Groce's, the army came upon a split in the road. The left fork continued east to Nacogdoches while the right fork veered south to Harrisburg. Taking the right fork likely meant an engagement with Santa Anna.

Without hesitation, the army turned south.

Whether this decision came from Houston, or whether his

men acted independently to force their choice on him, remains a question without a consensus answer. Nevertheless, Houston was still in charge on the day the Texians prepared to storm the enemy's camp at San Jacinto, and it was he who ordered and led the assault under bright sunshine at four in the afternoon.

Seth Swearingen had caught up with the army at Harrisburg, and joined a company of volunteers. In doing so, he at long last located his cousins from Kentucky. Their ship had put in at Velasco, up the coast from Copano, and they fell in with Houston as he was en route from the Colorado to San Felipe.

Standing at readiness on the edge of the San Jacinto plain, Seth and nearly nine hundred other Texians reflected on the slaughters of relatives, friends, and adopted compatriots at the Alamo and Goliad. The author of those atrocities was within reach, just across the grassy meadow. The Texians' rage, and their thirst for vengeance, had long since become corporate emotions.

Moseley Baker, temporarily putting aside his contempt for General Houston, made sure his company of infantry was in order. Three-Legged Willie Williamson, securely astride a black charger, was prepared to avenge the death of Buck Travis with a long rifle, a brace of pistols, a tomahawk, and a Bowie knife.

Among Houston's troops were Juan Seguin and a company of twenty *Tejanos.* Seguin had escaped death at the Alamo only because Travis sent him out as a courier prior to the fall. Several of Seguin's mestizo companions had perished in the fortress. They, too, would be avenged this day.

Houston, on a big white horse, moved to and fro before the double rank of infantrymen. Far to his right, newly anointed cavalry commander Mirabeau Lamar had organized the mounted riflemen. Splitting the ranks of infantry at the center were two six-pound cannon, the only Texian artillery. Recently given by the city of Cincinnati, Ohio, and dubbed the "Twin Sisters," they would have to be advanced across the soft ground with Herculean effort in order to support the assault.

Houston bawled the order to move forward. As quietly as it could, the ragged, dirty, hungry, angry, determined mob did so. Once onto the sunbathed plain, they had to wade waist-deep through lush spring grass. Incredibly, their steady advance on the dictator's camp went undetected until they had already traversed most of the intervening meadowland.

At a distance of around two hundred yards from their foe, the Texians heard the sudden bleating of a Mexican bugle. Then from behind the makeshift breastworks came puffs of smoke. A sporadic discharge of muskets sent balls whistling over and around the attackers' heads. Still, at Houston's insistence, the rebels held their fire. When most of the infantry had reached the top of the hump-backed rise, in plain view of their disorganized enemy, Houston ordered his men to return fire.

Within seconds, the regiment at the extreme left of the attacking force swept over the fortifications and into the Mexican camp. The centralists, thrown into confusion laced with panic, never formed an orderly resistance. The rest of the Texian foot soldiers, having discharged their rifles, broke ranks and raced headlong for the breastworks. Some paused to reload, but many utilized the heavy stocks of their guns as murderous clubs.

Screaming "Remember the Alamo! Remember Goliad!" at the top of their lungs, the long-suffering men of Houston gave vent to their darkest passions. Shooting, stabbing, clubbing, choking, they waded into the nest of the milling enemy to deliver death. Santa Anna, his reverie interrupted, came lurching out of his tent. One terrified look at the oncoming, demon-possessed Texians cleared his brain of the dregs of sleep and opium. *El Presidente,* wearing red slippers and a silk shirt, appropriated a horse and galloped off.

His men were not nearly as fortunate. Mexican resistance, never effective, lasted no more than twenty minutes. The engagement soon degenerated into a rout and mass extermination. This time, the Santanistas were on the receiving end.

Swearingen, towering over his terror-stricken prey, was among those who used their rifle butts as bludgeons. He crushed skull after skull, until the weapon broke in two, then yanked out his Bowie knife and continued his quest for gore. The long-legged Kentuckian ran down a number of screaming, begging *soldados* and answered their pleas with thrusts of his bloodied blade.

Finally, Swearingen stumbled onto a sight that served to curdle his blood lust.

In the hope of shaking their merciless pursuers, many of the retreating enemy plunged into a lake behind the Mexican camp.

When Seth arrived, a number of Texians were seated on the near bank, calmly taking turns loading rifles and shooting the swimmers through the head. The crimsoned water was becoming choked with bodies.

Seth found that his passion to kill had been satiated. He turned back toward the camp in search of active combat. There was none to be found.

The exact numbers might be debatable, but the basic results of the Battle of San Jacinto were staggering. More than six hundred Mexicans lay dead, most of them shamefully slain after the outcome had been decided. The remainder were taken as prisoners. Of the Texians, two or three died on the battlefield and another eight or nine perished afterward, either from their wounds or as a result of inadequate medical aid.

Santa Anna did not remain free for long. He was found cowering in the tall prairie grass the next morning, dressed in slave's clothing stolen from a nearby plantation. Apparently, the Napoleon of the West had mired his getaway horse in a marsh and continued his flight on foot. Mortally afraid of deep water, he tried to make his way around the twisting bayous and sloughs rather than wade across them. He wasn't very far from the battlefield at the time of his discovery and capture.

Chapter 64

*E*ager to pacify his captors, Santa Anna agreed to order the remaining segments of the centralist army out of Texas. His generals, especially Urrea, were at first reluctant to obey a command issued so obviously under duress; finally, though, they acquiesced and began the withdrawal.

Urrea's argument was that the Mexican forces in Texas were far superior in numbers and in every other respect to the army of the insurgents. For the moment, he was more right than wrong. But news of San Jacinto served to increase the number of armed Americans already streaming into the rebel province. Too, the Texians were on familiar ground, whereas the Santanista soldiers found the upper Gulf Coast a remote, alien land of flooding streams and treacherous marshes and wild, desperate foes who fought like Indians.

Frankly, the *soldados* had lost all stomach for the campaign, and their leaders sensed as much. The army headed home.

The shocking news made headlines in America as well as Europe. Across the United States, the event was hailed as a great blow for freedom in the tradition of the American Revolution. Among the most avid followers of events in Texas was a spry, urbane New Yorker enjoying his eightieth year.

"Well, well! I was right all along!" Aaron Burr said to no one in particular. "It's just that I was thirty years too soon! What they called treason in my day is now hailed as patriotism!"

The army's withdrawal did not, however, signify that the Mexican government summarily accepted the erstwhile province as an independent neighbor. The captive Santa Anna readily recognized the Republic of Texas; once set at liberty, he blithely ignored all he had agreed to. Over the ensuing decade, there were numerous plans made and efforts expended to recapture the lost territory. It took the Mexican War, following Texas's ascension to U.S. statehood in 1846, to finally and officially settle the issue.

The summer of 1836 produced an interesting contest for the first elected president of the republic. Although not an active candidate until less than two weeks remained before the election, Sam Houston swept the field over Henry Smith and Stephen Austin. Rather than choose the man who had done the most for Texas, voters chose the man who had done something big for Texas the most recently. After all, many among the electorate were living east of the Sabine when Austin's star was brightest.

Houston offered Austin the post of secretary of state. Austin accepted, but before the year was out he paid the ultimate price for his broken health. The Father of Texas died without a penny in his pocket.

By law, the president could not serve consecutive terms. Mirabeau Lamar, Houston's vice president, succeeded the general in 1838 in an election made easy because both his opponents committed suicide during the last days of the campaign.

Lamar used the opening months of his presidency to pursue a policy of running the Indians out of Texas. In one of the most disgraceful episodes in its history, the republic sent troops against the peaceable Cherokees of Chief Bowles.

For two decades, the tribe had tried to secure formal land rights from the powers in charge: first the Spanish, then the Mexicans, and finally the Texans. They had received nothing except empty promises. But Lamar's ultimatum of departure or destruction was not empty.

Houston, the Cherokees' champion and the negotiator of the all-important treaty during the Texas Revolution, happened to be out of the country when Texas soldiers rode into the Cherokee villages. They essentially forced the Indians to fight. The old warrior Bowles, well into his eighties, led his braves out against their oppressors and died on the battlefield from a pistol shot to the back of the head.

Mercifully for John Cumings, who had loved Bowles like a close relative, the roll-call for eternity had sounded just a few months before.

It took weeks following the triumph at San Jacinto for Rebecca to recover from her illness. Seth, having hustled back to Mill Creek with news of the victory, was saddened to see that she remained weak and feverish. Seth's mother was of the opinion, which she shared in private, that Rebecca would never again be "a whole woman."

In some respects, Seth's mother was right. Even when Rebecca had regained her physical health, she was no longer quite the same bright and cheerful individual everyone had known and loved. She evidenced a morbid fear of losing John, her last remaining family member in Texas. She discouraged all gentleman callers other than the protective Seth, who was far too frightened of somehow causing her further hurt to properly be termed a suitor.

And so things remained until, in the spring of 1839, John suddenly grew sick and died. Instead of suffering the expected emotional collapse, Rebecca, now in her fortieth year, turned her grief inward. With eyes of green flint, she focused on running the inn, raising stock, and amassing in her own name the extensive Cumings holdings. She suffered Seth's continual help and unwavering affection, but only rarely was he rewarded with a glimpse of the old Becky.

Nearly ten years after a redheaded, Southern lawyer first came to Mill Creek and claimed Rebecca's heart, another redheaded, Southern lawyer rode into San Felipe and established a law office. David Young Portis was a handsome man with winsome ways, and in a surprisingly short time he was representing the locality in the Texas Congress.

In addition to his political interests, Portis maintained a sharp eye for who owned what. It didn't take him long to figure out that the taciturn but attractive spinster on Mill Creek was the sole Texas heir to tens of thousands of fertile Brazos Bottom acres. Virtually Travis made over in some respects, Portis quickly overtook and outshone the bumbling Seth in the quest for Rebecca's hand.

In December 1843 Rebecca became the wife of David Portis, who was fourteen years her junior. He was not truly Travis, of course, nor for that matter did he measure up to James Bonham. Rebecca could not love Portis as she had loved the cousins. However, husband and wife did share a hearty appreciation of property and wealth.

By 1848, two years after the Lone Star republic achieved statehood, the Portises were doing very well on David's law practice and Rebecca's family estate. This, though, was also the year in which her brother William's son achieved his majority.

Raphael and Lucinda Thompson's existence in Maysville, Kentucky, in the 1830s seemed to consist of one crisis and tragedy after another. Whereas Lucinda's firstborn, Samuel Anthony Cumings, remained hale and hardy, his half-siblings from the Thompson union tended to be sickly and short-lived. Searching for a healthier climate, the Thompsons in 1842 moved to Missouri. They left behind four small graves on the south shore of the Ohio.

Raphael Thompson established a carpentry business at the corner of Third and Cedar streets in St. Louis, a couple of blocks from the busy Mississippi waterfront. Lucinda's brother, Moses Ruggles, made the move with them and opened a saddle shop a few streets over.

When he turned twenty-one, Sam Cumings journeyed to Texas in search of his birthright. Lucinda had done what she could in the probate courts of Texas to protect her son's inheritance, but almost as soon as Sam stepped off the steamboat in Brazoria, he learned that he was in for a long, bitter legal fight. Rebecca Portis declined to acknowledge who he was, let alone what he might own. To her he was Lucinda's brat and, besides, represented a real threat to the Portises' lifestyle.

To be precise, the fight lasted twenty-six years. At one point, it even reached the state supreme court before being remanded to the district court in Galveston. By the time the convoluted courthouse struggle ended in 1874, Sam Cumings was well established as a lawyer and surveyor, the father of eight sons and a daughter. The tussle cost both sides thousands of dollars, and the victory was essentially a hollow one for Sam.

Even so, the Portises had been reputed to be among the richest and most influential of Texas families. The U.S. Census in 1860 listed David Y. Portis of Austin County as owning seventeen slaves, property in excess of 35,000 acres valued at $100,000, plus personal property worth $20,000.

The Portises later removed to San Antonio, where David entered into a lucrative law partnership and Rebecca enjoyed as much of high society as she could tolerate. The prominent Mrs. Portis, though, was not a happy woman. The long legal fight with her nephew and the deterioration of her eyesight were troublesome enough. But the darkest shadow hanging over Rebecca's daily existence was cast by a crumbling old building located a few blocks from her posh residence.

Part V

The Storm
(1875)

Chapter 65

*H*aving lighted and adjusted the oil lamp, Kate Donahoo turned her attention to the yellowed square of folded paper she'd laid so carefully on the table.

Without, the oncoming hurricane hurled its vanguard across Matagorda Bay at defenseless Indianola. A fierce gust of wind drove the rain harder against the bayside windows of the Magnolia Hotel. Rebecca Portis, seated on the side of her bed, shivered and tugged at the wool shawl covering her hunched shoulders.

Gingerly, Kate unfolded the letter her aged mistress had safekept inside the antique book of the Gospels. The handwriting was strong and precise, that of a practiced penman. Dated "2 March" without citing a year, the missive was addressed simply to "R—." Kate read it aloud as she was bid, raising her voice over the drumming of the rain:

" 'This is being written by the light of a campfire, doubtless an imprudent display on the road between Goliad and Bexar. I wonder whether you will ever read these words.

" 'Little chance remains that Buck and his brave men are to be rescued. I choose to rejoin them, tell them the hard truth and share their fate. I could do nothing less and face myself.

" 'Too, I am honor-bound to present the ring to Buck, though I confess it will not be easy for me.

" 'You may as well know that you have managed, in a very brief but precious time, to kindle a fire such as never before consumed my heart. There burns within me a new and greater yearning to live, so that I might be with you once more. Yet, I am also compelled to

451

do my duty as a soldier and forfeit my life, if needs be, along with the others.

"'There! I have bared my soul and must beg forgiveness if you find the sight offensive. Pray do not judge me too harshly.'"

The letter was signed "J.B.B." Kate then read a scribbled postscript that had been added in different ink:

"'March 3 - Buck accepted the ring.'"

Hands trembling, Kate tenderly refolded and replaced the epistle while Rebecca stared wordlessly off into space. For some time there was no sound in the hotel room except for the raging of the storm.

"That's really a beautiful letter," Kate said at last, her voice husky with emotion. "Mrs. Portis," she continued, hesitantly, "do you mind if I ask you who Buck and J.B.B. were?"

Rebecca exhaled slowly. "Not at all, my dear," she answered. "They were two young fellows just beginning to discover life. Colonel William Travis was called Buck and the other man was his cousin, James Butler Bonham."

Kate's eyes widened. "The men of the Alamo!" she exclaimed, staring anew at the old book with its hidden treasure. Things were beginning to make sense to her. The kindly Mrs. Sutherland had known full well what the story of the fallen fortress meant to Rebecca, and chided her for continuing to live in the past.

A shiver convulsed the thin shoulders beneath the shawl. Kate knelt once more at the older woman's feet, removed the slippers, and helped her mistress slide back under the covers. The wind and rain tore at the windows like a living thing intent on forcing entry. It was now past six, and virtually black outside. Although Rebecca quickly dropped off to sleep, Kate decided to keep the lamp burning.

"Konrad! Can't you hear me, boy? Konrad!"

The young German sat up suddenly, and his hands went to each side of his head. Swearingen's whiskey had left him with a throbbing skull. At the other end of the dark hayloft, Enrique Guzman was also stirring. The voice that woke them belonged to Mr. Presig, the Magnolia's innkeeper. His agitated presence was further manifested by the bobbing light of a lantern.

Presig's anxious face, crowned with a dripping sou'wester, appeared at the top of the ladder. "Come, come, boys!" he ordered, his speech high-pitched and nervous. "The bay water is near half a foot high into the stable, and still rising! Get up, now! I need you to take the horses uptown, to Cassimir's livery stable. Things should be above water there. I hope so, anyway!"

"What time of mornin' is it, sir?" Konrad asked, stifling a grunt of pain as he groped for his trousers. Rain was beating a tattoo on the barn roof right over his head, and the wooden structure groaned and popped under the buffeting of the wind.

"Nearly four o'clock," Presig answered. "But there'll be someone on duty at Cassimir's," he added confidently. "Everybody from this end of Indianola will be sending them horses to keep, 'til the storm blows over and the town's clear of water. We need to hurry, while there still may be room!"

As he and Goose ambled through the blowing rain, riding bareback on two of the Magnolia's refugee horses and leading the others, Konrad decided he had never seen a storm so fierce. The town's new gas streetlights served as guiding beacons in the downpour. The mix of rainfall and bay water, driven by the wind and the high gulf tide, raced and foamed around the horses' fetlocks. Not a street surface was visible until they were nearly to Cassimir's, adjacent to the courthouse on the highest point in town.

Conversation at the commercial stable was all in the same vein: At first light, proprietors intended to board up their business houses. Everyone might as well stay home and keep dry. The foul weather would probably delay proceedings of the Bill Taylor murder trial.

In returning to the hotel on foot, the young men had to endure the sting of driving rain on their faces and saltwater splashing over the tops of their boots. Disgusted but not yet alarmed, they returned to the loft and managed to grab additional sleep.

Inside the hotel, Rebecca was seriously ill. She tossed to and fro in a restless half-sleep, not responding to anything the anxious Kate said to her. By early morning, she appeared to be enveloped in a high fever.

Dr. Fromme was summoned. Although irritated at receiving a summons in such bad weather, the physician saw at once the serious condition of the hotel's prize guest. He ordered the application of damp towels to the patient's face and neck, produced two bottles of liquid medicine for Kate to dispense, and left instructions that Rebecca not be moved before his return.

Fromme, though, would not return.

The people of Indianola realized belatedly that a storm of unprecedented strength and savagery was upon them. During the morning hours, many residents in the low-lying sections began abandoning their homes in search of higher places and sturdier shelter. But no spot on the long reef occupied by Indianola was high enough. And precious little shelter would prove to be sturdy enough.

By the time thoughts turned to wholesale evacuation, it was too late. The little city had in effect become a sinking island. The heavy rains and gale-driven flood tide inundated the roads leading in and out. The railroad bed would shortly be washed away in several places; besides, the boiler of the only locomotive in town had been drained, and suddenly there was no unpolluted source of water for a refill.

Around midmorning, bay water invaded the first floor of the Magnolia. The innkeeper Presig abruptly decided that he, his wife, and the other hotel occupants would be safer downtown in one of the brick buildings.

Following Presig's orders, Konrad and Goose closed and reinforced the storm shutters, then collected the finer lobby furnishings and carried them upstairs. Next, they securely joined themselves by rope to every willing hotel guest. Thus connected, the evacuees stumbled single-file through the surging water and lashing rain until they reached perceived safety at Sullivan's brick-walled bank.

Three of the guests had been either unable or unwilling to leave the hotel. Rebecca fell into the first category, and Kate and the ever-protective Seth Swearingen fit the second. Konrad was determined to rejoin them. At Sullivan's bank he said as much to Presig, and Goose volunteered to accompany him. The hotel proprietor, yielding to a sense of responsibility for those who had stayed behind, shrugged and nodded.

The way back led directly into the teeth of the storm and the rushing tidewater. The flood level had climbed to nearly three feet—waist high on Goose. Footing was uncertain at best, as the shell and gravel street surfaces were rapidly eroding under the constant flow.

Floundering along, the companions encountered a long, round-bottomed rowboat, empty of cargo and riding the storm crest. Goose recognized it as one of the lifeboats kept at the wharves. Labeling the happenstance a gift of Providence (despite the absence of any paddles), they took possession and managed to tow the vessel through the oncoming surf to the hotel. Using the painter and additional rope, they lashed the boat securely to the front-porch pillars.

Spent from their exertions, Konrad and Goose waded into the lobby and literally crawled up the stairs on their hands and knees until they were clear of the water. Then they rested.

Meanwhile, the central figure in the big murder trial was in the process of escaping the attention he had never wanted.

When the invading water became bunk-high in the jail, Bill Taylor and three other inmates were removed for their safety and escorted to the new courthouse. There, one of the prisoners surprised Sheriff Busch from behind, yanking a prized Colt revolver from its holster and training it on the dumbfounded lawman. As the infuriated sheriff and dismayed onlookers watched helplessly, the four newly armed desperadoes appropriated horses and rode away through the storm. It would be the last public sighting of Bill Taylor for many a year.

Seth Swearingen peered down from the landing at the top of the staircase. In the gloom of the shuttered building, it took him a moment to identify the two men whose bodies were draped limply on the carpeted stairs.

"All tuckered out, eh, boys?" Seth bellowed at last, easily heard over the racket of the hurricane. Two weary heads lifted in his direction. The old man chuckled. "You'd best try an' find some dry clothes," he advised. "Konrad, you kin make use o' my duds. They'll be a mite large, but that's all right. The Meskin kin go through the luggage up here 'til he finds somethin' suitable. I don't think th' guests will mind, since it was tendin' to them that got you-all soaked."

Konrad found his voice. "How's Mrs. Portis?" he asked.

Seth's face fell. "She's not doin' well at all."

"We caught a big rowboat," Konrad told him proudly. "It's tied up on the porch. We can take Mrs. Portis downtown in it."

"No, sir!" Seth snapped. "She's doin' too poorly t' be moved about. That damn sawbones said as much. I'm beginnin' t' wonder if we'll see him again. How bad are things out there?"

The young German wagged his head. "I've never seen anything like this," he replied. "We've had storms here before, with high winds and water in the streets. But nothing near this bad or for this long. Coming back from Sullivan's, we saw some small wood houses all busted up and about to collapse."

Swearingen nodded slowly. "Yep, it's one hell of a storm," he muttered, then added derisively, "That boat you found would prob'ly stay afloat 'bout half a minute before the water'd be into it. I don't believe we'd want t' try that route unless th' hotel blows down."

In what had become the sickroom, Kate was trying to save the meager supply of fresh water for her mistress to drink. She simply alternated the damp cloths she placed against Rebecca's face and throat as the doctor had ordered. Rebecca continued to toss fitfully, either sleeping or trying to sleep, and could not be prodded awake long enough to take her medicine.

The storm increased its fury, the rain roaring against the tile roof and wooden sides of the hotel. The rising tidal water pounded the building viciously from the bay side.

Waves cresting at five feet crashed through the streets of Indianola. Their strength intimidated both refugees and rescuers, who no longer dared to step into the churning water. Among the debris hurtling along with the torrents were wicked, nail-studded fragments of frame buildings. Ropes were strung across the streets, and passage from one side to the other was attempted only in boats drawn like makeshift ferries.

Shortly before dark, the wind driving the bay water and torrential rain reached a speed of ninety miles an hour. Many of the town's lesser structures were listing badly or had already been flattened and lay underneath the foam of the crashing surf. The stoutly built Magnolia was holding firm so far, but she shuddered and groaned under the brutal drubbing by the elements.

Above all other noises rose the demon shriek of the wind.

Painfully aware of having left their possessions in the stable, Konrad and Goose frequently peered out through the cross-barred shutters at the little building. At last, while Goose watched in dumb agony, it succumbed to the storm and broke into pieces. The wood-shingle roof slid beneath the waves.

With the arrival of nightfall, Swearingen organized a rotation of watches among the men. He did not want, he explained, to be caught napping by any unforeseen circumstance. Seth assumed the initial shift, commandeering an overstuffed chair in the hall midway between his room and those of Rebecca. He lighted a lantern and placed it beside the chair. Then he took up a cigar. Long before he finished the smoke, Konrad and Goose had fallen asleep in his room.

Sometime after ten, the big rancher was meditatively puffing on another cigar when the hotel lurched. No word better described the sickening sensation, which brought Seth out of his chair. He moved quickly along the hall in the direction of his room, hickory cane thumping, then halted in consternation. The passageway definitely inclined toward the front of the hotel! "Get up, boys!" he roared. "On your feet! We've begun t' list!"

However, the alarming movement did not immediately recur.

Kate poked a pale face out of the doorway. "What is it, Mr. Swearingen?" she asked anxiously. "What's happened?"

Seth turned to her. "Just a shift o' the buildin' is all, Little Miss," he said, with feigned indifference. "Everything's all right." But she was not fooled.

A moment later, Kate reappeared in the hall. "Mr. Swearingen," she said, "Mrs. Portis is conscious. She would like to talk to you." The old rancher, surprised and pleased, stepped quickly into her rooms.

Rebecca was sitting up in bed, propped against several pillows. A plaid shawl was pinned close under her chin and draped around her shoulders. Her face appeared flushed and haggard, and it was evident that just keeping her head up took considerable effort. The green eyes seemed alert, although preternaturally bright from the fever.

Swearingen moved within a few steps of her bed, so that the two of them could hear and understand each other.

"Seth," Rebecca began, her voice scratchy and thin, "I fear that you are all here because of me. Tell me precisely what danger I have placed us in. The truth, Seth—please."

Swearingen cleared his throat. "Why, we may not be in no danger at all, Becky," he replied evasively. "The old hotel seems t' be handlin' the storm okay. It did stir a bit, just a while ago, but I reckon we can still weather th' storm."

Nettled by his answer, Kate spoke up. "So then why was it, Mr. Swearingen," she asked pointedly, "that you woke up the other men when the hotel shifted?"

The rancher glowered at her. "We can't be for sure, Little Miss," he grunted, "just what this here hurricane's gonna do. It's best for the menfolk t' be up an' alert. Anyway, they'd been sleepin' a few hours."

At that very instant, the hotel lurched again. The oil lamp on the table rattled and shook, and a large picture frame dropped off its hook and struck the floor with a bang. From somewhere in the bowels of the building came the sound of breaking glass.

Wide-eyed, Konrad and Goose appeared at the door. Seth angrily gestured at them to leave, but Rebecca summoned her strength and cried out: "Young men! Wait! Come here, please!"

Her effort brought on a fit of coughing. When it had passed, Rebecca squinted at the two young faces, one ruddy and one swarthy. She beckoned feebly for them to come nearer. "I was just now asking Mr. Swearingen," she said in a virtual whisper, every word an effort, "about the predicament I have placed us in. All I can do is apologize to you. We must be in a very grave spot."

The popping and groaning of tortured wood came to their ears. The structure swayed once more. Toiletry items slid off the vanity and dropped onto the carpet. Goose dashed to the table, and with a bare hand steadied the rocking lamp.

For a moment, no one said a word. Outside, the wind screamed derisively. Then Rebecca motioned to Kate, who leaned close in order to hear. "You said you wanted to share something with me, Miss Donahoo," she said thinly, placing a slender, blue-veined hand to her throat. "Maybe you should share it with our friends, too."

Kate tossed off her hesitancy, nodded, and opened her New Testament. Without prelude, she began reading loudly and clearly:

" 'That if thou shalt confess with thy mouth the Lord Jesus, and shalt believe in thine heart that God hath raised him from the dead, thou shalt be saved.

" 'For with the heart, man believeth unto righteousness, and with the mouth confession is made unto salvation.' "

Kate looked around. Four sets of eyes were watching her in the sputtering light of the lamp. " 'For whosoever shall call upon the name of the Lord shall be saved,' " she concluded, and lowered and shut the book.

Boldly, chin thrust out, she asked, "Mrs. Portis, do you know Jesus Christ as your Lord and Savior?"

Her mistress nodded gently. Kate could just hear her whispered response: "Yes, my dear, I accepted Him at a very early age. I do confess, though," she added contritely, "that I have fallen away from that first love."

"The good news," Kate responded, "is that He is faithful to forgive us if we confess and repent of our sins." She turned her eyes to the men.

Suddenly, Goose went to his knees, squeezing his eyes shut and clasping his hands in supplication. He was shaking, and tears trickled down the dark cheeks. After a couple of sobs, he began a fervent monologue in Spanish.

Konrad stared in surprise at his co-worker. Then he too knelt, eyes closed and head bowed in audible prayer.

Swearingen remained standing, but directed a look of uncertainty at Rebecca. He saw her attempting to speak, and he inclined his ear very close to her lips. "Seth," she said, in a rasping yet tender voice, "no one but you . . . knows what your relationship is with the Lord. Considering the fix we've found ourselves in, you ought not take . . . any chances."

The old Kentuckian settled into a snugly fitting wooden chair and turned his face to the floor. Three male voices filled the sickroom, offering prayers in two different languages, muffling for the moment the belligerent din of the hurricane.

Chapter 66

*I*t may have been the sudden silence that woke Kate.

She had pulled up a chair alongside the bed of Rebecca Portis, who while hot to the touch appeared to be in a deep sleep. Despite the gravity of their plight, Kate was elated over the confessions and prayers she'd heard earlier in this very room. She was especially thrilled for Konrad. The howling hurricane continued to pummel the Magnolia, but she believed that now—regardless of the night's outcome—everyone's immortal soul was safe.

Satisfied that her mistress was resting as comfortably as could be expected, Kate once again changed out the damp cloths on Rebecca's neck and forehead before curling up in the chair under a knit coverlet. The sleep she had been robbed of across the past twenty-four hours swiftly overtook her.

Down the hall, Konrad sat at watch in the overstuffed chair first commandeered by Swearingen. He listened to the tempest voicing its rage, and he studied the shadows animated by the flickering light of the lantern at his feet. He also thought frequently—nay, constantly—of Kate. Further down the tilted passageway, in Swearingen's room, the big rancher and the little Mexican slept side by side.

Shortly, despite the best of intentions, Konrad's head settled onto his chest. He joined the others in slumber while the hurricane continued its march of destruction across Indianola.

A light touch on the shoulder did not rouse him, so Kate shook him vigorously. Konrad awoke with a start. "What is it?" he mumbled.

"The storm," she said, turning her eyes toward the ceiling as if scrutinizing the black heavens beyond. "It's stopped." And so it had. Konrad glanced down at Swearingen's pocket watch, which lay open in his lap. It was a half-hour past midnight.

Entertaining a cautious smile, he looked up at Kate. The hotel had absorbed the worst blows of the hurricane and still stood! Instinctively, their hands met in an exultant squeeze. Then Konrad picked up the lantern, went to the staircase landing and peered over. "The water in the lobby's dropped some, I think," he announced after his survey. Sticking his head into Swearingen's room, he woke up the slumberers with the welcome tidings.

Their celebration was short-lived.

Goose first noticed the low whine, but it became audible to everyone as soon as they stopped talking to listen. The wind had returned, and was rising quickly. This time the front of the building, the side facing away from the bay, was being impacted.

"Th' eye!" Swearingen exclaimed. "Th' center o' th' storm has passed over us, an' now we're gonna get it from th' other direction!"

Konrad again hoisted the lantern to view the lobby. Water was beginning to accumulate again, eddying through the wide-open double doors of the hotel entrance.

"Guess we thought it was over with before it was," he remarked lamely.

A far-off booming sound reached their ears. Mystified, they listened as it grew louder . . . and nearer. Finally, with a thunderous roar, the tidal wave threw itself against the front of the hotel. A foaming jet of water cascaded into the lobby. The violence of the impact knocked everyone off their feet.

Kate bounced up and scurried to Rebecca's rooms, where she discovered that the lamp next to the sick woman's bed had been thrown to the floor and shattered. Flaming oil, following the incline of the floor, poured across the carpet. Konrad, on Kate's heels, pushed past her and hastily rolled the burning portion of the carpet upon itself. Then he stomped on the roll until the fire was snuffed, sending the room into darkness.

Swearingen appeared at the door, cane in one hand and his lantern in the other. By this illumination, Kate examined Rebecca. Face and neck flushed, the patient remained unconscious, breathing weakly.

The hotel was shuddering without pause under the assault of the redirected wind and floodwater. Within moments, that most dreaded of sensations returned. The structure began a slow, jerking movement, ever increasing the severity of its incline into the screaming wind. The surf, blown by even greater power than before the lull, and 180 degrees from its prior flow, was washing the shell surface of the reef out from underneath the hotel foundation.

As the timber ribs of the building strained and snapped, Seth decided desperate measures were better than none. "Go see if your rowboat's still on the porch!" he bellowed at Konrad. Turning to Kate, he said, in a softer tone, "You need t' make Becky as ready as you can fer bein' moved."

Fortuitously, Konrad handed the lantern to Goose before he started down the staircase to the lobby. The dampness and exaggerated pitch of the steps caused him to lose his footing and plunge head-first into the water below. In spite of the circumstances, Goose laughed. Sputtering, Konrad stood up in the thigh-deep water. He wiped his eyes and peered around through the cloud of spray. Beyond the gaping hotel entrance he saw the boat still secure against the pillars of the porch, though vibrating like a windblown leaf.

How, he wondered, could human strength vie with the power of the storm and claim the boat for their use? Then he decided that if the craft were loosed, it might well be blown straight into the lobby.

Harnessing his determination, Konrad staggered through the churning water across the lobby and out the doorway. There the wind pinned him against the outside wall, and the tail of the frenzied painter whipped him viciously across the face. He seized the rope in both hands and pulled himself to the boat.

Left arm encircling a pillar, Konrad produced his pocket knife and began cutting away the hempen restraints.

Upstairs, Swearingen had concluded that his bad leg would not allow him to carry Rebecca safely over the slanting floor and down the stairs. That responsibility must now lie with Goose, the stunted Hercules. The old rancher took the lantern from Goose and brusquely ordered him to pick up the sick woman "an' be damn careful!" The little longshoreman eased the limp, blanket-wrapped form into his arms and cautiously started down the tilted hall toward the landing.

About that time, the hurricane hurled the freed rowboat against the outside wall of the hotel. There it clattered and danced precariously with the gale for several seconds before being propelled through the yawning doors into the lobby. Konrad sloshed along in pursuit. Reaching and righting the craft, he next wrestled it close to where the staircase disappeared into the water.

Goose, with Rebecca pressed against his chest, reached the balustrade of the landing and looked down at the foaming water in the lobby. Following him, Kate wondered—not without amusement—how her proud, aristocratic mistress might react should she suddenly revive and find herself in the arms of a Mexican man.

The stairs had become far too pitched for Goose to navigate with his burden. Unsure of what to do next, Goose looked over his shoulder for Swearingen. The latter emerged from the hallway bearing a large roll of bedclothes. With Kate's help, Swearingen quickly knotted several sheets together to produce a long and substantial sling.

A rivulet of water came crawling down the hallway floor and went spilling over the edge of the landing. The Magnolia Hotel, her foundation nearly undone, was being broken down by the power of the tempest.

The sling being assembled to the satisfaction of Swearingen, the big man told Kate in a kindly fashion to descend the stairs to the boat. "I'll see to it that Becky gets down to ya," he rumbled, a tender look on his rugged face.

He and Goose secured the limp body of Rebecca within the sling while Kate crept cautiously down the stairs. Konrad lifted Kate and placed her in the lifeboat. Then, joined by Goose, Konrad moved the craft to a point directly under the landing.

With big shoulders hunched and elbows propped against the balustrade, Seth Swearingen lowered Rebecca in the sling to those below. In a moment, all but the big Kentuckian were in or around the lifeboat.

Konrad had already determined the route they must take to exit the hotel.

The double windows on the south end of the lobby were set in a single frame large enough to admit the boat, and the water was already over the sill. The glass panes and wooden sashes had been smashed into fragments, and the gale-whipped shutters were nearly off their hinges.

Several mighty, well-placed blows with a metal hall-tree removed any impediments to their escape. The shutters blew away into the darkness.

As Konrad climbed into the boat, Kate clutched his arm. "We can't leave Mr. Swearingen!" she shouted, pointing to the upper landing.

Swearingen was leaning against the railing, holding his lantern high to illuminate the lobby. The doomed hotel sagged once more, and the occupants of the boat beckoned frantically for Seth to join them.

But the old rancher saw how low the boat seemed to ride in the turbulent water. Chances of its occupants' survival were remote enough, he reasoned, without adding his substantial weight. Seth shook his head at the pleading boatload. He flashed his crooked grin and waved farewell, then held the lantern close while he calmly ignited a cigar.

Upon further shifting of the hotel, a scowl replaced the smile on Swearingen's face and he gestured furiously at the others to leave.

It was clear that further imploration was not only useless but dangerous. Hall tree still in hand, Konrad directed the boat to the window frame. The hull grated against the sill. Heart sinking, Kate took a last look at Swearingen—then the storm angrily snatched up the craft and flung it into Matagorda Bay.

Kate lay in the bottom of the boat, huddled under two blankets and a poncho and almost on top of her comatose mistress. The covers and Kate's body were shielding Rebecca as much as possible from the elements.

As their vessel rocked along in the rainy, windswept blackness, Kate prayed without ceasing. *Lord, Lord! . . . Show your dominion over the elements! Calm the sea and the wind, Lord! Hide us in the shadow of your wings! . . .* Kate frantically rummaged her mind for scriptural passages promising rescue and safety, from New Testament and Old alike.

Although neither sea nor wind grew calm, the rolling surface of the bay did not threaten to capsize the lifeboat. The imminent danger came from the gusting rain and sea spray. As water threatened to accumulate in the boat, Rebecca was rearranged so as to elevate her head. Konrad and Goose began bailing furiously with their bare hands.

When Konrad sat up stiffly to relieve his aches, he took notice of something odd. Since their exodus from the hotel, he had been feeling the elements gusting against his back, indicating they were headed east across the bay. Now the windblown showers were stinging his face. Had the wind changed directions yet again? The mass of storm clouds rendered the night exceedingly dark, almost as though they were shut in a closet. Konrad concluded that his sense of direction had been hopelessly scuttled.

All they could do was to bail, and pray that the boat would not founder or be overturned.

After what seemed like hours, their bay cruise came to an abrupt, jarring end. Wood screeched upon wood, and the momentum of the boat halted so suddenly that Goose was nearly flung out.

Some great, indistinct shape, even darker than the night, loomed over them. The lifeboat was no longer afloat, but seemed instead to be resting on some sort of wooden structure. Indeed, the sensations of the bay surrounded them no more. The rain, though, continued its presence in gusts while the voice of the wind fluctuated between a moan and a roar.

Where the refugees had been carried, what they now rested on, were questions that only daylight could answer. Kate, attempting to share the warmth she retained, pressed herself against the chilled, still body of Rebecca. Periodically, she placed her hand on the older woman's breast in search of the weak but reassuring heartbeat.

At some point, the rain slackened to a drizzle and soon stopped completely.

Dawn, draped in gray, finally arrived in the company of a strong west wind but with no renewal of precipitation. First light revealed things the castaways were not prepared for.

Astonished, they saw that their boat had been driven into the wreckage of a beached schooner. Indeed, they were wedged securely in a tangled pile of salt-cured timbers, almost within the ship's shattered hull. The awkward angles at which masts and spars and rigging lay scattered about reminded Kate of a giant crushed insect.

"This ship, she the *Queen of Mobile*," Goose remarked. "I help unload her two days ago."

A second discovery proved just as surprising. The beach on which the schooner rested was that of Indianola! The waters of Matagorda Bay had been blown from the land and back into their natural basin. The desperate, gambling flight from the stricken hotel had come full circle. Apparently—perhaps due to the stalwart prayers of Kate—the runaway boat was intercepted in the bay by a strong countercurrent and directed back to the mainland. Konrad would hear later of others who, clinging to debris, were swept into the bay and rescued by the same quirk of Nature.

But for Indianola, ill fortune grossly outweighed the good. The port city had been leveled by the storm, and its families devastated and decimated. Where the bayside homes, shops, hotels, wharves and warehouses had stood, nothing remained. The former site of the Magnolia was marked only by flattened rows of oleanders and a few flagstones and roof tiles projecting out of the sand and crushed shell. Of the building itself, there was not a trace.

Staring in disbelief at the terrible spectacle of a thriving community laid to waste, Kate was startled by a light tug at her sleeve. The sodden fabric was caught quiveringly between a thumb and forefinger. Rebecca's eyelids flickered open, and green eyes attempted to focus on the freckled face before them. The parched lips moved, apparently in speech, but Kate could not hear what was being said.

She leaned over and virtually placed her ear against Rebecca's mouth. Thus she heard the final, whispered words of the prominent Mrs. Portis—words eliciting a poignant mixture of grief and hope within the heart of the young listener. What Kate couldn't know was that they had been used years ago by another who stood on the threshold of eternal life:

"Where I go you cannot follow."

Acknowledgments

Although what you have just read is labeled as historical fiction, many passages could as well be called novelized history. The great majority of *A Splendid Country* is in fact retold history, gleaned from a variety of sources.

For instance, the wilderness colony of New Ephrata has a solid basis in fact. Archaeologist-historian Dr. Donna Benson of Chagrin Falls, Ohio, has spent years authenticating the existence of a religious commune in the Ohio Valley during the border warfare era. New Ephrata was imbued with many of the factual elements found in Dr. Benson's work.

Though examining many other sources on Simon Kenton and Tecumseh, I leaned on Allan W. Eckert's *The Frontiersmen* (Little, Brown, 1967), a masterpiece of recounted research. I am also especially indebted to *Mr. Roosevelt's Steamboat* by Mary Helen Dohan (Dodd, Mead, 1981) and *The New Madrid Earthquakes* by James Lal Penick, Jr. (University of Missouri, 1981).

However, much of the data used came from local museums and libraries, state and county records, and regional research sites. I encountered particularly helpful staff at The Filson Club in Louisville, Kentucky, Northwestern State University in Natchitoches, Louisiana, the George Memorial Library in Richmond, Texas, and the Houston Public Library downtown and Clayton facilities.

Knowing the likelihood of omitting important names, I nevertheless wish to thank, for various reasons, Russell Autrey, Mickie Baldwin, Bill Butler, Wincie Campbell, Bud Childers, Darlene Cumings, Bettye Dillow, Ed Eakin, Les Fulgham, Kevin Harmon, Annie Ruth Jones, Joyce Claypool Kennerly, Bob Lutts, Antoinette

Reading, Melissa Locke Roberts, Deanne Rogers, Nancy Sparrow, Henri Spencer, W. M. Von Maszewski, J. C. Whitten, June Williams, Robin Wurzel, and the irrepressible Kevin Young. Special thanks also go to the Harrodsburg/Mercer County (Kentucky) Tourist Commission for the use of a photograph.

— T. AUSTIN CUMINGS

www.ingramcontent.com/pod-product-compliance
Lightning Source LLC
Chambersburg PA
CBHW050120030726
47505CB00007B/1964